THE WORLD OF MYTH

MAGAZINE
ANTHOLOGY
IV

www.darkmythpublications.com/

The following selections, in somewhat slightly different form, were previously published in the E-Zine The World of Myth @ www.theworldofmyth.com

Dark Myth Publications, a division of
The JayZoMon/Dark Myth Company.
21050 Little Beaver Rd, Apple Valley, CA 92308

ISBN: 978-1-7372947-6-4
First Printing December 2021
Dark Myth Publications is a registered trademark of The JayZoMon/Dark Myth Company

THE WORLD OF MYTH

MAGAZINE
ANTHOLOGY
IV

Table of Contents

Table of Contents (Cont'd)

Table of Contents (Cont'd)

Table of Contents (Cont'd)

POETRY SELECTION

Table of Contents (Cont'd)

Introduction

When I was asked to write this intro, I won't lie, I groaned. What could I possibly say that would honor the words contained in this anthology? Should I be witty? Charming? Sarcastic, that is, after all, my default setting. I decided I could be none of those things because I did not want my words here to take away from the words to follow. They are rich, inspired, wonderful works of literature.

You may think that I am being overly enthusiastic, fluffing up the actual pieces, but, as the Editor in Chief, I have personally read, edited, and chosen each one for our magazine. Nothing that is less than what I deemed acceptable was, and is, seen on our pages; I have a set, a level of quality that I hold our contributors to. So, what you see in this book, what you are about to read, really is just that good.

This anthology has been three years in the making. Three years of words, written by people, submitted to The World of Myth Magazine. Every Member of the Month winner for the last three years, myself included, are in this anthology, some with multiple wins, and some are Picks from the Publisher. Every single one is a work of art in and of itself. The tales range from horror to humor, fantasy to science fiction, drabbles, and poetry. The talent in this book is incredible, and I am more than honored to share space with them. This anthology is also the first that does not include Terry D. Scheerer, which is a solemn moment for those who knew him.

All of the previous anthologies have been filled with stories and poetry; this one includes our newest category, Drabbles. When I suggested adding that as a new option, I wasn't sure how it was going to go over. We had decided to give it two months to see if it was going to be well received, and here we are, with Members of the Month Drabbles included in the anthology. I would say it was a roaring success.

I am coming up on my third year as editor in some capacity for The World of Myth Magazine, and having read each story, each poem, each drabble that is in this book, to have had a part in putting it out into the world and now into this book, fills me with the same eager excitement and pride, that I felt on that first magazine that I edited. I feel very blessed to have the privilege of speaking to each contributor on some level. It has been a wonderful experience and one I do not see stopping any time soon.

This is the fourth incarnation of The World of Myth Anthology, and that in itself is a source of pride for all of us who work for the magazine. To be at this place in our literary history is something to be proud of, but it is also a place of immense gratitude. Without our contributors, without our readers, we would not be here.

At the risk of sounding like an Academy Award speech, I want to take a few lines of this intro to thank the man who made this all possible, the one who had the dream, so so long ago, to publish a magazine, offer it for free, and bring the world a little entertainment. David K Montoya, our fearless leader. He brought us all together, set the wheels in motion, and let us run with it. He codes the magazine, each book, and all the websites, podcasts included himself. We would be lost without him. There have been many changes over the years, many faces, but he has remained the one constant. So, and I am sure I speak for all of us, staff, contributors past and present, and readers, when I say, thank you, Sir.

Please sit back, grab a drink, and enjoy the hard work on these pages. Some will make you laugh; some will make you cry, some will make you think, but they will all keep you entertained from start to finish.

Thank you for believing in us and for your continued support.

Stephanie J Bardy,
Chief Financial Officer, JayZoMon/Dark Myth Company
Board of Directors, JayZoMon/Dark Myth Company
Editor in Chief Dark Myth Publications

ALSO FROM DARK MYTH PUBLICATIONS

- Book of Dreams
- Dragon Hunter and Other Fantasy Tails
- It's A Dark Ride
- The World of Myth Anthology: Volume # 1
- The World of Myth Anthology: Volume # 2
- The World of Myth Anthology: Volume # 3
- Eternally Bound
- SuperHorror Max
- Something Better
- Liberty's Run

OTHER ANTHOLOGIES

- Horrotica Online Magazine Anthology
- Natural Instincts: Tales of Witches and Warlocks

THE WORLD OF MYTH

MAGAZINE

ISSUE

67

NOVEMBER 2018

Sandy Parsons

Sandy's fiction has been published in *Escape Pod, Luna Station Quarterly, Nth Degree, the anthology Unparalleled Journeys, Tabard Inn, The World of Myth*, and *Everyday Fiction*. She has degrees in molecular biophysics and medical science. Sandy works as an anesthetist in Georgia and spends the rest of her time writing, reading, playing video games and working as an associate editor at Escape Pod. Sandy is a member of SFWA .

Find more information and links to stories at www.sandyparsons.com.

Friends and Food
By: Sandy Parsons

I CHECKED THE address on the crumpled piece of paper as I stepped from the cab. I hadn't been to this bar before, much less to this part of town. But Juvy asked me to come. And when Juvy asks me to go somewhere I go.

I peeled open the dilapidated door and almost keeled over from the smells. Smoke, sweat and something like citrus soaked in lighter fluid circled around me. I squeezed onto the only bar stool left and scanned the tables for Juvy. The place was crowded for a weeknight. The bartender tapped me on the shoulder.

"I'll just have some water," I said, only half–turning.

He scratched the stubble on his neck. "Two–drink minimum."

"What? Oh. Well then, a beer I guess."

He nodded, satisfied that I had come into line. Then, as if

to mollify me, he leaned in close and spoke from the side of his mouth, "The little tart's worth it. But the alcohol doesn't hurt either if you know what I mean."

I didn't, but I smiled and took a big swig, raised the bottle in his direction. Come on Juvy, I thought. This better be good.

The crowd was getting thicker, and the pitch in the background noise quickened in urgency. The house lights dimmed and the stage lights came up, momentarily blinding me. There was loud clapping, then hoots, then a hush as the curtains parted. I took a drink and gagged as my eyes took in the sight before me.

The alien was smaller than on TV. Her upper body was stuffed into a denim jacket and the lizard–like tail had been contorted into a sort of bun against her back. The lower set of eyes was ringed with blue makeup and the feather boa shaded the upper set. Sparkly earrings dangled from vestigial earlobes. Something akin to stilettos wobbled beneath the clawed feet, but the worst, by far the most incomprehensible sight, was the stockings. Mottled skin dripped like candle wax through the diamond mesh, and the nylon squeezed and stretched around the warty thighs, sagging and baggy at the knees and hindquarters.

I'd always considered myself a leg man until then. I'd never seen one of the fulgur queek in person, much less in drag. I shuddered a little when the alien waddled around and I caught sight of the zigzagging seam along the back of its legs. It took me so long to recover from my shock that I hadn't noticed the singing. I think it was "Strangers in the Night," but with all the squealing and grunting it was impossible to be sure.

I was on my fourth whiskey sour when Juvy showed up.

"Isn't she great? I've been dying for you to come out and see her." Her head swung to the side and her eyes rolled back as she emphasized the word dying.

I gestured somewhat shakily at the stage. "So, this really is what you wanted me to see? I thought it was some kind of joke."

She laughed, and as she slid into a bar stool and stretched her long legs I began to recover a bit from my revulsion. "So, why'd you want me to come out here?"

"To see the act for one. Didn't you think it was phenomenal?" She leaned in and her voice dropped to a conspiratorial whisper. "To be honest, I didn't even know they could make human sounds until I saw her perform."

"So what? Does this have anything to do with the big case you've been working on? Wait, don't tell me, you're representing the fulgur queek." I laughed, warming to my joke. I held my hand up, as if reading a newspaper headline. "I can see it now, Juvy Mallowtine inks million–dollar contract for flabby life form."

"That's way too long for a headline. And Marilyn isn't flabby, she's germinating or something."

"Germinating? Who's Marilyn? Oh wait, you aren't serious. I was only kidding about you representing those... them... the aliens. Aren't they like plants or something anyway?" I'd studied the discovery of life on one of Jupiter's moons like everyone else but it wasn't my best subject. My grandfather said the knowledge gave everyone on Earth a new respect for terrestrial life, but it's hard to imagine how different the world was back then. He even said that before interplanetary space travel, humans actually ate other Earth species.

Juvy was smiling at me over the rim of her drink.

"What?" I could tell she was up to something.

"I've got a surprise for you, that's all. I can't wait." "So Marilyn wasn't the surprise?" I gestured to the stage but realized the alien was gone. I was a little disappointed I had missed her final number. "She's coming back for a second act, right?"

"Hmm. Maybe. But no, the fulgur queek isn't the surprise. At least not that one." She drained her glass and signaled for another.

"What? You mean there's more than one that can squeeze into a pair of fishnet hose and belt out "I Gotta' Be Me"?"

She looked hurt. "I don't represent entertainment. I am strictly food and drink. Didn't I ever tell you about Simplicious Foods? That's my big client. The biggest. And you, as my ever–patient boyfriend, are getting the chance of a lifetime tonight."

I was glad to hear it, but I couldn't help turning my head every few seconds to see if Marilyn was coming back.

"Yes, tonight, baby, prepare to feel your taste buds sing. Are you hungry yet?"

Something to absorb all that nervous alcohol sounded good. "Yeah, I guess I'm ready. Where are we going? I hope it's not far."

"We're staying here," she said in her all–business voice, snapping fingers with sharp red nails over my shoulder. She mouthed something and made wiggling motions with her hands. Then she turned to me. "Great. It'll be out in a minute."

I shuffled my feet on the sticky concrete floor and

rubbed my elbows across the graffiti–laden bar top. I wouldn't have thought a place like this could raise enough in bribes to run a kitchen. But Juvy never let me down before. I decided to be optimistic. "What are we having?"

"Ah, that's the surprise. But I'll tell you this much. It's something you've never tried before."

"The last time someone told me that I got arrested."

She smiled wickedly. "No one told you to take all your clothes off."

I started to argue, but my mouth suddenly began to water so much I couldn't open it without fear of drooling. I felt light–headed from the aroma. I inhaled deeply, and my stomach, if it could, would have cried with joy.

Juvy rubbed her hands together in anticipation. "I think they braised it this time."

I wasn't listening to her. There was sizzling. There was steam. There was a plate in front plying my nostrils with a delicate yet pungent fragrance.

Juvy was already eating. "Dig in. You should really eat it when it's hot." Her chin was glistening, and her lips were a glossy ginger hue.

It was too good to be true. My suspicions were aroused. "What is it, Juvy? Is there some kind of drug in here?"

"No, no. Absolutely not."

My hand had already decided to pick up the fork. I raised the first bite to my lips. My tongue wriggled in anticipation.

"It's the fulgur queek. The chef's specialty."

My mouth clamped shut.

"What? Trust me, it's best if you eat it hot." She picked a little something from her teeth. It looked suspiciously like fishnet stocking fiber.

I turned back to the stage. It had a forlorn emptiness. "Marilyn?" I managed to croak. I was having a hard time making eye contact with Juvy.

She leaned her head back to laugh and her long mane of luxurious curls swung out around her. "You are so sweet. I've heard of people becoming attached to the fulgur queek before but that is just too rich."

My brain was preparing an angry response but my hand, stomach and mouth had their own plan. I can remember fighting it for only a second and the next thing I knew I was licking the last bit of gravy from the plate.

"Don't you have any manners?" grumbled Juvy, but she looked more satisfied than angry.

I pushed the plate away. "Oh Juvy, how could you have made me eat Marilyn?"

"You idiot, you weren't eating Marilyn. Do you have any idea how long it takes to train one of them to tolerate the costumes? Much less find one who can make enough sounds to mimic a human voice."

"Then what were we eating? A slow learner?"

She tossed her crumpled napkin on her plate. "I guess so. Although it wouldn't surprise me if this is last month's entertainment. People do get bored with the same old song and dance, you know?" She slid her tongue along her teeth and lips. "Now that beats seaweed stew any day, don't you think? Simplicious Foods is going to make me very rich. And you too, if you're smart enough to invest now."

I had to admit she had a point. At every table, people were merrily munching away. Still, I was bothered.

"But we aren't supposed to eat other species. Humans

decided long ago that that was wrong. I mean just because something tastes good…"

She stared at me innocently, with her lovely slanted eyes.

The waiter, who was clearing our plates, gave a knowing little laugh. "We hear that one all the time in here. Put your mind at ease, my friend. The fulgur queek are plants. They are plucked from the stem like fragrant onions, living only to be sautéed in a light cream sauce."

"But the singing… and the eyes…" During one song I kind of thought Marilyn was singing to me.

"Those are just tricks. Their minds, nothing but wheat. Their bodies, nothing but the ripe fruit of the vine."

I thought about the flesh oozing from the stockings, and wondered where he got his images from. "Don't be so conflicted," he continued, "It's okay to eat the fulgur queek."

Juvy piped up. "It better be okay, because they are just too delicious to give up."

"Juvy, I have to go."

"What? Wait, don't you want to discuss your investment options?"

I pushed away from the table and stood up. "No. I don't think this is the deal for me."

She looked crushed.

"Thanks though. Really. I'll see you 'round." I threw bills on the table and got out of there as fast as I could.

It wasn't easy finding the back alley entrance that would get me backstage. I had to bribe both a bouncer and a fat woman with hairy underarms guarding what I guess you could call the dressing room. But it was worth it.

I knew I had done the right thing when I saw the fishnet stockings, stretched in all the wrong places, folded neatly beside the denim jacket and the makeup kit. Plants didn't fold clothes.

I picked her up gently from the nest of newspapers she had been sitting in, rubbing her claw–like feet with her stumpy little appendages. She was smaller than she appeared on stage. "Come on, Marilyn," I whispered, turning my head a little so she couldn't smell the betrayal on my breath, "I won't let you become dinner." I tucked her gently into the crook of my arm, and before I had gotten a block she had fallen fast asleep.

THE END

THE WORLD OF MYTH

MAGAZINE

ISSUE

68

DECEMBER 2018

Matt Wall

Matt Wall is a booktuber and a writer. He is also the publisher of *Weird Mask zine* and the host of the *PulpFicLit Podcast*. Under the alias *Creep Creeperson*, he is known as a film director, musician, screenwriter, producer, actor and author. Matt has a long running history with this magazine as he is the son of *Terry D. Scheerer*.

The Killing of P3
By: Matt Wall

1

SO THERE I was. It was me I was sure of, but how sure is yet to remain seen. I was younger than I am now, by only a matter of minutes, but at the end of the day, that is really beside the point.

So there I was.

I know I used that line before but I am not that amazing of a writer, just hang on this will get good I swear. I showed up with D1, he was a good friend. Mainly because he offered to drive which is more than I can say about some other D's or P's or even E's!

What assholes.

A giant dark shadow just came over the front of my Hal the Cockroach and pushed up on my face. I know I am being watched now. I must try to figure out a better way of using code for fear that I might not be able to finish this tale without being put to death by the powers that be.

Anyway, when we got there R1, whose name for the sake of this story is P3, was late. That shouldn't surprise me. Every meeting we had before the mission, he was late too. Sometimes he would stop and get pizza or something to make it look like he was only late because he stopped to get us food, but the pizza that he got I already know was cooked and ready for pick up. At most, 3 ½ minutes were added to his ventures by this devise. Other times he would meet us at restaurants and talk loudly and shake his fists and yell obscenities in hopes that others would look to him and ask him more questions about the rambling that he spoke of just so he would have someone to talk to.

When we got there that morning, I was very happy to see that B1 was already there. It made a lot of the edge go away. The mission would not at all be easy, but I knew that B1 could get everyone's mind off of it. We parked and got out of our vehicle. Oh yes, I almost forgot, that day, A7 was riding in the back with us. She got out too.

I had my coffee, so that was good. I was smoking cigarettes, so that was good. Then to ruin all of it, P3 finally arrived and just as I feared, he was much more drooly than ever. He sat me down to talk to me. I couldn't really hear anything he said because I was too busy staring at the dead growth that kept the back of his neck warm on cold nights. It pulsated and moved up and down. If it weren't for the fact that he spat on me when he talked, I never would have awoken to hear anything that he had to say.

"How are we on time," P3 said, "You know, I don't want

to sit around here and wait all fucking morning before we start."

"I agree." I said. We would let him think that he had control a lot of the time just to keep him out of other more important things. In fact, D1 and P1 both decided, my main objective on this mission was to just keep P3 from knowing anything that was really going on and just to keep him away from all the D's, C's, P's, and A's during our mission. He was really only allowed to talk to civilians during our tenure. But I thought that alone would be enough to blow our cover, so I tried to interfere there too.

"You know I've done thousands of these things, and the one thing you always have to remember is to just hit the ground running," P3 stated. "So many times it seems to take everyone a long time to get in the zone and be able to all pull together and get shit done. Not this time. I will not stand for people sitting around waiting for the other guy to start something."

"Yeah. OK," I said, "What time is lunch?"

"How about like 2 or 2:30? I think that is a good time to break for lunch. What about you? Do you think that is a good time to break?"

"I think that is a lovely idea, P3."

P3 was gone. Thank God. That gives me time to assess the situation. What everyone on my team did not know, was that I was a double agent. There were things that I need to find out, get my hands on, and other classified things that I cannot tell you.

Later, I found out that P3 was really upset that D1 activated B1 without his consent. What he didn't know was that D1 didn't do it at all. It was me. I did it for a couple of

19

different reasons. 1. Because P1 had requested it. Not B1 by name, but someone with her skills. 2. Because she was the hottest female of the bunch, so I knew it would boost the troop's morale. 3. Because she talked like a sailor. Not that that's good in a homosexual way, but that she always talked about her tits and her ass. She often included them in stories about other female's parts and loved telling us what she would or could do with her mouth. All of these things were good.

I guess P3 and D1 had an agreement of how the protocol would work in activating a B and because I did it anyway, that broke their protocol. It was just my dumb luck that D1 didn't rat me out. It's not because he didn't want to, I think it was because he didn't know any better. See, this was only his second mission in this rank. And this mission, unlike his last one, was on a much grander scale; one that he was not familiar with. I would not be the only one to take advantage of this oversight during our mission, but more on that later.

I entered the war room and saw B1 preparing the troops. At this very moment I felt good about the mission. Our mission, or the only thing that I can share with you about the mission (which by the way, isn't that important and not even the focus of this story, just a mere subplot) was to get our secret weapon, A1 to take off her clothes. At that point we would slice her up really good until the blood came out, then she would kill the other A's. Mass murder missions like this were not the specialty of D1 who would much rather lead a charge of insertion or launching seals into battle. But because of an injury to his eye, he couldn't do that with the confidence that he used to. Back when D1 was a D2 or a P3, he followed me out on missions where I was his D1. He learned a lot under me and hopefully, he wouldn't fuck this mission up.

I had to go up into the tower once I spoke with D1 about what the hell was going on. He told me that most of the others were already up in the tower. When we got there, he was kind of right. C1, C2, C3, C4 and C5 were there getting ready to go. We even had A5 and A8 there ready to go. All we needed now was A1 to come and take off her clothes. A5 and A8 had no idea what was heading their way.

Immediately, C1 was trying to overstep his bounds and tell D1 what to do. I was getting pissed. I would have had that asshole killed if he would have done that to me if I was the D1, but D1 let it happen. I couldn't believe it. Once A1 arrived, I left. I went back down out of the tower, hoping that A1 would destroy A5 and A8 and then still be hungry and feast on C1. But no such luck. They couldn't get her clothes off. I could have done it, but that's not my mission.

I went back inside the war room and saw that many of the other A's have arrived. Little do they know that their days are numbered. One of them, A3, is a girl that I knew prior. A friend of mine would have intercourse with her on a regular basis for fun. The odd thing is that her ribs are inverted so her breasts seem small but are actually quite large and over–sized. You can't tell because they grow inward. In fact, in about 5 days, A4 will notice this and say something about it to me in secrecy and then I will rat him out in front of A3, thereby destroying their rocky trust in one another.

There were quite a few homosexuals there. More than I thought there would be.

All in all, the first day was good.

21

Matt Wall

We had chicken.

There were however a couple of problems. For instance, Operation 25 was a complete disaster. D1 was lost. And C1 wasn't helping at all. It took almost all day. And P3 was losing his mind. The good thing though, was that no one suspected A1 of anything other than being beautiful.

D1 was sinking fast. I stepped in and got things on track, but not without arousing suspicion of my motives and what my objective might be. At that point, we moved out into an alley. It was dirty and windy. Things back there were not good.

P3 showed up with a brilliant plan. (That was sarcasm by the way) . P3 was adamant about making sure that when your mouth moved, no sounds were to come out of it and to only talk when your mouth is shut. The idiot. He will ruin this whole mission with horrible orders like that. So I stood my ground and told him that was an awful idea and that we had to make sure that mouths and voices moved at the same time. He yelled at me in front of everyone because he had no idea that I was a P2. He was informed that I was only C6. So granted he yelled at me. He was about to break my cover. In fact, D1 and I were the only ones that knew P3 was in fact a R1.

I had to move quickly. I made a lunge at him like I was going on the offensive. This scared him and made him retreat. Now that P3 was away from the troops, I could chase him down and get to the bottom of this. I stopped him and pinned him up against a car. He screamed at me and I screamed right back. I convinced him that it was him who'd brought me onto the mission and that I was there to be the voice inside his head, on the outside. His tone quickly changed. Now, since he thought he brought me onto the mission, my cover could stay secure as long as P3 always collaborated my story.

I was still pissed and so was he. My job was done though. I am now his conscience. We walked back into the bunker and no one would make eye contact with me. This scared me a little bit. And just as I was staring at B1 and B2, D1 came in and called me over to tell me that P3 wanted to speak with us, in a secret room hidden off the rest of the building.

Once there, inside the large vacant room, P3 sat behind a large oak desk. I think this was just to put something between the two of us more so than to assert his dominance. He informed us that he did not like being questioned in front of the troops and his whole life he had to answer to people. This made him upset. He had fought long and hard to become a P3 and he wasn't about to let me take that away from him. D1 confirmed that he didn't know at all what was going on and had no clue what we were talking about. This put the focus on P3 and me. Soon, tears came out of his face and he wanted me to fuck him. This could not happen for reasons that I will go into later. D1 is a much stronger candidate for fucking, but that seemed out of the question. I did however notice that one of P3's forearms were much bigger than the other one which tells me that this doesn't come up too much and he does most of the fucking P3 himself.

I walked out after giving P3 a large hug that made him feel cared for.

The next day when we arrived, I was pissed. If A1 didn't get naked soon and start killing these people, I would just

23

scream!

Shit.

There I did it. I guess the cat is out of the bag.

2

When I said that I was a double agent, I wasn't lying. One of the tasks assigned to me was to make sure that when all of this is said and done, there are no witnesses. So if that means having A1 kill all the other A's and hopefully the C's too, then that is what will happen. P1 made that very clear to me when he made me P2. P1 also informed me that A1 was actually P4! No one knew this but P1 and me. If any of the A's or C's found out, her cover would be blown and no one would be caught dead alone with her for fear that they would be caught dead!

This day went a bit better than the last with only a few little hang ups. First off, we did manage to trick A1 (P4) to take her clothes off. This really wasn't that hard. Keeping them off was the hard part, for she wouldn't be completely okay with having nothing on until after coffee tomorrow. A1 also made some good moves throughout the day. She stabbed A10 in the ear with an ice pick and then strangled A11 (which made me quite sad because A11 was quite fun to be around. A11 was also a television) . While A1 was naked, we couldn't control her at first. Well, I should say D1 couldn't control her, see, if I haven't already mentioned it, he was not familiar with naked women. A1 while spinning around after stabbing A10, lopped off A8's head. This of course was an accident, but this is something D1 will have to fill out the paperwork for. This would never have happened if I was D1.

I went back into the bunker and saw B1.

It was time.

I motioned for her to follow me around the corner. She came to me with her white blonde hair sitting perfectly on her beautiful head and I grabbed her large, tan breast and squeezed it firmly. She looked deep into my eyes while I turned her nipple dial to "moist hand job". Her palm secreted just enough silicone vaginal secretion and she massaged me to climax and caught it in her mouth. I might have forgotten to tell you that B1 is a robot.

No one else really knew.

Some may have, but it really isn't an important part of the story.

I like to call ones like B1 – sexbots. It seems to make more sense. I hope that there is time later in this mission to actually have intercourse with B1; she was made to my specifications perfectly. B2 obviously is not a sexbot. She is just a general whore. She will fuck me for cigarettes. I don't know if I would really want to do that though. I like the sexbots because of their "self–cleaning" feature which makes any kind of STD, a fear of the past.

I couldn't find P3 anywhere. Then I heard that P1 was around. I walked into a room and found him with his mouth on parts of A6. He told me to not tell A1 about this due to the fact the mission would change and her "auto target lock" would take over. I understood. A6 did not however. She was Russian. He then told me two more things that would complicate my mission. One was that A12 was my responsibility, to which I asked if that meant I needed to kill him. Apparently, A12 is notorious for never being where he should be and it was my responsibility to get him to the warehouse tomorrow so A1 could do him in. I asked why A12 was so important and in P1's answer came the second thing that I learned. P1 told me that the Chinese needed A12 taken care of and had asked P1 as a favor. In fact as soon as A6 got the white liquid out of P1, he would be off to China to inform them that the deed was done.

The Chinese?!

This has gotten much deeper than I ever could have thought. This complicates matters greatly, especially since I have my own mission on top of being a double agent. My mission, above all others, is to kill P3. I believe that D1 knows why I'm there but honestly, he is so deep into his mission I don't think he would even notice.

The C's were out of control as well. I couldn't handle it anymore and I knew that everyone was busy. I had to blow off some steam. I found C5 alone in a room and walked over to him and very politely placed my hand inside of his belly and pull his innards out and then strangled him with them. Yes, I know that C5 would've died just from laying there with his inside parts on his outside but I needed to get the negative energy out of my system by pulling with great vigor the intestines tight around his neck.

I felt better. A lot better. Even more so when I pushed C4 off the top of the building so that his head would break his fall once he came into contact with the hard Earth below.

We had pizza.

3

This day started with B1's naked android body riding me to completion. So yes, this day started better than most. D1 picked me up and I told B1 to wait in the back then five minutes after I leave she can head over to the warehouse which is downtown in the heart of the slum district. This location will make it easy to dispose of the bodies after A1 is done with her part of the mission. I received a message from P1 while in transport with D1. The message stated that we need to complete the mission today; all of it. A1 needs to be ready as soon as we get there. The Chinese are pissed. They expect results and we have been dillydallying.

When we got there, I noticed that P3 was there. He was staring through me. He is onto me. I knew it. I had to come up with a way to get him off my scent. I explained to D1 that not only did we have to trick A1 to get out of her clothes but we then needed to quickly hide her coverings so that she would rage out and just annihilate everyone.

I saw B1 come in just in time. I asked her if she and B2 could spend the day running interference on P3. I didn't need his bullshit today. B1 told me how all she wants to do is help me (now if she was a real girl I would be touched, but I programmed her to say that) . They went over to P3 and started making out in front of him. I telepathically told her to make sure that she gives extra attention to his growth on the back of his neck.

She smiled.

The torture room had quite a few sub rooms connected to it. By the time I got in there, A1 was completely naked and was eating A15's face. We are on the right track. After it swallowed A15 whole, it was open, and it looked directly at me. I was horrified. I made eye contact with A1 who looked at me and smiled. It was a good thing that she was going through what we call in this line of work "food coma" or I would have been done for.

D1 grabbed me by the arm and reprimanded me. He reminded me of how dangerous looking into an A1 could be. Little did he know that even though it is dangerous, I have had my fair share of dealings while looking down the throats. Some even more powerful than an A1!

Back at the warehouse base camp, the rest of the A's sat around bored while one by one they were being called into a room to be lunch for the naked A1. I checked in on B1 and B2 to see how it was going with P3. All good over there. He was taking pictures with them while they had had intercourse across his lap. Just then, A14 pushed me out of her way and said some very nasty things to me. I understand that she doesn't know that I'm really P2 and most of the time a D1, but it still pissed me off. I looked at the rest of the A's and they seemed a little scared of what may happen next. Does this mean my cover has been exposed? Does this mean everyone knows?

I very quietly with a smile, followed A14 out into the hallway where I grabbed her by the neck and shoved my finger and thumb into her flesh on both sides of her throat, ripping it out onto the floor. She was very cute, but no sexbot. I pushed her corpse into what I thought was a closet but ended up being a bathroom where A13 sat pissing into a toilet. Of course her reaction was a loud one. I jumped over the corpse and filled her open mouth with my fist. I kept pushing my arm through her wet, toothy hole until I heard her jaw snap half way up my forearm. I pinched her nose shut with my other hand and calmly waited until she stopped breathing. Some of you might not see the problem here, so let me spell it out for you…

A1 needs to kill a certain amount of A's or else very bad things will happen to all of us.

In my rage I have dispatched two A's that were intended for A1. I would have to figure out a way to fix this. I felt like I was forgetting something but I couldn't be bothered with it at the moment due to the fact that C7 came up to me crying. She was the only C that was attractive but I'm pretty sure at one point she was a man. She was crying however because one of the weapons that P3 was really very adamant about having during this objective wasn't working. It was a stupid weapon to have in the first place but P3 couldn't be talked out of it in our briefings before we set out. She was afraid he would have her killed if he found out. I told her to take it easy for the time being since I knew he was being subdued. But, she had to try to fix it as soon as possible.

I checked on P3 and let's just say I'm super glad that B1 has a "self–cleaning" feature.

Once back in the torture room, I found D1 with C's 1–3. They were trying to figure out a way to keep A1 in this one sub room and still get another A in there for her to kill. Just then, A5 walked into that sub room not knowing what was going on. A1 leaped into action and ripped out A5's breasts. Blood was everywhere. I thought for sure A5 had breasts that were full of silicone, but I was wrong. The inside of a breast is one of the most disgusting things I have ever seen. I left them to clean up.

I still felt like I was forgetting something.

P3 came by and asked if I thought now was a good time for lunch because he felt like it was a good time for lunch (that is the R1 in him). I said sure. He asked if I thought Chinese would be okay with everyone...

Chinese?

Holy shit!

The Chinese!

A12!!!

I panicked. I asked P3 if he could find out where A12 was. He let me know that he outranks me and it's against protocol for me to ask him things like that or give him orders. I agreed. I let him know that Chinese would be fine and I hurried to find B1.

When I found her, she was finishing her last rinse cycle from her keeping P3 occupied. I told her how important it was that A12 get there soon and if she or B2 could go get him and make sure he was there. She left, still dripping.

I made it back into the room where the A's were waiting. They were getting upset. They knew something wasn't right. They started asking me questions. Questions I didn't want to answer. A4 jumped up and demanded to see D1. I thought maybe walking him into the lion's den wasn't a bad idea especially since he seemed to be a rebel rouser. A2 said he wanted to come as well. The problem with this situation is that A4 used to be close with D1 back when D1 was an A many years ago. D1 hasn't been jaded enough to set aside his feelings. I'm not sure how this will go. A2 was a closeted gay night club singer in his past life. Now, he's just a stupid fucking A.

So into the torture room I take A2 and A4. A1 just woke up from her dealing with A5 and jumped on A4 who thought she was coming onto him. Very quickly he disrobed in front of all of us and tried to have intercourse with A1 as she killed him. A2 freaked out as soon as the blood sprayed him in the face. A1 lunged at him. He quickly grabbed C3 and pushed him into her. This gave A2 a minute to figure out what to do and let the shock wear off while she bled C3 out. C3 was to be married next week.

A2 made it to the door and yelled, "RUN," just before he met his demise at the teeth of A1. I knew that I had to make it to the room with the A's to calm everyone down before this all got out of hand. I made a decision to jump over A1 while she fed on A2. That was by far the scariest moment in my long career. She could've grabbed me and pulled me into the carnage. But, I really think that she and I have a bond. I think she knows what I'm there for. I'm here to help her, to ensure that everything goes to plan. That look we shared when she was eyeballing me—there was a spark.

I rounded the corner to see the A's trying to run out of the room. My only hope was violence. I knew that if I knocked the biggest motherfucker down the rest would play by the book. There were only four left. Five if you count A12. A9 was the only man left, second if you count A12. A3, A6 and A7 were all that were left; all women, all beautiful. The Russian A6 was by far the best looking. So I cracked A9 in the knee cap and then punched A6 in the kidney. That was a bit sad considering, she doesn't speak English and most likely has no idea why anyone was running anyway. Regardless, it kept the rest quiet, scared and still. This isn't the best way this could've gone.

B1 finally showed up. A12 was nowhere to be seen. I asked her where he was and she said that he wanted to eat a ham sandwich over by the kitchen area. I ran over there to find him hitting on A1. Again, A1 is naked. So the idea that anyone eating a ham sandwich would have a beautiful naked woman in front of them is living in a fantasy world that I'm sure he didn't mind. His pickup lines were unnecessary and wouldn't have worked anyway, but he reached his hand out (the one without the sandwich) , and she ripped the arm off. A12 choked on his sandwich while trying to scream. It was good that no one heard him and it's a good thing that the Chinese will be off our backs. Now, I can get back to what I've been sent here to do.

When I came out I saw that P3 had returned with Chinese food. Everyone ate. P3 informed me that a HJSD would be coming by to see how things were going.

4

HJSD!!!

I was mortified. Those people take record of everything anyone ever says. My cover will be blown. HJSD will know me, will know who I've been, will know my status and will blow my cover. That's what they do. I don't have much time.

I found D1 who was interested to hear the news of HJSD's arrival. I tried to explain to him why this was a very bad thing but I couldn't without giving up why it bothers me so. I said some horrible things about P3 then turned around to see standing there before me, HJSD.

The HJSD showed great enthusiasm to see me and hear what I had to say. He then informed me that P3 said that he is going to really be throwing his weight around to show everyone who's the boss. This too did not sit well.

We made it back into the main area of the warehouse. There, I found that C1 and C2 were keeping the four A's at bay while P3 paced around. A1 was locked in a small room near the kitchen until she would become hungry again.

The A's asked what was going on, why are we doing this, the typical cries you hear from people before their lives are taken from them. I had to drown it out because D1 was freaking out. He wasn't sure how to make the rest of this go since the A's weren't supposed to know their fate. It's Operation 25 all over again. I let him know I was there for him with whatever he needed. He looked like he was about to ask me something when the cries of a woman from another room startled me.

I ran around the corner and found P3 holding C7 by her hair and smashing her face into the counter. I grabbed him by the head and threw him into the wall. After asking what was transpiring, C7 tried to talk but couldn't. Then P3 told me a story about how his weapon was broken. I knew something like this would happen. The worst part is HJSD is taking notes right behind me. This couldn't be worse. I grabbed P3 by the face and told him to just get out there and do his job or else I would do it for him. He said that I didn't have the right. To be fair as far as P3 knew, he was right. But that was about to change.

I made it out to the main room to see HJSD interviewing C7. I shook it off. D1 was quite panicked. There seemed to be a lot of that going on. D1 didn't know who to kill next. I told him it was very easy. If we open the door now, A1 will come in and kill A7 and could probably catch either A9 or

A3 before they make it into the next room. D1 was more worried about our safety and where we would hide to stay out of harm's way. I told him that I would handle it and to go hide behind the brick–a–brack. Right then, P3 stood up and made his presence known.

He screamed about how I dared try to take over his mission when I'm just a C6. And that if he wanted to kill every one of us he could and none of us would be missed. He screamed that he was the boss and that he called the shots. He looked me straight in the eye and told me to go fuck myself and then left.

HJSD had more than enough to write a proper report about how bad our team had completely fucked this mission up. There was nothing I could do, HJSD was very high up and if I tried to stop him or interfered in anyway it would be curtains for me. D1 however didn't know how horrible this could be. So I tried to convince him quickly that he should try to go stop HJSD while I let A1 out. So that he did.

C1 and C2 were all set but they didn't like that fact that I took over. See, they have been working under P3 for years, C1 the longest of anyone. They used to go cut up people for doctors, back when you could still make money doing that. Apparently on the black market, C1 still does those as solo shows. C2 is from another place. He shouldn't be here. But for some reason P3 has been able to hide him through paperwork.

While B1, B2 and C7 hid, C2 was ready to pop the door open for A1 to come out running. A7 was fighting me the whole time as I tried to put her close enough to the door for this to work. I screamed to the rest of the A's that the doorway on the right was their only way out and if they didn't believe me they would be dead for sure. C2 opened the door.

I jumped back as A1 devoured A7. A3, A6 and A9 ran as fast as they could, straight into the door on the right which I told them to go through, which of course was a tiny room with no exit. A1 leaped to her feet and threw a knife into A6's shoulder right before she made it into the room. They tried to get the door shut once they realized that there was no getting out but it was too late. A1 made it through the door and C2 ran over and shut it behind them while C1 locked it.

I didn't like C1 so as he stood up I unlocked the door and kicked him through it and quickly pulled the door back shut and locked it in time so that they were all still trapped. I hoped to god that this would be enough for A1's appetite.

Out of the corner of my eye I saw C2 hang up his phone and slowly make for the main entrance. I asked him where he was going. Seeing what I just did to C1 he was scared. And he had every right to be. I would definitely kill him if he tried anything. He informed me that P3 was waiting outside for him and was going to leave us all here. I broke one of C2's legs and picked up the phone when P3 called back.

I let him know that he had better come back into the warehouse because there was a problem that only he could fix. He then told me that he talked to the HJSD and knew I wasn't a C and that I could figure it out myself. I told him that P1 was up there and looking for him. This made him very nervous because P1 could have him executed. He wasn't sure if P1 was really back from China yet. But he knew that if he disobeyed an order from P1, it would be the end of him.

Moments later, P3 poked his ugly head through the entrance and I grabbed him by his fuzzy hair and threw him into a chair. I asked him many questions that he refused to answer. That's when he told me about the extermination papers. I couldn't believe it. P3 signed extermination papers for B1, B2, C7 and D1! I didn't understand.

Why? I thought.

He said that it was during that process he found out that I wasn't a C and that I actually outranked him. He found this out because he tried to put papers through on me. I told him that he had to put a hard stop on those papers and he said he couldn't. I knew he could because I know the process. He screamed as I beat his face into what resembled our lunch. He wasn't budging and I knew that if I hurried I could resend his orders.

D1 walked in right as P3 was breathing his last breath. Of course he was shocked. I knew I would have to debrief him. His eyes were wide and his jaw hit the floor. The door to the back room opened and out walked A1. She looked beautiful and tired. She thanked me, asked me for her clothes and kissed me on the cheek. D1 walked her to where we hid her belongings.

It seemed everything was fine. B1, B2 and C7 came out of their hiding spots just as C2 put bullets into the heads of B2 and C7. I quickly made his heart stop beating by puncturing it with sharp metal. Besides resending the extermination requests, our work was done there. I made everyone happy. The Chinese, P1, D1 and even P4 since she is no longer an A1. Her status might go up to P3 now but I really hate that rank.

After I debriefed him on everything I could tell him, D1 asked me what we were to do now. I told him that I was going to go home to sleep with my sexbot.

THE END

THE WORLD OF MYTH

MAGAZINE

ISSUE

69

JANUARY 2019

Steve Carr

Steve Carr, who lives in Richmond, Va., began his writing career as a military journalist and has had over a 130 short stories published internationally in print and online magazines, literary journals and anthologies. His collection of short stories published by Clarendon House Books, launched March 1, 2018.

A Murder in Rabbit Town
By: Steve Carr

IT WAS ONE of those nights. It was a night when every
lowlife and desperate bunny in Rabbit Town hopped up
from the bowels of the warrens and crowded the rain–
soaked streets. Thugs, mugs, dolls, dames, and pickpockets,
huddled in the darkened storefront doorways, waiting for a
break in the downpour before hightailing it to the nearest
sleazy nightclub, gin joint, and dive. I didn't have the time
to spare to try and avoid getting my new gray wool fedora
and tan trench coat wet. Anyways, as my mother always
said when she used to lick my unusually long ears, even for
a bunny, I wasn't made of sugar and a little water wouldn't
melt me.

I'm a copper, a flatfoot, a detective, a lepus chaser. My
name is Harry Rabbit and I was looking for a bunny with
an unsavory reputation who had suddenly disappeared.

The eyes of every bunny in every doorway was on me as

Steve Carr

I passed by them, splashing through the puddles with every
leap. They all knew me, or knew of me. I was well- known
in Rabbit Town, but loathed. Being a snitch is part of my
job, but I couldn't shake that label when I was off–duty. In
the warrens other rabbits didn't like sharing their burrows
with a bunny who had caused their son or uncle to be sent
to the slammer. I was always a private rabbit, so keeping to
myself suited me just fine.

In the glare of the flashing neon signs and under the
yellow orbs of light cast by streetlamps on Clover Street I
dashed into Lucky Rabbit's Tobacco Emporium, shook the
rain from my coat, and stepped up to the counter. The
heady aromas of a dozen different flavors of pipe and cigar
tobaccos hung in the air. Lucky was behind the counter
putting freshly rolled turnip leaf cigars in the glass case
under the counter. Lucky was a scrawny rabbit with one
bent ear and drooping gray whiskers. When he was
younger he spent several years in the big house for robbing
a carrot store and shooting its owner, fortunately only
injuring him. Murdering another rabbit was usually
punished with being fried, and no rabbit wanted to end
their life in a big skillet. The time in the hoosegow had
hardened him, but wizened him. That was before I was
even a kit. He kept his shop open late on Saturday nights to
cater to the swells and gangsters who bar–hopped, had
their pockets loaded with moola, and liked to show–off by
buying expensive cigars.

"What can I do for ya, Harry?" he asked, his upper lip
curled into a sneer, exposing his brown, tobacco–stained
buck teeth.

"A beet leaf cigar," I said. I reached into my coat pocket

44

and pulled out a slice of parsnip and tossed it on the counter. "And I need some information about your pal, Whitey Rabbit. He's missing."

Lucky grabbed a cigar from a box on the shelf behind him and tossed it on the counter. "What gives you the idea I'd tell you anything about Whitey?"

I picked up the cigar and rolled it between my fingers. "Because you wouldn't want to see him go to the joint and into the skillet on a bad rap for the murder of Snowy Rabbit," I said.

Lucky picked up the parsnip and put it in the cash register. He eyed me suspiciously. "What do you want to know?"

"Where was Whitey last Friday night?" I asked.

"Playin' poker in the back of Alice's Tavern," he said. "I know that 'cause I was there too. I lost a basketful of parsnips."

I put the cigar to my nose and inhaled the sweet fragrance of dried beets. "If you're lyin', Lucky, I'll make sure you end up back in the slammer."

Lucky glared at me, locking his eyes with mine. "If you're lookin' for Whitey go to Alice's and quit comin' to me every time you need information. I ain't a stooly."

"Why Alice's?" I asked.

"If you don't know it already, it was where Snowy hung out. He wasn't liked by some of the rabbits who swill their carrot juice there," he said. "Snowy had a habit of rubbing other rabbits the wrong way. He and Whitey didn't get along, but I'd bet a wheelbarrow of parsnips that Whitey didn't kill Snowy."

"I may hold you to that bet," I said.

45

I put the cigar in my mouth, turned, and hopped out of the shop. Rain fell in sheets. A fast flowing stream ran down the street gutter carrying pieces of celery and rabbit pellets with it. I pulled the collar of my coat up around my neck and hopped toward the sounds of croaking toads. Alice's Tavern sat on the edge of the algae–covered pond located on the outskirts of the city. In the two years that I had been a detective, I had only been to Alice's once. Its clientele was mainly the bucks on the verge of being outright down–and–outers and the does who followed them. It had little to offer the upper class partiers in search of slum–life thrills, or the mobsters and their molls who wanted to rub elbows with the rich.

I hopped down the street as fast as I could, stopping at times only to shake the water from my tail. At first I thought the sound of footsteps I heard behind me was coincidental, but then it became clear, they stopped when I did, and started again when I began. Before leaving the last light provided by streetlamps I stopped in front of a bookshop and pretended to peruse the used books shown in the window. After several minutes the rabbit came up to me.

"I'm sorry I was followin' ya, but you're Harry Rabbit ain't you?" she said.

The bunny was a pretty, albeit cheap appearing doe. She looked as if she was wearing her maiden aunt's ratty hand–me downs. She wore between her petite ears a small, red hat with a black veil, festooned with dead sparrows and berries that dripped rain onto her rain–soaked and moth–eaten faux fox stole. A small red purse hung from her arm. Her lips were thickly covered in fire engine red lipstick. She was chewing gum that frequently snapped.

"Yes, I am," I said. "Who are you?"

"I'm Beatrice Rabbit," she said. Her voice was high pitched and squeaky, as if she had inhaled helium. "I used to be Snowy Rabbit's girlfriend. That was before that floozy got her furry paws on him."

"What floozy?" I asked.

She looked around her nervously, up the street from where we had just come from, and at the stretch of dark street leading to Alice's. "I never found out what her name was but when I heard that Snowy had been murdered I knew she had to have been involved in one way or another." She raised the net and stared at me with lovesick eyes. "Snowy was so good to me. Whatever I wanted, Snowy gave it to me. I had more carrots than any bunny in the burrows. That was before she came along." Her paw shook as she adjusted her hat. "Snowy didn't deserve ending up in the pond with his body riddled with bullets."

This dame was itchin' to get back at the doll who took her buck and she'd say anything to do it. I'd seen it a hundred times before. With almost every crime there's a doe who's been done wrong involved in it some way. "Do you have any proof?"

"Proof?" she asked, gazing at me innocently. "She stole Snowy from me. Isn't that enough proof?" She wiped raindrops from her nose.

"You're just another dizzy doe," I said.

I expected tears to come next. That was the way it was with these types of does. Instead, she smacked me, right in the kisser. The surprise of it stunned me for a moment. I thought about punching her, to teach her that no bunny lays a paw on Harry Rabbit and gets away with it. Just then there were thudding footsteps behind us. She stared at the large hare walking through the shadows cast by the streetlamps and coming toward us. She bit into her rouged lower lip, let out a small squeal, and then hopped across the street, and rushed up the sidewalk toward the heart of the city.

As the hare came closer I recognized that he was Jack Hare, a surly, short–eared lupus with a scar across his cheek from a knife fight fought out in the cattail swamps on the far side of Rabbit Town. I knew him, but not well. Hares were a mean lot who mostly stuck to themselves, but Jack was a bit different. He was always looking for a fight with a rabbit. His black Homburg hat was slanted over his forehead, hiding his black, seedy eyes.

His nose twitched. "What are ya doin' down in this neck of the woods, Harry?" he asked.

"Lookin' into the murder of Snowy Rabbit," I answered. "You know anything about it?"

In the shadow of the hat, I could see the cold glint of hatred in his eyes.

"I'm just glad someone had the good sense to knock him off," he said. "I woulda shot him myself if he had provoked me even just a little. Jack always packed heat and though nothing had ever been pinned on him, rumor had it that he wasn't afraid to use his gun. "That doe you were just talkin' to owes a gamblin' debt to the lepus mob over on the East End. When Snowy left her she kept gamblin' but had no way to pay her debts."

"Why are you tellin' me this?" I asked.

"Even if she's not a lepus, I hate seeing a doe like her get

48

mixed up with the mob," he said. "it never ends well."

He was right. The lepus mob meant business when it came to being owed anything, especially parsnips. I suspected that Jack was a member of the mob, but I couldn't prove it.

"Do you know the whereabouts of Whitey Rabbit?" I asked.

"Nah, but someone in Alice's might be able to tell you. He was a fixture there until Snowy was murdered."

"That's what I heard," I said. "Where ya headed?"

"I was goin' down to Alice's for a bit of juice," he replied.

"That's where I'm headin'," I said. "I'll hop along with you."

His lips curled into a sardonic smile. "No thanks. Bein' seen goin' into Alice's with you would be like bein' asked to take poison. No decent lepus keeps any kind of company with a flatfoot. You go first and I'll come along later."

He leaned against the building and took a cigar from his black trench coat pocket. I turned and hopped to the tavern. The red neon sign above the door winked on and off. I could hear music from the jukebox and the low din of voices coming from inside the tavern. As I opened the door my nostrils were assaulted with the smell of fermented carrot juice. I had tried to kick the habit a few times, but even the slightest whiff of the juice immediately hooked me all over again. There were rabbits who shot it into their veins. They ended up down–and–outers begging for quick fixes in the back alleys of the city. I never got that bad. I stepped in and every rabbit in the joint turned and glared at me. Only the two rabbits doing a tango on the small dance floor seemed unaware that a copper had walked in. The tavern was dimly lit, which hid the peeling paint and ramshackle decor.

The dozen–or–so customers sitting at the round tables, quickly returned to swilling their juice. They were a motley group of petty criminals, floozies, and deadbeats. I scanned the room, looking for Whitey. That's when I saw the dame sitting alone at the bar. She had legs that stretched from here to the other side of the pond and they were covered in expensive silk stockings. She wore a silver lamé dress that clung to her curvaceous body like a second skin. A long string of black pearls hung around her neck. She toyed with them as she sipped on a glass of juice. On the bar was her silver purse.

I walked to the bar and sat on a stool two down from hers. I shook the rain from my hat and put it back on and laid my coat on the stool on the right of me, between she and I.

"I don't appreciate you comin' in here and depressin' my clientele," Bugsy Rabbit, the bartender, said.

"Knock it off and get me a juice, on the rocks," I said.

After Bugsy put the glass of juice on the bar in front of me, I swirled the juice with a celery stick making the ice tinkle. I took a sip and turned and looked at the dame.

Her eyes were on me like prison yard searchlights. She was a bunny that from the looks of her was born to plenty of parsnips. I'd seen plenty of dames just like her; dolls and molls that hung out in dives just to be noticed.

"Finally, I meet face–to–face with the famous Harry Rabbit," she said. You could have poured her voice over a stack of pancakes.

"I didn't catch your name," I said, and then gulped down

the rest of the juice. My attraction to this doll was dangerous, and toxic. This dame could have have easily turned me into a juice junkie.

"Pufftail Bunny," she said. She sipped from her glass, adding glossy pink lipstick to what already ringed it. "What brings you here tonight, Harry?" she asked.

"I'm lookin' for a guy named Whitey Rabbit," I said. "You heard of him?"

She nibbled on the celery stick. "Yeah, I've met him here once or twice. What has he done?"

"He's been missing since Snowy White's murder was discovered," I said.

The door to the tavern opened and Jack hopped in. His entrance caused a wave of hushed chatter among the rabbit patrons. He hopped across the tavern and sat down on the stool to the left of me. He placed a paw full of parsnip slices on the bar and said, "Give me a double juice with a mint chaser and keep 'em comin', barkeep."

Bugsy scooped up the slices and a moment later put a glass with the juice in it and a second glass of the green fermented mint next to it. The aroma of the mint wafted my direction. I never liked the stuff; it was too strong for my tastes, but was a popular drink among the lupus.

I turned my attention back to the dame. She was running her paw up and down her pearls like she was playing some kind of musical instrument. Dames like her displayed their jewelry the same way rabbits who were combat veterans displayed their medals. Dolls with jewels rarely spent time roosted on a bar stool in Alice's.

"Where were we?" I asked.

"You said something about Snowy Rabbit's murder," she

said.

"Did you know him?" I asked.

She straightened the seam in her left stocking. She coulda had her gams insured for a million parsnips. "Yeah, I knew him. He was one helluva a great rabbit. He didn't deserve to die that way."

The tone in her voice was a mixture of fire and ice. My thoughts of making kits with this dame had blinded me to who she was. There was no doubt in my mind that this was the dame Beatrice told me about.

"You were Snowy's squeeze, weren't you?" I said.

"Her eyes turned cold, as if they had been replaced with ice cubes. "It wasn't like that with Snowy. I loved the guy and that weasel Whitey murdered him 'cause he wanted me himself. I would shoot him and throw his body in the pond, just like he did with Snowy, all over again if I could."

The sudden surprised expression on her face revealed her awareness that she had accidentally confessed to the murder of Whitey Rabbit.

I flashed my badge. "You're under arrest for the murder of Whitey Rabbit," I said.

"No copper is going to take me to the stony lonesome to be fried in a skillet," she snarled.

As I bent over to get my gun from my coat, she opened her purse and took out a Smith and Wesson and aimed it at me. I lurched at her just as she fired the gun. The bullet missed me but hit Jack in the throat. He fell from his stool onto the dirty floor where he died, his legs twitching until his final breath. I wrestled the gun from her paw and turned it on her.

"Put me out of my misery and shoot me," she begged.

I took the cigar from my coat and put it in my mouth. "Sorry, sister," I said. "I'm not a judge or jury, I'm just a rabbit who's a cop doin' his job."

The End

THE WORLD OF MYTH

MAGAZINE

ISSUE

70

FEBRUARY 2019

Alan Russo

Lawrence Alan Russo Jr (AKA Alan Russo) is an American screenwriter, actor, film producer, and director, as well as a comic book writer and author.
In 2000, Russo co-wrote a comic book series called, "Smash," and throughout the years has written for several online publications. As of 2012, he left the film world and co-created, "Zombie Works Publications," where Alan works as the part-time CEO and Editor in Chief.

As of today, he enjoys the simple life with his wife and children in Arkansas, but makes no promise that he's actually retired from the entertainment business.

Through the Nose That's Hairy
By: Alan Russo

CHAPTER 1

DETECTIVE DENE DANDER walked up to the murder scene. Bambi Dumbimbo's slaughtered body was placed inside of a body bag.

"She was stabbed forty seven times with a Rambo knife, by a *Jack the Ripper* copycat," Dander said then paused for a moment. "And she cheats on her taxes."

The junior cop looked up from the corpse puzzled, and asked, "How do you know all that?"

"Because he's Dene Dander, the super detective, who is pissed off all the time," Said Detective Dick Stewart as he walked up to the others.

"Ha. Ha. Cute. Says the man who is named after Dick Grayson and Stewart Copeland from the rock band *Police.*"

Alan Russo

Dander retorted.

"H–How do you know that," the confused police officer asked.

"Because the writer is my best friend," he said with a wink.

"Ooh, okay," the confused officer said.

"So wrong place at the wrong time, partner?" Dick asked.

"No. It's a serial killer," Dander said, and on cue a heavy downpour begin. "Fuzzy hell," he continued and pulled out a pair of glasses from his pocket.

Dick looked at the confused officer and said, "Might as well have a seat, he's about to bust into his in–depth monologue."

"Well, for starters, I'm an old man and am secretly an all knowing wizard and two, there has been a couple of other murders that happened already, before the story even begin."

"What story?" The Confused Cop asked.

"Shh…" Dick hushed.

"So from the previous murders that happened, but you don't know about the because you didn't read them, this tells me that it is the same person." Dander explained. "For example, they have all been female victims and they are all found around the same location. Plus they have all been stabbed the same number of times, in the same places of the body and they are all prostitutes or former prostitutes anyway.

"Also, the name of the previous victims were Mary Ann Nichols, Annie Chapman and Elizabeth Stride," Dander said with a smile. "All names and in order of *Jack the Ripper*

60

victims. So we are—"

"But…but Detective this woman's name is Bambi Dumbimbo," the confused officer mumbled. "It can't be a copycat killer."

Detective Dander groaned.

"If you look boy–o, you'll find that Bambi Dumbimbo is her adult entertainer name and is actually Catherine Eddowes. Thus making the connection of a serial killer, in our ever raining, no named city, who is copying the method, and names of *Jack the Ripper*." Dander said and then bowed toward Stewart and the confused officer.

CHAPTER 2

Detective Dene Dander and his partner Dick Stewart walked into the morgue. Dene noticed that Dick seemed quite nervous and asked, "What's' wrong with you, gotta crap, son?"

"Uh, no. I…uh…just uncomfortable," Dick said while sweat flowed down his face.

"That's probably because of me," a woman with a white lab coat said.

Dander calculated for a moment, and then asked, "Who are you?"

"OH? I'm the sexy, yet nerdy, woman that Dick is secretly having an affair with, but everyone knows anyway. But, you can call me Cathy." Cathy said and then curtsied. "Okay, you two follow me and I will walk you over to the corpse."

"Okay." Dander said.

"And just to let you know the game plan, I will explain the forensic findings while I act like I'm not sleeping with Dick," Cathy said as she walked up to the freezer door.

"Perfect," Dick said. "I will also act like I don't know you, while I stare at your perky boobs creepily."

Cathy winked at Dick.

"Deal." Cathy said.

"Can we get on with this," Dander growled. "I have to get home and brood about how bad life is."

"How about this for quick! She was f*cked, knocked out and stabbed. The End." Cathy said in a snarky manner.

"Wrong story, but thanks for coming," Dick said. "So, on to chapter three?"

"Yeah, chapter three." Dander agreed.

CHAPTER 3

Dick walked out into the rain and over to his partner, who attempted to smoke a cigarette. Once he reached Detective Dander, he asked, "Hey Dene?"

"Yeah, Dick."

"Look, it's late and I wanna put this story to bed, can we just jump to were Cathy was kidnapped," Dick asked his partner, who continued to try and light his cigarette like a dumb ass in the pouring rain.

CHAPTER 40

While Cathy was kidnapped by the killer from her apartment, Detectives Stewart and Dander had problems of their own. That took over a year of storytelling to be told. (Don't worry, this writer isn't that kinda dude) and now the conclusion.

The Wild–Eyed man looked at Cathy with, well, wild eyes. She was nude and bound to a wooden chair (DON'T JUDGE ME! I didn't come up with this, it's that other guy who's been writing a year long murder mystery's kink shit and what not) , and he already had his way with her. Which was weird, because she totally did not put up a fight, she just kinda took it. Trust me, I saw the unedited version of this, it happened.

It was then when the cops busted in, which is odd, because since that was Dick's side piece of poontang pie, one would had thought that he was leading the raid. Anyhoo, back to the story. Once the area was cleared Dander and his partner Stewart (I only went with last name's because my wife said that my screen is full of dicks) , enter the house.

Each officer went to a different room, Dick (is it too late in the story to call him Richard, shit, you're right) , found Cathy where she was at the beginning of this chapter. Dander walked into the bathroom and found the Wild–Eyed man cutting on his ball sack with a small razor.

"What the hell are you doing," Dander said, and walked into the bathroom closing the door behind him.

"It's so hard to feel anything, but, I can always feel pain," The Wild–Eyed Man said with his trademark look to him.

"Ah. I see. You're one of those Emo wussy's that had mommy and daddy give you everything your little spoiled ass wanted, but they didn't spend time with you as a child," Dander mocked the killer. "So you became fascinated with

Jack the Ripper and started killing people because you are numb from not having your parents support even though you still live in their basement?"

"Holy shit, dude." The Wild–Eye Man said. "You are good. I'm not saying like just good, but you are like good, good!"

"All right jerk–off," Dander said while he removed his revolver. "This is so my partner, Dick, doesn't get any body on him."

"I have to say detective, that last comment sounded quite homoerotic. One wou—"

The Wild–Eyed Man was interrupted as Dander fired a slug into his forehead. As soon as the gunshot went off the bathroom door flew open and more police were in there. Dander sat his gun on the sink and lifted his hands.

"Easy boys," Dander said with a smile. "He came at me with a razor blade. It was self defense."

EPILOGUE

Dick and Cathy walked out of the Wild–Eyed Man's house holding hands. Dene Dander walked opposite of his partner.

"I'm so glad they let you walk, Dene." Dick said. "I guess we all get to live happily ever after."

"What about your wife, dude?" Dander asked sarcastically.

"Oh, man, I forgot about her." He replied.

"That's alright, you can take care of her after all of this dies down," Dander continued.

"What? What do you mean?' Dick Asked.

"Just wack her after all the heat dies down," Dander farther continued.

"I—"

"I mean after all, you are the real killer right?"

THE END

THE WORLD OF MYTH

MAGAZINE

ISSUE

71

MARCH 2019

Molly E. Hamilton

Molly E. Hamilton can be found spoiling a small dog and a large rabbit in the landlocked state of Missouri. To read more of Molly's work, please check out Scarlet Leaf Review, Orion's Child: Science Fiction and Fantasy Magazine, and Harvest Time, an anthology published by Inwood Indiana Press.

Ruanna's Dreams
By: Molly E. Hamilton

Part One

THERE WAS SOMETHING odd about the Berringers'
daughter. She was unusually good at skipping (almost to
the point to where it seemed as though she could fly), she
was borderline scary petite, and she had a faint glow to her
soft skin. Her hair was a golden red color, and she had
purple eyes that could be a beacon to your darkest
thoughts…if she was happy. Her name was Ruanna. She
was adopted, of course, because the Berringers believed it
was irresponsible, wrong even, to have children due to
"overpopulation" and the fact there were so many children
"already born and waiting for a family." They would even
decline every baby shower invitation.

Mr. and Mrs. Berringer had many extremes they lived

and swore by. They felt all food in their diet required measurement, along with the highest level of scrutiny. Anything worrn on their bodies needed to be natural. All "man–made" materials were detestable. The air filters in their home and car were cleaned daily and promised "top efficiency." They did their best to be surrounded by things that could be described as "real" and "organic." Every waking moment needed to be productive in some way. Sitting idly and letting thoughts roll through your mind was frowned upon, but the biggest offense to the Berringers was fantasy. Ruanna couldn't have fairy tales, television, unrealistic toys, or anything Disney (the plague). Their daughter would be just like them.

And yet, Ruanna began to trouble her parents once she started to speak. She was very fond of napping and bedtime, and she would awake from her happy slumbers saying her first word: Nana. The problem was that no one but Ruanna knew who Nana was. The grandmothers were called Mimi and Gram–gram. There was no sitter. Nobody was called Nana. It was very unsettling for the Berringers indeed. Where did she come up with that? They attempted to ease their worries by declaring "Nana" was simply a mispronunciation of her own name, but as the child continued to develop, that hypothesis was proven wrong. Nana was a constant. Little Ruanna would toddle around the house, sometimes in tears, calling for her Nana.

As words were added to Ruanna's vocabulary, the Berringers only fretted more about their daughter's nighttime adventures. She started to say forbidden words. Words like "magic," "fairy," and "unicorn." Despite the brigade against the world of pretend, she was not saved from such roaring nonsense. What was more disturbing was that "Nana" was teaching Ruanna things. The young girl mysteriously picked up on counting, the alphabet, writing her name, and moon phases before her parents could begin teaching her themselves. These were good things to learn, but unexpected.

"Who showed you how to do that?" her parents would ask.

The answer? "Nana." Nana was a secret help that no one understood. She even aided in potty training. Her bribes to use the potty were far better than Mommy and Daddy's bribes. Nana had chocolate, corn syrup, and a Pegasus ride for the grandest potty accomplishment.

When Ruanna turned five, Nana was trying to teach her something else. She was trying to teach her how to fly. This was not going well though. Not in dreamland and not in reality. Ruanna would leap down from the top of the stairs in the Berringers' house, run through the yard and spring into the air, but she couldn't achieve her goal. Practicing the art of flying only got Ruanna's beloved naps and early bedtimes restricted. The Berringers would watch for her dreamy gaze and clap their hands for her attention. They would get flashcards for her to stare at. They purchased more educational toys. However her sleep rebellion was a quiet one. The more the Berringers tried to ground her attention to their wiles, the more she sought the refuge of Nana.

"Something's wrong with my wings. Me and Nana don't know what it is," Ruanna would tell her mother. "They won't come out. They're stuck."

With eyes brimming with tears, Mrs. Berringer would

ask, "Ruanna, who is Nana?"

"My Nana," Ruanna would answer. "She takes care of me when I sleep."

The Berringers' feelings of devastation were building. It was getting harder and harder to rationalize Nana into the category of an imaginary friend. The only logical conclusion the *sensible* Berringers' could fathom was that Ruanna was schizophrenic.

"Nana's not real. You cannot fly. There are no Pegasuses," they always assured her. Then there were the doctors and the long, confusing visits that came with them. "Always listen to grown–ups." Ruanna wanted to believe them, but she also learned to keep her own world to herself. The taught silence masked Ruanna's "condition," but her dreaming never stopped. Her dreaming was becoming an escape. For she knew she could never be what the Berringers wanted her to be. She was not a "logical, efficient individual." She was a girl who believed in magic and savoring the moment. Hardly could she get peace but in her dreams.

As she got older it began to be harder to live in two worlds at once. She favored the dream world, but she knew she shouldn't. Nana always told her that she belonged in the dream world. Nana said Ruanna was special and a gift to all who weren't in the dream world. Nana was a fairy. Ruanna was supposed to be a fairy too. But Nana died when Ruanna was 14. She was old, but that didn't make it easier to take.

"Ruanna, why are you so depressed?" Mrs. Berringer asked one morning when Ruanna was sobbing in her cereal.

"I—I can't talk about it," she said softly.

Mr. Berringer was sitting across from her at the table. He had perfect posture and was elegantly drinking his black coffee; he had ground the beans himself. His composure was kept; he was unmoved by Ruanna's apparent sorrow. Mr. Berringer avoided eye contact with his daughter and only glanced at his wife. Mrs. Berringer frowned. "Those dreams again?" she asked impatiently.

"Nana…" Ruanna gulped and took a shuddering breath, "died," she whispered.

"That means you're growing up, dear," Mrs. Berringer said factually. She poured her daughter a glass of cold milk and plopped it beside her. "This is a good thing. Just like when we gave your stuffed animals away."

"But I loved her."

"Soon you will be old enough to take the medication," Mr. Berringer said adjusting his tie one last time. "Then you won't deal with these sorts of problems anymore." He stood up and patted Ruanna's head on his way out.

"I can't go to school today," Ruanna stammered.

Mrs. Berringer held her breath for a moment. "There are only so many mental health days you can use."

Ruanna couldn't respond. She cried more. Her head was now down on the table. The soggy Total cereal was pushed aside. The milk was untouched and became a part of the pristine background.

Mrs. Berringer sighed, "Alright. You can stay home today. At this point you will only be a distraction to your peers." There was no response. Mrs. Berringer watched her daughter's shoulders shake with grief. Carefully she slipped into a seat beside her and awkwardly slung an arm around Ruanna, who tensed at her mother's unfamiliar touch. Mrs. Berringer looked to the ceiling with slight disgust as she prepared herself to speak. "Can't you make her come back? It's your dreams." It was hard to encourage Ruanna to dream in the way she did, but Mrs. Berringer hated to see her daughter in a state of obvious dysfunction.

"No," Ruanna said. "It—it doesn't work," she lifted her head and buried her face in her mother's neck, "that way. I've tried."

Mrs. Berringer missed work that day. The death of Nana disrupted their lives for a short time. It disrupted Ruanna's much longer. She mourned Nana. She took her father's natural remedy sleeping pills to be sure to attend the funeral. Every night before sleep Ruanna would lay back in her bed and wonder how she could love someone so much who wasn't real. With her misery, she didn't want Nana to be real. But then she met Maverick, another being no one else knew.

The Berringers began noticing a change in their daughter. She became happier. She would smile at nothing. Giggle when she thought no one could hear. Her glow was brighter. There was more singing during chores, more skipping in halls. Ruanna was also much more eager to go to bed. Earlier and earlier it seemed she would rush to her room and go to sleep.

"Do you think she's really sleeping?" Mrs. Berringer asked as she was sitting on the couch one evening. It was 6 PM, and dinner was put away.

Mr. Berringer was sitting in his recliner, his files in hand. He slid his reading glasses to the tip of his nose and stared at his wife with a furrowed brow. "I thought she was."

"What if she's doing something up there?"

Mr. Berringer looked uncomfortable. He pushed his glasses back up, turning back to his papers.

"Like trying to get that near death high?" Mrs. Berringer said completely undisturbed. "I've read about kids putting belts around their necks. Or sniffing unsafe—"

"—Dear," he interrupted. And then back to his calm demeanor, "The child is sleeping."

"Kids get addicted to adrenaline," Mrs. Berringer continued.

Mr. Berringer stared at his wife while she babbled on. She had been reading forums about teenagers. Doing so made her more and more terrified. Mr. Berringer listened to her fret till she finally paused, waiting expectantly. She had given him permission to be listened to. It took Mr. Berringer a moment to realize he could speak.

"We can get cameras," he said.

So cameras were purchased and secretly installed into Ruanna's room while she skipped down the school hallways with a slight smile. Naturally the footage her parents captured was boring.

"Does it bother you that she never moves in her sleep?" Mrs. Berringer asked watching the footage with her husband. They were in their bed with pillows tucked properly behind their backs.

"She's just a heavy sleeper," Mr. Berringer insisted. Yet in his eyes was a quiet anger he would never discuss.

Mrs. Berringer watched on, "It's like she's not in there. It's like she's a doll."

Mr. Berringer frowned. He did another search on his Kindle about lucid dreaming. "In the REM stage there is always movement," he said with subtle damnation.

77

"Ruanna never even twitches. When do you suppose she will start dreaming?"

Mr. Berringer only glared into the darkness. He assured his wife he did not know.

Ruanna's grades began to decline. She was a very bright girl. Always overly diligent in her studies, but now she hardly cared. She earned a C on her history test, a B in math, and a D in English. Mr. and Mrs. Berringer were looking through Ruanna's backpack while she slept upstairs. Mrs. Berringer was holding the D paper in her hand, transfixed by the red, sloppy capital letter.

"She scored below average?" she asked her husband, needing confirmation.

Mr. Berringer was frowning at overdue and blank worksheets. In the tiniest of letters scrawled in the corner was the word *Maverick*. "Have you heard of a Maverick?" he asked, glaring more at the speck of a heart beside the name.

"Maverick?"

"Yes," he mused. "Maverick."

The school directory was torn through. The yearbook from last year was searched. There was no Maverick. "You go wake that girl up, this instant. She has a lot of explaining to do," Mrs. Berringer said. She still held the D paper in her hands. Mr. Berringer had the *Maverick* sheet folded neatly in his pocket.

The first confrontation was useless. Ruanna was very upset that her parents had been "snooping." She was more upset that her precious sleep had been disturbed. Ruanna said Maverick was just someone she met in a dream, and she didn't have feelings for him. Ruanna was in denial.

More rules were developed. She had to start calling them

during lunch at school to avoid little naps. When she got home from school the Berringers would have her sit down at the table. Her room was off limits. They would watch her do her homework. They would watch her read her textbooks. After assignments were taken care of, they would have Ruanna knit. Sometimes she would have extra chores; whatever was needed to keep her away from sleep would be done. On the weekends she wasn't allowed to sleep in. Mrs. Berringer developed a strict schedule. Ruanna would only get the minimum amount of slumber. But then teachers were reporting that she was snoozing in class. She slept through lunch after the ridiculous phone call she was obligated to make to her mother. Other times she would simply lose her phone. She was losing weight. Debates of homeschooling were muttered in the wee hours of the morning in the bedroom of the Berringers. Maverick was a distraction.

"Two years. In two years she will be 18, and giving her the medication won't be so dangerous to her developing brain," Mrs. Berringer said smoothing out the tablecloth Ruanna knitted. Mr. Berringer nodded.

Part Two

The Berringers continuously reinforced to their daughter that Maverick was not real—just like Nana. They consoled her with the promise of drugs when she turned 18. Ruanna's glow began to die away. Her giggles ceased. Her songs ended. The joy she had felt was diminishing as she was forced to focus on reality. Her time in her dream world was shortened and tainted by the nagging voice that said, "He isn't real." Soon, Ruanna tried not to sleep. It was too painful.

The depression was beginning to disturb the Berringers more and more. Therapists suggested getting her involved in activities. So they volunteered her to serve at the library. A respectable pastime, as long as she obeyed the rule of not entering the fantasy section. Although, with Ruanna's dismay over the ruin of her dreams, the fantasy section was not a fanged threat. The library was also good because the Berringers didn't want her to have a job yet, because they believed money "gave too much power." Ruanna had to be controlled. So after school, she went to the library for three hours. Then she would go home to eat and study and knit sometimes. Only then would she have some fleeting hours to herself. She took to the Internet to stay awake; she talked to strange peers online. She started sketching. Anything she could do to avoid falling asleep. Soon she became an avid reader. As she volunteered at the library, strange books began coming home with her from a strange librarian called George. George was certainly and tragically real.

George was a tall, thin man. He had masses of curly red locks piled on his great egg–shaped head and cynical blue eyes. His nose was long and skinny, and his lips rested in a straight line. He had taken an interest in Ruanna, who was steadily looking worse and worse by the day. From her depression she lost more weight. Her big, purple eyes were dull and neglected from view by the dark bags hanging below. Her hair was knotted, covered in flecks of dandruff. She was always nodding off behind the non–fiction shelves, and she would awaken with her face tight with terror.

George wanted to know why the young girl was the way she was. So he asked. George was never a shy person. He never had regards to social norms. When he asked, Ruanna told. She told about her love for a figment of her dream world. And how no matter what she did, what she read, what she thought, or what she watched—she dreamt of him every night.

"Always dream about the same world. Every night. And time passes? And he tells you he's real? You have conversations?"

Ruanna nodded, "And it's hard because I love him. I want to believe him, but I just can't."

George cricked his neck and slipped into his thinking posture. He slumped down in his chair from behind the research desk. His lower lip slipped forward and his brow sunk down. His eyes looked up at Ruanna. "Well what if it is real?" he asked quickly. His voice was a mix between a mutter and a growl, which was slightly nasally.

Ruanna stiffened, "What?" she asked in shock. She had never encountered anyone who made such an absurd suggestion.

"This Maverick kid—what if he's real? What if he's been trying to tell you the truth? You *love* him, don't you?" he asked, agitated by the idea.

"Well yes—"

"—And love is life's greatest lie," George said.

"George, please," Ruanna said. For she had heard many a time about George's philosophies.

"What I was saying," he said, "Before we get into the abstract manipulation of human emotion, have you ever considered that there's more to the Earth than what we can

81

see?"

Ruanna shook her head. She was taught to keep her "lunacy" to herself. She was a good little pretender. She was afraid George would end the conversation, but he made a speech to her delight. He talked about his firm belief in the paranormal, the spiritual, and other invisible forces. He complained about Karma earmarking him. He talked about scales of the universe constantly tipping and teetering, which brought him to the hidden function of a hero—to balance the scales. Then he went back to the unseen that shape every last human's life. Then back to the haunting in his friend's cellar. George finally began to end his rantings with, "So it stands to reason, if there are other plains with the dead, then there very well could be other plains that we simply do not know about. Dreams could be our subconscious picking up on it. Might I add, energy cannot be created nor destroyed?"

"Energy?" Ruanna echoed in a small voice. She was afraid someone else would overhear.

"There's something happening in these dreams. They aren't normal. You wouldn't understand it."

"I want to understand."

George, the great philosopher and physicist—the greatest dreamer of all time (who owned a genuine dragon scale key–chain) —smirked with satisfaction. "Then you need to read," he said. George prided himself for his research skills. He believed that the library held every answer in the universe. He, being so great, could find the truth of anything.

Thus came the books. The tireless amount of books that George could find relating to the quest of opening Ruanna's dream world seemed to have no end. Ruanna read them all. George did too. The Berringers began finding all types of physics books lying around their daughter's bedroom, and some science fiction. Books on various, non–taught theories began to appear and so did books on dreams. Ruanna was becoming happier again. She was eating food once more and sneaking naps. She wrote notes based on books that Maverick had in her dream world. A hidden stash of books: *The Dream Realm, Reality of Dreams, Dimension Physics Theories, Alternative Universes, and Energy Essence in Thought* were found in the back of Ruanna's closet. An outstanding library fine for *The Britannicus Veil* came for her in the mail. Apparently someone (George) couldn't wait his turn to read it and placed a reserve on it to force Ruanna to hurry up. Angrily the Berringers paid the fine. They waited for their daughter to come home. They demanded to know what she was doing. Also a report was mailed in from Ruanna's school to reveal that she had been skipping school. There was more to discuss.

This time Ruanna denied nothing. She beamed at her parents, her dancing, purple eyes forced them to smile. "I'm going to bring Maverick home!" she said.

She gushed about the late 1800s, before the fairies were forced into exile for the revenge of the witch trials. She explained how in 1901 the Witch and Fairy Wars ended with the fairies' surrender and decision to leave mankind. She talked about Sir John Rhys, Sabine Baring–Gould, Joseph Jacobs, and Andrew Lang and their studies and archeological evidence. She read to her parents the testimonies of Fiona Macleod and her fairy hunts. She brought down *the Britannicus Veil*. She opened it and linked it all to the "Dream Theory," founded by the William Butler Yeats Association.

"It is believed," she read, "that the fairies still secretly help mankind through intervening in their dreams. It is the only contact the fairies can have to avoid the witches, who still actively attack man today with curses." She glowed more and more. A bulge was developing between her shoulders.

"Call an ambulance!" Mrs. Berringer cried. "Our daughter is *mad!*"

Mr. Berringer stood hardly showing emotion. The anger was making his face quiver. "You can't possibly believe in that," he said.

Ruanna slammed her book shut. She smiled and stared into her father's eyes. "I believe in fairies!" she shouted, and wings slipped up from behind her. Gorgeous, silvery translucent wings that were delicately decorated with swirling and curling designs like the petals of flowers. She screamed joyously. She spun round and round trying to peek at them. "Oh look!" she cried.

But her parents did nothing. They stood and stared at her, for they could not see her wings, her glory.

"Oh, I must show George!" she cried out again. Tears of happiness streamed down her face from her jubilant eyes. "I must find a mirror!"

"Watch her!" Mrs. Berringer wailed to her husband. She rushed off to the phone. Mr. Berringer stood numb.

Ruanna began flying up the stairs. She went to her mirror and saw her wings. Her father quietly followed behind. "My wings!" she said in awe. "They're just as beautiful as Nana said they'd be. Oh, Nana!" she said, "How

I wish you could see them!"

"Ruanna," her father croaked out in a voice that he never heard himself use before.

Ruanna was mesmerized by her wings. She stared into the mirror continuously.

"Ruanna," her father said in an even deeper voice. In the far distance an ambulance was proclaiming its presence.

Ruanna glanced up and lost her breath when she looked at her father in the mirror. Something was different about him. He looked more angular. He looked darker. His face was ashen. He had great shears in his hands. She spun around covering her mouth with her hand to look at him fully.

When she did, he looked normal. He held no wing–cutting shears. "Ruanna, you do not have wings," he said.

Hurriedly, she looked back into the mirror. Her wings were there. Her father stepped closer with the blades.

"Get back!" she cried. She couldn't watch. She turned back around and looked at her father again, stopping the vision.

"Ruanna, you need help," he said in his guttural voice.

Ruanna stepped towards her window. "Get back or I'll fly out!" she yelled.

"You cannot fly," he said. He took a step.

Ruanna put her sweaty hands on the windowsill. "Come no closer!" she warned.

Her father halted. The ambulance was parking into the driveway. "Ruanna, please," he said. Mrs. Berringer was sobbing downstairs. "Ruanna, I don't believe in fa—"

"—Stop it!" she cried. Her wings were burning. They ached. "Don't say it!" she screamed. "Or I will jump from

85

this window and fly away! You're killing me!"

Paramedics pounded up the stairs and burst into the room. Ruanna tried to pull the window open, but her hands slipped. She tried again, but she was tackled. They gave her a shot of morphine, and she calmed down. Regardless, they bound her in a strait jacket, crushing her wings. The Berringers did nothing to comfort their daughter as they took her away. There were no promises of visiting, no following the ambulance, or words spoken to the medics. Mrs. Berringer only stood with quiet tears; Mr. Berringer stared straight ahead.

Ruanna was cold to her parents. It was either unforgiveness or the heavy amount of drugs they had her on. For two years she lived in the Behavioral Health Center. She was still and docile. She rarely spoke and never looked in the mirror. The institution was cold. There were alarms and thick locks on the doors. Kleenexes were on every flat surface. People were crying every time the Berringers were there to visit, which was never often. Ruanna said that tears were shed at least three times a day. Some of the patients would cycle in and out of the institution. Others lived there, like the lady who never spoke and only made sounds. Or the man with burns on his face. He told Ruanna that there was just enough water in the toilet to drown in. Five times a day would be "group time." Various doctors of the mind would sit down among the volunteering patients. They would talk. Different individuals would cry as they talked about their wrongs. Others would yell. Some were ashamed of what bothered them. They would laugh embarrassingly.

The counselors were never disturbed. The counselors were understanding, but the counselors never changed the rules. Ruanna could never have a pencil longer than three inches. They were always dull. Ruanna also couldn't have string. Not even the drawstring on her favorite sweatpants. No one could have anything sharp, for someone could kill themselves with it. Many patients came by ambulance.

Ruanna would frequently ask the nurses for paper. She would hide stubby pencils. She wrote letters to George. She wrote letters to Maverick. A few times a janitor snuck the letters to George to the mailbox. Maverick's letters had to be destroyed after they were written. The counselor insisted that Maverick was a delusion.

"Do you want a boyfriend?"

"I want Maverick," Ruanna would say quietly.

"Have you ever thought about meeting other people?"

Ruanna would only sigh. For now she couldn't meet many others, not that she wanted to. For the drugs administered every morning stole away Ruanna's dreams. Every morning every patient would gather around the desk. In little paper cups would be pills passed out accordingly. Every patient would take their cups. They would take their water. Not one could leave till the bitter pills were swallowed.

The Berringers decided to have her come home on her 18th birthday, a way to celebrate. She came home, reserved and agreeable. They administered her drugs accordingly, the same medication that took her dreams. At first, all was as the Berringers would have dreamed. She was polite, quiet, and logical. She made no reference to fantasy or the unknown. She was finally perfected. She did not rush to sleep. She was becoming like them. Deep down, the Berringers could feel a hollowness about her; they chose not to pay it any heed.

But as the days went on she started to change. She would eerily linger around her parents. She talked to them in short bursts. Other times she would creep into the corner and stand and watch until her parents noticed. She behaved as a ghost. Her gaze was always unsettling. Sometimes she would have a smirk on her lips. The days went on. The Berringers felt that their daughter needed social stimulation. However, she declined. The Berringers suggested getting a G.E.D. and applying for college, but she instead began to reside in the finished basement below. Mrs. Berringer was grateful for the sliding door in the basement—that way she got some sun. Ruanna wouldn't leave the house. At night Mrs. Berringer swore he heard her talking to herself down in the basement. Her soft, sweet voice—tainted by depression—would leak up through the vents. A few nights Mrs. Berringer swore she heard the basement sliding door and a masculine voice speaking as well, but whenever Mr. Berringer went to check, Ruanna was standing by the bottom of the stairs, looking up at the door frame alone. She waited for her father to check on her. Sometimes he would see a lost, vacant stare in her eyes. Other times it was a crooked little smile. She silently mocked him. Mr. and Mrs. Berringer whispered about her in their room late into the night. Each secretly began to fear her. Ruanna became increasingly quieter. She spoke only to herself at night in the basement.

Then one night she snuck out. While the Berringers frantically searched her basement for evidence for where she might be—they found an abundant amount of her medication and empty placebo bottles stored in prescription bottles that bore the name "George Giles" on the pharmacy sticker. The Berringers called the hospital. She replaced her medicine with a placebo. They called the police.

The next morning Ruanna came home with a young man whose name was Maverick. Mrs. Berringer grabbed her husband's arm and squeezed it as she caught herself from falling. "Won't you come in?" she asked. She was trying to look just above Maverick's head, trying to see what shimmering thing was catching the light behind him. Mr. Berringer only scowled at the young man with his daughter. He stepped aside and watched them come in as defeated men do.

The End

THE WORLD OF MYTH

MAGAZINE

ISSUE

72

APRIL 2019

DC Diamondopolous

DC Diamondopolous is an award-winning short story and flash fiction writer with over 150 stories published internationally in print and online magazines, literary journals, and anthologies. DC's stories have appeared in: So It Goes: The Literary Journal of the Kurt Vonnegut Museum and Library, Lunch Ticket, Raven Chronicles, Silver Pen, Scarlet Leaf Review, and many others. DC was nominated for Best of the Net Anthology.

She lives on the beautiful California central coast with her wife and animals. dcdiamondopolous.com

The Creep Factor
By: DC Diamondopolous

TAMMY HAD NIGHTMARES of the man she saw in her store window. His elongated face chased her through the streets of the San Fernando Valley, her terror mounting like a progression of staccato hits rising up the scales on an untuned piano. She always woke up screaming before the crescendo.

It all began after Rachel had a gun held to her head for a measly fifty dollars. How dumb could the thief be, holding up a pillow–and–accessory shop when Dazzles, Tammy's store three doors away sold jewelry? It was costume, plastic, some silver, a few pieces of gold, but, a pillow store?

After the police left, Rachel came in screaming and crying, "Why me?" her eyes red and twitching, mouth pinched. Tammy knew what Rachel was thinking: you take in more money than I do, why didn't he put a gun to your head?

DC Diamondopolous

She felt that the robbery at Rachel's had been a prelude to something bigger, a feeling—dread. It all came back to the dream. She was at the Pacoima county–fair, at an old–time taffy–pulling contest where the taffy wasn't taffy but the face of the man she saw outside staring in at the window display, his phantom shape morphing into multiple cells until a valley of identicals hunted her.

Tammy had a panic button under the cash register. The counter was next to the back door for a fast escape. A six–foot bank of back–to–back showcases stretched down the middle of the long, narrow store, and ten others lined the east and west walls. The glass doors reflected whoever looked into them and gave her time to assess people. Still, she thought of buying a gun.

Tammy stood at the counter with the computer on. She was browsing through listings of Bakelite necklaces on eBay when the door swung open, the buzzer alarmed. Since the robbery, Rachel entered her store like a bull in search of a red cape.

"They caught the asshole that held me up!"

"That's great."

"The douche spent my money. Cops said I won't get it back." Rachel stood just inside the door, her arms crossed, and her attractive face gaunt.

"At least he's off the streets," Tammy said.

"He'll be out soon enough. And probably come back to rob you."

Tammy sucked in her breath.

"I'm sorry. I shouldn't have said that. I hate coming to work. I'm so afraid."

"I understand." Tammy walked down the aisle. "At least

you weren't hurt."

"Emotionally, I was."

Outside, two women looked at the window display. One held a manila envelope, the other several letters. Three months earlier, new neighbors moved in with a shipping and PO Box store. Tammy's walk–in business increased. The customers were a mix of drifters, aspiring actors and models, hopeful reality stars, and self–published writers. They talked about themselves and shared intimate details, as if she were someone without judgment, and perhaps that was the reason, for Tammy saw the best in people, and she had to admit; it made a slow day go by faster.

The two women left.

Tammy was about to speak when the man in her nightmares looked into the window.

"What's the matter?" Rachel asked. "You look like you saw a ghost."

He stood hunched over, dressed in a long black coat, looking at the second shelf in the window display.

"Tammy?"

He was a giant but not really. He just appeared that way. His face and extremities belonged to a man seven feet or taller. His features all merged into the center of his enormous face, leaving his jaw and forehead a wasteland of acne craters. And his eyes, they were two dots of sub–zero tourmaline's.

Rachael turned around. "Ew, who's that?"

"I think he has a PO Box next door. He scares me."

"You've waited on him?"

"No."

"Probably just a looky–loo. It's the normal–looking guys

you have to watch out for. Like the asshole that robbed me."

The man left.

Rachel opened the door and looked back at Tammy. "I keep thinking the next time someone will kill me. Or you."

Tammy gasped.

"Oh, I'm sorry."

Was she really, Tammy wondered? Even so, Rachel left a chem–trail of gloom behind.

Tammy went back to the counter.

She entered her fourth decade of life without husband or child. She attracted men who used her, takers. It made her feel needed, in control, but they always left anyway. She wanted to change, but habits were stubborn, and men wanted younger women.

She dreamed of romances like those in a Nora Roberts novel. She wanted to love and be loved with a passion that could heat Pluto, someone to share in the distinctions of life, to be swept up a switchback of foreplay and countless orgasms.

She went on–line to meet guys, lowered her standards to the bell curve, where all she asked for was a man, under sixty, with a full set of teeth and a decent income. Not even the Internet helped.

She glanced at the large framed mirror—impossible not to look at—that hung on the back of the showcases at the end of the counter. There was no other place to hang it, and her customers needed to see their reflection when buying a necklace or earrings.

Tammy was without glamour, in a most glamorous town, lacked charisma in a city brimming with alluring women, but she did the best she could: added extensions to her lank dark hair, wore contacts that tinged her brown eyes green, ran five miles three times a week at Balboa Park. And she was short in a town where the average woman could play professional basketball. She might have a humdrum face, one that no boyfriend ever lied about by telling her she was beautiful, but she had compassion, could discover the kernel of beauty inside another no matter how hideous the person. So it distressed her, made her feel like she wasn't trying hard enough to discover the inner goodness of the man in the topcoat who looked into her window and tracked her in her dreams. He couldn't help what he looked like. She worried that she was turning into a shallow, selfie type of woman.

Tammy passed the day with customers and the occasional consignor who came in to pick up their check or add jewelry and knickknacks to a showcase.

It was a half–hour before closing. The January twilight cast a chill as darkness descended. The street lamps on Ventura Boulevard illuminated empty sidewalks. A light show of pink, blue and yellow neon flashed from the Thai restaurant across the boulevard and into Tammy's store.

She stood at the counter, matching receipts with money she had taken in for the day.

The door opened. The buzzer warned. A gust of cold wind swept exhaust and the smell of frying fish into the narrow store.

The man appeared.

As much as Tammy wanted to see his inner perfection, she felt the sensation of having her skin peeled.

She grabbed the money and the receipts, went into the bathroom, shut the door, and hid her day's worth in a bag behind the paper towels. She looked out the back window. Except for her Honda, the parking lot was empty. Her phone was under the first shelf of the counter. She told herself she was being ridiculous. It was always the ordinary–looking men who were rapists and murderers, not the ones with warped faces and mismatched body parts.

Tammy recited the affirmation that her Buddhist friend Qwan had given her: "I see beauty in all things and in everyone."

She opened the door. The blood evaporated from her brain and left her woozy with fear. "Can, I help you?" she stammered.

He stood in front of the counter, his long arms stretched from one end almost to the other, braced, an anchor for his gigantic head. "I'm looking for a jade ring." His voice garbled like nails thrashed about in a garbage disposal. His pinprick eyes seemed to enjoy Tammy's terror.

She thought about lying, but what if he saw the ring? "I, um, yes. A man's ring?"

"Yeah. A man's ring."

"There's one in the second case in the front," she said, hoping he'd walk away so she could open the back door. What for? To run out? And leave him alone in her store? Stop looking at his appearance, Tammy told herself.

"I want to try it on."

Tammy nodded. She hurried from behind the counter, went around the hanging mirror and down the west aisle with her key poised to unlock the case.

He lumbered toward her as if he wore concrete platforms, his expression smug.

He stood close beside her. Affixed to his long coat was a

100

metallic odor, iron, or was it blood?

Tammy reached in and gave him the ring.

Scars crisscrossed the top of his huge hands and knuckles. He jammed the ring onto his pinkie.

She glanced out the front window, hoping someone would come in.

"How much is it?"

His breath smelled like a jar of old pennies.

"$285.00."

"Gold."

"14 carat."

"Hmm." He stared at her and massaged the tip of his middle finger back and forth over the jade then tapped the stone with his teeth.

Tammy cringed.

"What's the best price?" he asked.

"I can take ten percent off."

"Hmm, $255.00, even."

"There's tax."

"Not with cash," the man said. He stared at her. There didn't seem to be any life coming from his eyes, not human, more reptilian. She expected a forked tongue to shoot out between his lips.

She'd pay the tax. She wanted him out of her store, out of her life, out of her dreams. "All right."

He held out his skillet sized hand—fingers that looked like they enjoyed pulling the wings off of sparrows—the gemstone dwarfed on his pinky.

"I'll think about it." He yanked off the ring and handed it to her. "I'll let you know, tomorrow."

"Tomorrow? Someone else is interested in it. It might be

gone by tomorrow."

"I'll take that chance," he said and walked away. The hem of his long coat touched her leg.

She shivered, watched him go out the front door and realized she had sweated through her blouse. The waistband of her skirt was damp. He did nothing overt. He could have knocked her down and run off with the ring. He could have raped her in the bathroom. He could have knotted his wiener like fingers around her neck and snuffed her.

He didn't want to pay tax. That was all he demanded. Tammy prayed he wouldn't return.

***

The next day was cold, but she kept the back door open. She turned the thermometer up to seventy–five, thankful for the people in the alley: car's parking, people shouting into their phones, UPS and Federal Express trucks screeching.

When she went home the night before, she had a glass of wine, then another. She had called Qwan, who suggested she meditate. She instructed Tammy to go beyond the physical to the spiritual world to seek answers. Tammy cried out, "I've tried that, and I'm still scared to death of him!" Qwan replied, "Focus not on his body but on his soul." "I don't think he has one," Tammy whispered. She said good–bye to Qwan and found divinity in another glass of wine.

At four in the morning, she shot up in bed, the monster in her dream the color of jade. The arms of his coat turned into green batwings. He chased her through the store until she dived into the mirror and vanished.

With three more hours before rising, she heaped the covers on top of her, shuddered, and squeezed her eyes shut. Tears streamed sideways across her cheek.

That morning she put on four–inch heels, and for the first time teased her hair—like her mother used to do—to make herself appear bigger. She carried the only weapon she could find at home, a souvenir from Disneyland: a tiny Swiss Army knife with scissors attached. She never harmed anyone, even spiders she'd toss outside. For Tammy, all God's creatures were worthy of respect. But nothing could quell her fear of the man.

Tammy polished the counter. She ran the vacuum, swept the sidewalk in front of her store. Her feet hurt from the high heels. When she'd bend over her teased hair would smash into showcases, and shelves.

So great was her anticipation of being murdered, that, she began to think of flower arrangements and who would give the eulogy at her funeral. Her mother would be in shock, her father forlorn. Rachel would be thinking, glad it wasn't me.

Tammy waited and waited. She peeked through the bathroom window whenever she heard a car, truck or motorcycle. She went out the front door and looked in at the PO Boxes. She glanced east then west. Cars backed up on Ventura. A skateboarder headed toward the Galleria, but no man.

That night, after she got home, she finished a bottle of wine, slipped into bed and closed her eyes like the lid on a coffin.

***

The next day Tammy dressed in her favorite sweater, lavender background with tiny pink hearts, and a navy blue skirt that showed off her athletic legs. Her hair obeyed the brush, and she wore just the right amount of make–up to enhance her features.

She felt invigorated from a good night's sleep and that the man had decided against the ring, and therefore, wouldn't return. How foolish, she thought, to work herself into a panic. Tammy hated being a victim.

She was sprucing up a case when the door opened the buzzer alerted.

A young Asian woman walked in, small and delicate, with long black hair parted down the middle. She went to the right aisle.

Tammy saw her looking into the second showcase. "Can I help you?" she asked, walking toward her.

The woman pressed her forehead against the glass. "My boyfriend wants me to see that jade ring."

"Your boyfriend?"

"Yeah."

"You mean—"

"He was here the other day."

The man had a girlfriend!

"He can't afford it, but he's up for a part in the new James Bond film."

"He's an actor?"

The woman looked at Tammy. "Yeah. He's up for the role of the new henchman."

"Henchman?"

"Yeah, the other actor died. They need to cast someone scary looking."

Tammy felt a hiccup launching in her stomach. "So, he's like getting into the role?" The hiccup expanded into a chuckle.

"I guess."

Tammy felt giddy. She laughed. "I have a feeling, he'll get the part."

"I hope. What's so funny?"

"Me. I'm laughing at myself. Can I take the ring out for you?" Tammy asked, feeling like the sun, the moon and the stars aligned instantly for her. She felt ashamed for judging him, stupid for being afraid, ridiculous for having nightmares about him.

The woman sighed and stared into the showcase. "No, I'd have to work overtime for a month if I were to buy it for him."

"Why buy it for him if he gets the role?"

"Even if he gets it, he can't afford it." She looked at Tammy. "He has a hard time finding work."

"Because of his," Tammy searched for a kind word, "distinctive looks?"

"That, too. People are picky about who they hire. So now he's trying to be an actor."

What did she mean by, that too, Tammy wondered?

"He thinks because I'm Chinese, I know good jade. I'm about as Chinese as Taylor Swift. It's a nice ring. But he's dreaming." She turned and walked out the door.

Tammy went back to the counter and sat on the stool. She pondered the meaning behind everything the woman told her. He was trying to be an actor, had a hard time finding work and not just because of his looks. What other reasons? Had he a prison record? Murdered someone? Would let his girlfriend work extra hours to buy him a ring —selfish, but so were a lot of men. She seemed intelligent. But Tammy knew love wasn't just blind. It could be deaf, too.

She was reaching for her phone to call Qwan when the ringtone let out, "All You Need is Love".

"Dazzles, Tammy speaking."

"I was in the other day."

Tammy's neck and arm hairs became stiff as antennas. "I remember."

"Don't sell the ring. I'll be in tomorrow."

"Congratulations," she said trying to keep the tremor out of her voice.

"What for?"

"The role, of the henchman, in the new James Bond movie. Congratulations." She heard his snicker and then the dial tone. Tammy glanced about as if something could save her. God help me!

THE WORLD OF MYTH

MAGAZINE

ISSUE

73

MAY 2019

Michael A. Arnold

Michael A. Arnold is a graduate of the University of Sunderland and Northumbria University. He is based in North East England, and has previously published essays and short fiction. His influences include George Orwell and Robert Frost.

There's No Trace of Numund Anymore
By: Michael A. Arnold

THERE IS, SOMEWHERE in the Sahara Desert, a small lake that is never fed and never disappears. Ancient stories say that the first great city, called Numund, once stood there but something strange and terrible happened.

Every version of the Numund story is different, since they survive in oral traditions – stories around campfires always change. After comparing all the different versions, and what papyri fragments might be related, I have found a basic story and will flesh it out here.

The tribe that made Numund's original population were migrating, following the wide river 'Nehilios' – probably what is now called the Nile. They had heard of a large, and largely unknown land in the north (possibly Europe) which was said to be very fertile and under populated. One night, while camped on the banks of the great Nehilios river, their tribal leader had a dream in which strange gods appeared to her. They said that her people were to settle a land nearby that would eventually meet their every imaginable need, and they would know it because of a small, white stone hill there which was sacred to those gods. The only request those gods made, that the people would not use stone from that hill in any way. In the morning she told her people about the dream, and yes they thought it must be a sign from the divines. Trusting those gods, they stopped their migration.

After half a day their scouts found a shallow valley with a thin stream running through it, and a small uncovered hill standing over it made of a stone so white it almost glowed in the sunlight. Even though they were some distance from the Nehilios River, and only a small stream ran through the valley, it was very fertile – wild grasses and fruit trees were scattered everywhere. They thought surely this must be the land their new gods had referred to, and when the people were gathered they started building a new home for themselves, calling their town Numund. Because Numund was in a valley, and because it was so far away from the great river, it was thought they would be both harder for raiders to find, and easier to defend; attacks from raiders were a constant worry in those early days.

Years passed, and the people of Numund began to feel settled. So, they thought, it was true, their new gods had blessed them, and they would be happy there. But tribes of wildmen eventually found Numund, and began raiding it for food and supplies. There was an especially savage tribe of wildmen who haunted Numund, and would even fight off other tribes for the right to raid — they appeared to enjoy killing. What they called themselves has been lost to the decay of history, but the Numundians called them 'eh therikai' (which sounds a lot like the later Greek word for 'enemy') . It was better for Numund to give in, and let the raiders do as they pleased — these were not people to be kind if resisted. While Numund had tools they did not have weapons, rocks and bronze tools were no defence against bronze swords and wooden shields. Instead the people of Numund prayed to their gods for help, but those gods who loved Numund's sacred hill were silent, and would remain silent.

Eventually one of the other wild tribes came to Numund, asking to talk in dignified and peaceful terms. I can only try to imagine the tension, the stone–faced anxiety on the people's faces as they watched a line of armed men walk through their town. An agreement was made after a long discussion with the town elders: these men would be given food if they stayed inside Numund and guarded it from others. While knowing all the risks, this sounded fair to all; in the celebration that followed this tribe of warriors officially became Numund's army.

So Numund made war with her great enemy, 'eh therikai', and drove them back to their camps in distant hills. However the soldiers of Numund followed them, and as night fell the screams of defeated wildmen rattled against the cooling sky. Numund's army came back victorious, and a holiday was declared to celebrate the battle. After that, other settlers starting coming to Numund as word of their victory spread, and the town grew quickly.

Numund became a thriving and proud city. War was soon made with its neighbours, and her army became feared and well respected in battle. Through war Numund became so rich, large halls had to be built to house all the spoils. In the land now called Ethiopia Numund soldiers attacked and overran a now unknown city, and seized a giant statue of the ancient water god Dagon. It was carried it back to Numund as a symbol of the victory, and the message was clear: Numund was now so powerful it could even face the gods themselves.

Because these first gods had gave no comfort to Numund, its people began to worship Dagon instead. They also began using the strangely white stone from the old gods' sacred hill to build huge, ambitious works, to show off their skill and wealth. Numund was soon building huge walls around itself, much like the high walls of Troy that would be built much later. Huge theatres were built where re–enactments of battles were staged for the people's enjoyment. Lavish bathing complexes, temples, and villas were also built, and even (which was unique in those days) paved roads with hanging flowers and lines of olive trees along all the major streets. The people became naturally proud of the city they had worked so hard to perfect and, with that strangely perfect–white stone, it was beautiful. From a distance Numund seemed to glow against the dark earth when night fell.

Then one day an old man came to Numund. He appeared to be a traveller, but strangely taller and more angular than was normal, and he moved with a great focus and strength while having all the folds and trenches of a man in the winter of life. The city guards were at first unsure, but seeing the man's advanced age and weathered appearance they thought they did not need to bother with any questions and let him into the city. The only thing they said to him was that Numund had laws, and one made sleeping on the streets forbidden. Those found doing so would be removed from the city, so he had to find a room at an inn by nightfall or leave the city.

Inside the city people mostly let him walk alone, but they watched him intently. They had grown too proud, and to dislike all who did not call Numund their home or did not look like a rich merchant. The old man did not talk with anyone, but found a small tavern he bought a cup of ale from, using strange coins made of a brilliantly white gold. Ale had recently became a delicacy in Numund, newly imported from the young city of Aegipton much further up the Nehilios River. This made people take notice; they watched him from the corners of their eyes as he sat, drinking and watching a street play nearby.

Later he went to find a room for the night. He walked alone through Numund's market places, under huge sheet towels that protected the Numundians from the burning sun, watching everyone move around him. He seemed to be conscious in his difference from them all. When he asked the people for advice soldiers nearby would laugh at him and taunt him, and none of the innkeepers seemed to want him staying because he looked poor. However the man never seemed to ever be put off by this, and kept trying to find a room for the night.

As the sun sank low, spreading an amber fire in the distance. He found a friendly innkeeper who was willing to take him in for a few pieces of gold. This was lucky, because word of the old man had been passed around the city soldiers, and they were looking out for him — knowing he had been told about the city laws and that he had to find a room for the night or be removed from the city. The innkeeper was poor, and accepted the man's strangely white gold without any questions – and even showed kindness to the old man with a supper of bread and olive oil, and a large jar of water. This was the first time the old man smiled.

The moon was nearly full in the heavens after a long and friendly conversation, and the old man thanked the innkeeper as he retired for the night. A great sense of peace fell over the room that the kind innkeeper felt but could not explain. It was something that almost seemed to radiate from the earth itself. Later, when the moon was starting to climb back toward the earth, two burglars snuck into the inn. They had been following the old man for most of the day, interested in his strange whitely golden coins.

As they crept through the rooms, lit dimly by the high moon above, they listened for any kind of movement from the old man. But when they slid back the cloth partition to the old man's room they found his bed empty. It did not look like it had even been disturbed. In that moment the thieves were overcome with an unending fear. A grim evil seemed to come from everything around them, as intense as it was inexplicable. They ran, but it was then already too late. That night the wells of the city quickly began to fill unnaturally, and a torrent of water burst from them like a volcanic eruption. The ground also started to gave way all over the city.

Only a few lucky ones managed to escape. The night–lit desert saw a small cloud of people fleeing, all moving in the direction of the great Nehilios River. When they looked back they saw what was happening in clear moonlight, the city was disappearing beneath the earth – water flying high into the air. The pace of destruction was far so swift for the people to properly understand it, and soon Numund had been eaten by the desert. All that remained was the lake that is still there today, that is not fed and does not disappear.

There's no trace of Numund anymore.

THE END

THE WORLD OF MYTH

MAGAZINE

ISSUE

74

JUNE 2019

Walt Giersbach

Walt Giersbach bounces between writing genres, from mystery to humor, speculative fiction to romance. His work has appeared in print and online in over a score of publications, including several stories published by *The World of Myth*. He's also bounced from Fortune 500 firms to university posts, and from homes in eight U.S. states and a couple of Asian countries.

Marty was a Jewel
By: Walt Giersbach

MY AUNT EDITH, up in the Riverdale section of the Bronx, is a funny woman. By that I don't mean ha–ha funny, but whimsical. Waggish and droll. Uncle Marty, she'd say, was on the road so much he should have bought stock in a highway.

Marty was what they call a jobber who represented denim manufacturers. He called himself the Denim Demon, wholesaling Levis, bluejeans, dungarees. Pants, vests, jackets — anything made out of denim.

Toward the end of a weeks–long trip some years ago he called Edith and said he'd grown a mustache. My cousin Bobby was still a little kid, so she bundled him up to meet his daddy's train when it pulled into Grand Central Terminal. With a sudden flight of fancy, she'd taken some of Bobby's hair trimmings and made a mustache that she pasted on his face with spirit gum.

She greeted the train at the station as Marty in his new mustache stepped down.

"Edith, what d'you mean putting that thing on an innocent baby!" were his first words.

"Well, Marty, it's been some time since we've seen you. I didn't know if you'd recognize your baby with his mustache."

"Not *that* long!" he snorted.

Just like that, she began giggling. As quickly as it had come, his glare died and they both began laughing at his outburst. See, that's what love does for you, even if you're both married.

Edith and Marty would occasionally shout at each other — in the street, at the market, wherever — and then they'd make up ten minutes later. They were like a kid's wooden paddle and rubber ball. Love was the rubber band that snapped them back together each tine. *Slap–slap–slap* all the time. Paddle ball, I thought when Aunt Edith called me from Riverdale.

"Your Uncle Marty is dead, Jake," she said. "He's gone and I need someone to advise me what to do. Can you come up?"

The rubber band had just snapped.

Marty was on the road when he died. Literally. Hit by a truck as he walked out of a store in Little Rock. Bobby was in the Army trying to stay out of trouble and I was the nearest relative. I said I'd come immediately.

I was in my office in midtown Manhattan where I edit *Laundry & Dry Cleaning Today*, a trade journal. I tell hard–working New Americans from India and the Caribbean how to defeat spots in worsted's and put new life in suede.

Thinking of Marty, I glanced at the bulletin board in my office where I'd stuck a press release that crossed my desk. An outfit had a technique for turning people into diamonds. Why that news came to me at my magazine I don't know, but I'd hung it up so I could think about it later. Now was a good time to think.

The release said this technique offered immortality. After all, people are just carbon molecules. This company simply refines a person's ashes — once they're dead, of course — and turns him or her into graphite. The graphite is put into a huge vise under a million pounds of pressure, heated to 3,500 degrees and — *presto!* — you're a diamond.

This didn't seem to be too far into the realm of the unbelievable. They say diamonds are forever, so Edith could secure Marty's memory while keeping him close to her.

I took the train up to Edith's condo at 252nd Street in Riverdale, plopping down in the living room across from her with a mixture of apprehension and expectation. Death isn't a good conversation starter. She slurped her tea while I nursed a glass of Dewar's from the bottle Marty kept in the closet.

Pretty quickly, she got around to discussing what she called "the arrangements."

"What'll I do, Jake? Something fitting should be done after the funeral. It's the right thing to do. God forbid the cleaning lady gets carried away seeing his ashes."

"Aunt Edith, burial or interment costs about five thousand. Let me suggest another idea."

I took out the news release from my office and she leaned forward to hear every word.

125

"If Uncle Marty was a diamond," I said, "you'd always have him in your hand. In fact, he'd be worth more dead than alive — about $2,300 for a quarter carat and $15,000 for a full one carat. Anyway, that's in the ballpark of funeral costs."

She picked at some imaginary lint on the chair and began figuring her options. "I think about half a carat," she said. "Marty wasn't very big when he was alive. He wore a size 40 regular."

The next day she called the memorials salesman, who was quick to admit the diamonds aren't flawless. Edith told him Marty had some anger issues and flawless would be too much to expect. Two weeks later, Marty's ashes were sent up from Little Rock. After the funeral service, Edith shipped him off to the giant pressure cooker in Illinois.

I was out of town myself, handling an event for advertisers. When I got back, I apologized that I was unable to be at the funeral and I asked Edith how everything had gone.

She snuffled, and then swore like my old platoon sergeant. Finally, she wheezed to a stop. It seems the Little Rock funeral parlor called and said they still had Marty's ashes and didn't know *who* was in the box she'd received for the funeral. Two days later, she got "Marty" back in a little velvet box. He was set in a plain gold band.

"I pondered this awhile, and you know, Jake, I tried to say even if it *isn't* Marty, it makes a nice memorial. After he was cremated, well, ashes are just ashes. It's the memories that count."

I uh–huhed sympathetically.

"Then," she continued, "on my way out of Gristede's

126

market a few days later, I went next door to the jewelry store. I asked the man to appraise Marty. Of course, I didn't identify exactly *who* the ring was. Well, he sniffed and said, 'Madam, this is a cubic zirconium.'"

That made Edith doubly disconcerted. Not only wasn't it Marty, he wasn't even a diamond.

"Aunt Edith, look at it this way," I told her. "Only you know the truth — and who's to doubt you?"

Her eyes got all squinty. "Are you just young or are you stupid, Jake? You give up too easy. I called the Little Rock funeral parlor and demanded my money back or said I'd tell the *New York Post* how they make bodies disappear. And I told Little Rock to send Marty up immediately so I could keep an eye on him right here in the Bronx.

"Further, I'm keeping the ring. It sparkles if you hold it in the sun. And," she almost winked, "Marty always liked a good joke."

# # #

THE WORLD OF MYTH

MAGAZINE

ISSUE

75

JULY 2019

Steven Bruce

Steven Bruce is the author of Thrown Up and co-author of Dark Matter 8. His work has featured in Picaroon Poetry, Building Bridges, No Tribal Dance, Forword, Lonesome October Lit, and the Black Light Engine Room Literary Magazine. Some of his poems have been translated into Polish. In 2018, he graduated from Teesside University with a Master's Degree in Creative Writing.

Chimaera
By: Steven Bruce

HER SLENDER FINGER brushed the palm of his hand.

"Your hands are rough," she said.

"Oh, thanks," he said.

"They're still my favorite part of you."

"What, my hands?"

"Yeah," she said, before bolting upright on the couch. "I had another scary dream last night."

"Oh?"

"Yeah, I was visiting my mother's grave and—"

"That is scary," he said, staring up at the nicotine-stained ceiling.

"No, that's not the scary part. When I walked away from her grave, this gaunt, yellow-faced man jumped out in front of me." She rubbed her bruised eyelid with the back of her hand. "His bony finger pointed behind me. I turned around, and this gigantic lion was standing there." He handed her a half-smoked cigarette. "Well, it wasn't actually a lion," she said.

"What was it then?"

"It had a lion's head, but its body was, well, something else. I remember it had wings and horns and scales."

"Holy shit," he said. "Then what happened?"

"The lion tore into my leg, and I woke up covered in sweat."

He pulled away from her, got up off the worn-out couch, put his underwear on, walked out of the living room. She picked his phone up from the grimy glass coffee table and skimmed through his messages.

"What are you doing?" he said, marching into the room.

He wrestled the phone from her.

"I was checking the time."

"What, in my messages? You're full of shit," he said, shaking his head.

"You're hiding something, then," she said to him.

He snatched a handful of her short hair and shoved the corner of the phone into her temple.

"After everything you've put me through," he said, twisting the phone.

"I'm sorry," she said, gripping his hairy forearm.

He dragged her up from the couch and smashed her through the coffee table.

"Fucking look at what you've made me do," he said, weeping into his hands.

She picked herself up from the shattered glass and hobbled over to him.

"I'm sorry," she said. "I never—"

"Oh, always *fucking* sorry. Well, no more. You can go,

134

crawl back to your bullshit family, see if they'll cope with you," he said, pacing the room.

She hobbled over to the window and looked out through the blinds. The street was empty, except for a young couple who were viewing a house for sale across the road.

"Looks like we'll have new neighbors soon," she said to him. "Do you remember when we came to see this place for the first time?"

"Of course," he said. "I remember you fell in love with the bathroom taps."

"Don't they look so happy?"

He peered out of the window, looked at her, and shook his head.

"Fuck this," he said. "I'm going out."

"Where to?" she said.

He stormed out of the house, slamming the door behind him.

Small blood crescents trailed up the cream stairway carpet into the bathroom. She tossed two olanzapine tablets into the sink and washed them down the plughole.

"I Forgot my wallet," he called out, coming back in through the front door.

She came out of the bathroom and smiled at him from the top of the stairs.

"You want me to make you something to eat, love?" she asked him.

"Fancy a chippy instead?"

"If you like. Get my usual," she said. "Oh, and a battered pineapple ring, if they have any."

He smiled at her, picked his wallet up from the sideboard, and left.

135

Steven Bruce

Hot water sputtered into the bathtub.

She sat on the edge of the toilet and raised her foot to her lap. A ragged chunk of glass protruded from her heel. She plucked it out. A thin line of blood trickled from the wound and settled on the floor.

She climbed into the water, closed her eyes, drifted into a half-asleep state.

A faint panting noise crawled out from the silence. A swift, hot gust of breath lashed her face. She shot up, her eyes scanning the empty room.

She hobbled down to the living room and spotted his phone among the coffee table debris. She picked it up and read the last message. It was from Lisa.

If you can get away early tonight, you can fuck me until it hurts.

She hurled the phone at the wall and growled into her hands.

He came in through the front door holding a white takeaway bag.

"They didn't have fish cakes, so I got you half-a-fish," he said, going into the kitchen.

He stepped into the living room, holding a long bread knife.

"You want a few slices of bread?"

"I'm not hungry anymore," she said. "And who the hell is Lisa?"

"What?" he said, looking at his broken phone. "Have you stopped taking your pills, you crazy cunt?"

He grabbed the collar of her shirt.

"You ungrateful bitch," he said.

She plunged a long, spiked shard of glass into his throat

136

and retracted it with a jerk. Blood splashed her face, splashed the yellow wallpaper, splashed the blue floral curtains. He stumbled around the room, clutching his throat, his eyes bulging with disbelief.

Her slender fingers brushed the palm of his hand.

"Your hands are rough," she said.

She hobbled into the bathroom and tossed his severed hands into the bathtub, atop his dead body. A wide-eye gazed up at her from the gore. When she moved around the room, it seemed to follow her.

She leaned on the sink, a bottle of gin in one blood-soaked hand, painkillers in the other.

A seascape painting hung askew on the wall above the bathtub. The sound of waves scraping the shore echoed around the room. It reminded her of the bread knife sawing through his wrist bones.

"I'm sorry, Eric," she said and guzzled down the gin and painkillers.

The bathroom door burst open. The young couple walked in.

"Please, help me, I didn't mean to do it," she said, staggering up from the floor.

The couple looked at the bathtub.

"Oh, my God, beautiful taps," said the young woman.

"Well, if the taps are beautiful, we should move in immediately," the young man replied.

"Please, help me," she said, holding her bloodstained hands out.

"Oh, I forgot to tell you, Auntie June rang yesterday."

"More nonsense?" the young man said, leveling the seascape painting.

"No, she was telling me about a house to let at the end of her street. Actually, yeah, she did mention something about her psychic."

"Oh, there's a surprise."

"Yeah, she said that in a previous life, she was a much-loved queen of Ancient Egypt."

"Sure she was, funny isn't it, how they never turn out to be gong farmers or 17th-century rapists."

The young woman rolled her eyes, took the young man's hand.

"We're going to be very happy here, I know it," she said, leading the young man out of the room.

"Wait, don't leave me here," she said, chasing after them.

The young couple vanished from the landing. She stumbled back into the bathroom and looked into the bathtub. It was empty.

"Eric?" she called out while searching through the house.

She lingered at the foot of the staircase. A spindly shadow shifted across the upstairs landing.

"Eric?" she said, climbing the staircase.

The yellow-faced man swung his head around the corner of the landing, his insane grin revealing a set of green, twisted teeth. Her fingers clutched the handrail.

He slithered onto the staircase, shuffling towards her, stopping inches away. He pushed his bony fingers into his forehead, breaking the skin, cracking the skull. He peeled the top of his head back, exposing his black, inky brains. With a shrill voice, he cried out,

"Taste the madness," and offered her a fistful of black brains.

She collapsed onto the hallway floor and sobbed. The

yellow-faced man stared down on her, laughing with insanity, inky blood dripping down his face.

The stink of decaying flesh filled the air. A fiery breath licked the back of her neck. She turned and was face-to-face with the chimaera. The beast let out a nerve-shattering roar. She scampered, backwards, into the living room and shouldered the door shut.

Her eyes darted around the room, stopping at the glass coffee table. It was as good as new. She slumped onto the floor, covered her face with her hands, and wept.

"Lisa, are you okay?"

She lowered her hands. Eric was on the couch, smoking a cigarette.

"Come and lay down," he said to her.

Her slender fingers brushed the palm of his hand.

"Your hands are rough," she said.

THE WORLD OF MYTH

MAGAZINE

ISSUE

76

AUGUST 2019

DC Diamondopolous

DC Diamondopolous is an award-winning short story and flash fiction writer with over 150 stories published internationally in print and online magazines, literary journals, and anthologies. DC's stories have appeared in: So It Goes: The Literary Journal of the Kurt Vonnegut Museum and Library, Lunch Ticket, Raven Chronicles, Silver Pen, Scarlet Leaf Review, and many others. DC was nominated for Best of the Net Anthology.

She lives on the beautiful California central coast with her wife and animals. dcdiamondopolous.com

Taps
By: DC Diamondopolous

PETER CROUCHED IN front of the attic window and
gazed down on old man Mueller's cornfield. The plow,
unhitched beyond the stalks, turned north like he meant to
continue but got interrupted. Peter looked toward the barn,
no sign of Mueller's horse and buggy. The Amish and
Mennonite neighbors, with their peculiar ways kept to
themselves. Mueller only talked to his pa when he accused
Rufus of killing his chickens, or a year ago, the day his
brother's mind broke when Gabe went screaming from the
veranda twisting his ears as he ran into Muller's cornfield.
That day Mueller shot out of the house, the top of his
unsnapped overalls flapping as he sprinted after Gabe,
Mueller's wife and five children dashed onto the porch, the
boys still in their pajamas.

   After that day, Gabe was never the same, and neither
was Peter.

DC Diamondopolous

At fourteen, he felt all grownup. His childhood ended when his brother and best friend came down with a cold inside his brain. Ma said h'd get better. They just had to pray harder. Pa wanted to send him somewhere, to a place where they removed part of the brain or shocked it into normal. Peter listened as they argued back and forth, Ma blaming herself and Pa's eyes wet with tears, as they tried to decide what was best for their eldest son; feelings of helplessness sat like a centerpiece on the dining room table.

"How come I don't hear the voices, Ma?"

"Thank the good Lord you don't, son."

Gab's trumpet playing now sailed out of his window across the beauty of the corn and wheat fields, the notes drifting as new ones began over the vast cloudless skies of Lancaster County. Gabe played Taps, Taps in the morning, Taps in the afternoon, and Taps at night. Peter thought it must have to do with the sadness inside him, but once in a while Gabe scratched the air with a different kind of song; it would sail smooth, cut off, spiral and dip. In those moments, he thought his brother had talent, enough to make Peter enjoy the fantasies they provoked. He coaxed Gabe to take lessons, maybe play at the church, learn *Come Thou Fount of Every Blessing,* so people would like him—that part he left out. Gabe had scowled, and Peter fell quiet, afraid h'd make his brother go to that place where a chorus of devils shuffled his mind.

Peter learned to rake words the way he did leaves. Words like sure, and *all right* calmed him, but others like before, and *used to,* could bring on a fit.

The kitchen screen door slammed as Gabe came out of the house and stood on the veranda. He brought the

146

trumpet to his lips and began to play. Peter bounded to his feet. Gabe had never taken the trumpet outside or played it in front of others. Peter hoped this meant h'd been healed, that his parents' prayers and his own were finally answered. Excited, he ran down the stairs wanting his parents to see. He passed the room he once shared with his brother until his pa separated them cause of the sickness. He jumped onto the landing and rode the banister sidesaddle down to the living room.

"Ma? Pa?"

Peter ran through the kitchen where his mother's cornbread sat on the stove. He caught a whiff of its warm, sweet smell and realized his brother had stopped playing.

He pushed the screen door open, but Gabe wasn't there.

"Rufus, come here boy!" he shouted from the porch. "Pa?" Where was everyone? His eyes darted from the tether ball, to the lawnmower, to the Troyer's house. The late September day was as still as the sun. It was Saturday. Life always had something going on. It didn't just stop.

Peter found it strange that his father's hammer, pliers, and screwdriver lay on the porch swing. Although his brother wouldn't hurt a gnat, h'd often hurt himself. And, his pa made sure to keep his guns and tools locked up.

Peter leaped off the steps and ran around the brick house they had moved into three years ago. The front yard looked no different from any other time, the '47 Buick station wagon parked in the driveway, nothing out of place, except the absence of his folks and Rufus.

Maybe they went to the Kerr's or the Troyers' cause someone got sick. But Rufus' disappearance downright confused him. That dog always came when called.

147

He'd better tend to Gabe.

Peter ran to the backyard and saw a swath cut in the cornfield. The Amish and Mennonites were acquainted with Gab's screams, his running away and hiding in their barns. And the time he sprinted all the way to the feed store and climbed into a grain sack to get away from the voices. Six months ago, Peter and his pa found Gabe in a dumpster. His pa picked him up by his armpits and dragged his crumpled body over the edge and placed him on the ground. Peter felt like something died that day; a corner of his heart just fell off. His pa helped Gabe get to his feet, put an arm around his shoulders and told him: It's gonna be okay. Peter wanted to believe. Later that day his father told him: *You're the older one now, son. Tend to him like a pup.*

He followed Gab's tracks, swatting through the rustling stalks, and batting away flies. "Gabe?" He felt trickles of sweat form on his brow as the smothering shoots closed behind him. "Where are you?"

"Go away."

"Wher's our folks and Rufus?"

"I don't know. Leave me alone."

Peter took careful steps so not to upset his brother. He wanted to make sure Gabe was all right and not doing weird things like banging his head against the ground, or clawing his ears until they turned purple blue.

Peter brushed his dark bangs out of his eyes and parted the stalks. Gabe sat cradling the trumpet, rocking back and forth.

"You seen Rufus?"

"No."

"Heard you playing outside." Peter parted the shoots to

give them more room. He stepped around his brother. "What's that on your shirt?"

"Nothin'."

"Somethin'. Looks like blood." He reached to touch the shirt. Gabe shoved his hand away.

"Leave me be."

"You tell me how you got blood on your shirt and I'll leave you be."

"It's not blood. It's ketchup."

"Hogwash."

Peter took hold of his brother's shoulders and gripped them as he leaned down and smelled the shirt. "It's blood." He ripped it open and saw slash marks on Gab's chest. "Jesus Gabriel."

"I'm cold."

"Wher's the knife?"

"You tore my shirt."

"Here put mine on."

Gabe did and started to blubber as he mismatched the buttons with the holes.

"Gimme the knife."

"Mueller has it."

"You're saying Mueller did this to you?"

Gabe nodded.

He couldn't trust a darn thing that came out of Gab's mouth.

Peter leaped on top of his brother and tried to roll him over, but Gabe fought back swinging his fists and grazed the side of his head. "I'm trying to keep you out of trouble," Peter said as he straddled Gab's legs and ran his hands along his brother's pockets. "Wher'd you throw it?" He rolled Gab's shirt into a ball, stood, and picked up the trumpet.

"Don't have it."

Peter glanced about. It could be anywhere. "Let's go find Rufus."

Gabe grabbed onto the stalks and pulled himself up. "Mueller killed him with the knife."

Peter swung around. He dropped the shirt and trumpet and lunged at his brother knocking him to the ground. "You're lyin'." He looked down at Gabe not feeling a bit sorry for him. "You can talk crazy all you want, but not about my dog." Peter felt a rush of trembles coming on. The kind he had as a kid when h'd wake up in his own piss. Sometimes his brother was just too much responsibility. Peter picked up the shirt and handed the trumpet to Gabe. "I'm goin' home."

Gabe followed.

Old man Mueller would never use a knife. He might shoot Rufus if he killed his chicks, but h'd never use a knife. And, when it came to hurting his brother, well sir, that just didn't make sense. It bugged Peter that Gabe could get to him like that, after all, his mind was sharp. He could grasp a situation and pluck its essence clean out.

When they reached the porch, his father's tools were still lying about. H'd put them away once he cleaned Gab's wounds and got rid of the shirt, no sense telling his parents. It would upset them, and they would send Gabe away.

The screen door slammed as the brothers went into the kitchen. "Take off my shirt. I'll clean those wounds," Peter said as he took the dishrag from the washbasin and soaked it in warm water. "Put the trumpet down." He reached into the cupboard and pulled out his pa's whiskey. "Come here." He poured a little onto the rag—his pa wouldn't notice—and wiped his brother's chest.

"Ouch! That's for drinkin'."

"It'll clean the wounds. Seen Pa?"

Gabe slowly moved his head to the left and the right, reminding Peter of an elephant he saw at the carnival in Hershypark.

"No."

Peter took the bloody shirt and put it in the sink. He lifted the lid of his Nanaw's bronze striker that hung on the wall, took out a wooden match and struck it, lighting the shirt on fire. When the flames licked it to ash, Peter ran the water. "Let's go upstairs. We gotta hide those wounds."

Gabe started to laugh. Peter saw the madness in his brother's eyes as if his mind hooked a corner and kept spinning unable to right itself. No amount of shaking, coaxing, or yelling could bring Gabe around. Peter remembered that same laugh Memorial Day when the Kerr's invited them to a picnic in their backyard. They all sat at the long wooden table eating ham, onions, coleslaw and pudding. Gabe scarfed down a slice of watermelon when he started to laugh. Course everyone wanted to know what was so funny. His laughter grew to hysterics. *Let us in on the joke*, Lester said. But Gabe kept laughing like it was his own private thing, even as the juice ran out his nose and into his mouth. The look in his eyes when Lester persisted, *come on, what's so funny*, was dark and ugly.

Peter would never forget the look on Gretchen's face, the girl with hair the color of wheat, and eyes as dark as the Blue Ridge Mountains. He wanted Gretchen for his girl the moment he saw her in the church choir. But on the day that Gabe snapped, and she brought her finger up to the side of her head and made fast circles laughing at his brother's torment, his feelings for her died.

Did he hear Rufus? Peter raced to the screen door and opened it. He stepped onto the veranda. "Rufus!" He took the stairs when he felt something strike the back of his head. The force was so great he toppled forward. He struggled to get away as he pulled himself along the ground. Crawling in his own blood, he was sure he heard his dog.

Rufus sprinted up to his master and barked. "Hey, boy," Peter moaned.

"Oh my God, Gabriel!"

The distant wail of his mother's voice reminded him of the way Gabe faded the final notes of Taps.

"Put that hammer down. Now Gabriel!" The fear he heard in his pa's voice scared him. Peter struggled to get up.

He felt a searing explosion and lost consciousness.

THE WORLD OF MYTH

MAGAZINE

ISSUE

77

OCTOBER 2019

Michelle E. Lowe

Michelle E. Lowe is a Georgia born native who has spent most of her life near the Atlanta area before pulling up stakes and moving clear across the country with her husband. She loves reading science–fiction and fantasy stories and enjoys old B horror and fun adventure films.
She is the author of *The Warning, Atlantic Pyramid, Cherished Thief,* and the *Legacy* series. Children's books, *Poe's Haunted House Tour,* and *The Hex Hunt* series. Her works in progress is *The Age of the Machine* series. Currently, she lives in Lake Forest, California with husband Ben, and their two daughters.www.michellelowe.net

Transition
By: Michelle E. Lowe

YESTERDAY, MOM AND Dad came home with the new baby. I'd been standing in a sunspot in the kitchen when they entered the room. Dad placed the baby down on the breakfast table for me to see.

"Introduce yourself to your little sister," he said, waving me forward.

Meeting her made me nervous, 'cause meeting something new doesn't, like, come along every day, y'know.

I approached the tank and leaned in close. "Hi sis, sis," I said, rapping my fingers on the glass. She twitched.

"Don't tap on the glass, Suzy," Mom scolded. "For her, the sound is twice as loud."

"Is she in freshwater or saltwater?" I asked.

"Fresh," Dad answered, going over to the hearth where a small fire burned under an iron pan. "No one can breathe under saltwater yet, but it won't be long before it's possible." He placed an oven mitt over his webbed hand, slid the pan out, and poured the tuna soup into a cup.

Mom's cold, damp hand gently stroked my smooth head as she said, "Isn't she beautiful?"

I returned my attention to the tank. My sister looked like a hairless albino monkey. She had reached what scientists called the Next Stage. Mom and Dad were so proud when they found out. She wasn't the only one to come this far, but the third. The very first to cross the finish line over to the Next Stage was a boy born in Africa twenty-four years ago. His parents named him Chiratidzo, meaning 'a sign'. The second like him was his son, born a few years back. I learned about them this year in school. For hundreds of years, ever since we began changing, scientists predicted we'd reach this stage and would gradually continue transforming so long as we existed.

Dad took large gulps of the tuna soup that I made for my parents before they came home. Tuna soup is easy to make, it's just chopped up tuna and fish broth, served really hot, the hotter the better 'cause it, like, warms the blood, y'know.

After draining his cup, Dad wiped his mouth with a cloth napkin and moved over toward the sunspot where I'd been standing. He warmed himself in the bright light that shone through the glass kitchen door like a water turtle sunbathing on a stone.

"We still need a name for her," he said.

"Would you like to give her one?" Mom asked me.

I pointed to myself. "Me? Really?"

"Sure," said Dad with a shrug. "We can't think of anything. Go for it."

For inspiration, I turned back to my sister, sleeping soundly in her plastic chair bolted down to the bottom of her small tank. Her tiny mouth opened and closed, sucking in water and breathing it out in tiny bubbles through the gills on either side of her neck. I slid my finger down my own neck. I have no gills. I still have a nose and my lungs need air, though I can stay underwater for, like, hours now. Mom got up from her granite chair and dunked her entire body under the three feet of water which covers our whole community. The area had been flooded for a while now. My teacher said the water reached the midlands some seven hundred years ago. As our bodies grow accustomed to the changes needed to survive, we had started building homes and furniture out of stone and cement since most other materials won't last long in water. We've basically turned homes into what I call 'stylish caves'. There are still warm-blooded air-breathing people out there, living on high mountain peaks, but not many, and with water levels constantly rising, they'll be extinct soon. It's funny, 'cause years ago *we* were considered the freaks, and like all outcasts, we were shunned by the majority that feared us. Now we dominate the planet two to one. Dad was right, it won't be long before we adapt to saltwater. When it does happen, everything we have left in which makes us human will be, like, y'know, *gone*. Funny, it took us millions of years to become humans, but it has only taken hundreds to return to our original state. After a minute went by, Mom reappeared with a refreshed look on her pastel face.

"Dehydrated, honey?" Dad asked as she sat back on her chair.

"Yeah. Having a baby takes the moisture right out of

you."

Mom carried the baby in her womb and gave birth, but they say in time females will lay eggs instead. YUCK! I don't want eggs plopping outta me. I believe that once we reach a certain stage, many things will vanish, like friendships, material want, and just about anything that once separated us from animals. Eventually, it'll be every man and woman for themselves. One day, surviving on a day-to-day basis will be the high priority, and instead of focusing on jobs, relationships, homework, or whatever, the new agenda will be finding food, hiding from predators, and breeding. Everything we owned will become useless to us, even our stylish caves. I mean, what will we need 'em for, shelter from the rain? Such a cold inevitability won't happen in my lifetime, or my children's, or my grandchildren's, but we're heading there, no doubt about it. As of now, we're still holding on to our species' traditions, like going to school, playing sports, and celebrating holidays. But many other things have disappeared like electricity, 'cause duh we're, like, surrounded by water!

My sister opened her eyes and looked at me. At least, I think she did. Her eyeballs were like solid glass marbles in a variety of swirling blues mixed with swirling lines of white. Mom and Dad's lipless mouths were shining with smiles. I could tell they were so thrilled about her. If they were capable, they'd have shed tears.

"The doctors say she'll need to eat raw foods," Dad said.

"That's disgusting!" I blurted.

Dad chuckled.

"Yeah," he agreed. "But I guess it'll be useful for her since it's getting harder to find dry wood for fires nowadays."

Two thousand years ago, the rising temperatures could've killed us off if we didn't adapt. When dry land became scarce, most people were forced to settle in water. After a while, their skin couldn't stay moist by itself anymore; they began depending on the wet conditions. Like needing lotion for severely dry skin, I guess. In my first-grade class last year, I learned about what's happening to us. It's called 'Transformation', some call it evolving. I think the word transformation makes more sense 'cause in order to evolve a species has to move forward. In my opinion it's more like we're moving backward, y'know, changing back into the very thing we started from billions of years ago before crawling onto shore. Some of my friends have these fantasies that we're all gonna turn into merpeople, but I know better. We're heading back to the drawing board, and my sister is the proof of it! We should've known better when the glaciers began melting. When time was still available, people often talked about improving the environment and preventing global warming from happening, but, like, not enough action took place. Then the hole in the ozone grew larger and before anyone had a chance to inflate a raft, the seas rose over their backyards. I think Earth will be okay now. There are no more factories billowing poisonous fumes into the air, and all the carbon dioxide has stopped when people couldn't drive anymore. Maybe millions of years from now, if the sun still burns, the water might recede, and we humans can start all over again. If so, I hope we use a little more common-sense next time around.

"Have you decided on a name, yet?" Mom asked.

"Aglaia," I told her. "Her name is Aglaia."

THE WORLD OF MYTH

MAGAZINE

ISSUE

78

NOVEMBER 2019

Steven Bruce

Steven Bruce is the author of Thrown Up and co-author of Dark Matter 8. His work has featured in Picaroon Poetry, Building Bridges, No Tribal Dance, Forword, Lonesome October Lit, and the Black Light Engine Room Literary Magazine. Some of his poems have been translated into Polish. In 2019, he graduated from Teesside University with a Master's Degree in Creative Writing.

Whimper
By: Steven Bruce

I NEVER MET my grandmother, a man named Arthur Jones strangled her before I was born.

Last week, in the middle of our Sunday roast, my mother called her a vile bitch. Said that when she was eight–years–old, her mother drowned two newborn puppies in the bathtub. And when her mother caught her crying about it, she made her climb in with them.

I didn't know what to say. None of us did. We all sat there, staring at our potatoes. I mean, what do you say to something like that? Never mind mother, malevolence wears no chains, could you pass the gravy, please.

The same night, my mother died of a heart attack in the bathtub. When I asked Uncle Rich if he thought it was weird, he said it was most likely a coincidence. I told him that Freud said there are no coincidences. At which point he picked up a sausage roll and hobbled off into the garden.

Steven Bruce

Yesterday I would have said that Freud was full of shit. But after this morning, well, I don't know what to think.

My mother's wake finished at four minutes past four. I got home for twenty–seven minutes past, leaving me three minutes before my cleaning routine began.

I start in the bathroom because it's the closest room to the front door. I use lemon–scented antibacterial wipes to clean the tiles, all sixty–one of them. I scrub the bathtub, sink, and toilet. Then mop the floor with bleach and boiling water.

Next, the living room, well, the living room slash bedroom. I live in a studio apartment at the moment. It's not much, but once my sci–fi novel's published, I'll be able to afford somewhere much better.

I strip off the bedding and spray the mattress with an antibacterial spray. Did you know that a single bed bug can lay up to two–hundred–and–fifty eggs?

While the mattress dries, I check the neighbour's house through the crack in the curtains. A few days ago, he was standing in his garden with his mouth ajar. I'm sure he was looking right at me. Once the mattress's dry, I stick the clean bedding on.

I give my writing desk a rub over with the lemon–scented antibacterial wipes. Then make sure my books are in alphabetical alignment. Asimov, Bradbury, Clarke, Herbert, King, Martin, Rowling, Tolkien, and Vonnegut. Then hoover the couch and carpet, twice.

Next, I wash down the one–hundred–and–four tiles, sink, worktops, fridge, kettle, and toaster. I refuse to own a cooker or a washing machine. Mother washed my clothes and cooked most of my meals for me, anyway.

Finally, I align the items in the food cupboard, chicken noodles, cookies, crisps, tea bags, and four cartons of soya milk. I did drink regular milk. But I read somewhere that cows develop abscesses during the milking process and puss seeps into the milk.

When my cleaning routine finished, I washed my entire body with hand sanitiser and waited to dry before putting on clean pyjamas.

At seven o'clock, I thought I heard a knock at the door. I checked through the crack in the curtains. My neighbour's front door was wide open, but I couldn't see him. I waited a few minutes and peeped through the spyhole in the front door. A spindly shadow lingered on the hall carpet, after a few seconds, it slipped away.

At nine o'clock, I locked the door, aligned my slippers with the pattern on the carpet, switched off the lights, and climbed into bed. I don't recall falling asleep. I never do, do you?

I woke up, in darkness, to animals whimpering. My front door staggered open, scraping over the carpet. A haggard woman drifted into the room, an ashy glow emanating from her body. She stooped at the bottom of the bed, eyes missing from the sockets. Her face like cracked concrete, her mouth drooping to one side. She crawled onto the bed with a gurgling hiss and climbed on top of me. My screams for help slipped out as small groans. Her face closed in on mine until her cold nose pressed into my cheek. She called me a gutless little shit, and before I knew it, she dragged me out of bed, by my feet.

The whimpering grew louder as she pulled me into the bathroom and slammed the door shut. A fleeting moment of darkness and her empty eye sockets lit up with a piercing white light. She grabbed my throat and held my face over the bathtub. Two newborn puppies struggled in the water. She pulled one out and shoved it into my mouth before throwing me into the bathtub.

I woke, to the sun punching through the curtains, feeling re–born. I wrote two chapters of my novel, began my cleaning routine and stopped dead when I noticed my lifeless body in the bathtub.

All morning, the non–stop whimpering, the hag's hand hanging out from under my bed. I had to get out of there, go somewhere quiet. I don't know how I ended up in your home, but I like what you've done with the place.

THE WORLD OF MYTH

MAGAZINE

ISSUE

79

DECEMBER 2019

Melissa Small

Melissa Small is a mother of two boys and her husband also shares all her nerdy hobbies. She has published seven short stories. A story in the book, The Way Through by Polar Expressions Publishing (Fate of the Sea Witch), Futuristic Canada by Dark Helix Press (Poutine, Bugs and Big Bessie) and five short stories in The World of Myth Magazine, (Wool of Time, Boom, Soleless and two SeaWitch stories). She is a member of the Star Wars 501st Canadian Garrison and she would love to write a Star Wars book someday.

Snow Magic!
By: Melissa Small

EVER WONDER HOW the first snow is made?

It's not all that science stuff you are told that just keeps the mundane happy.

It's Magic! Real Magic!

I guess I should explain who I am. I am Lord Pat'eli' McGynn the 4th. I'm a Snow Fairy not to be mistaken for a Frost Fairy, Blizzard Fairy or a Water Fairy. I'm a Snow Fairy I only deal with snow occasions like the First snow, Yule, The Jolly Santa route and now because it got written in to our contract Skier's snow. Like I have time to stop by every snow hill.

To make Magic snow we fairies start in the fall going as you call it door to door on our magical hares that give us a lift around checking on all the animals, the birds, the bugs and the trees. We make sure they are all ready for the first snow to fall and then we plan how it is to fall. As every first snow is not the same as the year before. We pride ourselves on each and every snow flake we make. All are unique and original.

That's correct every snow flake is made by hand by fairies. We can't tell you all the secrets but I can tell you this, every snow flake carries a magic to it and every snow flake carries a wish. Not just for humans but for all of nature.

For us Winter is a very busy time of the year. But most important is the first snow fall, Yule eve and Santa's visit of course but also ski hills, toboggan hills and snow days. We pride ourselves on getting more snow days then the Ice Fairies do.

So now you know where your snow comes from. Stop complaining about it or we will send more to your yard. Enjoy winter and all its magic.

I must go as Snow doesn't make itself.

THE WORLD OF MYTH

MAGAZINE

ISSUE

80

DECEMBER 2020

J. Agombar

J. Agombar resides near the treacherous waters of Southend–On–Sea, Essex, UK where visions of the speculative, criminal and supernatural have taken hold of his mind, (usually alongside a bottle of whiskey) . He holds a BA Hons in Humanities, where the creative writing module inspired his first published work with Luna Press.
He is a fan of the short story and inspired by classic authors such as Richard Matheson Ray Bradbury and H.P. Lovecraft. "The Night Cyclist" diverts from his usual style and touches on more heartwarming fantasy elements. He is currently working on his second collection. You can find his previously published works from his Facebook page: https://www.facebook.com/j.agombar.author

The Night Cyclist
By: J. Agombar

MY COFFEE STEAMS into the crisp midnight air as I glance upon the sparkling stars from my balcony. Living on the coast of Blavega is an experience full of wonder and magic, however, it can get crowded at this time of year with tourists, which is why my balcony becomes my retreat. On the night of every November 9th a grand race is held along the cobbled coastline road of Blavega, a twenty–eight–kilometer track that connects the top of Mount Cartlin to the peninsula of the Old Town where I reside. It calls to celebrate the world of cyclists that gather here, but this event serves merely as a facade for some, for the cobbled road is now twinned with a modern, smooth cycle path, and few cyclists actually consider it a 'race'. Nobody rushes this stretch where the coastal breeze changes the banal feeling of just existing into something more, a euphoric higher plane where the gulls above observe, matching the speed of even the more agile riders. The biggest secret is the least mentioned in advertising, but the most talked about in the town. The masses come in attempt to catch a glimpse of the 'Night Cyclist', a spirit that can be found on rare occasion, and even rarer, an encounter with a strange illusion where the rider is momentarily transported to another place.

I have been lucky; in my experience he can only be found on certain nights when the moon is fuller, and only reveals himself to a certain kind of person. Having lived here for several years, and initially not aware of this phantom cyclist, it so happens he was always more likely to reveal himself to someone like me. Each year after the event I find tourists and locals in café's and bars garrulous of their experience, flaunting some fanciful story as to how they were briefly haunted by the fearsome spirit world. But these stories are fabricated, mere poetics to impress the guileless masses who pass on the tale in a chain of whisper; a desperate grasp for attention.

The genuine ones are different. I know how they react, more subtle in their approach to the description. They are reserved, confused, and hesitant to reveal due to not expecting to witness such a strange occurrence. Some are lost in translation if their English is not so strong. But certain elements of what they say make it seem natural, certain perceptive intricacies concrete the validity of their experience. Firstly, they take the time, usually alone, to think about what they saw and ponder if reality had taken them away briefly, or perhaps if an overactive imagination had temporarily overcome them. Then they look around the bar, or coffee shop, not quite knowing who to tell, for they want someone who already knows, to assure them, to put their mind at ease, to let them know if they were actually just dreaming.

When I first moved here a few years ago in the height of autumn, my oblivion to such a graceful spirit was resolved by an old local man who had been climbing Blavega's steep inclines since his childhood. He was drunk, and initially I cast his tales aside before heading home. Then, after hearing about him, I was compelled and went looking, but that is how I learned that actively seeking him will always end fruitless. A year passed and another invasion of crimson and ochre leaves fell to the cobblestones. I'd forgotten all about him, until one September evening when the twilight battled with the antique street lamps, I saw him; saw something. I had rode less than 5km, leisurely; free of expectation, a classic trigger for his appearance. As I pulled up to where a low sea wall framed the last glimpse of the sunset, I stopped and released my drink from the bottle cage on the frame beneath me. A meek current of air; a slight zephyr, pushed across behind me. I turned my head to see him as he passed. His brown jacket and flat cap were what I noticed first. He half turned as he rode away, slightly tipping it to greet me, or so I believe. The bike was an odd shape which caused my main confusion at the sight of him, but as I completed my journey home that day, I realized exactly whom I had seen, and finally felt a sense of belonging in the town I still call home today.

Over a period of time I saw him sporadically from a distance, sometimes even from my balcony here. The visions were fleeting and barely noticeable, like passing through smoke only to find it disappearing as you disturb

183

it. Around three months ago was my longest and most profound experience of him. During a cycle home just before dusk, I had stopped for breath moments from my home. The rain had fell lightly for some time, and scattered dark clouds blocked the last remaining light that shone behind them causing them to glow at the edges, and a rainbow to form in the distance. It was the worst few days of the summer weather and followed a heatwave. Of course, I wasn't prepared for this weather and my hair helped soak my head. However, as I ducked under the canopy of a local bakers, which was closed, I noticed a man standing by the low sea wall, staring out to sea. I knew who he was immediately as it was too strange for anybody to be left on the coastal road in the rain, except for the odd tourist couple, perhaps. I watched him oversee the rippling bay for a moment before he moved and retrieved a bike that was not present, yet somehow leaning against the nearby lamppost. Like him and his bike, the lamppost also shimmered in the light like a prism turning and glinting. As he mounted it, it appeared to my vision with a blurred motion. He cocked his leg over the sturdy frame and rode away. I wasn't an expert in bikes, but I knew my way around one. I had not seen the type he had before, but I knew it was not from this modern age, and likely a relic of the past. I later researched the frame style. It was a Hercules, and furthermore, a trade bicycle which had a wider frame than usual with a kink in it so you could hang an advertisement board within it. There was also a basket frame below the handlebars. I didn't get much more from that moment, so I took a chance on getting a cold, jumped on my uncouth modern Ammaco Ethos mountain bike, and

184

followed him, taking me towards Mount Cartlin, and away from home.

I knew eagerness would likely collapse the vision so I calmly kept my distance. He seemed to follow the path of the cobblestones but found no friction from them, whereas I stuck to the modern cycle path that ran alongside them. As I trailed behind him, attempting to catch a closer glimpse of his bike, I felt a strange sensation. My body became numb, and the rain stopped. I felt heat as the temperature seemed to rise rapidly around me. The sun burst out from behind the clouds and the sky turned a bright blue with daylight once more. The ground in front of me unfolded differently. As I approached him, I slowed to stay in his wake. Vibrant colors burst from the ground and everything around me, dancing with incendiary motion. It was like the rippling effect a boat leaves on water behind it, but thickly applied like the strokes of a pastiche painting. Each color matching its component: the cobblestones, a gray and auburn; the ocean, an lazuline blue; the shops frames, umber and yellow, and the grass on the richer side of Mount Cartlin, a sensational green. Everything became a visual fantasy in lucid and eidetic form. Shortly, the colors then blended with their opposing tones with dark blues, violets and browns that transcended into an otherworldly night time. It injected a curious feeling of warmth and freedom with my mind as well as my body. I could no longer feel the aches of the day, nor the rain which had drenched me.

I continued my pursuit with lungs expanding to their full capacity and entranced by the imagery of another era that quivered before me. I gained a little momentum as I let the apparition take me on his beauteous journey toward the

185

mountain. Suddenly, the smell of bread in my nostrils, strong and fresh. It became hard to see him in the momentum, but his basket under his handlebars contained two loaves, stacked in equanimous fashion and separated with some apples. Although his attire was not a uniform, it was smart enough to warrant an occupation of some kind. His build was that of a regular working–class man and not the modern lycra lathered, agile visitors who crossed the same stones each year. I noticed his front wheel was slightly smaller than the rear, although his tyres seemed to be smooth, motionless circles in this strange parallel void, and his spokes near invisible. An array of souls, bursting with stop–motion color appeared around us and seemed to acknowledge him. A woman in a red coat waved a gloved hand at him, a small dog yanked at his masters lead to chase the wheels, he swerved a little to avoid the football of a young boy who darted across the promenade. I marveled at the now dark hues of the blue sky above which allowing the stars to glint with spectral, momentary beauty. I felt like my eyes were a prisoner of Van Gogh, and as I glanced at my own body, I found it had succumbed to the same artistic layered style the world around me had taken. Lines of flickering light blended with thick daubs of color which flaked away from my hands and shirt as my bike cut through the backwash of the unreal cyclist ahead of me.

My journey ended as he pulled over to a place just before the mountain. An old house with brown and red paneling, where the windows grilled with steel diamond emblems were lined with flowers stood. He slowed, leaned his bike against another lamppost, gathered the bread and apples from the basket, and glanced up to the house. A

186

woman emerged from the double doors and onto the balcony. She wore a long, stylish mauve coat with high heels, and a dark hat with a face veil. She smiled and blew him a kiss. I could see the cyclist's face clearly for the first time, a long, thin face and sturdy jaw with dark eyebrows against pale skin, although in reaction to her he adopted a florid expression and broad smile. The lady above retired into her house, leaving the balcony doors open. He stopped and looked at me. I froze. He sustained his broad grin, added a wink, and tossed me an apple. I instinctively went to catch it and did successfully as it swirled and resonated with restless sanguine shades in my palm. I snapped my head back up to him in bewilderment where his form lost its colorful shimmering flair and became a more ghostly transparent outline as he passed through the closed doorway of the house and disappeared. The balcony door above was then closed, or perhaps, in this moment of time, never opened. The vision faded, as did the bike against the lamppost, and I was left alone once more in the light rain of that evening.

So, I no longer strive to see the phantom the other cyclists speak of. They say the spirit of the night cyclist haunts this place as if with vendetta or malice, wandering lost with some developed torment. Yet they still seek him, wanting to believe in their own mindless folklore. My heuristic approach has taught me otherwise. To me the Night Cyclist represents the opposite nature. He is a happy soul and appears before those who achieve that same mindful clarity, free of judgment and stressful acquirement. To me he is the soul of a blessed man, a man in love with all aspects that he surrounds himself with, a rarity to be envied

J. Agombar

by many, and indeed, the soul of this very town.

THE WORLD OF MYTH

MAGAZINE

ISSUE

81

FEBRUARY 2020

Matt Lucas

I am an author represented by Labyrinth Literary Agency. I delve into paranormal, fantasy, sci-fi, and horror. My debut novel, *The Shadow Gospels*, is currently being pitched to publishers.

I've had several short stories published with Black Hare Press, Blood Song Books, and Eerie River Publishing. As my career progresses, I'm always looking for opportunities to expand my resume.

Writing is my passion and I hope to spend my days cultivating captivating stories with impactful messages.

Links:

https://twitter.com/MattDLuke

https://www.instagram.com/mattdluke/

Neo-Exodus
By: Matt Lucas

Part I

TERROR PERMEATED THE battalion as they desperately retreated across desert sands. Their enemy was in hot pursuit. An entire platoon of battle–hardened Allied troops had been decimated—reduced to ten soldiers. Fueled only by raw adrenaline, the survivors dashed towards their base at Ras Ghareb with the roars of unnatural beasts resonating from the shadows.

Private Isley looked over his shoulder into the black abyss. Just then, lightning struck, momentarily illuminating the torrid landscape. The visage of evil incarnate sent a shock wave of hopelessness reverberating through Isley's very soul.

A fleet of winged creatures blotted the night sky. They bore the roaring heads of lions and the wings of giant eagles. George Isley remembered how they'd swooped down, plucking off his comrades one by one. He shuddered, recalling how they ripped men limb from limb in the sky, raining blood upon the battalion.

On the ground, leopards with serpentine necks and the faces of cobras careened over the dunes. Acidic venom dripped from their fangs. A mere drop of their poison could sear a man's flesh to the bone.

Worst of all were the monsters riding on steel chariots alongside the horrific beasts. A regiment of Nazi tanks and vehicles bore down on the ten survivors with two Egyptian gods in tow. One was an imposing humanoid with a jackal's head. Visages of the beast adorned the temples walls, worshiped like some sort of god. There was also princely man with a cobra's crown. Images of him sitting on a throne littered the temples hieroglyphics.

"Don't look back!" Corporal Dolan, a ginger Brit, called to Isley.

When all hope was lost and Isley could smell the noxious stench of the monsters reaching for him, a glimmer of hope appeared. A set of headlights sped in their direction. Machine gun fire filled the desert air as a hail of bullets assaulted the winged terrors.

Isley realized two of his companions—Sherman and Owens— had made it back to base, jumped in a Humvee, and had driven back into hell for their comrades. Their counter assault bought the fleeing soldiers much needed time. Without Sherman and Owens' quick thinking, the rest of the squadron faced certain death.

Sherman—a grizzled brute from the backwaters of Pennsylvania—manned the gun, unleashing a murderous barrage against the mythical beasts while Owens, the battalion's most prolific killer, drove holding his Thompson sub-machine gun out the window, launching an assault of his own.

One after another the remnants of a once powerful force leapt into the back of the vehicle. Covered in blood and soot, they turned their weapons out the back, ready to join the fray. Instead, they received a stern warning from the senior–most officer, William Roberts, a curly haired Carolinian.

"Save your ammo!" Roberts shouted a midst the chaos. "We're gonna need every shot! Don't waste 'em!"

As Owens sped off, increasing the distance between the horde and survivors, the crew in the back stared into each other's sullen eyes. Distraught, they had no answers for what they had witnessed in that temple. Was it black magic, necromancy, or some other devilish plot devised by the world's most evil regime?

This was supposed to be a simple mission to eradicate the remaining Nazi forces from North Africa. Berlin would soon fall, and the war would be over. Tonight, however, everyone in the back of that Humvee knew the war was just beginning.

There was no time to waste when the ten weary combatants entered Ras Ghareb at the banks of the Red Sea. Many of the citizens had cleared out of the shantytown when Axis forces arrived in 1940. Four years later, they hadn't returned. The squadron was on their own.

"I need two guns on each side of the main alley!" Roberts barked. "Isley and Lee, I want you in the highest spot you can find to snipe! Get a roof over your heads! Keep those winged creatures from swoopin' in on ya!"

Isley and Lee—a Korean American soldier—grabbed their rifles and headed for the two highest peaks in the ghost town. Meanwhile, Gida, a boisterous Brooklynite, and Dolan scurried to move their machine guns into place.

"Let me, Sherman, and Claypool play bait down the main drag," Owens suggested. "They're gonna come at us full-bore. When they're too much for the gunners and snipers, have them fall back. If we've got men in the adjacent alleyways, they'll have broadside shots once those things break our line."

Roberts paused, leering at the three volunteers. "You sure you can outrun those things?"

Claypool, a blonde haired, blue-eyed Floridian cracked a grin. "I know I don' look like much, sir, but I'm deceptively quick."

The commander shrugged. "It's your funeral. Davis and Goldberg, I want you two in the alleys. Snipers and gunners will join you when the wave becomes too much."

Goldberg, a Polish Jew, who immigrated to America before the war, spoke up. "And what happens when we're overrun?"

"We'll get underground. Get them into close quarters in cellars," Roberts theorized.

Nodding in recognition, Davis, a stout Philadelphian with a deadly accurate shot, and Goldberg moved into position.

"It's not a good plan," Sherman nervously jested, aware of their impending doom.

"No," Roberts agreed, "but it's what we've got."

When the plans were laid, the calm before the storm

196

arrived. Each man nervously grasped the grips of their weapons with quaking hands. Sweat accumulated on their palms and the rhythm of their breathing became hard to control.

Soon, a black swarm of griffins blotted out the stars in the sky, the horde of serpopards covered every speck of sand, and the smell of Nazi tank engines permeated the air. Abruptly, the onslaught came to a halt outside the city walls. As the beasts awaited their next command, three figures strode to the front. The Jackal, cobra–crowned monarch, and a Nazi officer clad in black leather and adorned with medals stepped forward.

"Resistance is futile," the German office declared triumphantly, "lay down your arms."

Roberts shouted his reply while climbing atop the Humvee to man the sentry. "I think we're gonna hang onto our guns. We're quite fond of 'em."

The Nazi scoffed. "Ten men stand no chance against the union of ancient Egypt and the Third Reich. Abandon this silly resistance and witness the birth of a new empire."

Suddenly a shot rang out. The Nazi provocateur collapsed. Gore oozed from his forehead.

Isley, who fired the shot, smirked. "Now who looks silly?" he taunted.

A pause fell across the unholy army. The jackal and prince glanced down at the Nazi's corpse before refocusing on Ras Ghareb. With a blood–curdling screen the jackal thrust his arm forward. At their masters beckoning the army charged.

The initial onslaught took heavy damage. The griffins and serpopards spearheaded the charge ahead of their Nazi allies. Despite their fearsome appearance, the beasts were mere flesh and blood.

Gida and Dolan's machine guns shredded the serpopards' advance. Isley and Lee proved adept sharpshooters, blasting griffins from the night sky like pheasants. What few creatures that broke through the line were quickly dispatched by Owens, Claypool, and Sherman. At this point, Roberts, Davis, and Goldberg hadn't even fired a shot.

As the beasts' bodies began to litter the main drag, a murmur of hope exuded the battalion. Defiant confidence replaced their hopelessness. Their demise was no longer certain.

Their advantage, however, was short–lived. German tanks caught up with their supernatural counterparts. Now, the beaten and battered soldiers weren't simply dealing with mythical predators, they had to contend with mortars, tanks, and infantry. The familiar adversary turned the tide of the conflict.

A well–placed shot from a tank cannon careened into the Humvee just as Roberts leapt from the fiery plume. With their primary source of air defense rendered inept, the burden fell heavily on Isley and Lee. Despite their prowess, neither man could reload fast enough to counteract the bombardment of griffins swooping at the regiment with deadly intent.

Seeing the havoc Dolan and Gida wreaked on the preliminary charge also caught the German attention. Fixating their firepower on each machine gun nest, the Nazis forced the gunners to abandon their position. As they retreated down the side streets, a key cog in the battalion's defense crumbled.

Now, there was nothing to slow down the serpopard assault. The serpentine leopards flooded the main street, snarling as their acidic venom dripped onto the sands below. Still, Owens, Sherman, and Claypool stood defiant in the face of carnage.

"C'mon, 'ya goofy kitties," Sherman provoked the leopard–cobra hybrids, "it's chow time!"

Without hesitation the nightmarish beings gave chase, snapping at the trio's heels as they sped down the main drag. Quickly, the serpopards gained on their prey. Rearing back, the horde readied their killing blow.

Suddenly, a hail of gunfire erupted from each side of the alley. Davis, Dolan, and Roberts flanked from one side while Gida, Goldberg manned the other. It was a perfectly executed ambush, drawing the mongrels into a meat grinding crossfire.

Despite their brief success, there was no time to marvel at their tactical acumen. More explosions rocked the landscape. The heavy mortar fire drew too close for comfort as the Nazis littered the alleys with shells. Fortunately, the Nazis weren't just bombarding the platoon, they were cannibalizing the serpopard advance as well, buying enough time for the squadron to fall back deeper into Ras Ghareb.

Roberts located a storm cellar as they fled the carnage. "There!" He cried out, pointing to the entrance. "Get to cover!"

Some of the men skidded down the stairwell, but two stayed behind. Gida and Davis knew there were still two soldiers enveloped by the fray and they weren't about to leave a man behind.

Gida grasped Roberts' arm. "Sir, we can't leave Lee and Isley!"

"Look out for them, but as soon as it gets too hairy, you get into this cellar and lock the door!" Roberts commanded.

Emerging from cover, Gida and Davis gazed into the abyss. Blood pooled in the street. Many of the buildings were reduced to rubble. Smoke billowed from roaring fires. Hell was here.

The serpopards were fixated upwards, jumping and clawing at the sides of buildings. The duo shifted their focus to discern what caught the rabid monsters' interest. Astounded, they were shocked by what they saw.

On the rooftops of the buildings lining the main drag, Isley and Lee ran for their lives. Though out of the serpopards' clutches, the snipers were far from safety. Griffins dive–bombed with murderous intent; their assault masked by the dense smog.

Bounding from roof to roof, Isley and Lee were sitting ducks. Gida and Davis knew they needed to act fast. Raising their barrels to the heavens, the duo blindly fired into the black cloud. The bodies of griffins lifelessly plunged from the maelstrom, crash landing among their abominable kin.

Though they'd granted their cohorts a brief reprieve from danger, the duo also drew the ire of the serpopard pack. As the snake–like felines sped towards the soldiers while Isley came skidding down a fire escape ladder to rejoin his compatriots.

"You boys havin' fun yet?" Isley jested, lending his own firepower to the defense.

"We gotta knock 'em back!" Davis realized. "Hit 'em with grenades!"

In unison, the trio pull their pins and flung explosives into the onslaught. Three explosions rocked the land in quick succession. The serpopards recoiled as shrapnel shredded through their despicable ranks.

They might've bought Lee a few more seconds, but he wasn't out of the woods yet. The final structure he would've used to climb down was just then struck with a mortar. As the humble building crumbled, so did Lee's hope for escape.

Distressed, his eyes darted about, looking for some semblance of salvation. There was nothing. Jumping meant broken legs and certain death. Climbing would take too long. He had no way out.

"Alright, Adam," Lee murmured to himself, "time to get creative."

Clutching two Bowie knives from his belt, Adam Lee drew them with his eyes glued to a moving target. A rogue griffin was launching an offensive towards his fellow soldiers below.

The half lion, half eagle abomination crossed in front of Lee. Summoning all his strength, the sniper leapt from the rooftop. For a moment, time stood still. He hovered in the air, completely vulnerable. However, so was his target.

With two might stabs, Lee plunged his blades into the griffin's side. Blood spurted from the creature as it squealed in agony. With fluttering wings, the animal desperately flapped, accelerating its blood loss and helpless to halt their descent.

When they were a meter off the ground, Lee unstuck his

victim, dropping to the earth. With a graceful roll, he leapt to his feet and sprinted to rendezvous with the battalion. Pride swelled within him seeing his comrades gawking in amazement.

"That was one of the coolest things I've ever seen," Gida remarked, astounded.

"That was the coolest thing I've ever done," Lee agreed, delightfully shocked that his cockamamie plot had succeeded.

Davis grabbed his cohorts, leading them down the cellar stairs. "We gotta go! You can brag all about it down here."

Once the cellar door locked, the battalion sat in sullen silence. Some tried to rest, though their minds were wrought with disturbing visions of the atrocity they'd witnessed. Others stared into space, desperately working to erase the bloodshed from their memories.

Sounds of monsters prowling above their heads broke the silence. Hateful snarls and screeches plagued their ears as the predators sought out their prey. Each man knew they didn't have much time left. Ras Ghareb wasn't a large place. Their enemies would find them soon enough.

"What the hell happened at that temple?" Claypool broke the silence, keeping his voice slightly hushed.

"Black magic, necromancy, witchcraft," Sherman theorized possible explanations, "at least that's my guess?"

"How would you know?" Gida skeptically jibed.

"I read!" Sherman countered.

Gida turned quizzically to Davis. "Did you know he could read?"

Davis shrugged. "All I know is he's good at killing. Doesn't matter now, no book is gonna help us outta this fight."

Isley sighed. "Since when do the freakin' Krauts care so much about magic and Egypt?"

"Berlin's on its last leg," Owens interjected, "Hitler's desperate. I reckon he'll try anything."

Roberts lent his own knowledge. "Rumor has it that Hitler designed an agency to investigate the occult and mysticism since before the war. Obviously, they found something."

"Why Egypt though?" Lee pondered.

"Isn't it obvious?" Dolan chimed in.

"Not at all," Claypool answered for the group, "please enlighten us."

Dolan's lips pursed. His eyes darted towards Goldberg. He fidgeted nervously before outlining his explanation.

"We've all heard the reports out of Europe," Dolan began, "Jews and undesirables being slaughtered by the millions. Can anyone think of another historical empire bent on enslaving and massacring Hebrews?"

"Who is the Lord, that I should obey him and let Israel go?" Goldberg broke his silence, quoting scripture. "I do not know the Lord and I will not let Israel go. Pharaoh gave that charming tidbit to Moses in Exodus."

"Looks like they're still holdin' a grudge," Davis surmised.

Owen's chin tightened in anger. "Hitler wants to ensure that, if Germany falls, there's someone left to carry out his twisted endgame."

"I'd bet the farm that princely lookin' fella is the Pharaoh that got sideways with Moses," Gida wagered.

"Then what the hell's the dog headed guy?" Isley was

203

perplexed. "I don't recall any jackal men in Exodus."

Roberts shrugged. "Some Egyptian god, probably Anubis, given what I remember from third grade history."

Claypool boisterously threw up is hands in dismay. "They were nothing but myths! Even if some sorcery resurrected Pharaoh, those gods never existed! Neither did any of these other bizarre creatures!"

"The devil's got many tricks," Dolan speculated.

"And we've got front row seats to his newest one," Owens pensively added.

Sherman scoffed. "Somehow I knew this was gonna happen. Been having freaky dreams a week leading up to this operation."

"We don't need to hear about none of your perverted fantasies," Isley's jesting wit didn't cease, even in the worst circumstances.

"Not that kind of freaky," Sherman's solemn tone didn't waiver.

Roberts perked up, intrigued. "What are you talking about, soldier?"

"Been the same thing every night. I saw a shadow, racin' across the desert, consuming everything in its path," Sherman began. "I ran from it, towards the sea."

"Ain't no escape through the Red Sea," Davis noted skeptically.

Sherman shrugged. "I know it sounds crazy. But each night, I saw a dove fly over the sea into a sunrise. Never felt like I was gonna die."

Lee wasn't so hopeful. "Sure as hell feels like we're gonna die."

Claypool smirked, rolling up his sleeve. He turned his

arm, exposing a dark tattoo. It was an angelic figure, clad in black armor, wielding a scythe. The angel's feet trampled atop a serpent. Above his head was a verse of scripture.

"You are my war hammer, my weapon for battle," Claypool recited from the book of Jeremiah, "with you I shatter nations, with you I destroy kingdoms."

Owens stood to address the men. "It took ten plagues to defeat Egypt last time. Tonight, we're the embodiment of those ten plagues, reborn to send those demons back to hell."

Roberts lent his voice to the plotting, "We'll radio the Navy. Once we fight our way out of here, we make a beeline for the sea. No man left behind."

"No man left behind," the platoon echoed with courageous resilience.

Part II

The building was thankfully intact from the mortar fire. It was two stories, so the battalion divvied up into two squadrons of five between the first two floors. With guile they crept into their positions, silently observing their foes.

German tanks rolled into the main drag. Three of them hovered around the fighters' location, guarded by unnatural mongrels and sadistic Nazis. On the second floor, Roberts, Sherman, Lee, Gida, and Davis bided their time, awaiting their moment.

In a flurry of action, Goldberg, Owens, Claypool, Isley, and Dolan burst forth from the first floor, unleashing a vicious onslaught of bullets into the fray. Mercilessly they cut down serpopards as each man scattered in five separate

directions. The serpentine cats gave chase and a hail of
griffin's dive bombed the men.

The Nazis, however, whirled about in confusion. Chaos
reigned as they failed to decipher their targets' location
through a stampede of mythical monsters. Not only that,
they were guarding slow–moving, unagile tanks that
struggled to navigate Ras Ghareb's narrow streets.

Utilizing the Nazi confusion to their advantage, Roberts
gave the order to open fire on the bewildered soldiers. The
second–floor squadron released a barrage of gunfire down
on their adversaries, picking them off one by one. Their
onslaught would be abbreviated, however, as the tanks'
barrels began slowly shifting their direction.

Sensing their time was short, Lee, who was the eyes of
the operation, bellowed the order they all knew he would
eventually have to give.

"Jump!" Adam Lee roared.

The leap wasn't far, maybe about ten feet to the sandy
earth below. But that didn't make it any less disconcerting.
Fortunately for the team, the sounds of tank canons firing
provided the necessary motivation to take the leap of faith.

In unison, the five remnants soared out the windows.
Two missiles whizzed through the air, rocketing between
Roberts and Gida as well as Goldberg and Sherman. A
plume of fire mushroomed at their backs, searing their
necks with immense heat. The shock wave propelled them
forward, careening them towards the tanks.

Roberts, Lee, and Sherman landed with grace, deftly
rolling before bouncing back to their feet, seamlessly firing
into the Nazi squadron. Gida and Goldberg were less
fortunate. Goldberg crashed onto one of the tanks with a

bone crunching thud. Gida was sent skidding across the sand.

The Brooklynite desperately scrambled to his feet only to be instantly assaulted by a swooping griffin. The winged lion barreled into Gida. Its razor–sharp fangs clamped down on his meaty trapezius muscle between his neck and shoulder. The soldier bellowed in anguish as the monster violently shook its head, tearing flesh from bone.

As the griffin's mighty wings beat, Gida felt his feet lift from the earth. Despite his searing agony, the soldier refused to relent. His free hand scrambled near his belt buckle, clamoring for the hilt of his knife.

"I'm nobody's dinner!" Gida snarled through gritted teeth, thrusting his blade upwards, through the bottom of the lion's jaw and up into its skull.

With a guttural gurgling, the griffin released its prey. When his feet hit the ground, Gida realized his mangled left arm was immobile. He'd have to finish this fight with only his right.

"Screw it, a one–armed Italian from New York is worth a hundred Krauts," Gida reminded himself as he charged one of the tanks.

Leaping, Gida grasped the tank barrel and pulled himself up onto the platform. He charged the top hatch, wrested it open, and dropped into the cockpit. The inhabitants were caught by surprise.

The first whirled around, wide–eyed in terror, shocked by the bold maneuver. The look remained on his face even after Gida hurled his knife into the Kraut's chest. Once the first threat collapsed, the tank operator abandoned his captain's chair to charge Gida, drawing his German Luger.

Before he could fire a shot, Gida batted the pistol away, leaving his foe exposed. He delivered a swift punch to the tank pilot's face to stun. The big American then grasped the back of the German's head like a baseball and slammed it against the inner wall. Filled with rage, Gida repeated the bashing until the Nazi's cranium was little more than skull fragments and pink brain matter.

"I think you got him," Goldberg observed, peeking in from the top hatch before joining his comrade below.

"That was a little excessive," Gida sheepishly admitted.

Goldberg shrugged. "Best kind of Nazi is a dead Nazi. You know how to drive this thing?"

Gida inspected the controls. "Eh, sure. It's just buttons and levers. How hard could it be?"

Back outside, Sherman, Roberts, and Lee battled through the horde. Fortunately, they were able to use two of the Nazi tanks for cover, utilizing proximity to hide from the tank operators. The third machine, however, was being driven too erratically, so they avoided that one.

Griffins swooped down from the black sky, only to scrape their talons against metal, missing their targets. The Nazi soldiers fired wildly, but their bullets harmlessly ricocheted off the tanks' steel. The three Allied soldiers huddled for cover, savoring their tactical advantage.

They'd intermittently bob from cover to return fire like gophers bounding from tunnels to sunlight. Roberts, Lee, and Sherman kept their pattern of movement erratic, eliminating the chance of having their next move anticipated. The plot worked for a time, until reinforcements arrived.

A serpopard brigade charged onto the scene. Five

monstrosities led the assault. Three bounded atop the tank, while two others crept around the sides. Their elongated necks would prove to be an issue.

The three serpopards on top ferociously lurched forward, thrusting the poisoned fangs at the Allied trio. With no choice but to retreat from the safety of the tank, the human combatants backed away. However, the remaining two serpopards flanked the trio, encircling Roberts, Lee, and Sherman.

"How are you guys on ammo?" Roberts' voice quaked as the monsters approached.

"I'm damn near empty," Lee admitted, captivated by dread.

Sherman was in a similar predicament. "I got three shots and there's five of them."

"Shoot," Roberts cursed, "I'm out too."

The serpopards sensed their angst, bravely inching closer. From the right, one of the beasts lunged its neck forward. Roberts dodged to the left. When the serpentine neck was overextended, he clenched the creature's neck, just behind its head.

Summoning all the strength he could muster; Roberts pinned the serpopard's head under his armpit. As the monstrosity writhed, wrestling to free itself from his grip, Roberts plunged his knife into its neck.

Blood spurt from the mythical animal as it crooned in anguish. A searing sensation washed over Roberts' forearm. His clothes sizzled and his skin began to burn as flesh melted from his arm. The serpopard's blood was just as acidic as its venom.

"Bad idea! Very bad idea!" Roberts bellowed, releasing

the serpopard's neck.

"Screw it," Sherman growled, turning and firing a shot at the other hybrid creature prowling on their flank. Now only the three standing atop the tank remained.

"What do you suppose we do with them?" Lee pondered, knowing Sherman only had two bullets left.

Suddenly a faint whistling filled the air followed by a massive explosion. A melody of carnage resonated through the desert. A metallic symphony moaned, and beasts shrieked in agony. A ringing filled the trio's ears as they were propelled backwards from the shock wave

Once their senses returned, Roberts, Lee, and Sherman turned to see Goldberg's head peeking out from one of the other tanks. As Goldberg waved to them, they realized who'd provided their salvation when they saw the mangled tank they'd once used for cover.

"Get in!" Goldberg urged. "Time to go!"

In a frenzy Roberts, Lee, and Sherman scurried to rejoin their squadron. Lee and Sherman descended into the tank's bowels unscathed. However, Roberts wasn't so lucky.

A serpopard attacked, lunging through the air and striking out with its elongated neck. Its fangs plunged into his calf. The commanding officer wailed in agony as the acidic venom infected his bloodstream.

The vicious beast's onslaught didn't relent. Violently it shook its head, tearing away at Roberts' flesh and slinging the commander about like a rag doll. The serpopard soon slammed Roberts down against the tank.

Holding him in place with powerful jaws, the remainder of creature's body climbed atop the tank as if it were pulled by string. Placing a heavy paw on Roberts' chest, the monstrosity reared back, ready to unleash the killing stroke.

Baring its teeth, the jaws of death sped towards Roberts. The commander lost hope as a mouth teeming with razor–sharp, venomous teeth careened towards him with murderous intent. He closed his eyes and tried to remember home.

He'd left behind his wife, Vanessa, and child, Grace, to join the war effort. Now, at the end of his life, his mind drifted to Vanessa's warm embrace and declaration of pride in her husband's courage in the face of war. The smell of lavender filled his nostrils, recalling the last time he held his baby girl and pressing his lips to her chubby cheeks. At least his last thought would be a good one.

A brutish shout erupted from Roberts' right. Jolted, the officer was torn from his peaceful escape. When his eyes opened, salvation arrived.

Owens soared through the air with an axe raised over his head. The tracers of Nazi bullets zoomed past the soldier, but each one miraculously missed their target. It was as if time had stopped, allowing Roberts to witness the heated race between the axe blade and serpopard's deadly fangs with his life hanging in the balance.

Just as the creature's jaw got too close that its noxious venom dripped onto Roberts' shirt, its body went limp. Owens struck down with a mighty blow, severing the serpentine neck from its feline torso. Panting, Owens collapsed onto the tank's platform to recover from the dire sprint to save his commander. Leveraging the serpopard's corpse for cover, Owens found a brief moment of solitude a midst the chaos.

Owens contorted his neck, rolling to lock eyes with

211

Roberts. "You're not dyin' on me yet."

Roberts snorted. "I stormed Normandy, its gonna take a lot more than a damned snake bite to take me down."

Shortly thereafter the remainder of Owens' squad arrived to lay covering fire around the lone remaining tank. Goldberg pulled Roberts inside to join Gida, Lee, and Sherman. Meanwhile, Owens, Dolan, Davis, Isley, and Claypool reloaded and laid covering fire, hindering the Nazi advance.

Despite their recent success, a wave of caution permeated the battalion. The onslaught ominously slowed. Their enemy was plotting something and, whatever it was, it wasn't good.

Soon the shooting came to a halt. The Nazis instead formed a semi–circular, defensive formation around the Allied troops. The serpopards took a similar formation, while the griffins landed in droves atop buildings, biding their time to strike. The five soldiers outside the tank, stopped laying covering fire to conserve what little ammunition they had left in anticipation of what was to come.

The jackal–headed god and Pharaoh strode through their forces, taking their position at the front to face their much–maligned adversaries. A hush fell over Ras Ghareb. Only the guttural growls of the malicious serpopards could be heard.

"Hear me," Pharaoh proclaimed in a proud voice, "your valor is most impressive, but your resistance is futile! Abandon your iron chariot and swear fealty to me and I will grant you peace and prosperity during my reign!"

With Roberts out of commission, Davis stepped in to

assume authority. "I think we're gonna hang onto the tank. It's pretty cozy inside and we've grown accustomed to a certain lifestyle."

The resurrected Egyptian sneered at Davis' arrogance. "Two gods stand before you and an army unlike any the world has ever seen. Your choice is simple: kneel or die."

Claypool raised his hand with an observation like a child in school. "Excuse me, but there's only one God and I'm pretty sure he doesn't wear eye–liner."

Pharaoh scowled. "You insolent little—!"

"And also," Claypool interrupted, "I know you're new to English, but I think you're mixing up dog and god. Your buddy there's got a dog's head not a god's head. It's important to me that you understand the difference."

"Very well," Pharaoh relented, no longer interested in mercy towards his foes, "you'll have the death you deserve." He turned to the jackal–man hybrid and nodded.

The inter-species being snarled and placed its palms upwards. Fire emanated from nothing, consuming his fists. Undaunted by combat with mortal men, the monstrosity strode pretentiously into battle.

Sensing this battle wouldn't be easily won, Davis called to his comrades in the tank. "Goldberg and Sherman, get out here! Lee, keep watch over Roberts and Gida, they're useless in this fight!"

"I am not useless!" Gida protested from inside the tank's cockpit as Sherman and Goldberg climbed into out and into the fray.

"Out here you are!" Davis countered. "Try finding a way to help from in there!"

Within the confines of the steel machine Lee, Roberts,

213

and Gida contemplated their role in the fight. However, the serpopard's poison continued to permeate Roberts' blood stream. A dull, distant stare washed across his face as he entered a trance. Yet, before he dozed off, he had one last command for his men.

"Listen to Davis," Roberts ordered, "he's the commander now."

With Roberts drifting off to a state between life and death, Gida and Lee turned their attention to contributing to the fight at hand. While they sought out relevance in the refuge of the tank, the battle outside erupted. Their sense of urgency percolated as cries of distress resonated from their comrades.

Outside, the battle against the Egyptian god, Anubis, fared poorly for the remainder of the regimen. The glowering beast was supremely quick and seemed to possess the strength of ten or more men. Hurling balls of fire at his adversaries, Anubis ensured the combatants remained on the defensive.

The Egyptian god's strategy proved successful. Isley, Owens, Claypool, Goldberg, Davis, and Sherman spent much of the initial battle dodging for cover as explosive fireballs scorched the air. On a few occasions, a soldier was able to squeeze off a shot against the humanoid jackal, which seemed to intermittently hinder the monstrosity.

Interestingly, whenever a bullet struck Anubis, his serpopard and griffin subjects would recoil, screeching in pain. Owens and Davis, who'd found shelter behind a pile of rubble, noticed the peculiar phenomenon. They exchanged inquisitive glances, pondering how to leverage the first chink they'd unearthed in their enemies' armor.

"They feel his pain," Owens realized.

"If we can put enough lead in him, it might buy us enough time to escape," Davis theorized. "The Navy should be close to our location by now. All we have to do is hold them off for a few minutes."

Owens hopelessly sighed as flames impotently crashed into the wall of rubble at their backs. "That'll take hundreds of shots, we don't have that kind of ammo left."

Epiphany struck Davis. A devilish grin snuck across his face. "No, it'll only take one shot," he insisted, turning his eyes to fixate on the tank.

Owens smirked, grasping Davis' plot. He grabbed his radio to relay the message to his cohorts in the tank. "Boys, we need you to aim that gun at our canine friend."

"You see how fast that thing's movin'," Lee protested, "how are we gonna get him to stay still long enough for a shot? We've only got three more shells in here!"

"Leave that to us," Owens replied with a stoic confidence.

With new resolve, Owens and Davis sprinted from cover. Davis' Thompson sub–machine gun hurled bullets from his final clip at Anubis. Owens lent his sidearm to the fray, carrying the trusty axe as a supplemental weapon.

Anubis had been focused on Isley, Claypool, Sherman, and Goldberg, who'd been darting in different directions, when the hailstorm of bullets struck. When the barrage landed, Anubis backpedaled, freeing the others to unleash their own onslaughts.

With an enhanced attack, Anubis dropped to a knee, sporadically flinging fireballs at his foes to no avail. The offensive wasn't deadly, but it distracted the Egyptian god long enough for Owens and Davis to reach him. In the background, the tank cannon hummed as Gida shifted it into position.

Part III

Davis reached Anubis first, with a mighty swing, he bashed the butt of his Thompson against the beast's jaw. Undaunted, Anubis' powerful hand burst forward, gripping Davis' throat, squeezing the breath from his lungs. His scorching hand burned Davis' neck while simultaneously crushing his windpipe.

Air squeaked from Davis' esophagus. His eyes went dark as he smelled the flesh on his neck burning. Death was imminent. His only hope was that his sacrifice was enough to save his men.

Davis wasn't Roberts. He had no wife and no child waiting for him in Philadelphia. He wasn't a family man. That desire was never built into his heart. Instead, he spent his life in the Army, training to be a warrior and yearning for a warrior's death. There was no more honorable death that to lay down his life for the lives of others.

Just as he welcomed death's poisoned kiss, Davis felt himself falling back to the earth. Breath returned to his lungs as he gasped for air. His sight returned and his eyes darted about, searching to discern what caused his salvation.

Owens had buried his axe squarely into Anubis' chest. A symphony of anguish reverberated from a griffin and serpopard chorus. Anubis released Davis, wrestling to pull the axe plunged into his chest.

216

Summoning all his might, Owens grappled with the jackal, pressing forward and straining to push the blade deeper into the beast. Stunned by the turn of events, Davis watched in amazement as Claypool and Isley charged Anubis as well. Sherman, Dolan, and Goldberg, soon arrived on the scene as well, lifting Davis back to his feet.

The jackal roared in agony, straining against the might of mere mortals. Claypool and Isley pulled against Anubis' right arm, wresting it away from the axe and allowing Owens to bury it deeper into the monster's chest. As they struggled, resolve welled within Davis.

This was their moment. Anubis was rendered immobile. The tank's gun was in position. However, the soldier's strength waned against the jackal's supernatural might.

"Get back to the tank," Davis commanded Dolan, Goldberg, and Sherman with stern resolve, "tell Gida to fire the shot."

"What about you?" Goldberg queried.

"We're gonna hold him still," Davis confirmed, undaunted by what his order meant.

"Are you kidding me?" Dolan was astounded by the idea. "There's gotta be another way!"

"You'll die!" Sherman protested. "What happened to no man left behind?"

"This is war," Davis replied, "men are always left behind, but there are no men forgotten as long as those who knew them survive."

Without waiting for a reply, Davis rushed Anubis. Latching onto the terror's left arm, he pulled at it with all his strength. A spirit of faith fluttered in his soul, summoning a power he'd never known before. He wretched away the beast's arm, freeing Owens to release a final, vicious bombardment.

Understanding what was about to happen, Owens made his own contribution to the effort. He pulled the axe from Anubis' chest and began to swing away like he was chopping down a tree. With each powerful stroke, Anubis and his army wailed in strife.

It was a fitting conclusion. Owens had once been a promising baseball prospect before the war began. Known for his prowess with a bat, he'd been drafted to play for the Pittsburgh Pirates. Yet, when his country called for him to stand against the greatest evil this world has ever known, he answered the call.

Now, as it turned out, every swing Owens ever swung on the diamond came to fruition in this moment. He remembered his father, a pastor, teaching him to swing in the park behind his childhood home. Today, in his last moments, his father's wisdom returned for one last word of encouragement.

"Talent is what God taught you before He sent you to Earth," Owens heard his father's words in his head. "You've got a talent for swinging that bat. Rest assured, boy, He's gonna use that one day."

Goldberg, Sherman, and Dolan made a sprint for the tank. After, sliding down the hatch, they shared Davis' final order.

"Take the shot," Goldberg uttered with mournful sadness in his voice.

Gida reared back in disbelief. "Our men are still out there! I'm not taking the shot!"

"No way!" Lee lent his voice to Gida's defiance. "I'm not

killing my friends!"

"They know what they're doing," Dolan solemnly reckoned, "this was their plan. It's our only chance."

"No!" Gida bellowed. "I'm not—"

Gida's stand was viciously interrupted by Sherman, who shoved him aside with vengeful tears streaming down his face. Lee tried to block the husky brute, but he too was tossed aside. With his obstacles removed, Sherman clasped his fingers around the firing mechanism.

A brooding pause overtook Sherman. His hand quivered at the realization of what he was about to do. Those soldiers were his brothers, closer than any blood relative could ever be to him. He knew what he would do in their shoes.

"They'll die as soon as Anubis breaks free," Sherman reasoned, "every moment we waste is a second closer to them dying for nothing. If it were me, I'd want to die for something"

With a heavy heart, Sherman pulled the lever. A booming shot rang out, but none of the men in the tank heard it. Their sorrow was so great that it dulled their senses. The faint hum of griffins and serpopards bellowing in anguish confirmed they'd hit their mark, but every man knew the cost of that victory.

Goldberg mustered up the strength to stare through the periscope. Four bodies lay limp around a kneeling Anubis. Pools of blood surrounded Owens, Claypool, Isley, and Davis. The four brave warriors laid down their lives so the men in the tank could live to defeat the legion of evil.

Not lingering on his brothers' lifeless bodies, Goldberg shifted his focus to Anubis to see what they'd earned at the cost of their brethren's lives. The jackal's body was torn and mangled. Shards of bone were exposed, erratically jetting out in all directions. The heat of the blast scorched its flesh, leaving only the sinew below exposed. The bottom half of its jaw was blown off and its eyes hung limply from their sockets.

Parts of Anubis' limbs were blown off. The Egyptian god was missing its left arm at the shoulder and the bottom half of its right leg. The jackal's torso was split at its left shoulder as a bloody fissure line spread down to its naval.

"We got him," Goldberg declared numbly, in no mood to celebrate.

"Now's our chance," Dolan proclaimed, doing his best to remain focused on the task at hand, "if we go full–bore to the sea, the Navy should be waiting."

Sherman commandeered the driver's seat, pushing the lever forward. As the tank lurched down the main drag towards the sea, Goldberg refused to tear his eyes away from the scene at their backs. That was when he noticed something strange.

The Pharaoh approached Anubis' mangled corpse. He took a moment to inspect Claypool, Isley, Owens, and Davis' bodies. He spat on the ground, indignantly protesting their sacrifice. After he desecrated the memory of the fallen soldiers, Pharaoh laid his hands upon Anubis.

Goldberg watching in horror as new limbs sprouted in place of the old. The fissure in the abomination's body slowly fused together once more. Anubis' eyes retracted back to their sockets and its bottom jaw regenerated. The abomination was good as new, as if he'd never suffered a direct shot from a tank.

"Hey, guys!" Goldberg shouted in distress. "This isn't

over!"

"What's happening?" Dolan failed to hide the worried inflection in his voice.

"The Pharaoh healed Anubis," Goldberg confirmed.

Suddenly, a blood–curdling roar erupted from the Egyptian god. Anubis raised his fist in triumph and the griffins took flight. At their master's behest, the serpopards charged forward, careening across the desert sands in pursuit of the tank. The Nazi soldiers joined their supernatural counterparts and gave chase as well.

Desperately, Lee got on the radio, calling out in the hopes that a Navy ship had arrived on the scene. "Does anyone copy?"

"This is the USS Iowa," a voice confirmed on the other line, "we received a distress signal."

"I need you to fire every gun you've got on that ship into Ras Ghareb!" Lee urged.

"Sir, we would risk friendly fire," the naval officer answered in confusion.

"There are no friendlies left here!" Lee countered. "We stole a Nazi tank and are about to break through Ras Ghareb's outer wall, just blow this place to kingdom come!"

"Oh my God," the sound of disbelief came through the radio as the officer saw a legion of griffins blotting out the night sky. "Fire everything!"

A thunderous wave of explosions rocked Ras Ghareb. The tank quaked with each impact, rattling the men within. It was as if hell were unleashed on the tiny Egyptian town.

"What's happening out there, Goldberg?" Gida boomed in terror.

"Navy's slowin' 'em down!" Goldberg roared back. "I

think we're gonna make it!"

Just then a stray shell rocked the tank. The blast sent the steel chariot hurdling forward, rolling like a tire down a hill. The occupants violently bashed into the interior walls as they were flung about the cabin.

Thankfully their roll eventually came to a halt. The tank came to rest on its side as the occupants woozily stumbled to their feet.

"Everyone alive?" Dolan inquired while kicking the top of the hatch until it flung open.

"Depends on your definition of alive," Roberts groaned, waking from his poison induced trance.

When they emerged from the carnage, they turned around to find Ras Ghareb was nothing but a smoldering ruin. The main street they'd escaped through was littered with serpopard and Nazi bodies, still smoldering or aflame. A plume of smoke covered the entire area like morning fog.

The survivors found a shard of the tank's wheel that had been dislodged by the impact. They rested Roberts on it as a sled. Lee and Dolan began dragging their officer across the sands as the Red Sea came into view.

The USS Iowa floated in the water like an imposing monolith. Witnessing the devastation it had wrought on Ras Ghareb, filled the remaining fighters with hope that they might make it out of this alive. However, their hopes were dashed just as quickly.

Hundreds of griffins swarmed overhead. They mercilessly bombarded the vessel. The platoon looked on in horror as sailors were ripped from the deck and shredded alive in the sky.

Gunfire and desperate shouting filled the air as the

mythical beasts shredded the unprepared ship. Soon, an enormous fireball lurched through the sky, hurtling towards the Iowa. When the fireball crashed upon its target, the vessel was consumed in flames. As the Iowa sunk below the waves, their hope drowned with it.

Out of the smog, Anubis and Pharaoh emerged, accompanied by their conjoined Nazi and serpopard forces. Knowing their prey had no escape except swimming, the army calmly approached, confident in their absolute victory.

Unwilling to give up, Sherman, Dolan, Lee, Gida, Goldberg, and Roberts limped to the banks of the Red Sea. The sun was just beginning to crest above the horizon. The visage was bittersweet.

"At least we made it through the night," Gida attempted optimism a midst their imminent doom.

Lee proudly smiled. "We gave 'em one hell of a fight."

"Not a bad way to go out," Dolan agreed.

Sherman wasn't satisfied with this ending. "No, we've fought too hard. This isn't how it's supposed to end."

"Sometimes you just gotta embrace the inevitable," Roberts reasoned.

"No, we're not gonna die, I just know it," Sherman refused to surrender, "I can feel it in my bones."

"Listen, Sherman," Goldberg chimed in, "the ship is gone, and we're damn near out of ammo. There's no one left to save us."

Suddenly, a dove flew out over the water. Sherman wasn't sure if everyone else saw it, but he certainly did. White as snow, it gracefully flew over the sea.

Harkening back to the recurring dream he had before

this mission, Sherman was renewed with hope. The certainty of survival consumed him. As if he were controlled by something other than himself, Sherman stretched his hand out over the waters.

A strong easterly wind began to blow. Starting with the water at Sherman's feet, the waves began to part. In amazement, Sherman watched as the line that began at his feet stretched deeper and deeper into the sea.

The others' eyes widened in shock as they witnessed the miraculous phenomenon. Soon enough, the entire sea had parted, leaving an alleyway for the soldiers to cross. They looked around at each other, desperately trying to fathom what was taking place before their very eyes.

"Go," Gida breathed.

They broke into a full sprint down the tunnel of water. Oddly enough, the ground beneath their feet was dry, as if it had never been a seabed. With renewed stamina, they pressed on, failing to tire.

Roberts, who looked backwards, saw a look of terror overtake the Pharaoh's expression. He bellowed a command and his forces charged forward in pursuit. Despite the Allied soldiers' enhanced endurance, they were still no match for the serpopards' speed.

The beasts were quickly gaining on the retreating squadron. Pulling his pistol from his waistband, Roberts figured he'd make himself useful.

"Lee, hand me your sidearm," Roberts ordered.

Lee unquestionably obliged.

With the serpopard forces gaining and the griffins' refocused attention, the battalion wasn't out of the woods yet. Despite having lost use of his legs, Roberts remained in the fight. Dual–wielding pistols, he relentlessly fought to keep the advance at bay.

Unfortunately, there was no way to counteract the aerial assault that was about to be unleashed by the griffins. The escapees were sitting ducks, waiting to be picked off by the winged lions. Soon enough, the same horde of griffins that sunk the USS Iowa hovered above.

"Here they come!" Dolan shouted, announcing the death from above.

The mongrels careened towards their prey, growling and snarling with blood dripping from their salivating jowls. It was as if the beasts knew nothing stood between them and their next meal.

As they came parallel to the highest points of the walls of water, something peculiar happened. The walls instantaneously conjoined, creating a protective ceiling above the platoon. The waters engulfed the mythical creatures and a strong current funneled them to the depths where they were held to drown.

No matter how many barraged the group from above, the griffins could not break through the wall of water. Yet, they continued to try until their numbers waned to zero.

The chase continued for some time. However, the Nazi and Egyptian army couldn't gain on the survivors. While, the Allied soldiers walked across dry land, their counterparts traveled across dense, muddy sand. Throughout the entire duration of the ordeal, the distance between the two forces remained the same.

As the sun rose above the horizon, the Allied survivors reached the other side of the sea. They climbed from the depths onto the opposing shore with a wave of relief cascading over their souls. When they reached the opposite side, they turned back to watch the army in pursuit.

Pharaoh, Anubis, the Nazis, and the serpopards slid in the muck and mire of the sea floor. The pristine, powdered Pharaoh was covered in grime. The man who deemed himself a god looked more like a pauper than a prince.

Anubis fared no better. The malignant jackal desperately hurled fire at his enemies to no avail. Each fireball launched was immediately extinguished by splashes of seawater that whipped each attempt into impotence. This god was no match for the God who governed the sea.

When Lee and Dolan pulled Roberts onto the other shore, it happened. The dual walls of the Red Sea collapsed. Rushing water washed away the Pharaoh, Anubis, the Nazis, and the unnatural abominations.

The dove that had guided the soldiers through the sea glided over the waters once more. As it flew, steam began hovering over the surface. Curious, Dolan knelt and touched the water.

Wincing, Dolan pulled his fingers back after making contact. "It's boiling. They're being boiled alive." The was no empathy in Dolan for the maniacal men and heinous creatures.

Their eyes followed the dove as it soared over the sea. Soon it turned and flew past the surviving soldiers. It rose into the sky, disappearing into the sun.

Once the mysterious dove left, the soldiers shifted their gaze across the Red Sea. Smoke billowed from Ras Ghareb, though the decimated city was out of view. With the long night over, they reflected on the legacy their hellish night would leave.

"The world needs to know what happened here," Gida declared.

"They never will," Roberts advised, "as soon as we report this to command, they'll bury it. If people knew what happened here, the world would plunge into mass hysteria."

"Nazis wouldn't be the big bad anymore," Dolan agreed. "If they knew monsters and demons were real, humanity would descend into madness."

"Claypool, Isley, Owens, and Davis died," Lee mournfully reminded the group, "and you're telling me that no one is ever going to know why?"

"No," Sherman solemnly declared, "because that's the sacrifice we made when we signed up to wear the uniform. We spill our blood for people that we'll never know so they'll never know the horror we've seen."

THE END

THE WORLD OF MYTH

MAGAZINE

ISSUE

8 2

MARCH 2020

Ed Ahern

Ed Ahern resumed writing after forty odd years in foreign intelligence and international sales. He's had over two hundred fifty stories and poems published so far, and six books. Ed works the other side of writing at Bewildering Stories, where he sits on the review board and manages a posse of six review editors.

https://twitter.com/bottomstripper
https://www.facebook.com/EdAhern73/
https://www.instagram.com/edwardahern1860/

The Water of Life
Das Wasser des Lebens, Grimm # 97
By: Ed Ahern

JACOB KONIG OWNED a business as big as a kingdom.
But he was so sick that his expensive doctors thought he
was going to die. They cautioned him to make preparations.
So Jacob called his three sons together and told them that he
wouldn't be living much longer, and needed to name a
successor.

The sons thought there must be a way to save him, so
they asked doctors after doctors, until one said, "I read in
the AMA journal about a fluid administered orally that
might cure your father. But the doctor who wrote the article
disappeared before he told anyone where to find the
liquid."

The oldest son hoped that if he cured his father, he'd be
given control of the business. He spoke up before his
brothers could. "Dad, I'm the one to help you. Give me time

off so I can find the cure."

Jacob agreed, and the son left. Just after walking out of the building a beggar sitting on the sidewalk called to him.

"I'm hungry and need to eat, please help me."

The oldest son stared at the beggar- dirty, ugly and so short he could have been a dwarf. The son sneered. "No money for you, Little and Dirty. Get a job."

The beggar showed his teeth. "May you be trapped in a life search with no solution, like a man on a horse stuck in a narrow passage."

And so it happened. The oldest son disappeared. After a week the second son went to his father with the same request. "I demand the same chance as my brother."

The father was already afraid for his first son, but the second son insisted. And the father-owner reluctantly agreed.

As the second son left the building the same beggar was sitting on the sidewalk. "I'm hungry and need to eat. Please help me."

The second son saw how ugly, dirty and short the beggar was. "Go to work, Dirty and Little. Make some money. Leave me alone!"

The beggar snarled. "Your search will be in the dark room of your soul with no way out."

And so it happened. The second son never called, never returned.

After a week the youngest son went up to his father. "Father you are getting quickly worse. Please let me also search for this lifegiving water."

"My child, I may have already lost your brothers. Don't ask this."

"It's my duty and my right."

And the father reluctantly agreed.

The youngest son left the building, saw the beggar, and approached him. Before the beggar could speak the youngest son said, "You look miserable. Here's enough money for you to eat for a few days. I suggest taking a shower."

The beggar smiled, his teeth crooked and mossy. "You're good hearted. I'm the doctor you seek, and can answer your unasked question. The life-saving water flows from a fountain in an estate three time zones away. I'll give you directions. Take this tuning fork and two bread rolls. Rap the fork on the iron door of the palace, Its vibrations will unlock and open the door. Inside the door will be two guards with lion headdresses. Give each guard a bread roll (I know it doesn't make sense, just do it) and they will allow you to pass. Hustle to the fountain and take some water, then quickly leave. The door is on a timer and will shut and lock after one hour has passed."

The youngest son thanked the beggar and set off by plane, by ship and by long car drive to the palatial estate with the healing water. Once there he rapped the tuning fork on the door, which swung open. He handed the rolls to the guards and hurried down a long corridor toward the fountain.

Along the corridor were four locked doors, also solid iron. By the time he reached the fourth door the youngest was curious and knocked on it. From the room came the sounds of a woman crying. "Go away, leave me alone!"

Instead he rapped the tuning fork on the door, which flew open. Inside sat a beautiful young woman, still crying.

235

When she saw the man she jumped up, ran to him, and gave him a hug.

"I was cursed to quarantine in place, but you've rescued me. And, believe it or not, the man who frees me is entitled to share my estate and marry me if he wishes."

The young man kissed her. "Great idea, but it's a bit sudden. I must obtain the water of life and use it to heal my father, but I'll return before a year passes so we can marry. Now, where's the fountain?"

"A little further down the corridor. But first you should open the other three doors. Each room holds a guy who's really rich. They will, I'm sure, be grateful and generous. And, seriously, come back within a year and I'll marry you."

The youngest son tuned open the other three doors, and each captive blessed him and swore to honor their release with gold. The youngest was running short of time, so he quickly thanked them, grabbed an empty wine bottle, ran to the fountain, filled the bottle and ran back to the front of the mansion. The heavy door had begun to close just as he arrived and pinched his heel as he ran through the doorway.

Once outside the mansion he saw the beggar, cleaner, but still short and ugly. "Good," the beggar said, "you didn't screw up."

"My brothers. They must have asked you the same question?"

"They dissed me and are now more trapped than your girlfriend was."

"Please," said the son, "they're jerks but they're my brothers. Could you release them?"

"They're liars and cheats, and will do you dirt if they can.

Dump 'em."

"They Are scum, but they're family. Please let them go."
"Very well," the once beggar said, "if you insist. Look behind you."

The youngest son turned around to see his two brothers, wearing the same suits they'd had on the day of their departure. He turned back to thank the beggar, but he was gone. The two older sons joined the youngest by long car ride, by ship and by plane back to their father.

During the long car ride, the youngest brother explained what had happened, and showed the other two brothers the water of life. The older brothers sucked up to the youngest, telling him how pleased his father would be. But even while praising him they were planning his ruin. While on the ship, they snuck into the youngest son's cabin, drained the water of life into a flask, and poured rank bilge water into the wine bottle.

Immediately on returning to the family estate the youngest son hurried to his father, and poured him a glassful of what he thought was the water of life. But the father no sooner drank it than he cursed and vomited. "You've poisoned me!"

The youngest tried to tell his story to the father, but he barely heard it. "Leave my house immediately and never return! You're both fired and disinherited."

Once the youngest brother had been thrown out of the house, the two older brothers went to their father and offered him their water. The father cautiously drank, and within minutes felt healthy and virile again. "You have been my faithful sons," he said.

Two weeks passed, and three armored trucks arrived at

the father's office, each loaded down with gold bullion, and notes which each proclaimed:' For youngest son, who rescued me."

The father began to regret his anger, and suspect that the youngest son had been telling the truth. He ordered that announcements be put on billboards and on Twitter that he forgave his son and wished him to return.

But youngest son, realizing he'd been suckered, had already departed to return to his girlfriend, who after all had lots of money. The heiress, meanwhile, realizing she was contractually bound, had ordered that the path leading to her estate be painted in gold yellow as a sign of welcome.

The youngest son sprinted up the golden path and into his girlfriend's arms. After several tastefully undescribed days he looked over at her and said, "We need to visit my father so he can meet the woman I will marry."

"But he hates you."

"I know, but hate or not he's my father and may come around if there are grandchildren."

So the couple went by long car ride and ship and plane back to his father's office. When the father saw them he ran around his desk and embraced them both. "I know it was you who found the water of life for me. Tell me how to punish your brothers."

But the older brothers, learning of youngest brother's arrival, had cashed in their 401ks and departed, never to return.

THE END

THE WORLD OF MYTH

MAGAZINE

ISSUE

83

APRIL 2020

Shawn M. Klimek

Shawn M. Klimek is the author of Hungry Thing, an illustrated dark fantasy tale told in poems, plus more than 200 other poems and short stories, published in over 80 anthologies and e-zines. He specializes in speculative fiction with a touch of humor. He lives with their affectionate Maltese wherever his globetrotting wife, Sara, leads them.

Find a complete index of Shawn's published works on his creative writing blog "A Jot in the Dark": https://jotinthedark.blogspot.com/; or follow his writing adventures on Facebook: https://facebook.com/shawnmklimekauthor/ and Twitter @shawnmklimek

Dark Trek
By: Shawn M. Klimek

UNTIL THEY CAME, the missiles had never been a certainty. Now, Diana thanked God that she had taken her fiancé's advice and started up the mountains well before thousands of other evacuees had jammed the narrow roads. "I can't leave without you," she had protested. But Terence was the commander of the local guard unit and had gallantly volunteered to oversee the evacuation—at least until T–minus 48 hours. She couldn't bring herself yet to thank God for that.

"I'll catch up with you in three days," he had promised, looking tenderly into her eyes, and then added with a laugh, "I have access to a tank if need be. Meet your brother at the cabin, as we planned. Have him unload all our supplies into the root cellar—it's the least he can do to earn his keep. And then lock all the doors and keep the lights out until I get there."

They had shared a long kiss goodbye, and then he had sent her away in his truck loaded with supplies and survival gear.

The next morning, as she was detouring around a stalled big–rig, a gang of bandits had stopped Diana at gunpoint, pulled her out of the truck, then stolen it and all the supplies it contained. Frightened and shaking, she had just watched as it happened…until one of them made a grab for her engagement ring. Some feral impulse had awoken in her then, and before she could stop herself, she had struck out with her polished nails and clawed his face. Wild–eyed and enraged, the thug had pointed his gun at her, when both seemed to pause to process the same thought: *was she suicidal?* Diana braced herself for the bullet's impact. Instead, one of the mugger's friends, one who had been sifting through her groceries, turned swiftly at the commotion and clubbed her in the head with a can of spinach.

Diana awoke on her back, amazed, after consideration, to be still alive. Her shoulder was lodged against a broken tree stump jutting up from the edge of a precipice twenty feet or so below the highway railing. Apparently, she had been disposed of here. Her head and shoulder ached, and she could taste dried blood and tongue a loose tooth.

These miseries were temporarily put out of mind, however, by the hypnotic beauty of parallel supersonic contrails streaking across a sky of purest blue.

Steadying herself against the stump, Diana staggered to a sitting position, single–mindedly tracking the missiles with her eyes. Had they arrived early? Or had she really lain unconscious for half a week? Her aching muscles

244

seemed to make the latter plausible. Like long white fuses, the contrails curved sharply downwards towards the powder keg of her doomed city, converging to ignite in a blinding globe of marbled fire. As the earthly–nova dimmed to merely brilliant, it was crowned by a roiling mushroom cloud that punched rings into the sky. A lump came to Diana's throat as she thought of Terence and considered that he might have evacuated too late. She prayed that she had not just watched him, and thousands of other people disintegrate. As if in slow motion, a shockwave of searing heat and obliterating force flattened everything in the valley below her in a giant, expanding circle, turning the river into steam before her eyes. When the thunderous, freight–train boom finally reached her ears, it was accompanied by an extended blast of hot, corrosive, air that lifted her off the ground, pitching her roughly back onto the highway.

Diana lay stunned there for several more minutes—*or was it hours?* By the time she could rise again, it was rapidly becoming dusk—or seemed to be. It might even have been noon, but the sun already nearly eclipsed by a thick, sooty blanket of clouds, and continuous snow of fine, black ash. Eventually, the clouds would disgorge an acid rain, she supposed—the flushed nuclear sewage of these hellish heavens—but, even though it would clean the air of soot, it would quench no thirst but a thirst for death. She hoped to be indoors before the rains came.

Diana coughed and vomited ash. Taking the silk scarf from around her neck, she tied it into a mask for her nose and mouth—only then discovering how truly swollen her face had become. Thus prepared, she made her way deeper into the forest, away from the main highway, further away from the sounds of moaning, shouting, shooting and honking, and — by her reckoning — in the general direction of Terence's cabin. She no longer had the map her fiancé had given her, but she didn't really need it. She had hiked these mountains with Terence during the best summer of her life, and he had proposed to her on a walk in these woods. Mercifully, the deadly black snow seemed to fall somewhat more sparsely under the trees.

Diana trudged through the surreal landscape as though in a dream. Despite the burning in her eyes and lungs, she somehow willed her legs to keep moving forward. In a way, the physical discomfort helped to insulate her from the emotional hammer–blow poised ever above her heart: the loss of Terence.

She touched the blackened finger where her ring had been and put it to her lips. Like so many things, her beloved's last kiss was a memory buried under dust, soot, and blood. By the accident of her prolonged filth, she cherished a poetic notion that his loving touch yet lingered there, allowing her to kiss him goodbye one last time.

Torturous hours passed. Diana speculated that if she hadn't felt compelled to stop and hunker down every time she heard a twig snap, she might have reached the cabin already. She needed water and shelter desperately, and probably several other things as well: rest, calories, medical attention. Not far down the list, she ached for a friendly face. If Kyle was there—her lazy brother—she knew she would forgive him everything. They would patch things up on the spot; she would cry in his arms and he would console her about losing Terence.

For the last mile, as the sun fell, Diana made her way by touch, keeping her right hand on the wooden fence that outlined the private acres which included Terence's place. It was pitch–black night by the time she reached the driveway to the cabin. On her hands and knees, she felt her way to the wooden porch steps and ascended. At the door, she raised her fist to knock but then hesitated—forcing herself to think it through. What if there were more bandits inside? Or, just as fatal, what if her brother, greeting her disfigured visage, failed to recognize her and refused to let her in? Not only was it utterly dark, she considered, but even with a flashlight shining in her face, she might well be totally unrecognizable given how swollen, scraped and scorched she was, red–eyed, and coated in soot—not to mention that her clothes were black rags. If she were not recognized, would Kyle take pity on such a pathetic stranger?

There was little value in hesitating, she realized. Outside the door, her doom was certain. If it opened, she might yet be saved. Her hands found the cold stone which served as a doorstop, and she mustered the strength to hoist it with both hands. Pounding the door with this hefty stone would be heard by someone down in the cellar, she hoped. She knocked three times, loudly. There was no answer. Taking a breath, she pounded again and again and again, before dropping the stone in exhaustion. Finally, a man's voice, muffled, could be heard from beyond the door.

"Who is there? I'm armed!"

It must be Kyle, she thought. She needed but to say her name for him to open the door. But then when she tried to speak, nothing came from her throat but a gurgling hiss.

She heard him unbarring and unlatching the door and

247

then, as a beam of light hit her face, she heard her brother
gasp. "I have a gun," he repeated, nervously, apparently
startled by what he saw.

Behind her, an engine rumbled and then two distant
headlights turned a corner to pierce the forest and the black
snowfall, shining up the driveway and alighting on the
front doorway, illuminating her brother's frightened face.
She saw now that Kyle had a flashlight in one hand and a
pistol in the other, and that his boot was half–raised as if he
had been poised to kick her back out the door.

Remembering the mask she wore, Diana pulled down
the scarf and tried once more to speak—but still could only
rasp incoherently. Nonetheless, it was enough.

"Diana!" he exclaimed. "It's really you!" Lowering his
boot and putting down the gun, he took her by the arm and
pulled her inside. "Good lord, what has happened to you? I
almost didn't recognize you," he said.

His sister sagged to the floor, whimpering. Tears,
somehow held back until now, wet her cheeks.

"You poor thing," Kyle said. "I'll take good care of you.
But first, I've got to barricade this door." He turned to reach
for the two–by–four leaning against the wall and then
stopped. "I don't believe it," he exclaimed, staring under the
shadow of his hand. "It's Terence! That's Terence's truck,"
Dropping the two–by–four and then stepping full into the
headlights, he waved an encouraging welcome at the
truck's driver, gesture for him to hurry indoors as quickly
as possible. "And I think he brought some other guardsmen
with him."

Diana's brain was fogged with fatigue, but the sound of
her fiancé's name jolted her to awareness. Terence's truck?

248

But hijackers had taken that truck! *Oh no*, she thought. It's not Terence! Frantically, she began yanking at Kyle's pant leg and vigorously shaking her head. She tried to scream at her brother but succeeded only in hacking up more black sputum. Kyle looked down at her with concern and pity and then bent to take her dark shape in his arms.

"Shhh. It's alright now, Diana!" He insisted, hugging her sobbing form. As heavy bootsteps landed on the porch, he repeated, "Everything's going to be alright now."

THE END

THE WORLD OF MYTH

MAGAZINE

ISSUE

84

MAY 2020

Amber M. Simpson

Amber M. Simpson is a dark fiction writer from Northern Kentucky with a penchant for horror and fantasy. Her work has been featured in multiple anthologies, as well as online. She assists with editing for Fantasia Divinity Magazine & Publishing, where she has gotten to work with many talented authors from all over the world.

While she loves to create dark worlds and diverse characters, her greatest creations of all are her sons, Maxamus and Liam, who keep her feet on the ground even while her head is in the clouds. Find her online at: www.ambermsimpson.com   and www.facebook.com/authorambermsimpson/

Marked
By: Amber M. Simpson

"**BURN! THE! WITCH!**" The crowd of villagers chanted, thrusting their torches to the sky. "Burn! The! Witch!"

Twelve–year–old Pippa stood among them in the darkening village square, biting her lower lip. When the witch was dragged out by a thick rope knotted around her neck, the villagers cheered. Women tossed their skirts; men threw their hats in the air.

Pippa watched with dread as the woman was hauled up the crudely built wooden steps leading up the side of the pyre. The evening breeze blew her long hair in her face, obscuring the dark eyes that seemed to glitter with fury at the man awaiting her there—Pippa's own father, his priestly robes billowing around her feet.

As her father motioned for the jailer to tie the witch to the stake, the crowd's excitement grew to a fever pitch, thrilled with this rarity of amusement from their dull daily lives.

"I heard she sleeps with the devil and eats her own offspring," a tall toothless woman beside Pippa cackled.

"I heard she seduces any man foolish enough, then cuts off his member to aid in her spells," an emaciated woman to the other side of her added.

"Let her burn!" a gruff male voice near the back of the crowd shouted. "Kill the witch!"

Frenzied cries of "Kill the witch!" washed over the throng of villagers like a wave, increasing in volume and intensity until Pippa had to cover both her ears with her hands.

Fighting her way to the front of the crowd, she found her brother, Abram, whose own loud cries added to the swelling chants. Pippa knew it was Abram's dream to someday be a holy priest as well, yet it still made her stomach turn to see the pride in his eyes as he looked up at their father. Didn't God preach love and forgiveness above all else? Surely, he would not condone the burning alive of a human being out of what Pippa knew to be simple fear.

"Abram," she croaked, tugging at his arm. "Must they burn her? What if she is not truly a witch?"

Abram laughed down at her and tweaked her nose, immediately dismissing her concerns. "Then our glorious father is not the renowned priest of Meere!"

"But—" Pippa started, but Abram shushed her with a finger to the lips as their father began to speak.

"Villagers of Meere!" he cried, throwing his arms wide as if embracing the whole of them. "This woman stands accused and charged of witchcraft and evil intent! Therefore, tonight is a special night, indeed! Tonight, we banish the darkness that has invaded our homes! We destroy the evil that has infiltrated our lives!" The villagers cheered, Abram as loud as the rest, and Pippa shrank back away from him.

As her father continued his zealous rant, Pippa stared at the witch, realizing for the first time just how beautiful she was. It was hard to believe her capable of the supernatural atrocities of which she was accused. Even now, as she stood bound to the stake that would soon be lit to burn her alive, she did not lose her beauty, the corners of her lips turned up ever so slightly as she glared at the crowd amassed before her. Her eyes swept over the crowd, as if looking for someone in particular. When they landed on Pippa, holding her hostage in their glare, all the air left Pippa's body and she struggled to breathe.

Her father's voice droned into a dull buzz in her ears as the witch held her with those dark, scorching eyes. The mark on Pippa's forearm burned as if on fire itself and she was transported to the nightmare she had had the night before—the nightmare where the witch had crawled through her window and come to her bed, grabbed her arm and spoke in an unfamiliar language. Pippa had wanted to scream, to call out for her father or Abram, but the witch's eyes had paralyzed her, held her down, mute, to the bed. Not until she finished speaking in that strange, garbled tongue did she release Pippa's arm and slither back out the window to disappear into the night.

Pippa had remembered nothing else until she had woken in the morning and had even almost forgotten the dream… until she saw the deep red marks on her arm, raised like welts, in the shape of gripping fingers. She had made it through the day by reasoning she had done it herself while having the nightmare, but now, she was not so sure. The longer the witch stared at her, the hotter the mark burned, until Pippa was yelling as loud as the crowd of villagers around her.

"Have ye any last words, witch?" her father asked, drawing the witch's eyes away from Pippa. Instantly, the burning on Pippa's arm ceased as the witch glared at her father, her lips pulled back in a hateful sneer.

"You are a fool," she growled, straining toward him against the ropes which bound her to the stake. "You cannot rid yourself of me. I will haunt you until you go insane, then I will slit your throat in bed. I will strangle your children. Cook them. [Eat] them. Your God will not protect you. Your God is a bigger fool than [you]."

The crowd hissed and made the cross sign in front of them. Someone threw a rock at the witch, striking her above the left eye. A stream of blood gushed from the wound down her face.

"Burn! The! Witch!" The chanting resumed as more rocks flew through the air. One of them struck her father, who quickly commanded the pyre be lit before rushing down the steps. Several men stepped forward and touched their torches to the dry wood at the witch's feet. Immediately, it ignited, the gust of heat shooting out at the crowd. They jumped back with a collective gasp.

Pippa watched in horror as the fire licked up the witch's legs, catching her tattered skirts aflame. The mad crowd did a wild dance of excitement, and Pippa was jostled about roughly. She looked back and forth between her father's and brother's faces, sickened at the sight of delight she found there.

As the witch burned, Pippa saw her dark eyes on her once again, her thin lips moving quickly as if in prayer. A dawning realization struck her just as the witch's hair caught fire, going up in a bright halo of flame.

But it was too late.

With the witch's last ululating scream, Pippa's body stiffened and seized, her eyes rolling to the back of her head. The witch's melting face appeared in her mind's eye, and she felt the sensation of being torn apart from the inside out.

Pippa tried to resist—struggling to remember all the prayers her father had ever taught her to ward off evil spirits—but it was no use; the witch was too powerful. Twelve–year–old Pippa was simply no match for a centuries–old woods witch.

A dazzling bright light shot through Pippa's head like a bolt of lightning, and she lost control of her body. Going limp, she collapsed against her brother who barely caught her before she hit the ground. From somewhere deep inside, Pippa's consciousness screamed for help, but the witch snuffed it out as easily as putting out a candle.

"Are you all right, Pip?" Abram peered into her eyes, helping her resume balance on her feet. Straightening and smoothing her skirts, she nodded and looked up at the charred remains on the burning pyre, the priest reading to the crowd from his ridiculous bible.

"Wonderful," she answered with a smile, eyes dancing with reflected flame. Satan would have to wait for her a while longer yet—she had unfinished business with a foolish priest to tend to.

THE WORLD OF MYTH

MAGAZINE

ISSUE

8 5

JUNE 2020

Ximena Escobar

Ximena is an emerging author of literary fiction and poetry. Originally from Chile, she lives in Nottingham with her husband and three children. Contact me on FaceBook and Twitter

Plato's Apprentice
By: Ximena Escobar

THREADS OF HIS hair billowed, veiling his sight of the Parthenon. *Oh, to be Architecture! Majestically permanent and complete!*

The apprentice sighed, releasing his ephemeral fulfillment into the breeze—leaves and light stirring, his ever-moving mind shifting from a changing cloud onto the porous rock he sat on—perpetual in its concept but, ironically, constantly eroding with imperceptible Time.

What shape is timelessness, if not rock? Which is death, if not the straight line? Which is life, if not the undular wave only fathomable upon it?

As a snake slithered out from under his seat, time stopped—for the apprentice.

THE WORLD OF MYTH

MAGAZINE

ISSUE

8 6

JULY 2020

Nora Jean Garcia

Nora Jean Garcia lives in Arizona with her two plants and a collection of cookbooks. She makes pasta and dumplings in between writing and editing. She loves to travel. She is an MFA candidate at Lindenwood University.

The End
By: Nora Jean Garcia

"**IF I TELL** you not to be afraid at The End, will your knees shake? When you face the monster? Will you fight," her head tilts. She watches me.

I'm scared. Dragons -The End's tomorrow. The End'll come when I'm eleven. I haven't grown the extra inch. I'm too old to stay with The Mother. I'm too short to take The Journey.

I sink my fingers into the flesh of The Garden. Verdant earth rises around me. I'd rather keep working. Yet, I contemplate the question.

"The monster," I try to be brave. I can't. "Yes, I'll be afraid."

"I won't lie to you. Fighting death's useless," She tells The Truth.

We work in The Yard. It's a human grave site. We work Free Land to make The Garden to feed The Community.

Nora Jean Garcia

364 days ago I was sent to here to be Of Purpose. Being ten years old is tough in The Yard. I'm too short to reach the water. I'm barely strong enough to push the empty wheel barrow. Better me than my little sister. She's Sparrow. Sparrow's just five. I've toiled. I rake human bone fragments. I carry water. It's hard but doesn't matter because we eat.

"Let's lunch here." She pours water over of my hands. She hands me a plump, purpled tomato.

The purpled tomato's special; fertilized with fish meal to give it more protein.

"Happy Birthday, kid."

My mouth sinks into the firm, succulent flesh. It tastes bitter instead of sweet.

"Don't worry, kid. Monsters only come when someone doesn't need you."

"Why's it taste funny?" I ask too late. My eyes, blurry with sleep betray me.

"Sleep. Dragons aren't worth fighting." Her strong hands pull the soft soil over my feet.

Warm soil covers my torso.

"No worries, kid." She whispers.

THE WORLD OF MYTH

MAGAZINE

ISSUE

87

AUGUST 2020

Molly Liu

Molly Liu is a CSM Chinese student. She has won the second prize for young adult prose in 2019 SoulMakingContest with "Minds off" and published on FreedomFiction.com with "Tilt" in August 2020. She is engaged in writing science fiction, memoirs, and short analytical works in writer's groups.

The Flat Man's Guide to The Galaxy
By: Molly Liu

JULIA:

I kissed someone.

We were walking down the street. He asked me once before if he could take the next move, holding my hands or more. He said he was always bad with timing.

I said I can help out. And then I asked him: "Can I take your hands?"

He laughed and said sure. So I reached out and held his hands, fingers crossed. It was wet and big, his hand.

I got tired, so we sat on the branch we found on the street. He asked to kiss me again, and I said ok.

His lips were parted, eyes were open. They were small lips, and they were soft. We adjusted our positions and sucked on each other a little bit. After the fifth or sixth time, I pushed him away, saying that I needed to breathe.

Molly Liu

It was our first date. And I was 17.

Robert:

The aliens were everywhere. It was the end of all. You can't get out of your home. You can't go on the street. And when something like this happens, you gotta breathe.

"Uncle, let me in." The nephew thing was downstairs, smiling and yelling. What he didn't know was that he would never be able to step in my home again. Ever.

"OK, just go in." My daughter, Julia yelled back. I took one step forward, covered her mouth, and pulled her back from the window.

"Did you leave the door open?" I cursed, "I told you never leave the door open, and nobody is coming in!"

"I didn't leave the damn door open." She pulled my hand away and spit, but her face was pale. But the nephew thing had already disappeared from the street and entered the apartment building.

Our whole family held our breath. My wife Rebecca hugged her belly tight, and Julia turned away from me.

Some small, kitten steps from the front door. The sound of something heavy being pushed open. Singing and humming. Gentle knocking on the bedroom door.

"Uncle? Let me in." The youthful voice sounded so pure and unbearable. Time is paused. The door remained locked.

"You know that you're paranoid, right? I'm just here to deliver some dinner from my mom. Auntie, Julia? Please let me in."

After 10 minutes, the alien placed a roasted turkey before the bedroom door and left.

I dumped it in the trash. This is the second time it does this. I dumped it below all trash so the neighbors would not notice like the last time they did.

Julia:

Once again, I snuck out of the apartment and entered the street. The street is covered with ashes, just because the government said smoke can cast out the aliens. My dad said it's nonsense.

"The only key is to never let them into your house." he said. I wanted to say it was an apartment.

But before I went, there was one thing I needed to do. I sat down under the apartment door and watched my body transform into liquids, and then through the door, transform back.

Today is the second date. I thought about what would happen. I kind of dislike him, but I wanted to experience things other girls have experienced too. So even though his hands were too big, his muscles were too much, and his hair was too thick and black, I was still going to hold his hands.

After that, I was going to go back, let myself into the apartment, transformed to liquid under the apartment door, and return home after I transformed back.

Robert:

"It's possible," The TV said, "that this alien disease is transformed through sex. That means, if you had sex with an alien attached person accidentally, you will become one

Molly Liu

of THEM. They're like parasites, you know? Enters the human body through holes and transforms you. And then you start talking nonsense like..."

"Don't ever go out again." I turned off the TV, pointed to Julia, "I know you have been sneaking out. Crawling under my eyesight, huh? Don't go out unless you want to become one of them."

"You always said we are the less, the vulnerable, but if the aliens are everywhere on the street like the government said, why don't they just rule us?"

"Sit down," I heard myself talking, but it sounded like bubbles under the water, distance and unclear, for I know a speech was coming, "I will show you why."

I opened the notebook, which is full of graphs and tables, "I calculated. Since the dinosaur, to the Egyptians, every 3000 years, he will kill off the dominant species on earth, possibly this universe, until what remains fits his heart. Now, we are developing special talents like telepathy, the one I have, dream prophecy, the one your mom has, and transforming, the one you have. Your baby

brother Paul, he will have talents too. By the time humans own ultimate special talents, our doom is..."

"So what? God doesn't like our superpower? They proved that God didn't exist years ago..." "Not God," I heard my flat voice; my heart was pumping and my mouth felt bitter, "The Flat Man. And he is sending out these aliens to kill us."

She looked at me, paused for a second, and laughed. I laughed too. We laughed so hard that we couldn't catch our breath.

We know about The Flat Man, since when, 17 years ago?

280

Now it has become a bitter joke, pretending not to know it.

"I really wished we could go out." She said quietly, "If we managed to get through this 3000 years."

Paul:

It feels warm inside the cocoon, an island in the dark. His heart is thumping steadily, and the amniotic fluid was tender. The womb is his support. His ship. But one day he is going to get out of there. He just didn't know yet. All children leave their mom.

He puts his hand to his mouth and giggles. He doesn't feel like an "I", or that he is living in the past; it's always present to him as he always has the power to transpose into universes.

What is this universe(0) ? He dives into it. It is filled with dark energy, and a fat guy made of it lies within the universe, a huge body consuming the light of the sun, the quality of air, everything that is made of light energy, the energy he senses with eyes and fingers, not mind.

"You're not the one I 'm looking for." he thinks."What is the fun being in a universe where the darks just consume the light to keep everything dark, and you're the darkness itself?" In one

universe(1) , he and Julia are twins and they both have the power to transpose. But he won't understand that now, what he does understand is that he wants comfort and joy, and this universe is too cold.

He dives into another universe(2) , where he is an only child, and his parents are named Ye and Liu after their grandpas, and they're all original Chinese without talents.

281

Molly Liu

Ye, his mom, drives him to school using a motorcycle every day, and she drives fast.

He pushes his face to his mom's green jacket and feels the hushed wind that brushes through the city road. There are so many things in this universe, he makes a note of returning which he will forget within seconds and dives away with the image of his mom's lip as a thin line as she cooks him two eggs for breakfast in his mind.

He dreams of being inside another womb(3). Inside a psycho rabbit's. "How is it going," He talks to the rabbit, "still devorando un hijo?" "None of your business." The rabbit turns her ass to him.

"They say you like carrots," He says, "How about carrots?" "Bullshit. I like carrots." The rabbit continues eating on the grass.

The stars that rotate in the sky, one of them becomes him. He feels dizzy. The wind brushed through his flaming body, adding up to the flame.

Suddenly he is in a spaceship. It was kind of like the womb he was in before, but chiller. His sense all reduces to the smallest amount. He feels like a caption, but he is the only one on the ships so either way.

"I love you," His twin sister, in another universe, said to him, blurry, "now tell me you love me back."

"You are just saying that to win the line back." He concentrates on fumbling on the console on the front of the ship.

"It's so dark there. You are running out of resources. When would you leave?" His sister says.

"After the bodies run out." He responded.

"Dumb ass." She pulls a face. The bored look is gone

though.

The dream stops. He is alone in the womb. His heart is still thumping. The water feels warm. He's just going to give it one last try.

Here. This is the universe(3) he's been looking for. He is a whale, happily swimming in the ocean. He rises, brushes through tons of water, feels the coldness, saltiness, and heaviness on his back, and reaches the blue, warm surface on the top. The blowhole opens up, spilling out a rainbow. The mist floats above his head, and the water covers his body back under the surface. He opens his mouth, and the secrets of the sea swim in.

This is the universe he likes.

He dives deep and disappears soon after.

Rebecca (When 17):

Mom, I love you. You love me too, I know, even though your love is hard and you don't know how to love me.

When I was little, in our country villa, you told me: "People in our height ought to have resonance with only a certain amount of people." What you mean is that do not play with people with different skin colors unless they live in a castle higher than ours; do not talk with boys with shiny fingers; spend your whole life waiting for a prince charming to come should be your life purpose.

"If you sleep with anyone before that, I will break your leg."

You don't know me, you think I am a pretty daughter, both in mind and body, but you don't know me.

When I was 13, I walked down the city street and saw

the thing.

It was lying right at the street, all black and small, cowering on the corner, silence. It looked strange. Was it the leftover of an alien? Trash that falls out of the trash car?

"Here." He passed, handing over a scarf to it. It opened up its shell. It was an homeless alien, sitting on a street full of cocaine, used condom and waste, receiving the old scarf, before retreating back to its shell.

"What the hell are you looking at?" That's your first reaction when you hear it, "Stop talking and shut up. Do you want to marry them? Thieves and beggars? You want them to propose to you?"

You don't know, that's the first time I have delusions. He is not a thief, nonetheless.

You remember a month ago, I went into delusion and had my accident in the bathroom? You made a comment I can never quite forget. You said that what I said is untrue and suggested my father not to believe me after I told you I was suffering from delusion because of my special talent(Yes, that is a thing), and that I think I am going to have a baby.

This is not a suicide note or a makeup note. This is to explain why I'm leaving with this stranger. He is nice, good to me, and he loves me despite my mental issues and believes in my talent.

I love you.

Paul (talking with The Flat Man):

"Are you going to resolve the future war yourself?" He says, "The war human rises against you, light and dark

Matter conversion, because they're scared that they might die, which will eventually destroy all of them?"

The Fat Man's heavy eyelashes shutters and opens. An eye-full of pupils looks directly at him.

"If not, how are you going to protect yourself? If you do want to protect yourself, you can trap yourself in a different time so they can never reach you. But you don't wanna do that, right?"

The Fat Man blinks.

"All the aliens you send. Human fears that you send them out to kill them, but they're just messengers, and the message, the nonsense they said, about everything has to keep balance, that this is all destined, for the balance of the dark and light matter, so that all universe can remain stable until they reached their end and restarts, is true.

Every 3000 years, the light matter becomes too much, so some of them convert to dark matter, and after the convection, new life can be born. It happens every 3000 years since the beginning of universes, and will continue to happen until the restart."

The meat under the Fat man's chin crumbles together. "And you're just an agent to deliver this."

The Fat Man nods again. Under his head, the stars rotate and send out fabulous white light. "How are you going to do it then?"

The Fat Man paused. A while after, the Fat Man opens the big hand and touches his fingertips.

Paul (talking to "imaginary friends"):

He is talking in his head. All the friends exist in his

mind, his eyesight, his sense. They're real to him.

"I'm going to fix this," He tells the stranger in the street sadly, who looks at him strangely, shakes his head and walks away; "fix here," the fire-spitting dragon pats its face and hiccups; "fix the universe I'm in." The five-headed man nods.

He looks at the other him in another universe, who will be tossing a ball to a white soft wall and catching it when it bounces back in the future, "I shouldn't ask you this. The other universe, can you fix that? Fix your universe?"

The other him nods. They all nod. "We're leaving together then."

Julia:

I had a dream. In my dream, I was 13 and walking on the street with you, which can't happen in reality, because you are always so intent about getting out home, and you hugged my shoulder. I was short, wore small shoes, sucked up snots, and reached out to hold your hands.

"Is he real?" After much gibbish, I asked you, "Dad, is The Flat Man real?"

"He made every idol statue of every religion maximize, stand up, everywhere was a disaster brought by this event, so that he can prove to us that Gods don't exist. After this, the aliens came and replaced humans. They still had the same shell, but their spirit changed. Before this we didn't give a damn about science, so we couldn't defend ourselves now; we paid."

"But if we do care about science, the cobalt bomb would have already been invented and earth would be doomed."

"The Flat Man is still going to destroy us. Maybe by making us all die suddenly, or by making aliens kill or replace us all. All this is like a dream of his, he can add or subtract things in the dream, or even end the dream at a thought. All these can even happen unconsciously," His eyebrows are tightly knitted, "After Doctor Hawking died, our knowledge about him remains still."

"Did Hawking say it's a guy?"

"He did. He left audio about him, and we identified it through computers, found out that he named him The Flat Man."

"Dad, how did mom and you get together?" I asked.

"She was an uptown girl who looked really nice when she smiled. I like her a lot, and swear that if not her I will marry no one." You said.

What you didn't tell me is that she didn't even mention your name to a single party of her divorced parents, and after four months of your dating you made her pregnant, and then you elope together.

I wiped out the tears when I woke up. You're still sleeping on the bed.

I had prepared. Before this third date, I am going to reject him, telling him despite all the fondness, he is a friend. And that I only used him for kisses. He is going to hug me, and we're going to cancel our date and say goodbye. I would go back to the apartment, feel hard to breathe, sit down and watch myself transform into liquids.

Ever since I'm a child, the one about aliens has always been the priority of our family. I have never had the chance to go out, to live. And when I had it, I didn't feel like cherishing it as well.

Molly Liu

You Trapped in a cage, you are so desperate to get out that you become a part of it, and when you finally have the chance to get out, you ended up chasing the thing you don't know what it is.

I turned back at the door, looked, imagined you said:" go," and then walked out.

Robert:

Back when we were 17 when Rebecca was crying in the bathroom from another mental breakdown, I told her we are going to be together and we can make everything better, and there she agreed to run away with me, telling me that we are going to have a baby.

But I don't know how to love them. Ever since the date I married Rebecca, The Flat Man has been the center of our life. I don't let them go out and only leave home for work. The intent was to protect them, but we ended up all exhausted.

In her life, her mother did the same thing. She doesn't let her make contact with anybody in the real world, for class standard. I am doing the same thing to Julia, for some ridiculous thing called protection. Maybe one day all of these can stop, but I don't feel like having the key to all these.

If everything passes, and we can climb up the waterdog mountain, all four together, setting up tents under the blue stars, lying down under the cool wind, how beautiful would it be?

Family:

The day it came, the endpoint of this 3000 years, they were sitting around the empty dinner table. Both the apartment and the home were locked, no aliens could come in; parents have turned on their superpower, ready to take their kids and leave if anything happened.

The clock was ticking. The time was about to come. Robert stood up from his chair, stopped in front of the black window, folded his arms. Julia looked down at her hands.

"It's going to be fine. Everything." Rebecca said. Her hands were shivering.

"Oh, come on," Julia said, and before her father gave her sights of disapproval, she hugged her mother the first time since she was 15. Rebecca laughed, with some tears in her eyes.

Under Julia's arms, Rebecca's belly shines out white light. Outside the window, inside every room of every family, big and small, all the mothers' swelling belly shines out white light.

Julia and Rebecca didn't see it with their closed eyes.

Paul (The Flat Man) :

He feels like swimming upwards and ready to grasp the one breath. There is a tornado of light in the center of the universe where everything used to be dark.

He is going to become a part of that holiness, and Robert, Rebecca, and Julia will become that too, all will. In a way, it's the future him, the new births, that end his present life, but he doesn't feel like dying, he is just going to be alive as The Flat Man. The Flat Man, other than a single figure, is more like a concept of the universe: it's all the deaths. All deaths will become him; and all will die, every 3000 years, again and again, to give out new births.

Paul giggles. It feels peaceful. What was he worried about before? He forgets. He opens his eyes and disappears into the night skies.

Epilogue: Robert (mind reader):

"I was only experimenting. You see, after the scientists typed out the truth that they left for our sake to balance The Flat Man, I thought, I had the talent, and he was my son, so we might have a human type of connection and this, climbing up a mountain so high that I might be able to read his sense, might actually work. Didn't expect it worked though."

"If I was a much detailed man, I would tell you about my wife, the breakfast, the news, probably the climbing. But I would only going to tell you how I felt him, with my brain and my heart, in the very top of the hill, and how he didn't felt me back. It made sense, he was in such a broad place now. His mind was so broad. He saw the stone rainfall on Centaur, the first time the angels shed wings, the earth crumbled to a drop of tear at the end of the universe. He saw everything without focus, and in his focus, there were so many souls, so many deaths inside, making him a combination of thoughts other than a man."

"I could tell you I cried. Every child left their parents at some point, but he was never mine, not this moment, not ever was, and as long as this universe still exists, he would be The Flat Man only."

If a time travelers pass by at this season, he would ofter saw a man under these stars, mouth opened, eyes tearing. How could this little man climb a mountain this high is a strange thing the time traveler wound not understood. His hair was dripping with rain, hands fisting beneath sport sleeves, sweater all soaked up. Hours later, he covered his hands on his face and his head fell. The wind flowed by pleasantly, pasting his body, leaving small circles on the puddles on the ground.

Far away, the forest was shaking inside the dropping waterfall. The leaves were dense, so the water couldn't hit them flat. Still, the forest was shaking in the rain, singing an indirect song.

High above, the stars shined like birds' eyes.

"But he would see me one day."

The End

THE WORLD OF MYTH

MAGAZINE

ISSUE

88

SEPTEMBER 2020

Robert Masterson

Robert Masterson, English professor with CUNY-BMCC in New York City, has authored Garnish Trouble, Artificial Rats & Electric Cats, and Trial by Water. First published in 1978, his creative writing, literary criticism, photography, and journalism has appeared in dozens of magazines, newspapers, galleries, and journals. Masterson holds degrees from the University of New Mexico; the Jack Kerouac School of Disembodied Poetics; and Shaanxi Normal University. Masterson's work has taken him to Ukraine, Japan, India, inside men's and women's prisons in the United States as an instructor and mentor, and to nuclear reactor stations in Brookhaven, New York; Los Alamos, New Mexico; Three Mile Island, Pennsylvania; and Chernobyl, Ukraine as an observer and reporter.

The Source of Fr. Santiago de Guerra de Vargas' Monstrous Crimes
By: Robert Masterson

Part One

THEY RODE, THOSE who had horses, and they walked, those who did not, south from Mexico, south from the Aztec capital, Tenochtitlan, brought low. Led by el Caballero Pedro de Alvarado under orders from His Most Catholic Commander Hernán Cortés, the expedition bore letters of marque to explore, locate, and conquer every pagan country to be found. Under the flags of His Holiness Pope Pius IV and His Majesty King Phillip II, every devil, demon, and dybbuk berobed in the drifting ash of that once floating imperial city rode with them and, in particular with the priest de Vargas. Armor and arms glittering in the New World's sun, banners and streamers afloat from pike and pole, soldiered ranks and mounted gentlemen of adventure, trains of mules and two-wheeled carts baggage laden, the mass of native fighters conscripted, chained slaves and women, and with the religious processioned holding Holy Cross and icon before them, a slow clot of dust loosed into the air to rise and mark their journey. The corridor they laid upon the ground was both deep and broad, ignored the native highways leading who knew where, and would remain after their passing to become *nueva carretera* for any to follow. The enterprise moved south from the marshy, high plano surrounding the Mexican capital to climb the pass between the Sierra Madre Oriental and the Sierra Madre del Sur skirting the snow-capped Pico de Orizaba, the dormant volcano of "pleasing waters," and down, down into the green maelstrom of Yucatán with only two directives: find gold and save souls.

#

Santiago de Guerra de Vargas returned to his wooden hut after bearing witness to the day's mass baptisms/executions. He had duly recorded, as was his wont and duty, the number of converted and the number of those propelled to the welcoming arms of their new Savior. Though watching so many people die upset his scholarly tendencies (today's total was 783 bound heathens sprinkled with the Holy Water that would cleanse their blackened souls before they were hung and then sent straight to Paradise before the opportunity to sin tempted them from the true path of Righteousness) , he was compelled to silently rejoice at the bounty of new adherents to the One True Faith, how God the Father and Jesus Christ His Son would smile upon their efforts to induce the growth of the Holy Mother Church in this New World. The voices that droned in his ears were his and his alone, their constant tintination a familiar commentary on all to which he was witness, a devilish, native criticism of all the expedition accomplished. He waved his hand around his head as if to banish flies, but the voices persisted in their Nahuatl interpretation of events.

Unlike other expeditions franchised by His Majesty Charles V, Lord over the Holy Roman Empire, Austria, the Burgundian Low Countries, Naples, Sicily, Sardinia, and the wonderous New World, this expedition followed the True Cross. They were intent on finding not merely riches, but souls, human souls, to feed the always hungry Church. His Excellency, the Most Revered Bishop Diego de Landa rode his black gelding on the right hand of el Señor Alvarado to lead them all in service to God with plunder a most secondary consideration. To Santiago, the entire troop seemed to glow with the holiness of its mission, to become the beacon of light that would guide these monstrous pagan idolaters to salvation, death, and Glory. And it appeared to be working. Santiago wrote:

Pedro de Alvarado, there to take the heathen enclave of Q'umarkaj, moved forward with 180 armored cavalry, 300 men-at-arms in infantry, 4 barking cannons, and five hundred allied native warriors from the conquered north. Three and twenty friars, priests, and the Bishop himself observed the battle from a nearby hill, and they blessed and prayed for the fighting contingent and its victory in this New World's Valley of Elah. The assembled force did there meet in the field more than five thousand Mayan warriors in full war display. The profane horde carried mahogany macahuitl glittering with knapped obsidian

299

*shards and they voiced Nahuatl chants while costumed in feather
cloaks and headdresses and masks of remarkable beauty and form.
There followed slaughter as Spanish steel and crazed war-horses
engaged the massed pagan horde with cries of "a Dios!" and
"Jesucristo!" that overwhelmed the skirling whistles and flutes
shaped from human bone and played as Mayan war cry. The
befeathered warriors, all from noble Mayan families, fell like ripe
wheat under a new scythe. Smoke from the cannon, the harquebus
and matchlock drifted heavy over the battle. Slavering dogs of
war, horses mad and flailing spiked shoes, Spanish footmen gone
blood-mad collapsed the Mayan line, folded in the Mayan flanks.
The northern native warriors, all newly converts, exerted and
concluded ancient vendetta. Short and brutal, the conflict ended
in prolonged massacre. Above the field did fly the banners of
Church, its Saints, and God.*

Santiago entered his cubicle and prepared to create the
day's document. He enjoyed his work and, with the
seemingly limitless supply of blank Mayan paper the
expedition had confiscated, Santiago could indulge his
propensity toward expansive narrative. He was in love with
details, the small sights and sounds and odors and textures,
that supported the veracity of his chronicle. Santiago
understood the importance of numbers, the exact counts of
objects and entities that proved the expedition's importance
and worth. So many miles from Mexico, so many casks of
wine in baggage, so many men-at-arms, so much
gunpowder and so much shot, so many priests and
prisoners and converts. Numbers were the logos of the
mission. But the pathos and the ethos lived in the details,
and Santiago was dedicated to ensuring the legacy of their
endeavors there in the jungle rot and pagan ruin would

resonate with readers yet unborn.

The drops of blessed water shimmered in the afternoon sun as they flew from the aspergillum. There in the thick and weighty air of Yucatan, they seemed to pause for a moment, as if to savor their freedom before splashing down upon the brows, thick and heavy, of the assembled savages. Their cleansing and blessing was inspiration to every assembled Christian and the miracle of Holy Communion uplifted even the heaviest heart.

Santiago stopped his pen to reread his writing.

Every Christ-loving soul was swollen with awe when the brothers sang the Auroras for salvation at the end of a rope when the reborn creatures were prodded to the gallows for their triumphant convention at the Throne of God. Many a soldier drew his sword to thrust into the soft earth and knelt to pray before a holy warrior's cross. Three and eighty and seven hundred cleansed and perfect souls were sent to the outstretched arms of our Lord and Savior, Jesus Christ. Our miracles are daily and magnificent to behold.

Santiago was moved by his own words. He actually ached toward poetry, to fulfill the lover's quest of expression, to capture the blinding instant in perfect prose. The Mayan paper, pounded out from the bark of certain trees, seemed to not just take his strokes upon its surface but to absorb the meaning of his words beyond their definition. The voices buzzed angrily in counterpoint to his enraptured prose.

Still, there were details Santiago would not record. How could he write the truth of what he'd seen to then offend His Excellency? The reluctance of the newly baptized to discard their mortality and embrace the Savior. The thin lines of urine that outlined the contours of their legs when they dangled there in the Yucatan sun. The gasping, the gagging, the choking, the struggles both earnest and sincere for even one last gasp of humid air. These were secret images.

The box and the hut, he both had fashioned himself from lumber torn from idolatrous structures. Planks of tropical wood he'd pounded into a frame, some still fragrant with perfumed sap, and a roof of fronds all pointing downward to direct the rain away from the interior, formed his crude abode on the outskirts of the camp away from the bonfires and tents and huts of both church and army. From lighter planking had he fashioned the box, the casket, the repository of his history most secret. A door, no windows, a rope bed, a writing table, a stool, his garments and linens, and the box were his dwelling's only contents. A stark carven crucifix and a single, fat candle stub adhered to the edge of the table provided the only illumination, day or night, to enter his monastic cell.

He was afraid to devise a lock for his rough door assuming that someone of the party would venture into his chamber. There were, indeed, thieves and brigands among the company and, espying a bolted door, such men would be tempted to think it treasure inside and such men would take the box to a secret place, an unseen place there to open it by force to reveal not gold nor jade but the priceless record of their true adventure. He was afraid to leave it unlocked, and upon this dilemma he fretted almost constantly. Santiago was afraid his words would send him gallows-wise and to there dangle among the newly Christianized, the newly deceased Mayan. Instead, he left it on the pounded dirt floor, but he threw a coverlet upon it.

He prayed every night and every morning and, in those prayers, offered with humility and fearful love, he asked the Lord to protect his secret history enclosed in pagan carpentry. He found himself unwilling to venture too far or for too long away from its sight.

They whisper among themselves, these foul and bloodied miscreants, during the ceremonies of redemption, their horrid language all clicks and throaty exhalation. They seem deliberately ignorant of the gift of eternal life, and, instead, accept our blessings as they accept their meals without thanks or recognition.

Their jungle empire is broken, shattered under Spanish steel and cleansing fire, and so, they, too, are broken. They speak of devilish prophecy, a forewarning from their demonic gods, and bow their heads to annihilation. They are disgusting and more deserving of Satan than of Saints, but His Excellency proclaims them bounty for the Church, and so we force the Body of Christ into their clacking maws, pour the Holy Blood across their clenched lips, anoint them, bless them, and kill them all in one stroke.

I think it, though, a kind of madness that justifies murder with Christ's limitless bounty, and each evening the soldier-hangmen confess their sins and receive absolution to go and sin tomorrow. But, the Inquisition is ever zealous. Every commandment is shattered hourly in drunken, licentious abandon and every soul is whitened through Confession and Communion by sunset. The piles of gold and jade and skillfully worked flints are made small by the mounds of dead converts that smolder constantly to foul the air with the stink of human grease.

And the books. All of them. Satanic by His Excellency's decree, and every book plundered is thrown upon the pyre to be

303

consumed with their authors. Only God will know what they contain—laundry lists or tallies of maize, unholy curses to breach the gates of Hell or songs of love and courage. The flare of their ignition gives brief outline to the skulls upon which they burn. From the gallows and the libraries, we have made another kind of Inferno for ourselves, one that will burn long after these fires have burned away. But my voices keep the Great Library alive, and describe to me the secrets and the spells where once therein they lay. Yum Kaax, the lord of the forest, Chaac, the bringer and the withholder of rain, Yumil Kaxob, who lives in flowers, and great Itzamna, who rules the heavens themselves in splendor and fearsome beauty all are known to me through them, and I feel their torment in my Christian soul. I long to and cannot bear to desire the warmth of human blood and the joy of a beating human heart in my hands as benefaction of dark faith older and more powerful than that of Jesus Christ, our Lord and Beloved Savior.
I am lost.

Part 2

Santiago returned the paper to the casket, and he returned the casket to its hidden-in-plain-sight corner. He knelt in silent, futile prayer. He lay himself down upon his rope bed, pulled a thin blanket up across his chest, and closed his eyes. His dreams, if dreams came to him, were dark and full of confusing, disturbing turns. The tick-tock, click-clack of Mayan whispers insinuated his heated torpor, the meaning of the hellish syllables dancing just outside his consciousness. He moaned his heresy while his eyes jittered beneath their lids.

There is spectacle in the rise and fall of empire. Around

such calamity lives the drama of all things human and the struggle to become and remain human in the grand gesture of civilization. But, so, too, there is marvel in the crossing of rivers, in the weaving of cloth from cotton fiber, in the simmer of beans in a kettle suspended over fire.

This army, if such a name can be rightly applied to such a gathering, quavers in near constant state of mutiny and drunken rebellion. His Excellency chooses to blind-eye the egregious nature of the assembled felons and sodomites and brigands that form his company. He speaks of them as children, reprobate children, in need of firm guidance and massive lashings of pulque and bacanora, daily confession and communion, and the leadership of true warriors of the Cross. His most considered opinion on the expedition is that of Crusade, that his crusaders are therefore divinely attributed, and that which is guided by Providence cannot be sinful. Our passage through the forest left the imprint of misdeed upon our trail, but His Excellency is manifestly incapable of looking back.

They are still here, these horribles with their feathers and with their drums, though we have slain them in multitudes. The essence of their being, their refusal to become past tense and "has been," remains to pollute our souls, and I alone can hear the doom to which we plunge.

Santiago drew his daily rations of corn, beans, and goat to deliver to the mute Sacniete, his designated and personal Mayan slave, for her to cook. She was a pretty girl with a smear of small pimples across her cheeks. While she labored over grindstone and hearth outside the hut, he removed his secret casket and placed it upon the table that was his.

'So small a thing,' he measured. 'So small a thing to be

Robert Masterson

the largest thing left of the city from which it was
fashioned. So many buildings, so much wilderness labored
into angled form and structure, with this the largest
unburnt fragment. That the whole of the city Nojpetén,
burnt now with only its stone shell survived, should be
reduced to this small box...'

He removed the sheaf of bark-paper and began to write.

When we burned the library at Zaculeu, the priests and
monks and friars rejoiced. They chanted the Prayer to St. Michael
the Archangel Eph., 6:12.

In the Name of the Father,
and of the Son,
and of the Holy Ghost.
Amen.

Most glorious Prince of the Heavenly Armies,
Saint Michael the Archangel,
defend us in our battle against principalities and powers,
against the rulers of this world of darkness,
against the spirits of wickedness in the high places.

The flames of the bonfire created a new kind of Inferno, and I
turned to weep alone at such treasure incinerated. Oh! The
Alexandrian Calamity and now this. The tongues of flame
reached into my heart and burned my faith away. The language
and the voice of murdered authors invaded me. I stood alone in
the light of wisdom lost forever and prayed to nothing, felt no
Divinity remained in this shattered world, as drunken caballeros
sang barroom filth and danced intoxicated fandango in the light
of Armageddon. I became the Keeper of Hosts, the Guardian of

306

Forbidden and Forgotten Learning, the man to whom the ghosts and spirits spoke.

Impoverished Santiago lay himself down upon the thin pallet that served as his mattress, the secret box behind his head, and there he fell asleep again to dream confused betrayal and benighted landscapes. He twitched and groaned in desperate lethargy.

And the box moaned back.

The faithless priest jolted upright, unsure what had pulled him back to consciousness. The box made its presence known.

"Tick tock. Click clack," it said in Nahuatl.

Santiago, somehow now fluent in the language of the boxed specters of ruined countries, the language of ten times ten thousand murdered souls, could understand each rattle issued from the box.

"Kenin chiua teuatl continue? Tlein propels teuatl axkan ikamo neltokokayotl ipan amoyolotl? Kenin uehka s teuatl ya nik kuepiltia mo sacred Christ?" the box asked with blood-sodden gloom. "How do you continue? What propels you now without Faith in your heart? How far will you go to avenge your sacred Christ?"

Santiago could not answer. He looked for Christ in his heart, looked for the shape of the Holy Cross, and found only emptiness where it had once been.

"I am bereft," he told the box. "I have nothing in my heart, my soul, my hands."

"S teuatl kuepiltia mo omopolo neltokokayotl? Teuatl kuepiltia in murder iuik to civilization? Teuatl kui ako ahkoltin nik ueikapa in itlakamiktilistli?" the box sang. "Will you avenge your lost Faith? Will you avenge the murder of our civilization? Will

you take up arms to stop the slaughter?"

"I was a man of Divine Peace," he replied. "I came to carry the Holy Word to those souls doomed by ignorance. I watched the library burn and it burned my soul to nothing."

"Tikpia in uelilistli. Teuatl uel amotlaxtlauas in yolilistin teuatl trapped between mo paradise iuan to mahtlaktli omeyi heavens. Teuatl moneki xiximi in estli iuik omeyolomeh nik release tehuantin. Teuatl moneki carry forward ika mo task iuan amotlaxtlauas in yolilistin teuatl've enslaved ipan ayauitl between tlaltikpaktin," the box moaned. "You have the power. You can free the souls you trapped between your Paradise and our Thirteen Heavens. You must spill the blood of Papist hypocrites to release us. You must carry forward with your task and free the souls you've enslaved in darkness between worlds. You must murder the murderers."

"Break in hispantlahtolli teposmekameh teuatl forged nik tekipanoa tehuantin ueika iuikpa teotl. Kaua tehuantin ualtepotstoka se trail iuik estli toward melauak freedom," the box continued. "Break the Spanish chains you forged to keep us away from our Gods. Let us follow a trail of blood toward true freedom."

Santiago sat with his consternation, his dilemma, his last true test of Faith. Could he break all vows and assertions to become a new kind of Christian, an assassin for the Lamb?

The box grew and changed its form before him. Santiago was witness to wonder as the box became something entirely else, something that contained more than it could, a moving, shimmering tesseract of Divine Intervention, the Deus ex Machina which would define the end of his story. He held the world in his trembling hands, he felt the movement of multitudes, the cry of slain races for mercy and revenge, the music from broken drums and shattered flutes throbbing and shimmering the very atmosphere surrounding him.

"*Notsa forth, niman, iaxka temamautik holiness, in ueytlahtoani yum cimil, in teotl iuik mikistli, iuan kaua yeuatl guide mo maitl nik to retribution. Kui se knife iuik tonaya tepostli iuan kaua yeuatl drink iaxka fill,*" the box intoned. "Call forth, then, his Terrible Holiness, the emperor Yum Cimil, the God of Death, and let him guide your hand to our retribution. Take a knife of shining metal and let it drink its fill."

Leaving his worn sandals upon the hard-packed dirt floor of the hut, Santiago insinuated himself into the camp. It was an easy matter to find a displaced *falcata* amidst the tumble of baggage and gear. The hand that had never filled itself with aught but Crucifix and Communion and Holy Text marveled at the dead iron weight of the thing, at its loathsome hunger to kill. Santiago licked the blade.

A Mighty Ghost followed him, a spirit composed of spirits, the multitude made one. It stalked him on his mission and wore the sacred raiment of befeathered divinity. For each step the Ghost took, it carried the weight of the hundreds, the thousands, the millions of murdered *indios,* and deep were the prints it left in the tampened soil of the camp. The Ghost sang, it chanted, it murmured, it howled in all the tongues of the slain, but only Santiago could hear its damn-ed voices. He continued as barefoot as that which trailed him, the fallen thorns and sharp pebbles a path of penance before him. He feared to look back, could feel the Ghost and its hot exhalation on his nape, but was compelled to stealth as he moved about the camp.

The first *soldado* that Santiago the priest approached was nodding in fermented stupor at the flames of a dying fire. His name, the priest remembered, was Pedro Alacard.

"*Oye,* Pedro," Santiago said for greeting. "Still awake this lonely night?"

The drunken Pedro roused himself to see it was the good Father, the one with the pen who remarked the company's adventure.

"*Oye,* Padre," he slurred. "Awake and dreaming. Yes. Awake and dreaming both, I think."

He looked around and behind the priest to better ascertain the figure at the edge of firelight, the disturbance of the atmosphere with the glittering blackstone eyes.

"Who's that with you there?" Pedro asked. "Who have you brought with you?"

"This is my friend," Santiago replied. "This is my friend and my tormentor, my shadow and my Ghost. This is my devil and my redeemer."

"Huh?" Pedro grunted as he turned his slitted, bloodshot eyes up to glean Santiago's face.

And just that quickly, the priest's war-knife found and buried itself in poor Pedro's throat. The warm gush of blood washed hot and thick over Santiago's hand, the cry of surprise and outrage Pedro attempted reduced to gurgle and gasp as the priest drove him down into the Yucatan soil, the ashy margin of the firepit, there to choke and sputter his sinner's life-breath away.

"*Por Jesús y maldita sea tu alma,*" Santiago whispered and made the sign of the cross upon the fresh corpse. "For Jesus and damn your soul."

The Ghost upon his heels raised spectral baying of hard

delight. The priest wrenched the *falcata* free with some trouble. He would need a soldier's practice to handle the weapon with more skill.

With slow stealth and Mayan glamour encloaked, Santiago moved deeper into the camp. He walked a ring around the next smoldering fire, three men-at-arms asleep in their clothes with armor heaped behind them. The first, the priest dispatched by, again, ruining the man's throat with his blade. The two others stirred but did not awaken. Pulque dulled their wits and senses. Their dreams were too loud to properly hear the world around them, their doom approaching. The second, a large man who kept a beard and known to the camp as El Oso, clawed his way to consciousness and wrapped his weighty hands around Santiago's slender wrists and there to struggle against the thick bladed already sunk to the hilt in his chest. The priest recoiled in mortal terror having lost any sense of spiritual fear. Their push-pull enraged the Ghost who stamped its feet and shrieked its impatience.

"Tepopololiztli! Tepopololiztli!" it shouted a whirlwind into the priest's ears. "Kill! Kill the thing!"

The third soldier was awake and staring at the blood-soaked cleric with eyes wide open.

"Padre?" he said softy. "What are you doing, Padre?"

Santiago propelled himself in a lurching crawl to the man's side. His name was Porfirio.

"I have come to give you peace, my son," He told the drowsy, drunken, confused soldier. "I have come to send you home."

Porfirio did not understand, was troubled by the blood spatters the priest wore on his face and cassock. Santiago laid his palm against the man's wet mouth, and he slipped the blade under his ribs. When the tip touched Porfirio's beating heart, he could feel the vibration in the handle.

The Ghost was sniggering tick-tock click-clack glottal laughter.

"*Yollo Tetecuiquiliztili,*" it snickered. "Take the pain of the heart."

And the murderous priest began to pry and lever his way through poor Porfirio's ribcage to make known the heart of the man. He cut, he pried, he pulled until the organ snapped free dangling vessels and webbed by pericardium. Santiago looked to the Ghost for instruction.

The Ghost, all feathers and black glass, brought its hand to its yawning chops. It repeated the gesture. And again, it pantomimed the directive.

Santiago had received and given innumerable Holy Communion, brought the Blood and the Body to lips in supplication and received the Sacrament himself inside the eloquent cathedrals of Spain as well as along the blood-choked dust of the conquistadors' highway. How, then, his brain churned, was this so different? Weren't all men possessed of God? Did God not bestow His Holiness on all creation? Was not all Blood and all Flesh both sacred and holy?

The murderous priest brought the late Porfirio's hot heart to his mouth, stretched his mouth to receive the essence of divinity manifest in blood and flesh. But the muscle was strong and tough and resisted his effort to tear from it enough to swallow. Blood emptied from its ventricles and poured down his jawline, a thin tissue of membrane all he could wrench from its perfection. He

312

swallowed the meat from the man and, again, tried to tear a mouthful away from the whole. He ground and sawed his teeth against its fibrous resistance, and he succeeded in pulling a slight shred of muscle free. He swallowed it as whole as any other Host he had received, blessed himself with its passing into himself, and made the sign of the Cross in blood at forehead, shoulder, and core.

The Ghost was ecstatic. It twirled in a vaporous enchantment, phantasmic feathers awhirl such as the columns of dust that rose from the northern plains. It barked its wonderous approval. It grinned a terrible grin.

The assassinations followed quick one upon the other with each that much more uncomplicated than the last. He moved from rough fire to greasy tent to lonely picket in each case propelled and guided by the spectral dervish whose grunts and yowls only Santiago could hear, the exhortations high-pitched and cadenced ceremonial.

"Yes," the priest would whisper at each blade thrust. "Yes. Yes."

The blood filled him, it covered him, it glistened on his face and hands even as it dried to be layered upon with blood anew. His cassock soaked in blood, it gathered the ground's particulates along the hem and at the knees where he genuflected to dispatch more souls. His holy costume grew heavy and made a new kind of sound, a rattle that would be his undoing.

Diego del Esparanza heard the murderous priest's approach and, springing to his feet, drew his long sword in challenge and in terrified awe at the apparition of the foul creature he'd only known in passing as Fr. Santiago. When the cleric refused to halt or acknowledge Diego's challenge, the miserable soldier ran his blade into the flesh of Santiago's left thigh. And still, while falling to the earth, the priest stretched out his killing hand as if to stab Diego despite his incapacitation. The Ghost was enraged at Santiago's failure and kicked him there in the dust. Diego saw the priest curl as if in pain, unknowing of the ghostly blows that drove the breath from his body.

"Alarm!" Diego cried, keeping the point of his sword upon the felled priest. "Alarm!"

As the camp aroused itself in reply, men ran, stumbled, shambled, and some even crawled to the spot still besotted with native alcohol. There was much shouting, calls of confusion and despair as torchlight revealed the desecrated bodies of their *compañeros*. They could not position the evidence of foul deeds and the man of the cloth writhing before them in the same place. It was beyond their ken to imagine the man and those deeds conjoined. They called for the captain. They called for His Excellency himself.

The caballero and the bishop considered the men, the events, and the evidence before them. Santiago's hut was searched and his precious box uncovered. The Bishop read the manuscript therein. The captain himself could not read, but accepted the clergyman's summation of the blasphemous narrative. The bleeding priest lay before them, the testimony of his very state of being the harshest of evidence for his conviction. The representative of the Spanish throne and the representative of the Crown of Thorns conferred swiftly. Their conclusion and their verdict was both precipitate, unanimous, and terminal. Santiago's brief rampage ended in the mud at his superiors' feet. Whatever consternation he had brought to the camp would be expelled with his summary execution. The verdict pronounced, his tonsured head pulled back, his heretical throat exposed and gashed open by firelight, the mad priest's blood contributed nothing so much as more thick liquid for the expedition's thirsty and already muddied camp.

They threw Santiago de Guerra de Vargas' body, his box, and his heretical scribblings on the same bonfire that consumed the corpses of the converted and the books that held their heathen history. Beyond the light of the conflagration, before the Maya and long after the Spaniards, green Yucatan chittered, whistled, ticked, and roared. As the poor, lost priest oxidized to lacy ash, the Ghost in the flames danced a glimmering dance of welcome for his soul.

The End

315

THE WORLD OF MYTH

MAGAZINE

ISSUE

8 9

OCTOBER 2020

Clark Zlotchew

Only three of Clark Zlotchew's 17 books consist of fiction: Two espionage/thriller novels and an award-winning collection of his short stories. Newer work of his has appeared in literary journals of the U.S., U.K, Australia, Canada, Germany, South Africa and Ireland from 2016 through 2020.
www.clarkzlotchew.com

Merrow
By: Clark Zlotchew

Part One

IT WAS A chilly evening in September. A bitter Atlantic
wind drove rain through the streets of Waterville, a seaside
village on the Ring of Kerry. Jeff MacNamara, a recent
American college graduate on holiday, head bowed against
wind and rain, lumbered past the varicolored two-story
structures on his right, searching for the *Mermaid Inn*. Over
the roaring of the black and white billows that smashed
against the rock-strewn beach to his left, he heard the
music. It was a wild and merry tune that surged in patches
between the crashes of surf on shore. It made Jeff want to
dance. Or run. Or fight. It was a surprisingly strong feeling,
yet diffuse, bearing no specific goal. He accelerated his
pace.

Almost all the structures –some painted white, some

blue or yellow or violet-- on this sea front promenade were illuminated by lamps in windows and lanterns over doorways, except for the location he sought. Within thirty seconds he caught sight of it. Jeff might have walked past it in the darkness, he realized, if it hadn't been for a lightning strike on the ocean that intensely lit the entire area for a split second. It flashed a brilliant light on the structures along the sea front, allowing him to catch sight of the small green building with the red door. In that instant he glimpsed a sign that read Mermaid Inn and displayed a crude painting of a bare-breasted mermaid combing her golden tresses with one hand, holding a lyre in the other. Her smile was inviting, and her eyes seemed to focus directly on Jeff.

The American opened the door to the Mermaid Inn and entered. A wave of warmth chased the smell of fresh salt air, replacing it with various aromas that washed over him, and seeped into his clothing: beer, both fresh and stale, fish and chips frying. He scanned the people on the barstools as well as those at the round oak tables. Every barstool was occupied, and people drank and chatted while standing between and behind the fortunate ones seated at the bar.

The rousing music emanated from a group of young men and women in jeans and sweaters sitting at a table in a far corner. There were two fiddlers, an accordionist and a pennywhistle player whipping out a reel. Jeff stood behind the barstools, caught the attention of the burly middle-aged bartender who smiled and walked over. "Good evening, sir. And what's your pleasure this evening?"

The American ordered a Murphy's Stout. While waiting for his drink, Jeff vaguely became aware that the pub was

322

bathed in soft lighting that threw the entire room into a mellow setting of brown and beige, which somehow put him at ease. He struck up a conversation about the weather with the man standing next to him but stopped in the middle of a sentence when he noticed a strikingly attractive girl at the table with one unoccupied chair. She wore a bright red cap at a jaunty angle.

Mike, the bartender, plunked the pint down on the bar and wiped his hands on his white apron. Jeff took his frothy glass, strolled over to the vacant chair next to the girl, and said, "Excuse me. All right with you if I sit here?"

She looked up at him and smiled. That smile produced an odd feeling in him: a surge of adrenaline, and a sensation somewhere between pleasure and fear. She answered, "And why not? I don't see anyone's name on it."

He seated himself and said, "Hi, my name is Jeff."

She regarded him for a moment, then indignantly asked, "And who was it that even *asked* you your name?"

Jeff turned red and just gaped at her. He didn't know what to say at this rebuff.

Enjoying his discomfort, the girl chuckled and said, "Ah, I'm just pulling your leg, Jeff. My name is Merrow." Her chair was next to his, but he had the odd impression that her voice came from a distance. He'd been listening to too much high-decibel rock music back in Dublin, he decided.

"Tell me, Merrow," he said, "Do you live here in Waterville?"

"Not exactly."

"Just visiting, then?"

"Well, sure, and you could say that, but my home is not all that far from here."

323

Jeff was about to ask her exactly where she lived, but she said, "Well, then, Jeff, where in the States are you from?"

"Boston. But how did you know I was American?"

She threw her head back and laughed. "Oh, come on now, Jeff, do you really think you sound like everyone else around here?"

Her laughter had a musical ring to it. *I bet she has a great singing voice..*

"I do," she said.

"Huh? You do *what?*

"I've a beautiful singing voice. Or at least that's what people tell me." She paused, then added, "Some even tell me I have a voice to die for." She chuckled.

He stared at her for a moment, then stammered, "But how did you know what I was thinking?"

She smiled and placed her hand on his shoulder, looked deeply into his eyes. "Just thinkin', was it? And did ya not just tell me ya thought I must have a great singin' voice. If you were thinkin' it, then you were thinkin' aloud, Jeff."

There was something about this girl that intrigued Jeff. Intrigued and strongly attracted him. Still, that uncomfortable feeling he had experienced when she first smiled at him persisted. The attraction stemmed from her beautiful oval face, the shape of her wide mouth, the gleaming white teeth behind her pink lips, and the way her nose crinkled when she laughed. She was playful with her wicked sense of humor. Even the musical sound of her voice charmed him. She was enveloped in a light scent that reminded him of the fresh salt smell of the open sea. But most of all, he loved the way she gave him her entire attention when he spoke, as though his thoughts were the most fascinating ideas imaginable. Which he knew they were not. Even the way she had of touching his shoulder or upper arm when she wanted to make a point enchanted him.

And her eyes, those grey eyes –eyes that seemed unfathomable, bottomless, vertiginous, that swirled like whirlpools that one could be sucked into and gladly fall, fall, fall forever– eyes shaded by thick brown lashes that partially obscured those beckoning depths. And the long, wavy golden hair that coiled around her face and neck and draped over her shoulders to cascade down to her hips, seemed to glow with a life of its own. The vague unease she inspired disturbed him, but not enough to cancel out everything else about her, which he found truly alluring.

Although he had felt warm while standing at the bar, Jeff felt a bit chilled while seated at the table. *No doubt a draft from under the front door.* He looked at his watch; it was almost midnight.

Merrow suddenly stood. "I've got to be off now, Jeff."

"Oh, so soon?

She nodded.

"Can I take you home?"

"No, Jeff, I'm not in need of an escort, but I thank you for the offer." She thought for a moment and said, "Will I be seein' you next Saturday, then?"

This simple question produced a feeling of joy in Jeff. It was like the sound of an orchestra suddenly striking up Beethoven's Ninth Symphony. But the young American had not planned to stay more than two nights in Waterville, after which he would go back to Dublin before flying home. He had by now a good taste of Ireland and was ready to

Clark Zlotchew

return to Boston.

His wanderlust had decreased dramatically yesterday when he visited the Cliffs of Moher, on a rare bright sunny day. Jeff had gazed at the Atlantic horizon, and wistfully pictured his home across the sea. He experienced a sudden pang of homesickness, a feeling of being too far from home, a sense of detachment, irreversible separation from family, friends, everything he knew and loved. The American shifted his gaze to look down at the breakers below and experienced an attack of vertigo. He turned and moved away from the cliff's edge. He was ready to go home. And now, here in Waterville, this beautiful, exciting young woman asked if she would see him the following Saturday.

Jeff stood and offhandedly answered, "Sure." He didn't want to show he felt the idea of seeing her again was thrilling, didn't want to seem too anxious. This young American wanted to be "cool," or at least seem so. He limited himself to replying, "So, I'll see you next Saturday." Dilemma resolved.

During the week he did some touring, but always returned to Waterville where he stayed in an inexpensive little hotel. Evenings he would spend at the Mermaid Inn, enjoying the impromptu music while having a pint or two of Murphy's Stout, and sometimes chatting with locals. During that week, which seemed to creep along sloth like, Merrow's face, misty eyes, golden tresses, her touch and her silken voice kept haunting his thoughts and his dreams. Sometimes, in those dreams, he saw Merrow, her grey eyes like ocean waves that swelled and heaved and crashed and foamed and sank back and swelled again. He heard her beautiful voice croon haunting melodies in a language he could not understand. He heard strange murmurings like *Teacht chugam* and *Tabhair grádom* and yet he felt those incomprehensible words or commands, or incantations, were carrying a message meant for him, for him alone and no one else. As he heard those strange words in song, he seemed to hear, in English, a feminine voice whispering: "Come to me. Give me love."

In some dreams he saw a sailing ship in a raging sea driven by a fierce wind to crash against huge rocks, splinter and sink, while crewmen were dashed by mountainous waves against those same rocks and then slid below the surface. He felt a wave thrusting him toward the rocks, but just as he was about to be dashed to pulp, he awoke in a sweat, sitting up in bed, heart rapidly beating against his ribs as though it would break out of his chest.

Part 2

Saturday evening arrived, after what felt to Jeff like a month. He showered, shaved his cheeks, leaving his reddish mustache and chin beard intact, and wore his grey tweed sports jacket and good black wool trousers in place of his usual sweater and jeans. He carried his raincoat over his arm. It was chilly, and the leaden sky glowered at him. A strong wind blew off the Atlantic, and the wild surf boomed and hissed as it lashed the shore. His breathing became more rapid as he made his way toward the Mermaid Inn. He felt as though he might explode into a thousand pieces.

He opened the familiar red door and was greeted by the same comforting warmth and aromas as always, though

 Zlotchew

attenuated by the early hour. The sound of human voices had not yet reached the usual decibel levels, and only two musicians had arrived. The fiddler and the spoons player chatted and drank while apparently awaiting the arrival of at least one more musician. The American hung his raincoat on a peg and glanced at his watch. Of course, it was only a little after seven o'clock, too early for the place to be crowded. There were only four other patrons seated at the bar, and five at one of the tables. He was going to order his usual Murphy's Stout but felt the need for something stronger first.

The ruddy-faced bartender ambled over to him and said, "Evening, Jeff. I'll draw you your usual," and placed his large hands on the tap lever.

Jeff said, "Hold it, Mike. Make it a shot of Jameson."

The bartender nodded and said, "Jameson it is. On the rocks?"

"No, no rocks!" He realized he almost shouted it. The bartender narrowed his eyes. Jeff cleared his throat and more calmly said, "No, Mike, no rocks. Just straight up." As the bartender turned to grab a bottle and shot glass, Jeff added, "Make it a double."

"Right." The bartender, one eyebrow raised, grabbed the whiskey bottle and tossed two jiggers into his customer's empty glass. He moved away from Jeff and took the orders of other patrons. While the barman was engaged in lively conversation with a couple of old-timers in tweed flat caps, cable sweaters and baggy corduroy trousers, he noticed the American waving him over.

#

328

By nine-thirty, the pub had filled with regulars, the musicians were in full swing, the hubbub of voices had increased appreciably, and the smell of beer and fried fish had intensified. The bartender noticed that the American consulted his watch more frequently and looked increasingly morose.

"Expecting someone, are ya?"

"Huh?"

"I asked if you were expecting someone."

Jeff stared at the bartender for a moment, then, "Yeah, I think so." He sounded irritated. The young man's speech was slurred due to the double Jamesons followed by three pints. He stared at the bartender, then, "Mike, tell me: Bartenders are supposed to be amateur psychologists, right?"

The bartender thought for a moment, shrugged and said, "I guess so. But no extra charge for the head shrinking." He chuckled. "So, what's the story, then, Yank?"

Jeff took a deep breath, held it for a moment, and exhaled in a long sigh. He looked at Mike and said, "There was a girl here last Saturday night, you know?"

"There were tons of girls here, as usual."

"Okay, yeah. But this one was really pretty."

"There were quite a few good-lookers, as always. What was so different about this one, then?"

Jeff closed his eyes, picturing Merrow. He said, "She wasn't wearing jeans, and…"

The bartender cocked his head, a quizzical look on his face. "No jeans, was it?"

Jeff continued, "Well, just about every girl comes in here

329

wearing jeans or tights, right?"

The bartender nodded.

"Well, this one was wearing a skirt. An actual skirt! A kind of *long* skirt."

Mike narrowed his eyes. "Wearing a long skirt, was she? Wait a minute, Yank! Did you catch her name?"

"Yeah. Merrow." He nodded." Yes, it was Merrow."

"Jesus, Joseph and Mary! Herself was it?" The bartender stared at Jeff for five seconds.

Jeff said, "What?!"

Mike wiped the bar down mechanically while in deep thought. Finally, he looked straight at Jeff, tugged at the collar of his turtleneck, and said, "Look, Jeff, you'd be best off forgetting about that one and finding some other girl. There are plenty of them around."

Jeff wrinkled his brow, and demanded, "Why are you telling me to forget her?"

Mike muttered, "I have my reasons."

Jeff squinted at the bartender. "Why? You interested in her?"

Mike frowned. "Is it a joke you're after makin'? I'm a married, middle-aged man."

"Well, why, then?"

Some customers at the other end of the bar were calling for service. Mike said, "Hold on for a minute. I work here, you know. Be back in a jiff."

Jeff stared at the bartender's retreating figure, and nervously drummed his fingers on the bar. He watched Mike serve some other patrons and experienced a growing tension. He gazed at his half-empty glass of the deep blackish brown beer topped by a now-thinning white foam.

It brought to mind the breakers that foamed as they crashed against the stony beach just feet from where he stood. In his present hyper-sensitive condition, the fragrance of bitter hops seemed to intensify, as did the odor of fish. His stomach felt queasy.

Mike returned to face Jeff, wiped his weather-reddened hands on his apron, and silently stared at him for a long moment. Then, "Would ya tell me somethin', Jeff."

"Sure. What?"

Did you notice what brand of beer she was drinking?"

"What kind of a question is that?"

"Humor me, would ya."

Jeff thought for a moment, "Yeah, she was drinking a beer I never heard of."

"What brand?"

"Wait, let me think. Umm..., *Beamish.* Yes, definitely *Beamish Stout.*"

The bartender's ruddy face turned pale, and then flushed. He stared at Jeff.

Jeff demanded, "What!"

Mike inhaled deeply, looked down at the bar and sighed. Finally, he raised his eyes and said, "Well, you see, *Beamish Stout* is a very fine beer, and no mistake. Beamish started brewing it way back in the 18th-Century, I believe. 'Tis just that we haven't carried that brand for a very long time, probably since the 1950s. Simply because we can't carry every single beer brewed in Ireland. Plus the popular foreign beers. We have a limited clientele."

Jeff cocked his head, a puzzled expression on his face.

The bartender asked, "When you first spotted her, was she talkin' to anyone?"

"Well, no, she wasn't."

"She didn't have any girl friends with her?"

"No, she didn't."

"Now, she's quite a beauty, you say. Yet none of the lads made any conversation with her?"

"Well, *I* did."

"Aye, I know. I mean besides you, like before you sat down."

Jeff thought for a moment. "No. She just sat there, smoking a cigarette."

Mike's eyes widened. "Smokin' a cigarette, you're sayin'?!"

Jeff nodded.

"And have you not noticed 'tis illegal to smoke in public houses in Ireland? Has been for quite a while now. I stick strictly to the law, so you'll not see anyone smokin' in here, my boy. Now, I know the place was full of customers when you were here. And this Merrow had to have been sitting next to at least one person that night, and not far from the others at the same table. But there was no conversation she was involved in. Right?"

"Yeah, that's what I just said. So…?"

"And do you not think that's a bit strange?"

"What's so strange about that? Maybe she was just enjoying the music."

The bartender said, "Listen, my lad, I saw you sitting at that table, and you were sitting next to an empty chair on your left. The rest of the table was filled with young men."

Jeff stared at the bartender in silence.

Mike added, "And when I eyeballed you every now and again, it looked like you were talkin' to an empty chair."

332

Jeff turned pale. "What are you saying?"

"I'm just telling you what I saw, lad."

Jeff put his elbows on the bar and leaned his face on his open palms. He murmured, "I don't get it. I just don't understand."

"Jeff, when I bought this bar from old Sean Milligan, the previous owner, six years ago, he told me something weird."

"He told you…what?"

"I thought he was just telling a tall tale, Jeff, but now I don't know."

"Damn it, Mike, would you make some sense?"

Mike looked down at the bar, wiped away non-existent dirt with his towel. He looked at Jeff, then stared at the ceiling and said, "I thought it was just one of those idiotic urban legends, but Milligan said that back in 1958 something terrible happened in this place."

"Terrible? Like what?"

Mike stared at Jeff and said, "Like there was a girl named…" The bartender hesitated and looked directly at Jeff. "It was a girl named Merrow…"

"Okay, so what?" He shrugged. "So, her name was Merrow. Anyone can have the name."

"Oh? And have you ever met any other Merrow, then?"

Jeff wrinkled his brow in puzzlement and placed his hand on the nape of his neck but said nothing.

A very old man was inclined over the drink he was nursing a few feet down the bar. He had a long white beard, deep creases in his windburned face, and white hair peeking out from under his black watch cap. He muttered, "*Tá sí ina maighdean mara.*"

333

Jeff stared at the old man.

The bartender explained, "He says she's a maiden of the sea. You know, a mermaid." He nodded at the old man, turned back to Jeff and continued, "Right. Now just listen, Jeff. You've listened this far, so keep listenin'." He wiped his hands on his apron and continued. "Right. First of all, Merrow is the name of a mermaid, as the old stories would have it, a beauty with a fine voice, who lured men to their deaths in the sea out there past the Aran Islands." He stretched his arm and pointed to the west.

"Okay. A mythical mermaid. So, what…"

The bartender interrupted to continue. "Now, mind you, this real flesh and blood Merrow had a boyfriend named Sean. Good looking lad, apparently. They were engaged. Had been for about seven months, according to the story. One night, there she was, waiting for Sean. He came in, sauntered over to where she was sitting, like he didn't have a care in the world —didn't sit down himself, mind you— and told her it just wasn't working." Mike gave a mirthless laugh. "Now there's one hell of a statement, *just wasn't working*." He shook his head. "Now get this, will ya: as he's standing over her, dumping her right there in public, smiling, no less, this fine-lookin' redhead parades her way over to him. He puts his arm around the redhead's waist and they kiss. And a real long kiss it was. Talk about insult to injury." He clicked his tongue and shook his head.

The music of the two fiddles, the deep-voiced accordion, the shrill pennywhistle and the clacking of the spoons grew louder, further agitating the American. The wild reel seemed to be saying something to Jeff. He felt it as a sort of warning, an alarm.

334

Jeff said nothing; he just gazed at the bartender, who continued, "So, Merrow jumps up, knocking her chair over, grabs a half-empty bottle —of *Beamish Stout*, by the way— that was on the table, and smashes it over his head! It killed him on the spot."

"My God! Right here in this pub?"

Mike nodded. "Aye, right here, at that same table you were sittin' at. Talkin' to yourself."

The music seemed even louder to Jeff, and wilder.

Jeff shivered, despite the warm indoor temperature. "So, what are you saying?"

"What am *I* sayin' is it?" The bartender sighed. "I'm just tellin' you what Milligan told me. Anyway, Milligan said that Merrow streaked out of here like a bat out of hell, screamin' like a banshee with a hot poker up her arse, and scampered across all those stones on the beach, then dashed head first into the breakers and disappeared. It was too dark for anyone to see more than that through the windows."

"Are you trying to tell me…"

The bartender held his hand up, palm outward, as a signal for the American to stop talking and to just listen. "Look, lad, I'm just telling you what Milligan told me."

"Okay, so what are you saying? That I was talking to a, a, a …?"

"I don't know, Yank. *You tell me.*" He paused, then, "Something else: Milligan said that he was told that over the years there've been five other lads who claimed they were talking to a girl named Merrow, but no one else in the room saw the young woman he described, and people thought they had seen him talking to himself."

335

Clark Zlotchew

Jeff shivered again, even though the heat was building as the crowd increased. The music grew louder and the smell of frying cod and stale beer became unbearable.

"Oh," the bartender added, "Milligan told me that each of those five other lads died under mysterious circumstances. *Crazy* circumstances is what *I'd* say. One of them who'd been looking for this Merrow character, who no one else knew, got so drunk one night, because she didn't show up, that he went and bashed his head against that wall right over there, and died of a cerebral hemorrhage. Another one bought a gun and blew his brains out. This all happened several years apart." Mike scratched his head and added, "The others all simply flew out the door, ran into the ocean and vanished. Bodies were found washed up on the shore shortly after each incident."

Jeff remained silent for a couple of minutes, gazing blankly at the rows of liquor bottles behind the bartender. "Okay, okay, it's a fascinating legend." Jeff said this, but his face had turned pale.

"You don't believe it?" The bartender shrugged. "Well, what do I know? I'm just a barman. But it seems to me that just clapping your eyes on that one is fatal."

At that moment the door was flung open and two men boisterously entered the room. Jeff looked at the door and thought he glimpsed, just outside in the darkness, Merrow's face. The door closed.

Jeff stood, glanced around one last time to be certain Merrow was not inside. He took his wallet out of his back pocket, fished out a bunch of Euros and plunked them down on the bar, and without saying goodbye or even looking at Mike, staggered toward the door.

336

The bartender gaped at the money, then yelled, "Hey, Jeff, this is far too much! Wait for your change, will ya.!"

Without even grabbing his raincoat, Jeff opened the door and lurched out into the darkness. He didn't seem to notice —or care—that it had started to pour again, driven by a fierce wind. In the humming of the wind he heard a lovely voice, Merrow's voice, crooning mysterious words that he somehow understood to be urging him on, promising joy unending. He stumbled his way over the black and gray stones when an even stronger gust whipped the cap off his head. He stared after it for a moment, then walked out into the raging sea.

The End

THE WORLD OF MYTH

MAGAZINE

ISSUE

90

NOVEMBER 2020

Lynne Phillips

Lynne Phillips lives in the Northern Rivers area of New South Wales Australia. Her stories have been published by Zombie Pirate Publishing, Black Hare Press, Fantasia Divinity Publishing,Our Wonderful Anthology, Black Ink Fiction, and in various online magazines. She enjoys exploring the craft of writing stories and the challenge it presents. Her priority is spending time with her family while her passions are reading, writing, keeping fit and spending time at her farm.

Connect with her on Facebook: https://www.facebook.com/lynne.phillips.505

The Three Wishes
By: Lynne Phillips

MARCI RACED UP the steps, but it was futile, the train pulled away from the station, leaving her exhausted and angry.

"That's tops off a shitty day," she fumed as she collapsed onto a seat. The next train wouldn't arrive for half an hour.

"At least I don't have to stand, my feet are aching," she sighed. Removing her shoes, she rubbed her feet.

The day unravelled at Uni. Her tutor said her thesis needed work, her mother sent a text saying Grandma was ill, and her boyfriend of three months, Grant, dumped her for Marilyn with the big tits.

"It's certainly been a day I'd rather forget," she muttered closing her eyes, forcing back tears.

"Had a bad day love?" Startled, Marci turned seeking the questioner. An old lady smiled kindly at her.

"Well, it's not been a good one. I missed my train and I

promised my mother I would walk the dog. I have to work on my thesis, and my Grandma is poorly." Marci rustled around in her carryall and produced two chocolate bars, offering one to the woman.

"Why, thank you love, that's very generous of you."

They sat in silence nibbling the chocolate.

"One good turn deserves another," the old woman said. "I have something which will change your day. Close your hand and shut your eyes." She winked at Marci.

"You don't need to give me anything," Marci said, embarrassed, but closed her eyes and put out her hand. She felt something small and cold being placed in her hand. When she opened her eyes, a tiny green stone shimmered as the sun reflected of its surface. Marci looked for the old woman to give it back, but she had disappeared.

She slipped the stone into her pocket, feeling its warmth through the cloth. *Maybe my luck will change* she thought as the train hummed along.

Baxter, her mother's dog, greeted her with his leash as soon as she entered the house.

"Okay sport, but it will be a short one; it looks like it will rain."

Placing her laptop in the study she changed into joggers. They did three circuits of the park before the first raindrops fell and they raced for home,

The microwave pinged. Marci ate standing up, needing to work on her thesis. She filled Baxter's bowl and headed to the study.

The clock struck midnight before she printed off the final copy. She was happy with the result, but tired and ready for bed. She hoped sleep came quickly.

The green stone fell onto the floor as Marci took off her jacket. Picking it up and idly fingering it, she recalled the old woman and her promise the stone would change her day. She smiled at the thought, placed the crystal beside her bed, closed her eyes, and fell asleep.

During the night the crystal morphed into a black cat. It jumped onto Marci's bed and snuggled in close.

The sunlight filtered through the blinds wakening Marci. Her hand touched something soft. She was surprised to see the cat. "Where did you come from?" She stroked the cat which purred in appreciation. "I wish you could talk."

"That's your first wish taken care of. You only have two more. Don't waste them." The cat's green eyes blinked sardonically as its tail swished. It stretched its legs and arched its back.

"Close your mouth, it's not attractive. Haven't you seen a cat before? What are your other two wishes, I haven't got all day?"

Marci thought long and hard.

The black cat rubbed against her legs, disconcerting her.

"For my second wish I would like my thesis to pass."

"Oh, that's an easy one." The cat touched the cover of the thesis. The words *First Class Honors* appeared across the page. "That should do it."

The cat paced the room impatiently. "I should warn you be very careful what you wish for."

Marci thought about her grandmother. "I'd wish my grandmother was young and happy again,"

"Well, that will be a bit harder, but if you are sure, I'll try."

The cat blinked and began to fade. "Don't forget to pass

345

the stone on to someone else who needs good fortune." He blinked twice and disappeared.

Marci picked up the green crystal. Its lustre was gone. It just looked like a green pebble.

The phone in the hall was ringing. It was Marci's mother. "I 'm sorry Marci, Grandma passed away this morning."

"Oh mum, that's sad. Are you okay?"

"I'm fine. A bit upset, but Gran was old and in pain. She was ready to go. I'll have to organise the funeral, but I'll be home tomorrow."

As she put the phone down Marci thought about her third wish. She wished her grandmother was young again, how could she be dead. She picked up a photograph of her grandparents on their wedding day. They looked so young and happy. Lightly touching the photo to her lips, she whispered, "I hope Grandpa was there to meet you."

Marci emailed her thesis to her tutor and packed away her laptop. She took Baxter for a walk.

Looking in the mirror as she cleaned her teeth, she asked her reflection, "Did I dream it all?"

Sleep eventually came, but it was a troubled sleep. The clock in the hall struck one. Marci woke.

The green stone shimmered, giving the room a soft green glow. Marci realised she wasn't alone. Grandma and Grandpa stood at the end of her bed, no wrinkles, no grey hair. They were young, vibrant and so much in love.

"Thank you, Marci," they both said with soft smiles. Grandma blew a kiss and Grandpa bowed low. Marci's eyes filled with tears. When she blinked them away her grandparents were gone, and the tiny crystal slowly faded leaving the room dark. Marci smiled, turned over and went to sleep knowing she would find someone to pass the stone on to the next day.

The End

THE WORLD OF MYTH

MAGAZINE

ISSUE

91

DECEMBER 2020

James Rumpel

James Rumpel is a recently retired high school math teacher who has greatly appreciated spending some of his newfound free time rekindling his love for science fiction and the written word. Writing also provides him with an excellent opportunity to ignore the household chores his wife assigns. He lives in Wisconsin with his forgiving wife, Mary.

Christmas Mission
By: James Rumpel

STNICK HATED HIS job. He hated everything about it. He despised being stranded on this backwater planet. He couldn't stand the incredible amount of downtime, having to wait a full planet rotation between missions. Each day he dreaded having to work with the E1VE5's. The automatons were the loudest and most annoying creation he could imagine. They constantly chattered with their high-pitched synthetic voices and bounced around the compound, constantly hammering and drilling.

The only thing that Stnick liked less than being stuck in the compound three hundred sixty-four days a year was the one day when he had to leave. His mission called for him to stifle the development of the creatures of this world. Once a year, he had to traverse the globe and distribute mind-numbing devices to as many of the planet's youth as possible. That duty involved climbing into an outdated time-space inversion unit and warping from home to home. The SPACE-LOCATION-ENIGMATIC-INTERVAL-GENERATING-HOVERCRAFT or SLEIGH should have been replaced years ago. The eight robotic facsimiles of one of the planet's bovine creatures that gave the SLEIGH the appearance of being pulled by magical creatures only served to make the entire thing look even more ridiculous than it was. He completed his annual task in one of the planet's rotations, but for him, it felt like years of constant labor.

This year was proving to be the worst that Stnick had ever had to endure. The popular intelligence inhibiting device for this season was a large stuffed animal that sang one of thirteen idiotic songs whenever it was shaken. Needless to say, every time his time-space inversion unit came to a sudden halt atop of one of the planet denizens' homes, the entire supply of singing toys would burst into song. He swore that if he had to hear one more verse of "Be Your Beary Best" he would disassemble every E1VE5 at the northern compound.

Luckily, Stnick was nearing the end of this particular round of deliveries. Upon completion of the final drop off, he would travel back in time and space to return to the compound and pick up another load of items to deliver. If timed correctly, and it always was, he would reappear at the workshop immediately after his last departure.

The SLEIGH came to a stop on the inclined roof of one of the planet's homes. The adhering base of the craft allowed it to stay in position without sliding off the side of the building. Stnick, unfortunately, did not have an adhering base. He crawled along the snow-covered slippery surface;

354

a bag of singing animals slung over his back. Eventually, he reached the peak and found a position where he could stand steady enough to use the short-range transporter, which would allow him to beam into the interior of the home. He activated the device. As always, his insides felt like they were being squeezed in some gigantic vice and his head pounded to the verge of exploding. The effects only last a few seconds and Stnick materialized inside the home.

Not wanting to be discovered and forced to go through the trouble of erasing his discoverer's memory, he quickly checked his belt buckle computer for the gifts that were to be left at this locale. He reached into his bag and withdrew a singing bear and a handheld video game. The latter was an especially effective brain-numbing device. He was just starting to straighten up when he heard a quiet cough behind him. He quickly made certain his large, prosthetic beard was in place. He did not want one of the humans to see his distorted face and fanged mouth. The screaming such a revelation would cause was certain to wake everyone in the neighborhood and that would mean Stnick would be stuck doing way too many mind erasures.

With his beard snuggly in place, Stnick turned to see a young female human child. She was so tiny and cute that he immediately wondered why the leaders had not decided to destroy this planet years ago. They would be an easy opponent.

"Is that you, Santa?" she asked.

Protocol stated that it would be permissible to allow an occasional human child to see Stnick, as long as that child still believed. This appeared to be such a case.

"Yes," he glanced at his belt buckle, "Tammy. Now you

355

need to go back to bed, so I can finish giving you and the rest of the children their numbin... toys."

"Ok, but please, Santa, take one of the cookies that Mommy and I made for you." She pointed to a tray that contained a number of weirdly shaped conglomerations of sugar. Stnick's digestive system did not respond well to sugar. However, he had his role to play.

"Of course," he said, picking up one of the cookies and stuffing it into his mouth. He covered his mouth with his hand as he did so. He forced the noxious baked confection down his throat.

"Mmmmm," he said, not too convincingly. "Now, you go back to bed, please."

"OK, Santa," said the little girl as she turned on her heels and began strolling towards the stairs. As she turned, Stnick noticed the cellular phone in her left hand. She had been recording the entire encounter.

"I hate this job," said Stnick as he pulled the blaster from his belt. He didn't even check to make certain it was set to stun; he really didn't care. One small, silent ray shot from the nozzle of the weapon and the girl fell to the carpet, unconscious. The alien quickly used a cane-shaped, striped instrument to erase the child's memory. He also erased the entire contents of the cell phone, before transporting back to the SLEIGH.

As the hover-craft left the home and Stnick prepared to make a space-time jump, he had an uncontrollable impulse. It was against all the rules, but at this moment, he was too frustrated to care.

He loudly exclaimed as he disappeared into the night: "Merry Christmas to all and if I had my way, I'd blow you all out of sight."

The End

THE WORLD OF MYTH

MAGAZINE

ISSUE

92

JANUARY 2021

Timothy Law

Timothy Law is a writer of fantasy, horror, detective and general fiction from a little town in Southern Australia called Murray Bridge. A happily married father of three children, family is very important to him. Currently working at the Murray Bridge Library in the role of Library Manager he has dreamed since his early high school years of becoming a full-time author. Working for a library, surrounded by so many wonderful authors it is difficult not to be inspired to write.

Many of his short stories and general musings can be found on his blog http://somecallmetimmy.blogspot.com.au/ or on Parenting Express website.

The Missing
By: Timothy Law

"**LISTEN TO ME** officer, please," begged the woman.

Inspector Davidson tried not to sigh audibly. It had been a long shift, the pub was calling.

"It's my son Michael… He's been missing three days now and…"

"Ma'am, report this to your local station. Surely they would know the area better?" the Inspector suggested.

"We've tried everything, friends, family, we involved the police but that text we received from Michael has confused us all…"

Inspector Davidson had been on the trail of the Messenger for over a year. The mention of a text quickly awoke his interest.

"Ma'am may I please ask you to email me that message?"

The Inspector suddenly found his exhaustion vanished. Pub forgotten he eagerly prepared for a long night.

As usual the message was a row of five symbols. The first picture was possibly a gimp or a sign for silence. Following that was a crescent. Inspector Davidson took that to literally mean the moon, perhaps a clue to the date of a planned meeting. Open, inverted scissors with a red handle followed from the crescent shape. After that there came a handshake and a spider's web.

"Bring up the other three," suggested Davidson to the other officer he'd roped in to help.

Another three lines of symbols appeared above the one sent from Michael.

"Thanks George," the Inspector murmured, focused on the images.

"So far we know only boys missing, fifteen years of age, all nabbed within two hundred miles of London..."

"Look there!" pointed the Inspector eagerly, showing no sign of the tiredness felt hours before. "Those two messages have scimitars while Michael and the first boy have the moon."

"Maybe it means Crescent, like Street or Terrace?" suggested George, stifling a yawn.

"Bingo, George!" announced Davidson, giving the other officer a punch. "Silent Crescent! There's one in Retford!"

The other messages had variants on this so Davidson thought it had to be right.

"What about this then?" George asked, pointing to the scissors and handshake. The other messages all had the handshake but one had a plane, one a tree, one the cat with heart eyes. All four messages ended with a spider, web or something arachnid.

"Who are the other missing lads?" Davidson asked

suddenly.

"Jethro, Blade, Terrance, Felix…" replied George.

"Jet… Stump… Felix… Michael was to meet Blade at the Spider Inn…"

"You got it Inspector!"

"Too right, George! Call back-up to meet me there…"

Within three hours Inspector Davidson was outside the Spider. Local officers were already onsite. The pub looked like it hadn't functioned for years. On his count Davidson breached the front door. What he discovered shocked him. There were 11 boys in the room. All dressed in black, pale of skin, their blood drained. Each lay out on the floor as if drunk or sleeping, except for their eyes, opened wide and glassed over. Each was raven haired, those eyes the color of the bluest summer day. From each came not a sound, just lifeless silence.

The End

THE WORLD OF MYTH

MAGAZINE

ISSUE

93

FEBRUARY 2021

Christopher Bice

Growing up in Brantford Ontario, I moved West with my family to a small village in Northern BC.

After many years I returned to the East and met my wife. We later came to Coalhurst Alberta (just outside of Lethbridge) to retire. I enjoy fishing and camping and I find my inspiration while out in nature.

My Valentine
By: Christopher Bice

ANOTHER VALENTINE'S DAY, a new year, and love is still in the air. Slowly I walk up and sit beside you. Throwing my arms around you I give you a soft loving kiss.

"Happy Valentines my love. I told you I wouldn't forget the day we met." I whisper

From out of my jacket I produce a small bouquet of carnations, your absolute favorite flowers.

"Honey I love you so much, I always will," I say quietly.

With tears flowing freely I lay the flowers at your headstone. One more kiss and a promise to see you again next year.

The End

THE WORLD OF MYTH

MAGAZINE

ISSUE

94

MARCH 2021

David K. Montoya

For a good part of two decades David K. Montoya was an active writer, artist and business entrepreneur in the micro-publication world. In 2013, turned his pen in for a microphone and became a podcaster for the following five years—and even did a small stent in independent Hollywood. But, now, he's come home and is ready to begin weaving new tales for this magazine.

Day of the Easter Bunny
By: David K. Montoya

THE SKY, DARK, the dirt-stained red from the blood of the innocent, Taylor emerged from behind a framed rustic vehicle and found her friend Pham who jumped at the sight of her.

"Jesus, Taylor," Pham cried. "I thought you were *it*."

"Shhh!" Taylor hushed. "You want *it* to hear you?"

"It's *Good Friday* you know as well as I do it's awake n—"

Before Pham finished his thought, from nowhere, the large creature known as the Easter Bunny bounced up behind him, swallowed him whole. Taylor was frozen as she knew her fate was next.

The End

THE WORLD OF MYTH

MAGAZINE

ISSUE

95

APRIL 2021

Dawn DeBraal

Dawn DeBraal lives in rural Wisconsin with her husband Red, two rescue dogs, and a stray cat. Dawn has published over 400 stories in many online magazines and anthologies, including Spillwords, Potato Soup Journal, Zimbell House Publishing, Black Hare Press, Clarendon House, Blood Song Books, Cafelit, Reanimated Writers, The World of Myth, Dastaan World, Vamp Cat, Runcible Spoon, Siren's Call, Setu, Kandisha Press, Terror House Magazine, D & T Publishing, Sammie Sands, Iron Horse Publishing, Impspired Magazine, Black Ink Fiction and others. She was the Falling Star Magazine's 2019 Pushcart nominee.
https://linktr.ee/dawndebraal
https://www.amazon.com/Dawn-DeBraal/e/B07STL8DLX
https://www.facebook.com/All-The-Clever-Names-Were-Taken-114783950248991

Abducted
By: Dawn DeBraal

BREANNA MALCOMB WAS expecting a delivery. She and Lee paid for a baby, and the child would be delivered to their doorstep. She knew this was the due date week of the birth mother. The nursery was ready. The agreement with the attorney was the delivery of a healthy child, nothing more. She would get the child, a clean bill of health, along with legal adoption papers.

When Breanna told her boss, she was adopting a baby, her work was very supportive. The nursery was ready, a very non-committal yellow and green, so any sex they got would fit the room. Everything was laid out, diapers, cotton balls, onesies, cans of formula, bottles, rocking chair, cradle, and a crib.

Breanna loved to go into the room and sit, looking at the night light shining stars onto the ceiling as it played soft lullabies. What baby wouldn't love this room?

Dawn DeBraal

The attorney had called her at work yesterday, saying labor had started that she shouldn't go too far from home. Breanna punched out for her last day of work for the next two months and came home to wait. Today or tomorrow, she supposed, pacing the floor.

The doorbell chimed. Breanna raced down the hall, flinging the front door open. A basket. She picked it up, looking to see if someone had waited around, there was no one.

Breanna set the basket on the couch and pulled back the covers. Pink, everything was pink. They had a girl. Oh, what would Lee think about a little girl?

Breanna took the basket down to the nursery, took the baby out, and put her on the dressing table. Counted fingers, undressed the baby seeing the umbilical cord fresh in a clip, counted ten toes, changed the baby's diaper. She was perfect. Putting the precious package in the cradle she hurried to the kitchen to sterilize the nipples for the bottles and to make formula. She was a mom! Breanna was waiting when her child woke up crying. She entered the nursery, whispering as she approached the crib, lifting the baby while telling her it would be alright. She placed her forefinger near the baby's mouth and brought the bottle to her face. The baby eagerly took the bottle. Breanna contentedly rocked while she fed her. Everything was perfect.

Lee came through the door. She had called him to come home, that they had a daughter.

"Oh, look at her. Don't worry, I washed up in the kitchen before coming in. Can I hold her?" Breanna nodded through her tears of joy.

All those hormone shots and invasive tests had produced nothing for them. Adoption was a long wait, but when she found a friend of a friend who specialized in secret adoptions, they jumped at it. The adoption had cost them a fortune. Providing prenatal care for the mother, paying for the delivery, and making the child legally theirs, but she was so worth the money. Lee sat down, accepting the baby in his arms.

"What do we name her?" he looked up at his wife. Breanna had been thinking since the baby's arrival.

"How about a combination of our mother's names, Helen and Anna? How about Hannah?"

"Hannah. I love it." Lee cooed her name. "Hannah banana is such a little monkey!" She fell back to sleep, Lee put her in the cradle, turning on the baby monitor, he took the handheld unit with him.

"Oh, Breanna, we are parents!" Lee was all smiles as he handed the monitor to her.

"We are parents," she said back to him in disbelief. It was a long night. Every three hours, Hannah demanded to be fed and changed. Lee took the first shift. Breanna the next. Lee had taken off a few weeks himself so they could get this parenting thing down, and bond with their new daughter.

New daughter, Breanna, beamed when she said that to herself. How long they had waited for this day. At two-forty-five in the morning, Breanna walked into the baby's room, surprised that Hannah had rolled over. Her head was up like a baby bird! How could that be, she was a newborn? She flipped on the light. Hannah was on her back, crying like crazy. It must have been the night light playing tricks on her eyes. Breanna fed Hannah and changed her. It seemed as if Hannah had grown overnight. She felt good and solid.

Lee came in during the feeding. "Wow, she is growing fast. Is that normal?" Breanna was thinking the same thing. She didn't think this was normal, but she didn't tell this to her husband.

Breanna stroked Hannah's face. Hannah bit Breanna's finger, drawing blood.

"Ouch!" Breanna couldn't quite believe what happened. How could the baby have teeth? She'd heard of it, some babies born with teeth. She looked down at her finger and put it in her mouth. She finished feeding Hannah and put her in the cradle, Breanna walked to the bathroom, scrubbing her hands with soap and water. She took a bandage out of the cupboard. It was a deep cut, and it hurt.

The doorbell chimed. Breanna looked at the clock in the hall as she peeked out the door. It was after three a.m. Who would be out this late ringing her doorbell? She saw a basket on the stoop.

Breanna opened the door. Another baby? She looked out into the darkness. How could she tell them they delivered to the wrong house?

She put the basket on the couch, pulled back the covers in the basket, everything was blue. A boy? Something was wrong. They couldn't afford two children. What was going on? Lee came yawning out of the bedroom.

"Who was that? What is that?"

"Lee, it's another baby. There must be some mistake!" Lee pulled back the basket. Counting fingers. It's a boy, he said after pulling off the baby's clothes.

"We should call the attorney tomorrow. I can't believe

they would screw up this bad." Breanna fed the child and put him in the crib. He looked so tiny. She left to get some sleep.

She called the attorney early the next morning. His assistant said he was on another call but would get right back to her. Breanna was so glad Lee had taken off. They were both busy changing, bathing, feeding the new babies. They were afraid, what if they had bonded with the wrong child. Were they supposed to get the boy or the girl?

"Hello, Brianna, did you get your little guy last night? We could finish the paperwork do you have a name?" Breanna told him they got a little boy last night. But the day before, they had gotten a little girl. "That's impossible." The mother of your child delivered yesterday afternoon.

"Well, there must be some mistake; we have two babies. Are you saying the boy child is ours?" Breanna wanted to cry, it had only been two nights, but she had fallen for Hannah.

"The boy baby is the baby you received from us. I have no idea who the other child is. I will get to the bottom of this. In the meantime, will you accept the boy?"

"Of course, we will. Please get this straightened out for us!" Breanna put the phone down. Lee was standing next to her, holding his son.

"This is our son?" He asked matter-of-factly. Breanna nodded, yes. How could she turn away from her daughter? She was here first. How could the agency make such a horrible screw up? She started to cry. Lee put his arm around her.

"Don't, maybe we can keep both. It's their mistake!" Hannah cried. Breanna went to get her.

"Lee!" she screamed. When he came into the nursery, he handed the boy to Breanna, and he tried to extricate Hannah who had outgrown the cradle. Her arms and legs went through the bars, and she was stuck in the bed.

"There is something not right!" Breanna hissed at him. Lee put Hannah on the changing table she was fine. The newborn size diapers didn't fit her. Luckily the sample pack had some larger diapers.

"She's into the twelve to fifteen-pound diapers," he said as he took the bottle from Breanna. Hannah nursed as Lee rocked her back and forth in the rocker.

"Ouch!" he shrieked.

"Lee. What?

"She bit me!" Breanna put her son in the cradle and took her daughter while Lee went to wash the bite. Breanna pulled down Hannah's lip. A row of razor-edged teeth filled her mouth. Breanna gasped. Hannah had grown a full set of teeth last night. Hannah was not a normal baby. Breanna shivered. She was afraid of her daughter.

Breanna was still holding Hannah when she answered the door.

"Oh, thank God, you have her!" The couple shouted as they stood on her front porch.

"Excuse me?" Breanna looked at the couple in her doorway. They didn't appear to be human, though they could pass for human from a distance. The size of them, both well over six feet. The woman smiled her teeth were rows of sharp razor-edged points, just like the ones in Hannah's mouth.

"I'm sorry, were the Mork's, and our daughter was delivered to the wrong house. As soon as we found out about the mistake, we came, the attorney called us this morning.

"What?" Breanna held Hannah to her tighter. "Lee!" she called out to her husband.

"Here's the card of our adoption attorney." Breanna saw the same business card that she possessed. "Thank you for taking such good care of her." Before Breanna could say a word, the large woman snatched the baby out of her hands. Hannah was now the size of an eighteen-month-old.

Lee came up behind his wife.

"What's going on here?" Lee could see how the baby stopped crying as it snuggled into its mother's arms. "You can't do that. This is our daughter, Hannah. He reached to grab the child from the woman's arms. The new mother screeched an unearthly sound. Hannah reared out of her mother's arms, biting Lee's hand ripping two fingers off. Lee screamed as the blood spurt. The couple ran with the baby to a spaceship parked on the front lawn. Lee and Breanna chased them, not far behind when the door closed, they stared in disbelief as they watched the ship hover and fly off.

"Hannah!" Breanna cried, but then she saw her husband bleeding profusely. Breanna ran into the house grabbed a dish towel wrapping it around Lee's hand, trying to stem the flow of blood. "We need to go to the hospital."

#

"What happened to you?" The doctor asked.

"Meatgrinder, I was making sausage. Lee replied, "My hand got pulled in. Needless to say, there are no fingers to

389

bring back to you. The doctor stitched Lee up in the emergency room and gave him a tetanus shot.

"Cute kid, what's his name?" The doctor asked.

"Lee." Breanna blurted.

"Bradley," Lee said. Both parents answered at the same time. They glared at one another. The doctor looked at them strangely.

"He is so new, how old?"

"Born yesterday, and we are still discussing the names," Breanna said covering her tracks. They hadn't finalized the adoption yet.

"Wow, he is new. Alright, we're almost done here, I will get the nurse to come in and discharge you. I am putting you on an antibiotic and some painkillers."

"Thanks, doctor." Lee and Breanna turned to one another.

"Bradley? Where did that name come from?" Breanna asked.

"A combination of my name, Lee, and your name Breanna. It just came out. Sorry." They sat in silence, waiting for the nurse who came in a short time later. She went through instructions with Lee. There was a rap on the door. Several officers burst into the room as the nurse quickly left.

"Breanna and Lee Malcomb, you are under arrest for kidnapping."

"Wait? What? Call our lawyer. We paid for a legal adoption through Thomas Vanguor call his office. Please." Breanna handed the business card to the officer, who left to make the call.

"The number has been disconnected," said the officer when he came back.

"That's impossible. I just talked to the attorney this morning." The two were led out of the room while the woman who gave birth to "Bradley" came in.

"Oh my God, you found him. Thank you so much." She scooped the baby out of the carrier holding him to her.

"Why are we being arrested?" Breanna asked the officer.

"That baby was born here yesterday, taken from the nursery. He was kidnapped."

"But we're innocent!" Breanna shouted. "What about our daughter?"

"Daughter?" the officer asked.

"Yes, the abnormally tall couple took her away in a spaceship." The officer looked at his partner and put his finger up, circling it at his temple, the sign for being crazy. Breanna protested struggling all the way to the squad. She couldn't believe it. This morning she and Lee had two children, now they had none, and they were going to jail.

The End

THE WORLD OF MYTH

MAGAZINE

ISSUE

96

MAY 2021

Stephanie J. Bardy

Stephanie J. Bardy is an accomplished author, poet and editor. She is Editor in Chief at *The World of Myth Magazine* and has held an editing position with them for over 2 years. She is also Editor in Chief for *Dark Myth Publications* and holds a position on the Board of Directors for T*he JayZoMon/DarkMyth Company*.

Her published works include *Eternally Bound, Eternally Bound PCE Exclusive Edition, The Chosen, The World of Myth Anthology Volume 3,* all under *Dark Myth Publications*. She also appears in *Full Moon & Howlin: A Werewolf Anthology Monsterthology 2* and *Natural Instincts: Tales of Witches and Warlocks* published by *Zombie Works*.

She has several short stories to her credit on *The World of Myth Magazine*, and several works of poetry.

Her editing credits include *Full Moon & Howlin: A Werewolf Anthology, Natural Instincts: Tales of Witches and Warlocks* and all of the works on *The World of Myth Magazine* for the last two years.

Penance
By: Stephanie J. Bardy

THE SMELL OF decay surrounded Reese as she lay as still
as she could. He would be back. He always came back.
Something slithered nearby and she cringed just a bit. He
had never left her like this before. Just lying on the cold
stone. It was always in the hole. This time he had just
dropped her like a ragdoll and left. She could feel the damp
beginning to seep into her bones.

"I have to get up." She thought. She almost laughed out
loud because that is what she always thought. "I have to get
out of here."

She moved her left hand slowly across the floor until it
was beside her. The arm was broken at the joint and she
knew it was going to hurt like a bitch to put it back. She grit
her teeth as hard as she could and twisted her arm back to
its rightful angle. Bones popped and snapped as she did.
The sound of flesh tearing almost made her gag but the

searing pain that quickly followed it made all her senses shut down. She neither saw nor felt beyond that pain. Then there was a loud pop, and the arm was again as it should be. She took a moment to catch her breath, tears flowing freely from her eyes and getting lost in her hair. She continued to stare up at what she assumed was the ceiling. She never saw the sun, the stars, or the moon, never felt a breeze or heard the sound of the trees, so she assumed she was inside somewhere.

Slowly she moved her legs and repeated the same process she had with her arm. After what seemed like hours, her limbs were back to rights and she could push herself up to a sitting position. She looked down and realized that her feet were not where they were supposed to be. Sighing sadly, she turned her head back around to face the right direction. Once she was as she had begun, she wiped the tears from her face, and stood. Her legs shook beneath her, but she remained upright. Sheer determination and the will to survive rode her and she lifted one foot and then the other. When she reached the door at the far end of the room, she gave it a hard push.

Nothing.

She pushed again and still nothing. Not even a slight movement.

Sliding down the door she crumbled on to the small step and lay her head on the cold stone. If she had any tears left, she would have shed them.

The smell of dry leaves, wet dirt, and the cold blew across her face. She raised her eyes slightly and she could see a small line of light under the door. Every time the wind blew, the line got bigger, then smaller as the wind stopped.

She watched it closely. It was blowing inwards, not out.

She stood again, a small spark of hope igniting in her chest. If she had a heart, it would have beat faster as she placed her hand on the door handle and pulled inward.

The door stuck for a second then came loose and swung open. Light burst in and engulfed her. She threw her arm up and shielded her eyes and shrank back into the shadows.

"Get it together Reese!" she said out loud. It almost sounded like words. She had not used her throat or her voice in over a hundred years. What came out was harsh, dry, and raspy. She crept towards the light again and felt the warmth on her skin. Paper thin and cold she just stood for a moment and drank it in. She could smell freedom. Feel it. She just had to make her feet step beyond the threshold of her prison. One step and she was free. One movement of her foot. She stood, swaying slightly as she fought with herself.

A deep male chuckle echoed from the room behind her.

"It's always the same Reese. I do not hold you here. You do."

Her head fell forward, and her shoulders dropped.

"You built this prison. Each stone, each board, every nail. Created by each sin, by each life you took. Every soul extinguished by you; built the prison you now can not escape."

Marlon pushed himself off the far wall where he had been leaning, watching Reese go through the same ritual she put herself through every night.

"Do you not think you have suffered enough?" he asked, "Do you not feel that your penance has been paid?"

399

Stephanie J. Bardy

Reese stepped back into the shadows, pushing the door closed. The room was engulfed in darkness once again.

"No." she said. "It will never be enough."

She walked over to the stone slab in the middle of the room and lay down on it.

"Begin." She said.

Marlon walked over to the door and opened it. Again, the room was flooded with light.

"No." was all he said and then disappeared outside.

Reese lay on the slab staring up at what she now could see was the ceiling of a crypt. Each stone bore a name. A life. Marlon was right.

She sat up and looked around the room. It was not an ordinary crypt although it passed as one from the outside. There were no slots for bodies. No human had ever been laid to rest here. Each stone, each board had a name carved into it. Each name, a life she had taken. A soul she had destroyed.

She slid down off the slab and the sun hit her again. The warmth crept into her. She stood for a moment, again soaking it in. It would be so easy to just walk out, breath in the fresh air instead of the fetid stench of this prison. She had spent a hundred years trying to do penance for the sins she had been accused of. Marlon had been her jailer at the beginning. Her persecutor. Some how over time, he had become her guardian.

Each night he would pull her, limb after limb, breaking bones, tearing flesh, rendering unbearable pain upon her, then he would place her into the hole. She would wipe her memory, heal, she would try and escape, and she would fail. Just as all those who's names taunted her from every

400

angle, had. She would clear her mind of the memory of what was to come, clear her mind of her duty to pay such a price, and begin the fear, the anguish, again each day. The night was her reprieve. Her moment of peace. That is how she had come to know Marlon as more than just the one tasked with her sentence.

He was once a man. Not an overly good one, but an honest one. Which is why he had been given the job. He would carry out the punishment, without fail, no more, no less. Until she told him to stop. She had not removed his free will, just the ability to leave her permanently. His body would not allow him to venture to far from her side. She knew he would be just beyond the door, sitting sullenly on the stoop.

She walked to the open door. This was new. This defiance.

"Marlon." She said. He grunted from the sunlight.

"You can't ignore me." Reese stepped closer to the threshold.

"No, I can't. You took that away from me. I have to tear you apart every day, watch you scream and writhe in pain, and then talk to you like an old friend every night." He stood angrily.

"I can't do it anymore Reese. Physically I cannot stop, but inside, I am dying."

Reese chuckled a bit. Marlon glared at her. "You know what I mean."

"Marlon, we are immortal. We cannot die. Outside or in. You know what I was accused of. You know that I do not remember my time of change. Until I know for sure one way or another, this is how it must be." She turned back towards the shadows.

Marlon stormed after her. "How are we to find out if we never leave this place? If we never seek out those who know the truth?" he waved his arm, "This is not your prison, I see that now, it is your escape. You do not want to know the truth. It is easier to hide here, bear the pain, and play what they painted you to be, than to seek the truth. You are a coward. Nothing more."

Reese's eyes became slits, a fire burning in them. "Tread carefully jailer. You live because I will it. Should that change, your name can be added to the stones that you stand upon."

Marlon huffed angrily and stormed out of the crypt again. She knew he would pout for a while and come back. He always did. After all the years of torture and pain, there were moments, during the night, as she reknit her bones and mended her torn flesh, that they had become something akin to friends. He had never loved so when she bound him to her, he had nothing to lose but an honorable death. He had hated her for that for a long time, taking his frustration and anger out on her day after day. She had welcomed it. Sinking into the devastation he caused her, to pay for what she had done. She was guilty, no matter what Marlon said. Maybe not of all she was accused of, but she had taken lives. Many of them. Each a name now in stone.

She stared at the sunlight streaming in the open door. To just step beyond that threshold, to feel the warmth, to relinquish her penance. It was so easy, but one of the hardest things she would ever do. She inched closer to the door and stepped into the sun. The threshold lay before her, small, insignificant, dull. She stood here every evening, during the "great escape". She always turned away. What if she did not this time? What if she lifted her foot and stepped over that threshold? What would happen.

"Nothing." Said Marlon from the stoop outside. "Nothing would happen. The world would keep turning, the sun would keep shining, and the souls you took would still be gone. You would remain immortal, and I tied to you."

Reese looked down at him. "Since when did you learn to read my thoughts?" she asked.

He snorted in disgust. "I don't have to. I have seen it every evening for a hundred years. You come to the door, you mimic wanting to escape, you ponder the reality of said escape, then you close the door, and lay on the altar and I tear you apart until full dark. It is not easy to know what you are thinking. It is written all over your face. Your eyes take on this faraway look."

Marlon stood and reached up for her hand. "You are eternal, you have made me as such. Why can we not have a life outside of this crypt? You have paid dearly for your crimes, real and otherwise. You are the Mother of All, let us go and look for your children. Those they created from your flesh. You no longer need to be alone."

Reese stared into Marlon's eyes. Those beautifully gold flecked eyes. She ached to step out into the light with him. To take his hand, let him pull her out. She closed her eyes, took a deep breath, and lifted her foot. Slowly she moved it forward and put it down. She waivered for a moment and Marlon took her hand and gently tugged her the rest of the way.

Warmth surrounded her. The fetid air of the crypt faded

back, and the scent of cherry blossoms filled her. The birds, who always sounded hollow and distant, chirped loudly. The breeze teased her hair and tickled her face. She opened her eyes and immediately squinted.

"We may have to find you a bonnet to shield your eyes until you adjust." Said Marlon. He pulled her close to him and turned her to view the forest they were in.

"It's so…so…green!" She exclaimed. Marlon laughed. "Yes, it is, and in the fall, it is red, and orange and brown."

Distant barking caused Reese to tense. Marlon moved to stand in front of her as a black and brown dog burst out of the brush and skidded to a halt in front of them.

"Biscuit!" a male voice shouted, "Get back here you fool!"

A man, dressed in britches that were missing the bottom half, and a strange kind of shirt with a triangle on it came running after the dog.

He too came to a skidding halt. He looked around and then back at Marlon and Reese.

"Hey, you guys, ok? Did I interrupt some kind of cosplay thing?" he asked grinning slyly at Marlon. "You know this is private property, right?"

Reese sniffed. "Of course, it is. It belongs to the Duke and Duchess of Highton."

The man laughed. "Not for about a billion years it hasn't. It's a B and B now. My cousin owns it." His eyes narrowed slightly.

"Who did you say you were?"

Marlon again moved to put Reese behind him, not trusting this strange loud man.

"I am Marlon Gibson, and this woman is my prisoner. Who be you?"

404

The man laughed. "Dude, you can drop the character. No one is around. Name's Chris. Chris Martin. That's my dog Biscuit."

Reese moved around Marlon and walked toward Chris. She could feel the frailty of his spirit. He would be easy prey, and it had been so long. She licked her lips and suddenly she had Chris's full attention.

"Tell me…Chris…is there shelter and nourishment at this B and B place?"

Chris nodded.

"Wonderful." She smiled, giving just a bit more pull, his energy came easily. "Take us there."

Chris smiled and without question, turned and led them out of the forest to a small country home.

Reese looked around panicked. "What has happened?"

Marlon looked down at her and grinned. "It has been a hundred years. Did you think things would not change?"

Reese looked around again and grimaced.

"Not quite for the better I see."

Chris opened the front door and immediately they were bombarded by loud music.

Reese and Marlon both recoiled.

Chris furrowed his brow. "Megadeath not your thing?" he asked.

"Mega…what?" questioned Reese.

"Never mind, you don't look like you listen to much rock."

Reese stepped close to Chris and captured his gaze.

"Let me make this clear. So, there is no misunderstanding. We are not from this time. The last time we saw the light of day, it was 1921. You will be our guide

405

in this new land."

Chris shrugged. "Sure." He turned and sauntered towards the back of the house. "Kitchen is this way."

Marlon looked down at Reese. "I see your powers of persuasion are still intact."

Reese looked up at him puzzled. "I didn't use them."

They both turned and looked down the hallway towards where Chris had disappeared. Strange noises had started to emanate from the kitchen.

"Strange." Said Reese. "Very strange indeed."

THE WORLD OF MYTH

MAGAZINE

ISSUE

97

JUNE 2021

Walter G. Esselman

Apparently, I'm supposed to write this bio to humanize me. It is bold of them to assume that I am a carbon-based lifeform from Earth, but regardless...

I grew up in Michigan, practically on the campus of MSU. Not that I follow sports, humorously enough. I've been writing forever but never really sent anything out. So, I pushed myself to get short stories out there and became a regular contributor at World of Myth and Dark Dossier. I recently started turning my eye towards novels, which is the first step in that process.

My wife Amy and I still live in Michigan because it's the most beautiful state. Not that I like to go outdoors, humorously enough. I mean, seriously, there are bears out there, Sharks! I even saw a Bearshark once. A chilling sight.

After tooling around the Commonwealth with Cait for many years in Fallout 4, I'm back in the land of Skyrim once again.

Khajit will shoot arrows if you have the coin. Or, it's a dungeon with a lot of loot.

I hope you have a wonderful day!

The Kingfisher
By: Walter G. Esselman

Part I

I'M FALLING.
   Maybe even plummeting.
   …
   Yep. Definitely plummeting.
   Fast, but I feel like it's happening in slow motion.
   …
   Behind me, the night sky suddenly lit up like fireworks
as the airplane exploded, diving down.
   Not quite sure why I jumped out.
   DANGER! They were trying to kill me.
   Must hide. Get away!
   River down there. Big city lights.
   Maybe I'll hit the river.
   Not that it matters at this height.

Pancake.

Large chunks of the burning plane hit the river. Lucky plane.

But I was definitely going to miss the river.

…

…

…

This is going to hurt.

…

…

My left side slammed—Hard!—into the lip of a building. I bounced off and spun into the alley.

Immediately, I smacked into the opposite wall and then dropped straight down. Falling towards a huge mound of garbage, I easily passed through it to crushing against concrete below.

The End.

I waited.

Patiently, I waited for that whole White-Tunnel-Filled-With-Light-Thing. But it must've been running late.

Surrounding me was the aroma of moldy chow mein, cabbage and used diapers.

Experimentally, I tried moving one limb, and then another. Standing, my hand brushed my leg. I froze.

I had nothing around my waist.

Yikes!

Desperately scanning around, I snatched up a large piece of dark canvas and wrapped it around myself. It was not going to tie easily at my throat. Reaching down, I snapped a piece of wire off an old mattress and quickly straightened it out.

Something told me I needed to stay low. A chill, persistent paranoia that I couldn't shake. Fashioning a crude hood, I used the wire to tie the canvas around my neck. It probably looked ugly, but it would at least afford me some cover.

Now that I was somewhat decent, I looked towards the end of the alley. It was partially lit up by an unseen streetlamp. The light further reflected off a damp street. A step forward seemed a lot for me. My head felt heavy, and my eyes were drooping.

Someone tried to kill me, and I did just fall from a great height.

Maybe if I should lay down for a second.

#

A sharp light played across my garbage heap.

Blinking, I saw a car at the mouth of the alley. The spotlight played over the interior of the alley, checking every corner. When it moved to one side, I saw two uniformed officers, and if I focused, I could just hear them.

"We should check it out," said the first officer. He sounded young and eager.

"**NO!** WE should **absolutely** not check it out," snapped the second officer tartly. "My gram, when she walked this beat, would say that this neighborhood had been abandoned by God. And that was before things had gotten worse."

"But...," started the first officer. "These people here, we need to make sure they're safe."

"People," scoffed the second officer dismissively. "Let's

413

go."

"But....," started the first.

"NOW!" barked the second.

The light snapped off and the car went away. Before I knew it, I was asleep.

#

Occasionally, I woke, but I was too tired to move.

The sun felt good, so I pulled my cloak away and allowed it to beat down upon me.

Then, I closed my eyes once again.

#

I must've been half-awake when a backpack nearly took my head off. It dropped like a ton of bricks, scattering trash.

A male voice called out. "Hey! Didja see how far I got?"

"I didn't even see it land!" grinned another male voice with a malicious glee.

"Hey! Let...let go of me!" growled another voice in outrage. A girl, it sounded like.

The sun had passed overhead, and now the alley was bathed in shadows once again. Raising my head, I saw people—No, kids!—at the mouth of the alley.

One was on the ground. I couldn't tell who, but a boy of maybe-twelve straddled the person. Beyond the boy were two others watching, just inside the mouth of the alley, and a fourth leaning against a car in the street.

Bullies, I determined with fiery certainty.

"What did I say?" asked the bully who was doing the

414

straddling.

"Get off me!" snapped the person on the ground. It was a girl, and she didn't sound any older than him. "Get! Off!"

The bully ignored her and kept talking. "I said…" He spoke like a teacher talking to a bad student. "I said that Winter Run Academy is not for people like you. Didn't I?"

"Let me go," demanded the girl.

"And what kind of name is Sydney for a girl?" asked the bully. "I mean, why not Mary, or Rebecca."

"You asshole," growled the girl, Sydney.

"Now, that's not very nice," said the bully. "Tsk tsk."

Just as I was about to move forward, an older man came into view, and I relaxed. He would help the girl. The older man looked into the alley and saw the girl on the ground.

"Help!" cried Sydney.

"What're you looking at?" growled the kid by the car, and he pulled up his shirt, just enough to show the gun. "Don't make me 'Stand My Ground'."

The older man flinched at that. His eyes darted towards the girl, but then he ran off.

"Please! Please don't leave!" pleaded Sydney.

However, the older man was gone.

The boy by the car took his gun into his hand and flashed it about. A few other people ran by on the other side of the street, and then it was empty.

"Tsk, tsk," said the bully. "Where have all the heroes gone?"

"Listen, get off me!" growled Sydney. "I *earned* my right to be at Winter's Run! I've got a scholarship."

"My Dad said that you took that scholarship from someone more qualified," replied the bully. "That you only got in because of your skin color. To show some diversity."

"I got in because I can do calculus, and you're still in algebra 1," said Sydney. "And struggling, I hear."

Without warning, the bully smacked her forehead. The back of her head rapped hard against the concrete.

Blinking, she tried to focus, her voice slurred. "Sttoop."

The bully pointed down at her. "You! Shut up! I didn't give you permission to speak."

Deep in the alley, my eyes narrowed with a cold rage.

But again, some deep paranoia stopped me from charging right out, revealing myself. Looking up, I saw that there were no convenient fire escapes to rush up. However, I went to the wall looking for handholds. I needed to climb up. Putting out a hand, I grabbed the brick, and something held fast.

Grappling the wall, I pulled myself up, and when I was high enough, my toes gripped too. Distantly, I knew that this wasn't right; that there was something weird about this.

I heard a guttural cry from Sydney.

Swiftly, I scaled up the wall. The moment that I was on the roof, I ran silently to the front of the building.

Cautiously, I looked over and saw the boy with his car, still leaning, lurking.

No one else was on the street. They were probably all trying to plug their ears.

"Hel...help!" cried Sydney, though I couldn't see her.

And deep down inside, a fiery part of me wondered if we could really tear their arms off. Shaking my head, I forced myself to focus on a plan of attack.

\#

In the alley, Sydney tried to lift her head.

Suddenly, she saw someone grab the boy by the car.

Someone who was dark, a shadow.

And the boy was gone.

There was a distant clang.

Above her, the bully was talking, talking, talking.

Then, only Sydney saw the boy, who was closest to the mouth of the alley, suddenly whip away.

No time to scream. *Clang.*

The other gawker turned around in confusion.

"Hey? Where'd everyone go?" he asked.

"Shut up," growled the Bullyboy. "I'm working here."

The other boy took two steps out of the alley, and he was grabbed.

Clang.

The Bullyboy turned his head at the final clang.

"Guys?" he asked, a little tentatively.

No one answered.

Standing up a little awkwardly over the girl, the Bullyboy now looked around more.

Without warning, Sydney kicked up, hard.

The Bullyboy's eyes grew wide as he grabbed his crotch and fell over.

But then Sydney twisted onto her side and threw up. Her head tried to lift back up.

"You....! You...," raged the Bullyboy as he tried to stand.

However, the bully did not see the figure above him. But Sydney looked right at me as I descended, upside-down.

Seeing the girl look past him in shock, the Bullyboy turned around.

417

Like lightning, I lifted him off his feet as I dropped to the ground. The moment my feet hit concrete; I ran away with my prize.

Clang.

There was still no one on the street, or even at the windows, so I leapt back into the alley, in the shadows. I was fretting that someone had seen me when I spotted a piece of metal near the car. The one boy had dropped their gun.

It was just lying on the sidewalk for anyone to pick up. Jumping out of the shadows, I scooped it up and brought it back into the darkness with me. It was heavier than I had expected. Somewhere distantly, I knew that the bullets needed to be removed.

But, I wondered, how did you do that without setting it off?

"Do you know anything about guns?" I asked the girl.

As I inspected the weapon, I suddenly realized, with growing concern, that she had not answered.

"Um, Miss?"

The girl— Sydney! Yes, that was her name— was still laying by a pool of sick, virtually motionless.

Terror spiked and my hand closed around the gun.

I shot forward. Dropping the weapon, I knelt by Sydney's side. Dressed in gym clothes, I could see that she was breathing.

"Hello?" I said.

Squatting down, I nudged her upper arm.

"Hello? Wake up!"

Not waking up was a bad thing…very, very bad. If someone passed out, they should go to the hospital. And if they're not waking up...

"I'm going to pick you up an' take you to a doctor," I said, but there was no response. It really worried me that there wasn't one.

It took me a moment to figure out how to pick up a girl, who was not related to you, and definitely avoid any place that would be covered by a bathing suit. Though distantly, I couldn't remember why this was important, just that it was.

Anyway! I told myself harshly.

Carefully picking up the girl, we reached the mouth of the alley. I had really hoped that there would be someone there. Someone to hand her to. But everyone was still staying indoors, hands over their ears.

There were only six story apartment buildings, up and down the street.

Nothing else for it, I thought.

Cradling Sydney in one arm, I leapt up and grabbed onto the light red brick of the alley. Somewhere inside me, as my toes dug in, I felt thousands and thousands of nano hooks gripping. In no time, I was up and over the top.

It felt safer up here. It was still slightly exposed, but better than the street. And the sun felt so good. Moving across the rooftops, I pulled back my hood and felt the sun hit my hair. It felt great.

"Wha...No, No...," moaned a voice from my arms.

Sydney was looking up at me fearfully. One of her eyes —half shut—twitched.

"You're awake! That's great. It's going to be alright," I said quickly. "I'm taking you to a doctor." I scanned over the edge of the building. More apartments. "If, I can find one. Do you know where the hospital is?"

419

Walter G. Esselman

Sydney's eyes closed.

Is she just sleeping, or...I could not bring myself to think anything worse. But then, I heard her heart beating. However, it didn't sound very strong.

Pouring on the speed, I raced across the rooftops. The neighborhood was giving way to more restaurants.

Suddenly, I saw a door on the opposite street which read 'Dr. Craig Spangler, D.D.S.'.

That would have to do.

Near me, there was an alley leading down between the buildings. Descending, I came to peer out. A car slid by, but its driver was looking at the road. Here, there were more people.

Fear swiftly began to override me, paralyze me. Unconsciously, I took a step back, deeper into the shadows. But then, in my arms, Sydney made a little noise.

Straightening, I pulled the makeshift hood over my head, but I didn't run out.

People notice someone running, so go slow, I reminded myself. Though I wasn't sure where I had learned that.

After another car passed, I walked out, casually. Just a guy out for a stroll.

On my side of the street, there were two people looking in a shop window, but they didn't even glance over. As I walked, I started to worry that I was trying too hard to be casual.

Across the street, I went up the stairs to the dentist's office. There was a glass door, but I hesitated to go in.

Stepping back, I gently—ever so gently—set Sydney down and leaned her back against the metal rail. Once I was sure that she wouldn't tip over, I turned to knock on the window.

No one moved in there.

I tried to knock a bit louder.

The glass door shattered under my hard knuckles!

Wide-eyed, I saw people moving through the second glass door.

"Sorry!" I blurted out reflexively.

Springing back, I jumped clean over Sydney, and tore on back into the alley. This time the people did look up, but I was already in the shadows, scaling up the side.

The moment I reached the rooftop, I carefully went back to look off the top. In front of the dentist's office, two women in scrubs were looking around in confusion. But then one, Stephanie, turned to the other woman.

"Call 911!"

The other woman disappeared as Stephanie looked over Sydney. Finding the blood matting the hair on the back of the girl's head, Stephanie spoke soothingly.

Shortly, the other woman returned and said breathlessly. "They say it'll be an hour or two. Budget cutbacks."

The older woman swore. "Tell Craig I'll be back."

Before the other woman could reply, Stephanie picked up Sydney. Taking the girl to her car, Stephanie drove off, quickly.

Even as the car was leaving, I wondered what to do. But somehow, I couldn't leave it like this. Not without knowing that Sydney was safe.

Running once more across the rooftops, I followed the car to a nearby clinic. It was so close. But really, I probably wouldn't have found it, just wandering about. The clinic was in an old storefront with alleys on either side.

421

Stephanie carried Sydney in, but soon came out by herself.

I looked back to where I had come from. Suddenly, I realized that I had no idea where I was. The apartment buildings were all uniformly built. And further away were taller buildings, but I didn't recognize the city skyline.

In fact, everything was unrecognizable. And through the fog in my head, I included my hands, which were a dark blue grey. Something told me that normal-people hands didn't look like this, but I was having trouble focusing.

My eyes went back to the clinic, and I forgot what I was worrying about.

Nothing happened. The sun felt so good on my arms. So, I moved aside the cloak to let the light beat down on my back as well.

Suddenly exhausted, I waited, half-dozing.

It was getting close to dark. Storm clouds were marching towards the city.

A side door to the clinic opened up and light spilled out.

A little girl snuck out.

Part II

I straightened as Sydney walked out onto the street, and casually walked away. When she was far enough away, the girl went across the street and kept going, a little quicker.

Curious, I started to follow. With occasional glances down, I trailed her back to her alley. The bully's car was now gone. Still, Sydney stopped and checked her alley before going down it. Wearily, she moved inside, however she suddenly stopped to look at something on the ground.

"What the hell?" she muttered to herself in a low voice. "Is…is that a gun?"

A roll of thunder came, and Sydney shook her head. She escaped deeper into the alley.

Sydney stopped by a 6 foot by 4 piece of plywood, which was flush against the brick wall. Grabbing the edge, the board swung open, and the girl disappeared inside as it closed.

The rain started to pater down. I waited a moment, but she didn't come back out.

Maybe that's her home, I reasoned, and it was not a happy thought. Poor kid.

That explained why she was even in the alley earlier. Vaguely, the little voice in my head was telling me that alleys were bad, but it was not clear why. Something about muggers, pearls and people turning into bats.

"Okay," I grumbled out loud with weary frustration. "That one doesn't even make sense."

Lightning lit up the sky, and it was immediately followed by a peal of thunder.

With Sydney sorted out, I needed try go back down into the alley and try to sort myself out, if possible. The little voice in my head was telling me to not stand out in the rain, because it would be bad for my health.

Using the nano hooks on my hands and toes, I climbed down into the alley and headed deeper in.

A second before I stepped on it, I noticed the pink backpack.

For a long moment, I stared at it in confusion. But then it hit me.

This was the backpack that had nearly taken my head off

earlier. It was the girl's. Hunching over the pack—to keep the rain off it—I walked back to the plywood and almost pulled it open.

Luckily, I froze. The little voice in my head told me that that would be wrong, though it was a little fuzzy on the 'why'.

A little bit of light shone under the bottom.

I decided to put the backpack down, right by the door. I knocked gently this time, and then went back to the shadows.

The light went off under the plywood.

I suddenly decided that it was weird to stand outside a child's door, so I turned away and slid deeper into the alley. Despite the fog in my head, it did surprise me how well I could see in this dark alley. Unfortunately, mostly what I saw was that there was little to hide under.

"Thank you for my backpack," called out a voice behind him. "But..." There was a pause, and then she continued. Her voice was frightened but determined. "But, I still wish you hadn't killed those boys. Ijusthadtosaythat!"

Blinking in confusion, I turned around. "What?"

Sydney was standing within a jagged opening in the brick wall.

"The boys were...," started Sydney, but she faltered for a moment before rallying. "They weren't good, but they didn't deserve...that. To be killed." She said the word, as if she were biting into a lemon.

"Um, I don't know what you're talking about," I said tentatively.

"I saw you grab the boys who were...being mean to me," said Sydney. "And I have no doubt that it would have been worse for me. A lot worse. But, I saw you grab them and then…" She stopped. "There was a terrible noise, like a 'clang'."

Understanding now, I chuckled with relief. "Oh! That was the manhole cover."

"The what?" asked Sydney.

"I couldn't show myself, but I also didn't want to hurt the kids," I explained. "So, I pulled up a manhole cover and dropped them down. Though they might have gotten bumped up going down…but…"

"So…Wait! They're not dead?" asked Sydney with relief.

"They…shouldn't be. They were trying to get out from underneath each other, last I saw them."

Sydney gave a little laugh. "You threw them in the sewer?"

"The car's trunk would have also worked, but I didn't have that kind of time, and…I'm sorry for worrying you."

Sydney peered into the darkness for a moment, but then she continued. "The dentist's office said someone broke their window and left me in front. Was that you?"

"Yes," I admitted.

Sydney stood in silence for a moment. "Why?"

I blinked in confusion. "Um, you were hurt." Now that I heard it more, my voice sounded odd, with a slightly mechanical undertone.

"Oh," replied Sydney. "I guess I did kinda need a hand there. Thank you."

"You're welcome," I replied. "I'm just glad that you're alright." Suddenly, there was an awkward feeling. He had no idea what to say next. "Well, take care."

Sydney stepped back into her hole in the wall and closed

the plywood door.

Looking around, I searched for something, other than her plywood, that would keep the rain off.

"I have a concussion," said Sydney's voice suddenly.

Turning, I looked back at her. The door was open once again, and she looked down at the ground uncertainly.

"But, I thought you were okay?" I asked.

"I...," started Sydney. Then she made an unhappy noise and held up a camp lantern. "Can you come forward a little? It's weird talking to a shadow. Makes me think that I'm crazy."

Stepping forward, I walked to the edge of the light. She raised the lamp a little higher and got a good look at me.

Giving a little cry, she dropped the lamp and jumped back in her hovel. The board slammed shut.

The LED lamp clattered to the ground.

Blinking in confusion, I looked down at myself. Somewhere in my mind, the little voice told me that something was wrong. My skin was a dark blue gray, which was almost black. I started to reach towards my face when the board opened up again.

"I'm sorry," said Sydney immediately. Her voice prim and proper. "I should not have slammed the door in your face. That was rude."

"Oh?" I said hesitantly. "It's okay."

Reached down slowly, I picked up the lamp and handed it to her. She hesitated for only a moment, but then she took it.

"Thank you," said Sydney.

"*Da nada*," he replied.

"You speak Spanish?" she asked.

My eyes widened, not sure of what to say.

"It's okay, it's okay," said Sydney quickly. "I ask too many questions."

"Nothing wrong with that," I replied though I wondered where that idea had come from.

"Maybe," she murmured.

I reached up to my face and touched the lines across my nose and something else. It gave me a start. "Do…do I have tusks?"

Blinking, Sydney leaned out a little further. "Don't you know?"

"I'm…a little fuzzy on what's going on." Probing my face, I decided that maybe they weren't tusks, but rather large fangs jutting up and out of my lower jaw. "Someone tried to kill me, and I jumped out of a plane. Then it exploded."

"You! You were in the plane that exploded?" asked the girl.

"Um, oh yes," I replied.

"Oh my God! That's all they was talking about at the clinic," said Sydney with breathless excitement. "It's a big mystery, because there was not supposed to be a plane flying over the city."

I shrugged. "Um. I don't remember. Sorry."

"Well, that's okay. I should probably know your name. Mine is Sydney. What's yours?" she asked.

Opening my mouth, I started to speak, but then he stopped. "Um…"

"You…don't remember your name?"

I just shrugged once again. "I…I don't know. I'm just… tired. Can we talk about this later?"

427

"Sure," said Sydney quickly. "Of course."

"Thanks," I said.

Turning, I started deeper into the alley as Sydney closed the plywood behind. Right now, I wasn't even worried about finding something to hide under. I needed sleep so desperately.

"Hey!" called out Sydney from her doorway once again. "You still out there?"

"Yes," I replied.

"Are you going home?"

"Home?" I asked. "Um, I'm not sure where home is. But, I'll find something to keep the rain off." He realized that he only said that because he didn't want her to worry about him.

"Why don't you have a...," she started, but then she stopped herself suddenly. "No! That's a rude question Sydney." She was about to start again but stopped.

I waited, suddenly realizing—somewhere deep inside me— that the rain would not hurt me. Something separate than the little voice in my head.

"At the clinic, they said my brain got knocked around," said Sydney. "They say if I hadn't gotten to the clinic when I did...it could have been bad. Really bad."

In the shadow, I straightened in surprise, but did not respond.

Sydney started to close the board again.

"Are you okay?" I asked.

"Hmmm? What?" she replied uncertainly.

"Are you okay?" I repeated. "You look worried."

"Well, I do have someone I've never met outside my house," chuckled Sydney, but even she heard the

428

defensiveness in her voice.

I just waited in the rain.

Sydney gave a long sigh. "Okay. The nurses were worried about me going to sleep because of my concussion."

Still carrying her lamp, the girl moved inside the small space that was her home. She began to pace back and forth, talking out loud. She would appear and then disappear in the so-called doorway. "I had heard that if you go to sleep with a concussion, you might not wake up, an' I don't want to do that. But I'm getting really sleepy, an' I have school tomorrow."

"You might want to call in sick," I suggested gently.

"I can't risk it," said Sydney.

"Because of those boys?"

"No, they were just bullies," she said, waving the idea away. "No, I'm on a scholarship, and I have to be better than anyone else. Smarter, faster…and always First in my class."

"I think they'll understand."

Sydney shook her head quickly, and that made her wobble a bit. She stopped and got her bearings. I almost stepped forward.

"Maybe you should lie down," I suggested with concern.

"But if I go to sleep, I might not wake up again," said Sydney in almost a wail.

"Actually, that's a myth," I said, quickly and surely. "That's what I thought at first too. But, you're not having trouble walking…"

"But I…"

"Unless you shake your head really hard," I smoothed over. "And you're certainly able to talk with me." I stopped to poke the little voice in my head to help here.

"How do you know that?" asked Sydney.

I opened my mouth to answer, but then shrugged. "Not sure. But I am sure that what I'm saying is solid." I stopped. "I...just don't know why."

"It's okay," said Sydney quickly. "What else do you remember?"

"Oh. We should also check to see if your pupils are dilated."

"Can you do that?" she asked.

"Sure," I said. "But...I'd have to step closer."

Sydney stopped pacing in the so-called doorway. "An' if they're not dilated?"

"As long as you're talking, walking okay and your pupils aren't dilated." I counted on my fingers. "Then, you can sleep. But someone should wake you a couple times during the night, just in case."

"And...what if I don't wake up?" asked Sydney with cold terror in her voice.

I took a small step forward. "Then I'd take you back to the clinic immediately. And I'd try not to break their glass door."

Sydney chuckled, and then immediately reached for her head. "Ow, don't make me laugh. I still have a headache."

"Two presidents walk into a bar...,"

"Stop it," grinned Sydney with real mirth. She looked down and then nodded slowly, so as not to hurt her head. "I would be able to sleep better, if you could check on me."

Slowly, I stepped forward.

Sydney's eyes widened as I came into the light, and I wondered what she saw. But I resisted an urge to touch my face. Instead, I stopped for a moment, a little ways away. And then started forward until I could see her brown eyes.

The camping lamp hung near her knee, but I could see that her pupils were wide in the shadows.

"Can you lift your lamp up?" I asked.

"But...," she started.

"Your health is most important right now," I said, and I heard the surety in my voice. "And, if any problems come out of that clinic, I'll help you with them."

"Why?" asked the girl suddenly.

I blinked. "Being healthy is essential because it's..."

"No," she said quickly, interrupting him. "Why are you helping me?"

I stopped. "Um, because you're hurt."

"You're just hanging out in an alley in some suit, helping young girls?" asked Sydney pointedly.

Stuttering, I tried to form words, but I was having trouble.

"I just need to know," said Sydney. "Because I don't have any money, and I'm not into guys."

"Wait? What?" I exclaimed as I stepped back. "I don't want money, and I definitely wasn't thinking of the other thing. You're way too young." I rubbed the bridge of my nose, feeling worn.

Sydney was watching me carefully.

"I...I'll just go to the back of the alley," I sighed. "Or, I can find a new one, if that makes you more comfortable. There has to be..."

"You passed," said Sydney happily with a bounce.

Blinking, I looked back at her, confused.

"I just needed to...make sure," said Sydney. "Sorry."

431

Nodding, I understood. "No, it makes sense. You have to be careful."

"I guess, I just haven't gotten a lot of help…these past few years," said Sydney softly. "Not without someone wanting something, usually something bad. I've gotten lucky, but…"

"Luck runs out," I said softly. I held up a dark blue-grey hand. "Maybe mine ran out as well." He looked at her. "But, right now, I don't know what's going on with me. But I can at least help you. Even if it's in some small way."

"Are you just going to head off after you help me?" asked Sydney.

"I…I wouldn't even know which direction to go in," I admitted.

Sydney stepped a little closer.

"I would appreciate it, if you could check my pupils," she said. "To see if they dilate."

"It's better to know, than to hope," I said. "And everything comes out in the wash anyway."

Sydney cocked her head questioningly as I held my hand out.

"Could I have the lamp?" I asked.

I found myself looking at the dark blue-grey skin of my hand. But then she put the camping lantern into it.

Raising it up, the light shone in her face, and her pupils immediately dilated.

Stepping back, I handed her the lamp and spoke with mock gruffness. "Your pupils are fine, go to bed!"

Sydney gave a little chuckle.

"I can wait out here, and then I'll knock on your door every couple of hours, until you get up," I said.

432

"Okay," said the girl, but she did not move at first.

"Seriously," I said. "Bed."

Sydney pointed to me. "What's that?"

My cloak had fallen open at the waist. I immediately pulled it shut. "Sorry...sorry!"

"It's okay," said Sydney quickly. "I...I think you're in something, like Iron Man's armor."

Turning a little, I opened the robe. What could be seen was definitely not anatomically correct. My shoulders slumped. Everything important, especially *that*, must be under the dark blue-gray skin.

"I was kinda worried about that," I said.

"What's that?" she asked.

Absolutely not wanting to talk about anatomy, especially mine, I turned back to her and left the cloak open, since it was safe. "What's wrong?"

"Oh, you have writing there," Sydney. "On your left side."

Blinking, I looked down and lifted my left arm. There was definitely something there. I pulled the cloak over my shoulder, trying to see.

Sydney lifted her lamp. "Turn to the right a bit."

As I did so, the girl leaned in closer. "It's a bit hard to read. Like part got scraped off."

"Oh! I did hit a building when I was falling from the plane," I explained. "Before I dropped into this alley."

Sydney suddenly called out. "Kingfisher."

"What?"

"I can't make out much," said Sydney. "There are some letters, E, C, T, and then 'Kingfisher'."

"Wonder what that means," I muttered.

433

Sydney suddenly gave a big yawn. She wobbled a little. I looked at her seriously. "You really need to go to sleep."

"But I got this big mystery now," she whined. Her face contorted as she tried to suppress another yawn.

Picking up the plywood door, I put it right in front of her.

"Is this your way of trying to get me back inside?" asked Sydney's voice behind it, somewhere between amusement and grumpiness.

I moved the plywood forward a little to cover the door and gently bumped into her.

"Okay! Okay!" she grumbled. She walked back into her small home as I set the door in place.

"I'll knock in a few hours," I called through the door. "But, if you don't reply, I'll probably have to come in."

"I'll wake," replied Sydney from the other side. "Good night Kingfisher, thanks for your help."

"Good night," I replied, and sat in front of the door.

Sydney suddenly cried out from inside.

"Wait? What do you mean you fell out of an airplane!"

The End, for now

THE WORLD OF MYTH

MAGAZINE

ISSUE

98

JULY 2021

Gabriella Balcom

Gabriella Balcom, who is from Texas, writes fantasy, horror/thriller, romance, sci-fi, and more. She likes traveling, music, photography, great stories, history and movies. Gabriella says she loves forests, mountains, and back roads. She has a weakness for lasagna, garlic bread, tacos, cheese and chocolate. Check out her author page: https://facebook.com/GabriellaBalcom.lonestarauthor

Not Catching On
By: Gabriella Balcom

"**STOP WIGGLING, BREEA**," Sylene said, her voice soft and calm. "Try to be still and pay attention."

"But I don't wanna do lessons, Mama," her six-year-old daughter complained. "I wanna play." She stared longingly at the nearby swing set, then looked at her small trampoline and wading pool, and fidgeted even more.

Their dog, Doodles, let out a sharp bark before charging toward a squirrel making its way across the edge of the backyard. Breea's eyes lit up as she watched the animals. Standing, she took a step toward them.

"Honey, sit down," Sylene told her.

"*Mama,*" Breea wailed. "I haven't gotten to play in *forever.*"

"You've played every single day."

"Not outside. You said I could when summer came. But you've been making me stay in. And you won't let me play now. That's not fair."

Sylene smiled and gently tousled her daughter's hair. "I didn't let you go out for a while because we were getting so much rain. Before that, it was too cold, and you could've gotten sick."

"It's not cold now," Breea accused. "It's *nice.*"

"Yes, today is very nice." Taking a deep breath, Sylene smelled the fragrance of the flowers blooming around their home. A gentle breeze rustled leaves on the nearby trees. Two blue jays squawked at one another, and a robin flew to the ground and began to peck at the dirt. Other birds soared overhead. Enjoying the lovely weather, Sylene had to admit she'd also love to skip lessons and go swimming at the lake less than a mile from their home. But she forced her attention back to Breea. "Sweetie, sit down and take a breath—nice and slow."

"I wanna play." Although she plunked down onto the ground, Breea sulked and gave her mother a dirty look.

Stifling her laughter, Sylene replied, "I know, but what I'm trying to teach you is important. It can be a lot of fun, too. When we're done, I thought we'd go to the lake and—."

Breea gasped. "It's *beautiful!*" Shooting to her feet, she ran after a butterfly which had flown by.

Hearing a muffled sound behind her, Sylene whirled to see her husband Lukar standing a few feet away. He tried unsuccessfully to stifle his chuckles behind his hand. She glared at him, but he only laughed harder.

"You're no help at all," she chided him. "Lessons are serious business."

"I know," he chortled. "Still, you have to admit this is funny."

"No, it's not." Her lips twitched.

"I saw that." Lukar nodded knowingly.

Sylene's eyes sparkled as she grinned at him. "I'm smiling because it's your turn now."

He frowned.

#

A few minutes later, Lukar explained, "Energy is everywhere. In the air around us, the ground, plants, trees. Inside us, too."

Breea giggled. That's when he realized she wasn't even paying attention to him. Instead, she watched a caterpillar crawling up her arm. After gently transferring the crawler to a bush, he looked hard at his daughter.

She blinked at him before studying the ground. "Sorry, Daddy."

He urged her to close her eyes, be still, and breathe slowly—the same way that Sylene had—but Breea only fidgeted. "Listen," he said. "What do you hear?" She shrugged, so he answered his own question. "That chattering sound is a squirrel, and I hear birds. Some insects are chirping—maybe crickets. And do you hear the tap-tap-tap in the woods?"

"That's a woodpecker," Breea replied.

"Yes. All kinds of animals are around us. They're probably enjoying this beautiful day just like we are. Now, I want you to think about how warm it is." When she looked at him as though he'd spoken a language she didn't know, he talked more about the temperature, but she claimed she didn't feel it. He wasn't sure what to think, because earlier she'd complained about being too hot. She'd changed from jeans into shorts for that very reason.

Lukar frowned but had no intentions of giving up. Briefly going into their home, he ran hot tap water into a large bowl, returned outside with it, and called his daughter away from her trampoline. "Do what I'm doing," he told her, ignoring her pout. He dipped his hand into the liquid he'd brought. She did, too, and they both held some in their cupped palms. She acknowledged it was warm, but within seconds her interest shifted to flicking droplets at him and Doodles. The whole point of the exercise was lost on her.

Sighing, Lukar exchanged a glance with his wife who'd quietly seated herself beside them, and he chose to try something different. Extending his hand palm-up, he produced flames there.

"The colors are pretty." Breea stared wide-eyed at them. Grabbing fallen, dried leaves which were close to where they sat, she begged him to burn them.

"All right. Make a small pile." He reasoned at least she'd have no trouble feeling the heat. However, instead of focusing on that, all she wanted to do was add more leaves to the flames. She grabbed a twig, stuck it into the fire until it caught flame, and began to jab things with it. He was barely able to prevent her from setting Doodles' fur on fire, after which she ran away after another butterfly.

"You did well," Sylene murmured. She rubbed Lukar's shoulders before hugging him. "I'm sure you tried everything you could think of. I did, too."

"Yeah, but we've done the same things for months and nothing's working." He rubbed his forehead. "She's not catching on. Since I have Fire and you have Fire and Air, I thought she'd at least have one of them."

"Some children take longer. You know that. And some don't have any magic. I hate to say it, but maybe she doesn't."

He bit his lip, then admitted, "I'm trying not to worry."

"Me, too. And I'm sure we'll think of something else."

#

The next day

"Mama! Daddy!" Breea yelled. "Look who's here."

Lukar and Sylene hurried in the direction of her voice and found her at the front door which she'd opened. There, they exchanged greetings with Bryndon and Mayelle, their friends from a nearby town. The couple, Water and Fire Masters, had brought their six-year-old son Marken with them. He'd begun his lessons almost a year earlier. After a slow start, he'd caught on, and continued to make good progress with both elements at which his parents excelled.

"We have a surprise for you, Breea," Sylene announced.

The adults began a magic demonstration in the back yard. First, they created small yellow, red, and orange sparks, then showers of them. They produced flames of the same colors, added blue, and made the flames rhythmically shrink and expand again and again. Materializing baseball-sized fireballs next, they tossed them back and forth, then made some the size of basketballs. They juggled them and sent long bursts of fire toward the sky.

Using air and fire, Lukar and Selene lifted one another off their feet. The other couple did the same thing with

water and fire. Their clothing remained untouched.
Bryndon and Mayelle made flames and waves dance, and
Marken joined in at the end of the demonstration, using fire
to create animals which floated through the air.

Breea, obviously delighted, clapped and laughed
throughout the "show." However, she made no attempt to
use magic herself.

Eventually, Sylene and Mayelle went indoors to prepare
a meal, while Lukar and Bryndon remained outside to
watch the children.

#

"Ooh," Breea murmured, staring at a bright green bug
crawling on the ground. "You're pretty."

Marken ran over to join her, looked at the creature, and
smashed it with his foot.

"No!" Breea wailed. Shoving him away, she examined
the insect. "It's not moving now," she accused.

"So?" Marken shrugged. "It's nothing but a stupid old
bug. I'm glad it's dead." He walked away without a
backward glance.

Breea glared at his back and her face began to darken.
Tiny sparks appeared in her eyes. A faint glow came from
her palms. Small flames appeared and danced across their
surface before her hands were enveloped in flames. Eyes
widening, Breea studied them, giggled, and ran after
Marken.

#

Lukar, who'd dozed off in a chair, opened his eyes when something poked his shoulder. "What?" he mumbled.

Bryndon poked him again. "You didn't try anger with Breea, did you?" he asked.

"Huh?"

"Look at your daughter."

Once Lukar did, he grinned widely. "It's about time."

The men studied the grass and leaves burning on the ground. More caught fire as Breea ran over them.

Lukar waved his hand, and the flames went out. "Not bad," he commented as she threw a handful of flames at Marken. The boy stepped out of their way, but they hit a plant and it caught fire. Marken doused it with water he produced.

Breea screeched, stomped her foot, and glared at the boy. Small fireballs shot from her eyes, hitting a tree beside him.

"Wow!" Bryndon commented. "She's got a temper." He extinguished the fire licking at the trunk of the tree with a snap of his fingers. When flames appeared on the top of Breea's head, he chuckled.

Lukar laughed so hard he couldn't even speak.

"What's so funny?" Sylene asked as she came out their back door holding platters of food. But she dropped the food when she saw Breea knock Marken off his feet with a surge of fire.

Mayelle froze beside Sylene and stared open-mouthed at the children. "Idiots!" she snapped at the men. "They could hurt each other." She gasped and her face went pale as Marken engulfed Breea in towering flames.

But Breea walked right out of the fire unscathed. Her entire body flamed now, not just her hands and head.

445

Gabriella Balcom

"We don't need to wonder if she has magic anymore," Lukar murmured. Grinning at his wife, he put his arm around her waist and pulled her tightly against him.

Sylene sighed. Then she snickered.

The End

THE WORLD OF MYTH

MAGAZINE

ISSUE

99

AUGUST 2021

Josh Poole

25-year-old working-class hero writing his way through the pandemic. I make visual art out of soda cans, cartoon for a variety of newspapers and magazines, and have been writing short stories and poetry for a few years now.

A Fight Amongst the Ruin
By: Josh Poole

HOW THE HELL did I use up my missiles? Ryder Farley
shook his head, and the giant mech that he was inside
mirrored his frustration. The robot stood in the rubble of a
city long ruined by war, its foot planted in a school bus like
it was a slipper. Only blocks away, another Gundam, one
that was much bulkier than his own with an enormous
shoulder-mounted cannon lined up its shot. His entire
squad had been slain, leaving only him to continue the
good fight.

"Oh hell, it's a goddamn Tyger-III," Ryder's eyes
widened as he crossed his arms, activating the deployable
shield that would retract into the mech's forearms.

The shield fell, a fifteen-ton curtain of titanium, carbon
nanotube, and ceramic composites built to withstand
anything up to a 355mm armor-piercing round. What
Ryder knew, however, with only a brief glance, was that the

shoulder-mounted cannon currently eyeing him from a few streets down was a 501mm bunker killer, a weapon that could not only remove mountaintop bases, but remove the mountains themselves.

Ryder's mech hid entirely behind the shield as he waited. There was a flash of light across the HUD, but he felt no impact.

Systems critical! The kind, female voice of the mech's systems informed.

"I didn't feel impact! Negative impact!" Ryder yelled back at the computer.

Reactor compromised. Resorting to auxiliary power cell. Auxiliary power cell at 77%, approximately seven minutes remaining in current combat engagement.

Ryder looked at the HUD and realized in an instant the damage he'd just taken. There was a 501mm pinhole through the shield and a hole the size of a train through his mech's torso, right in the vitals.

That's no good. He thought, retracting the shield quickly into the mech's forearms only to see that other mech barreling towards him. He shifted his feet, knowing if he tried to brace and survive the blow that the compromised mid-section would fail and the mech would fall into a crumpled heap to be stomp-terminated. The Tyger lowered its shoulder, preparing to bulldoze Ryder into the pavement with its heavier build. A second before impact, however, Ryder rolled out of the way, slamming into a nearby building as the other mech tried to slow itself down.

"You're big, but you aren't fast!" Ryder yelled as he whipped an arm around and actuated the internal weaponry.

The mech's fist broke into several smaller pieces, forming a muzzle-brake with its digits before an enormous bombard fired from within the arm. A projectile the size of car lobbed through the air no faster than a thrown football, its warhead making contact just as the larger mech finished turning around to engage. The explosion obscured Ryder's vision with a flash of instant rubble, and pushed his own mech deeper into the building until pieces of the structure hung over the mech itself. He lowered his arm, exhausted after three days of constant combat in the city, and exhaled.

Warning! The computer managed only the one word before a giant fist smashed into the face of Ryder's mech.

"Shit!" He yelled; his body flung all around the inside as the safety mechanisms struggled to distribute the G-forces in a way that wouldn't turn his organs into pudding.

He crossed his arms, deploying the shield in the middle of the melee just as the Tyger was throwing a body shot with a hook. The curtain dropped down, slicing right through the other mech's arm at the wrist, severing its hand like a guillotine. Ryder retracted the shield, anticipating that the Tyger would take a step back to regroup. The other mech, however, had other ideas.

The severed hand crawled up the leg of Ryder's mech while, with its intact hand, his foe palmed his face with a crunching sound that surrounded the cockpit. The hand locked against his leg exploded, blowing out his mech's knee as the other mech slammed Ryder down face-first into the rubble.

"Damn outmode," Ryder groaned, staring at the rubble his mech's head was buried in.

There was a heavy pressure from behind as the other

mech stomped the back of Ryder's head. Rather than panic, however, Ryder simply laughed, activating the transport thrusters on the back of his mech and blasting nearly four million pounds of directed thrust into the air. The force buried his own mech deeper into the rubble, but blasted off the entirety of the Tyger's damaged arm and shoulder-cannon along with disintegrating the upper half of a nearby building.

Ryder rolled his mech over, just in time to look up as the Tyger swung down with a heavy fist than forced its way into the gaping hole in his mech's abdomen.

"Activate the reactor at full capacity!" Ryder yelled.

Reactor is compro—

"Activate it!" Ryder yelled again as he grabbed the Tyger's arm by the wrist.

The computer obliged, activating the reactor for only an instant. There was a huge flash at Ryder's mech's abdomen, a small-scale uncontrolled nuclear reaction before the systems redirected everything back to auxiliary to avoid a complete meltdown of the core. The Tyger pulled its arm out, ripping itself from Ryder's grip with no more than a molten nub for a hand.

Ryder sprung to his feet, his mech following suit in a slower shadowing of his own movements. The Tyger took several steps back and regrouped. Ryder looked at the disabled shoulder-cannon and at the Tyger's ruined hands, feeling his confidence return. The bombard round had done a number on the other mech as well, with a giant black stain of damaged armor and internals covering most of the mech's torso and shoulder. Ryder motioned as if he were unsheathing a sword from his hip, and the sheets of metal

454

that had made the shield slid out of his mech's arm and formed a rigid, single-edged sword complete with a large handle. The Tyger took another step back, firing out countless flares that filled the street with dense smoke.

"Oh no you don't!" Ryder yelled as he charged into the unknown, gripping the sword with both hands and swinging wildly through the ether.

He didn't make contact with any of the swings, and he could see nothing. He paused, listening intently to his surroundings, trying to catch the movements of the enormous Tyger. In an instant, however, the Tyger emerged from behind him and wrapped him up in its lumbering arms. The force began crushing Ryder's mech at the chest, compressing the armor plates and breaking the dense outermost layer of ceramic composite.

"Wrong move," Ryder smirked, spinning the sword around, and plunging it through the hole in his own mech's abdomen until the blade shot through the Tyger.

He released the sword, pulling his mech away from the Tyger. Without the added weight of the shield, his mech was faster than ever. Ryder spun around, swinging a heavy hook into the sword, spinning it around inside the Tyger and slicing through an entire half of the mech's torso before the blade clattered to the ground.

"80% thrust to the right foot!" Ryder yelled, and his mech suddenly shot into the air with a flying knee that landed squarely in the Tyger's chest.

He could sense the damage he'd dealt, feeling the force of the impact even as his own mech stabilized the blow for him. The Tyger stumbled backwards, falling to the ground as Ryder's mech fell from the air and landed awkwardly beside it. Ryder smiled, activating the bombard again and pointing it directly at the Tyger as it sprawled helplessly in the rubble.

"Good fight," Ryder said, and fired the weapon.

The instant he did, however, the Tyger swung its melted stump through the muzzle-brake and into Ryder's mech's forearm.

"No, no, no!" Ryder shrieked, but it was too late, the bombard fired, and the explosion blew his mech completely through a nearby skyscraper.

Ryder blacked out for an instant, his mech unable to compensate for the immense G-forces from the blast. He came to a few seconds later with fireworks in his vision and a headache from hell. He was concussed, the last thing he wanted to be in the middle of combat. He staggered to his feet, his shifting vision trying to make out the large hole that he'd just made through the building and the sauntering figure that approached him from within.

"Gun volley," Ryder mumbled, barely able to stand and feeling nauseous.

The armor around his mech's collar opened up to reveal dozens of 30mm chain guns, and the row of weapons began to thunder with hundreds of rounds firing over mere seconds. The small rounds would do little to the armor of a Tyger, but focused on the exposed mid-section, Ryder could damage it further or bifurcate the thing entirely.

The Tyger, however, quickly covered its wounds with its remaining arm, allowing the limb to absorb the bulk of the damage, and continued its approach.

"Alright," Ryder swayed in the cockpit, realizing that his mech was also missing a right arm, the same as the Tyger,

456

"we're even now."

The Tyger swung with a heavy hook, but Ryder ducked it awkwardly before firing a swift jab into its abdomen that swept out a rain of internals. The foe adjusted, swinging back with an elbow that just barely missed Ryder's mech. It left its body open again, and Ryder fired another jab into the same area, taking more internals out and sending the Tyger stumbling backwards.

His opponent kept pressure on their abdomen, trying to prevent any further leaking of its internals. Ryder diagnosed their predicament, a mech without any ammo, running its huge mass on auxiliary power, with one arm that has to constantly hold its battered stomach. It was, Ryder thought, more or less a sitting duck.

Ryder pressed forth, rushing towards the Tyger with a cocked arm ready to deliver a crippling blow. Before he could land it, however, the Tyger ducked, sending its shoulder into Ryder's stomach, and flinging his mech through the air in a somersault. He crashed hard on his back; his brain felt like it had been smacked around inside his skull. The Tyger slowly turned, unable to move quickly and risk furthering the damage it had sustained. It raised its leg, preparing to stomp Ryder into oblivion. Ryder attempted to raise the mech, but was only able to move the head into a vertical position.

Before stomping, however, the Tyger staggered, and collapsed to the ground in a boisterous fall.

"Out of juice," Ryder laughed before realized that he, too, was out of auxiliary power.

He stripped himself away from the mechanical harness, feeling the bruises that had accumulated all over his body in the past few days. His pilot's suit was bulky, covered in armor plating designed to protect his body against the jarring movements of combat and to provide some protection against small arms and bladed weapons. The cockpit was open, with equipment sparking all around him. Once out of the harness, he staggered to a small compartment in the wall and removed the standard issue assault rifle along with three spare magazines of ammo. With the rifle slung over his shoulder, he climbed up a ladder, and opened the escape hatch before emerging from the mech.

Ryder stood with his feet still on the ladder, using the head of his mech as a brace to scan the fallen Tyger with his riflescope. There were no signs of life, but he knew the other pilot had the same idea as him, to get into a defensible position and hope they made the first lucky shot. Ryder continued to scan the Tyger as a light wind blew through the stress, carrying with it the dust and debris from their battle. He struggled to focus, his brain firing on compromised cylinders and his vision filled with polychromatic flashes.

The was a sudden hum that turned into a loud buzz before a crisp, metallic crack sounded right next to him followed by the buzz of a ricocheting bullet. He scanned his scope, knowing that he'd have only an instant before his enemy corrected for the wind and range. At last, he found the silhouetted, perched on the chest of the Tyger.

Dammit, I forgot the location of the cockpit! Ryder thought as he took aim and fired a volley towards the figure from a football field's distance. The figure hid behind a section of peeled armor, which provided more than ample protection against the small projectiles. Ryder continued firing in the direction as he mantled the rest of the ladder and took cover behind a large chunk of concrete rubble that clung to his mech's head.

The enemy continued their volley, placing shots consistently against the concrete cover as Ryder reloaded his weapon. With a shove, he pushed the bolt of his rifle forward and took aim again at the pilot, spraying an imprecise volley at the piece of cover before ducking behind his own. He worked up the courage to spray again, mounting the concrete to get a good rest and sending a few rounds towards the hidden pilot. Ryder ducked again, counting the number of rounds he had left.

47. He thought, wondering if his best option wasn't to simply scurry off his mech and flee into the surrounding city with the hopes of an evacuation when reinforcements arrived for the next wave. He held his rifle close to his chest, trying to shake off the effects of the concussion. With heavy breathing, he twisted back around and mounted the block again, scanning the Tyger for the pilot.

When several minutes had elapsed, it was apparent to him that the other pilot had had the same idea, to flee into the city and wait to be evacuated when more of their own units arrived. Ryder turned back around, settling with the gun in his lap and a weary look on his face. He soon fell asleep, his first break from the exhaustion of combat in three days.

#

"I'll take that," a woman's voice stirred him. Ryder woke up to find that his rifle was gone, scooped up by a woman wearing a pilot's uniform similar to his own in all aspects but color.

Ryder said nothing for a moment, realizing that he was completely helpless.

"Why do you fight?" The pilot asked, her weapon trained on Ryder's head.

"I was drafted when I was five years old, trained to pilot a mech, THIS mech."

"What do you fight for?" She asked, sounding irritated.

"I fight to protect the citizens of Ark from you Osiris invaders," Ryder said, disgust in his voice.

"Strange," the pilot lowered the gun, a look of confusion on her face that quickly morphed into a look of reticent understanding, "I was trained from the age of five, and told that I was to defend the citizens of Osiris from the Ark invasion."

"And?" Ryder asked.

"This city. I'd never heard of it until I deployed here. I'd never heard of anything but you, you Ark soldiers, how you were savages, deserters, terrorists."

"That's not true!" Ryder hissed, "I swore an oath when I was a child to defend the citizens of Ark! To defend it from you savages and—" Ryder stopped, realizing he was merely illustrating the pilot's statement.

"The war isn't real," she said, "but why? What is this for?" She turned her back to Ryder, who did nothing but slump further against the concrete slab. In the distance, dozens of mechs from both factions deployed from the air in the distance, slowly descending to the surface to continue the war.

"We're entertainment," the pilot laughed, "everything is surveilled. Our cockpits record everything, we're gladiators."

Ryder bit his tongue, wishing to chastise her for such a ridiculous idea, but having no counter-argument of his own he replied, "so what do we do?"

"Well," the pilot turned back around to look at him, "our mechs are shot, we've got no way of contacting the others, and I'm out of ammo." She tossed her gun off the head of the mech.

"I've got ammo in my rifle, but it won't do us any good with those mechs coming in. They'll kill us both." Ryder laughed.

"Yeah, probably." The pilot laughed with him.

"What a life," Ryder muttered as the mechs started fighting all around them.

THE END

THE WORLD OF MYTH

MAGAZINE

ISSUE

100

SEPTEMBER 2021

Linda M. Sauve

An avid reader from a young age, Linda developed an addiction to books in her childhood that has intensified into an obsession that is getting more expensive by the day. Although she had been writing for some time, prior to publishing as "L. M. Mercer" her work had not been viewed by the public at large. Linda had mainly used (and still does use) writing as a release for life's stressful times (never intending for others to read her poems) , but she eventually allowed herself to be badgered into submitting some pieces by friend and coworker, Kevin Magnus, who told her to "Stop wasting your talent." She did finally admit to him that she is very grateful for his badgering.

Linda is returning to *The World of Myth* after years of consistent encouragement (pestering) from good friend, David K. Montoya. While making no guarantees on the frequency with which she will be able to submit pieces, Linda has decided to end her hiatus and return to *The World of Myth*.

465

A Hotel California Night
By: Linda M. Sauve

Part One

ANASTASIA CONNER ROLLED the driver-side window down all the way and delighted in the cool breeze that entered the car as they sped down the deserted desert highway. Although it was minutes before midnight, it was still ninety degrees outside, and her brother's very old car had no functioning air conditioning. At least the wind created by the vehicle as it sliced through the night circulated the air within and blew away some of the smell of marijuana and alcohol that wafted forward from the back seat. The stench had been lingering in the smothering air for the last hundred miles since her brother had decided he had to light up, yet again.

Looking into the rearview mirror, Ana focused on her brother's reflection and shook her head. She had been

Linda M. Sauve

bailing Nicholas out of trouble for as long as she could remember and this time, like so many times before, she swore was the last. Lifting her long ebony braid off the back of her neck with one hand to allow the air to cool her warm skin, she glanced at her brother in the mirror again. "Unbelievable," she thought with disdain. "Here he is, on his way to court-appointed rehabilitation in the Mojave Desert—rehab that *I* managed to fast-talk the judge into ordering, and he's passed out, drunk on tequila, and stoned out of his mind. Leaving me to drive through the night to get him to the rehabilitation center—an out in the middle of nowhere rehabilitation center—by the court-ordered date. Un-freaking-believable!"

Facing a long, lonely night behind the wheel, Ana flicked the dial turning on the car's radio, and started searching for a station but found only static. After a few unsuccessful minutes, she bounced her palm off the steering wheel and turned off the radio, resolved to spend the night in silence. "Damn him, anyway," she thought angrily, "the least Nicholas could have done was stay awake, let alone remain sober."

#

Ana drove on through the empty Southern California desert, the long hours passing without seeing another living soul. The monotony of the scenery and the gentle humming of the tires on asphalt were just lulling her to sleep, her head slowly dropping to her chest, when the engine began to sputter and knock.

Instantly awake, Ana's eyes frantically searched the
468

instrument panel, trying to determine the trouble. After a few moments, the noises from the engine ceased—as did the engine itself—and the car began to slow down, coasting to a stop at the top of a hill. Glancing at the useless and dark idiot lights again, she was unable to figure out what was wrong with the engine. Then Ana looked out the windshield and noticed some lights up ahead in the distance.

Not wanting to sleep the rest of the night in the car and walk the desert road during the hot part of the day, Ana released her seatbelt, turned on the dome light, and turned to face her drooling brother.

"Nich," she said softly, not wanting to startle him. "Nich. Wake up." When her brother didn't even grumble or twitch, she yelled, her voice echoing in the small car, "Nicholas, you horse's ass, WAKE UP!" Receiving only a sigh and a change of position in response, the usually even-tempered woman began to get upset. Looking around the front seat, she chuckled when her eyes came to rest on a half-full bottle of water. Grabbing the plastic container, Anna removed the lid, thankful she had purchased the wide-mouth bottle, and leaning over the back seat, yelled, "WAKE UP, NICHOLAS, DAMN YOU!" as she upended the bottle, pouring the warm liquid on his face.

Nicholas sat up suddenly, sputtering and spitting water out of his mouth, "Hey, what the fu…"

"Don't even say it," Ana cut off his tirade mid-word, raising her hand and pointing her index finger at her younger brother. "Say it, and I swear, I'll leave your ass sitting here, all alone in the middle of nowhere, with a warrant out for your arrest for failing to appear for your

469

rehab."

"Geez, Ana, chill," Nicholas began, climbing into the front passenger seat. "What the hell did you wake me up for?" he inquired and looked out the window. "And why did you stop here?"

"I didn't stop," Ana said, opening the driver's door and leaning out into the cooler night air. "Your damn twenty-six-year-old P.O.S. did."

He pushed in the cigarette lighter and tapped a cigarette from a crumpled pack he had pulled from his jean pocket before saying, "It's probably out of gas."

Nicholas was shifting the cigarette from the left side of his mouth to the right and back, waiting for the lighter to pop. Anastasia said, "No, I already checked that; the gauge is on 'Full.' Guess again."

He lit the cigarette and took a long drag, then, leaning back against the headrest, said, "It's busted. The damn thing *always* shows the tank as full." Smoke puffed from his mouth as he spoke.

Ana turned her head to stare at her brother in disbelief. "And you didn't think that was something I needed to know BEFORE we started this little road trip?" Without another word, she grabbed her shoulder bag from the dashboard, got out of the car, slammed the door, and started walking toward the lights, hoping to find people and a phone there.

Staggering out of the car, Nicholas jogged a few steps to catch up. "So, where are we going?"

She pointed her finger at the vague outline of a building, barely visible on the graying horizon. "I don't know where you're going, but *I'm* going there. Maybe they have a phone

I could use, or maybe someone there wouldn't mind giving me a ride into town."

The pair walked in silence for a few minutes before Nicholas began complaining about everything: from the cops that arrested him for the use of a controlled substance and the judge at his trial to the rising temperature as the sky began to lighten on the horizon. Unable to stand listening to him another moment, Ana sped up and was soon walking half a dozen steps ahead of him and could no longer hear his endless ranting.

A short time later, as Anastasia was passing through an open gate in a large stone wall, Nicholas caught back up to her and as the sun rose over the horizon and told her, "Let me do all the talking, sis."

Ana continued walking without saying anything, and upon reaching the oak doors of a large Spanish Mission-style home, she waved her hand toward the entrance and said, "After you."

Nicholas knocked on the iron-studded oak as the first yellow rays of light shone into the desert valley, and a large silver bell in the tower above them began to ring. The siblings were looking around at the stark landscaping when the door opened silently behind them.

"Can I help you?" a voice whispered from the darkened interior. The raspy voice startled Ana, and sucking in a gasping breath, she turned towards the door, grabbing at her heart and expecting to see someone standing behind them. Nich and Ana stared into the darkness for a few moments before hearing the same whispery voice say a little louder, "Can I be of assistance?"

Ana looked at her brother expectantly and nodded her

471

head toward the open door. Instead of speaking up, he just shook his head and jerked his head toward the door himself. With a weary sigh, she said, "Sorry to bother you so early, sir."

"It's not too early," the response came from within. "In truth, it is actually rather late for us," he chuckled. "We are creatures of the night around here."

Puzzled by the man's words, her eyes nervously searching the dark interior for the voice's source, Ana continued. "Our car broke down up the road, and we were wondering if we could use your phone to call for a tow truck."

"That is for the master to decide. Please, come in."

When they just stood there on the threshold, the voice came again, more insistently, "Please, come in."

Nicholas strode in without a backward glance. Anastasia was not as confident, and looking around once more, she took in the complete solitude of their isolated location. Turning back to the house, she heard the same whispery voice say, "Miss?" Without answering, she slowly took a step and crossed into the cool interior of the house.

They stood in the large foyer, their eyes adjusting to the dimness when the door closed behind them with a ring of finality. Ana and Nich started at the sound, then turned to face an old man standing by the door, previously hidden in the shadows. Looking at the man's appearance, Ana's fear was replaced with concern for the frail little man. Even in the minimal light, she was able to see the emaciated man's pale skin was thin as an onion's, while bruises in various stages of healing were speckled across the translucent flesh. His cloudy white, unseeing eyes staring straight through her, the man limped his way around the siblings and began shuffling down the hallway. "This way, please," he said softly over his shoulder.

Following him down a long windowless hallway, Ana said, "I apologize for our intrusion."

Turning his head slightly to the left, permitting his voice to drift back down the hall, the old man told her, "No trouble at all, my dear. We so rarely have guests here."

They came to a closed door at the end of the corridor, where the elderly man knocked and opened the door a few inches, then announced, "You have visitors, Master."

From deep within the room came the muffled reply, "Show our guests in, Jennings."

The servant opened the door and stepping away from the opening, then executed an awkwardly shaking bow and said, "After you."

Nicholas swaggered through in his usual arrogant nature, ignoring the small man holding the door open, while Anastasia paused at the door for a moment to smile at the old man and whisper, "Thank you, Mr. Jennings, for your help this morning." Once the pair was within the room, Jennings pulled the door closed, and they were left facing a seemingly empty room.

Ana looked around the candlelit room, taking in an impressive array of museum-quality furniture, while the surrounding walls were lined from floor to ceiling with a startling collection of books. Hearing someone clear their throat, she fixed her eyes on the outline of a man sitting behind a huge oak desk at the far end of the room. He was leaning back in a large leather wing-back chair, his hands steepled before him.

"Please, do come in," a deep voice called from the shadows. The honeyed tone seemed to echo in her mind, caressing its inner reaches and caused a shiver to run down Ana's spine, instantly putting her nerves on edge as her senses became acutely aware of the mysterious stranger. Slowly they began walking forward, carefully navigating around the chairs and small tables, which were topped with dark reading lamps. When the siblings were standing a few feet before the desk and Ana could just see his icy blue eyes watching them, the man asked, "To what do I owe this," he paused as his gaze raked over Ana's form, "pleasant surprise?"

Although she was still unnerved by the man sitting partially hidden in the shadows created by the heavy, burgundy velvet curtains and the wings of his chair, and sensing that her brother would not be speaking, Ana said, "I apologize for the intrusion so early this morning. I'm Anastasia Conner, and this is my brother, Nicholas."

"Anastasia," the man whispered, his eastern European accent turning her name into a caress. "It is a pleasure to make your acquaintance," he continued his deep, husky voice hinting of forbidden secrets. Then, as if added as an afterthought, he said, "Nicholas, likewise a joy."

Ana's jaw dropped slightly at the intimate way their host spoke her name, and she stared at him bewildered for a moment. When her brother turned to her and raised an eyebrow at her pause, she quickly stated their reason for appearing, unannounced, in his home, "Our car..." she began, but suddenly nervous under the man's intense observation, her voice faded off, and she began fidgeting like a small child on public display.

Seeming to notice her unease, the man rose from his seat and stood behind the desk, his hands resting gently on its smooth surface. Lifting his left hand to indicate the two smaller chairs positioned before him, he said, "You must be exhausted from walking. Please, have a seat."

Part Two

Before Ana could politely decline the offer, her brother strode forward and swung his leg over the back of a chair, a cloud of dust rising into the air off his tattered jeans. "Don't mind if I do," Nich stated as he slid down into the seat and propped his feet atop the desk, ankles crossed, dirt falling off his sneakers. "My feet are beat."

Seeing no other course of action left, especially after her brother's behavior, Ana moved slowly forward and carefully sat down in the other chair but remained perched on the edge of her seat. Leaning over slightly, she pinched a chunk of Nich's flesh through a hole in his jeans and twisted savagely.

Instantly his feet fell to the floor, landing with a thud, as he turned toward his sister and asked in a hoarse whisper, "What the hell was that for?"

Even more, mortified than she was moments before, Ana ignored her brother and, bravely meeting an icy blue stare, said, "Please excuse my brother's complete lack of manners this morning. He is not usually this rude."

Once more, taking his seat, the man smiled when he spoke to her. "There is nothing for you to apologize for, my dear. It was your brother's transgression, not your own."

Unaware that he had just been insulted, Nicholas started

picking at a hole in his pants and said, "Since it doesn't appear my sister is going to get to the point any time soon. Ana here," he jerked his thumb at her face, "ran the car out of gas a couple of miles up the road." Catching her angry glare out the corner of his eye, he whispered to her, "Well, you did," before continuing for their host, "So we were hoping that you had a phone we could use to call for a tow." When the other man just sat in his chair and continued to stare intently at Ana, Nich became bolder and asked, "Well, do you?"

The man tore his gaze away from her, as if it caused him great pain to do so and looked at Nich. Under the man's stare, Ana's brother began to sit up straight and seemed to suddenly become aware of his disheveled appearance. "Unfortunately, the house phone is not functioning and will not be repaired until later this evening." Seeing Nicholas open his mouth as if to speak again, their host continued, "And one of the servants took my car into town to visit with an ailing family member and restock the cupboards and will not return until tomorrow morning."

Leaning forward to stand, Ana, tapped her brother's arm and said, "Come on, Nicholas, we really shouldn't take any more of this nice gentleman's time; we have taken enough already."

"Do you expect me to walk all damn day?" her brother whined, disgust over the impending physical activity oozing off his words.

"Nicho…" Ana began to reprimand him when their host raised his hand, interrupting her.

"Please," he said as he stood up from his chair. "Do not consider walking through this desert in the heat of the day."

Moving around the side of the desk, he added, "You wouldn't even make it three miles, and the nearest town is over ten miles away. Devil's Valley may not be as hot as Death Valley, but it has four times more deaths per year." Smiling, he reached up and pulled a tasseled satin rope hanging from the ceiling. "Please, I insist that you remain here today and rest. Then after dinner, we can try to fix your car problems."

"Oh no," Ana said quickly, "We couldn't possibly impose on your generosity."

Stepping forward, he extended his hand to her, offering to assist her up. "Anastasia, my dear, you are so tired you can barely keep your beautiful eyes open."

Rising from the chair with his assistance, Ana was just beginning to stutter out a response when the door behind them opened.

Glancing at the door for an instant, their host said, "Ah, ladies," before returning his eyes to Ana. "Please show Nicholas to a *room* and make sure he is comfortable." Unable to resist, Ana looked over her shoulder and gasped when she saw two of the most exotically beautiful women, she had ever seen enter the room.

The two women moved to stand on either side of Nicholas, their flawless bodies barely concealed by sheer clothing. Looking like proverbial genies escaped from a bejeweled jar, they knelt down, bowed their heads, and waited to be introduced. Positioned on Nicholas' left, slits in her blood-red pants showing her olive skin from ankle to hip, her large breasts barely hidden behind cascading waves of ebony hair, Giovanna rose when her name was spoken. On his right rose the heavenly Angelica, her blonde

477

curls piled high atop her head revealing the silk toga she wore, made of the palest blue imaginable and held in place by a silver brooch on one shoulder, while silver cords tied beneath her breast. Once introduced, the women quickly grasped Nich's hands and began trying to pull him out of the chair.

Smiling foolishly, he allowed the women to help him up and lead him toward the door. As he left the study, Nicholas called over his shoulder, "I don't know about you, sis, but I'm not leaving."

Suddenly left alone with the mysterious man and becoming increasingly aware of his nearness, Ana muttered, "Thank you for allowing us to rest in your home." She blushed when he lifted her hand to his lips and gently kissed her knuckles.

"Think nothing of it, my dear. It is the least I could offer." Her nervousness was apparent; he let her hand slip from his grasp and waved toward the door. Trying to put her at ease, he spoke gently, "Please allow me to show you to your room. After you."

Ana had taken a few steps toward the door before she stopped and, with a weak chuckle, said, "I don't know anything about you. You could be some psycho killer, planning to murder me in my sleep, and I wouldn't know it. I don't even know your name."

"Gabriel," was his response as he joined her and showed her from the room.

As the pair left the study, Gabriel said to her in a voice so quiet and seductive, for an instant, it was as if the words were spoken in her mind, "You have nothing to fear in my home, Anastasia. You are my guest, and no harm will come to you while you sleep."

They moved in silence down the same hallway she had recently traveled. They had almost reached the front door when Gabriel turned and guided her through a doorway that opened into an exposed courtyard. Careful to remain in the shadows created by the balcony of a second floor, he led Ana toward a set of stairs. Gently cupping her elbow in his hand to steady her, he guided her up the stairs and, upon reaching the top, slid his hand down to rest lightly on the small of her back. Using this one point of contact to direct her, Gabriel showed Ana to a door at the end of the hall, where he turned her to face him.

"This will be your room while you stay here. Please make yourself at home," he said softly.

"Thank you," Ana whispered, unable to take her eyes off his face. She watched as his eyes roamed her own face, and the instant their eyes met, she was unable to look away. Ana felt herself being pulled forward into their icy depths, a sense of peace and calm closing in on her.

Tentatively she reached forward and rested her hand on his arm to steady herself as the hallway spun around her, and she remained unable to break eye contact with Gabriel. Her eyelids drifted downward as he moved closer and lowered his lips to hers. Gently he applied pressure until slowly she parted her lips and allowed his probing tongue entrance. Responding on instinct alone, she followed his lead and began exploring his mouth with her tongue, finding the sweet taste intoxicating. She heard a moan of pleasure and was startled to realize it was her own.

Lifting his lips from hers, he stared down at her upturned face. Slowly his hands trailed up along her rib cage and traced the underside of her breasts to the center of her chest. His fingers deftly loosened the first few buttons of her blouse.

Suddenly nervous with him, her hand moved to the top of her shirt, holding it closed, and her eyes flew open, her uncertainty clearly visible with their sparkling depths. She quietly uttered a single word, "Don't."

Leaning down, he whispered huskily in her ear, "Trust me."

When her hand loosened and fell back to her side, he kissed the tender pulse point behind her ear. Feeling her relax against the wall, he slowly began trailing kisses down the length of her slender neck. Reaching the base of her neck, he playfully nipped the muscle at the start of her shoulder. He paused and inhaled her scent deeply when a shiver of delight ran through her body.

After a few moments, he continued his journey, placing kisses along her smooth flesh in a path following the curve of her shoulders. Reaching her bra strap, he slowly slid his silky wet tongue into the hollow along the ridge of her collar bone and thus maneuvered it beneath the elastic strap. Softly he caressed the sensitive skin beneath the strap with his tongue, enjoying the slightly salty taste of her skin beneath its sheen of excitement.

Her sigh of pleasure caught his attention, and he began retracing the trail of kisses he had traveled across her flesh, only this time he drew his moist tongue along her flesh and stopped when he reached the tender underside of her jaw. He placed tiny nipping kisses along the underside of her jaw from one ear to the other. Then he slowly pulled her ear lobe into his mouth, gently sucking on it and teasing the sensitive area behind it with the tip of his tongue.

When she moaned and began to slide down the wall, he stepped closer to her, trapping her fully between his body and the wall. Effortlessly supporting her weight with the pressure of his embrace, he began trailing kisses down this shoulder, the silk of her shirt caressing his cheek as he pushed it out the way as he went. Reaching that side's bra strap, he again slid his tongue beneath to tease the tender flesh beneath.

After a few moments, a whimper escaped her lips, and hearing a tone of emotional pain laced beneath the pleasure, he ceased his caress and lifted his face from her skin to look down at her. When he saw a single tear form in the corner of her eye, then spill out to roll down her cheek, he slowly pulled her shirt together and, using his hands at her elbows to support her, stepped back. When he was sure she would no longer fall without his assistance, he released her and dropped his hands to his sides.

With a sigh, Ana opened her eyes and noticed they were just walking the last steps to her door. Puzzled, she looked up at him.

Lifting his hand from the small of her back, Gabriel said, "Dinner is at nine." Then he turned and walked away, leaving her confused, standing next to the door of her room.

Feeling silly and contributing the vivid daydream to lack of sleep, she opened the door and entered the room, closing the door behind her. Hearing an odd series of clicks after the door shut, she turned the knob and tried to open the door again but found it had locked behind her. Ana stood there for a few minutes, trying to get it open before becoming resolved that it would not be opening from the

481

inside. A little unnerved by being locked in, she rubbed her arms to ward off a sudden chill she inexplicably felt. After she thought about it for a moment, Ana decided that Gabriel only wanted her to have an undisturbed sleep and most likely merely locked the door for her own security and a more peaceful rest. At least, she hoped that's all it was.

Ana decided to explore the room, and she trailed her hand down the soft, thin draperies surrounding the queen-sized bed, centered on a raised dais. Moving slowly around the bed, she found a fully stocked walk-in closet complete with a lovely oak vanity. Ana left the closet to continue her exploration and soon found herself standing in a bathroom fit for royalty. A shell-shaped whirlpool tub took up an entire corner with shelves of blooming plants separating it from the glass-walled shower.

Ana turned on the water in the shower and adjusted the temperature, then began taking off her clothes as she closed the bathroom door to contain the steam. Locking the door, she noticed a fluffy white terry cloth robe hanging from a hook behind it. She rubbed the material between her fingers and said to herself, "Wow, they thought of everything."

Part Three

Forty minutes later, Anastasia emerged from the bathroom amid a cloud of steam, a towel draped around her shoulders and a comb in her hand. She moved to sit on the bed and was just pulling the comb through her damp hair when a loud noise came from the hall outside her room. Ana dropped the comb on the bed and went to the door, where she listened closely, trying to determine what was going on in the hallway and courtyard outside her room.

She stood beside the door; she pressed her ear to the wood but then jumped back when she heard what sounded like savage animals violently fighting right on the other side of the door. Frightened by the vicious sounds, Ana looked around quickly, searching for something to prop against the door. Thankful now that her door was securely locked, she remembered seeing a small chair in front of the vanity and rushed into the closet to grab it. She was just returning to the bedroom when the door shook within its frame as if something were ramming against it, and then the handle turned slightly, stopping when it reached the locking mechanism. Ana quickly wedged the chair beneath the doorknob and took a few steps backward, feeling a little more protected. The doorknob stopped turning, and eventually, the noises seemed to fade away.

Shaken and still frightened, she climbed into the bed and pulled the satin covers up to her chin, then lay there staring at the door, waiting for the knob to turn again. Sometime later, exhaustion overpowered fear, and Ana began drifting off to sleep. Just as her lids were slowly lowering, Gabriel's accented voice echoed through her mind, "You have nothing to fear in my home, Anastasia. You are my guest, and no harm will come to you while you sleep."

#

Anastasia awoke when she felt the mattress give next to her. Opening her eyes, she gasped when she saw Giovanna and Angelica climbing into the bed on either side of her. Anastasia tried to push the covers back and get out of bed

483

but was unable to move more than an inch. When she started to open her mouth to protest this intrusion, Angelica laid a single finger against her lips and leaned forward, and whispered, "Relax, Anastasia, we're not really here. This is all a dream. Allow yourself to feel."

Slowly Giovanna skimmed her hand down Ana's body, following the peaks and valleys of her upper torso, then down over the flat plane of her abdomen. Caressing her waistline, she followed the swell of her hip to the spot between her legs and the ebony curls there. Ana shivered as Giovanna spread her tanned thighs apart, then smiled when she found her warm and wet when she slid her fingers inside.

Giovanna slowly thrust her fingers in and out of Anastasia's sex as her thumb found the swollen nub of Ana's clitoris. When she touched her, Anastasia stiffened, and her back arched off the bed for a moment, then she moaned and rotated her hips against the other woman's seeking hand. Slowly her thumb circled over and around Ana's clitoris as her fingers continued their rhythmic thrusts at an increasing rate of speed.

Not wanting to be left out, Angelica eased herself down and leaned over Anastasia, then trailed her mouth over the girl's trembling body, placing kisses against her blushing skin. Angelica's teeth nipped at tender flesh as her mouth continued its journey over Ana's body, taking first one breast then the other into its moist cavity. She circled her tongue around Ana's hardened nipple in a pattern that matched the movements of Giovanna's thumb, eliciting a strangled moan.

When Anastasia tried to move her arms, she found she

was able to lift them, and she tangled her fingers into Angelica's hair, clutching her head to her breast. Angelica smiled against Anastasia's flesh and lightly bit the pointed mound. Ana moaned and arched her back, thrusting her breast further into the blonde woman's mouth. Giovanna's thumb increased its pressure against her clitoris, causing Anastasia to moan again, and she began to frantically rock her hips against Giovanna's hand, her body searching for release.

Anastasia's excitement was reaching a frenzied pitch, and Giovanna could tell she was moments away from her climax. The dark-haired woman removed her hand from between Anastasia's legs, and when she gasped in surprise, Giovanna slid down in the bed and positioned herself between Anastasia's legs, her face just inches away from the ebony tangle of Ana's pubis. Knowing what Giovanna's intentions were, Anastasia spread her legs and panted in anticipation. She untangled one hand from Angelica's blonde locks and reached down to wrap Giovanna's hair around her hand, and then she tried to push Giovanna's face against her moist triangle. Not ready to let the pleasure end just yet, Giovanna held back, her mouth mere inches from Ana's glistening pink lips. She softly exhaled warm breath against the flushed skin, and Anastasia's body quivered.

All the while Giovanna was repositioning herself; Angelica had continued nibbling on Anastasia's nipple and massaging her breasts, causing Ana to thrash her head back and forth on the pillow. She winced in pain for a brief second and flinched after a particularly hard bite, but the momentary discomfort turned into a drawn-out sigh of pleasure. Arching herself off the bed, Ana forced her breast further into Angelica's mouth. Angelica placed her hand between Ana's breasts and pushed downward while she pulled her head backward slowly, allowing Ana's breast to slide from her mouth, catching Ana's nipple between her teeth. Angelica licked the tip of her rosy mound before releasing her.

Anastasia moaned and raised her legs, resting her ankles on Giovanna's back, as she bent in and lightly brushed the swollen clit with her tongue. Anastasia gasped and squeezed her legs against Giovanna's shoulders. Still an inch or so away from Ana's sex, Giovanna flicked her tongue back and forth, the tip sliding over and around the now throbbing clitoris, then down and around her wet inner lips, bringing forth another series of gasps and moans.

Moving closer, Giovanna let her mouth cover Anastasia's clit and pressed her tongue against the hardened knob. Feeling it twitch beneath her hot tongue. Grabbing Anastasia's ass cheeks in her hands, she lifted Ana's hips up slightly and let her tongue drop down to circle the outside edge of her vagina. She could taste her hot juices, and Ana tightened her legs around Giovanna's head.

Moaning and rocking her hips back and forth, Anastasia had released Giovanna's hair and now clenched her fists in handfuls of satin sheets as her passion mounted, even coming up off the bed, knocking Angelica off her chest and nearly sitting up.

Without warning, Giovanna thrust her tongue between Anastasia's pussy lips, deep inside her hot hole, and Anastasia cried out in surprise and delight, nearly ripping the sheet apart as she threw herself back onto the bed.

Her mouth locked against Ana's pussy; Giovanna let her tongue thrust in and out and rotate around the outside of her vagina, occasionally brushing her clitoris. As her own excitement mounted, Giovanna herself became more aroused, and she slid her hand between her own legs, stroking herself with the same fury she used on Ana as she literally attacked Anastasia's clit with her hot tongue. Pressing harder and circling the hardened nub more rapidly. Anastasia's hips rocked beneath Giovanna's expert ministrations.

Her breath coming in ragged gasps, Giovanna pressed her face against Anastasia, her tongue a whirlwind over and around Ana's clit. Anastasia's body suddenly went rigid. Her thighs becoming a vise against the sides of the other woman's head, and then she exploded.

With a scream, her body began shaking, and her climax rocked them both as the pent-up anger and stress of constantly cleaning up her brother's mistakes burst loose in a frenzied orgasm. Giovanna thrust her fingers in and out of her own pussy and kept her mouth locked over Ana's quivering slit, her tongue continuing to abuse Ana's clit as she rocked back and forth as wave after wave of ecstasy broke over her. Anastasia's body trembled, then tensed as yet another orgasm washed over her, and she finally had to push Giovanna's head away, as she could not take any more of the intense pleasure.

Gasping and panting, she squeezed her legs against the other woman's head one more time before finally relaxing and releasing her near stranglehold on her. Giovanna slowly lowered her head and lightly kissed Ana's sweaty inner thighs, then blew cool air onto her overheated pussy and clitoris.

Anastasia smiled and sighed, then allowed her arms to fall to the bed. When she tried to lift them again, she was once more unable to move. She watched helplessly as first one woman then the other dragged her tongue up her body, ending just below her jawline. Closing her eyes, she pursed her lips, her face tilted upwards. After waiting a few seconds to feel the pressure of a mouth against hers, Anastasia opened her eyes and found that she could once more move, and she was alone.

She looked around the room and noticed a strip of daylight spilling in between the drawn curtains. With a contented sigh, she decided that she has just experienced the best fantasy of her life, then rolled over in the bed and fell back asleep.

#

Several hours later, Anastasia awoke to find the room around her cast in darkness, broken only by a small flickering point of light hovering a few feet off the floor. When her eyes adjusted to the pulsing light, she discovered it came from a tall candle formed of red wax, which stood on a table across the room. Focusing on the candle, she watched as a drop of wax well up and slowly flowed over the edge, sliding down the length of the taper like oozing blood. She suddenly sat up in bed with the realization that there hadn't been a candle on the table when she went to sleep.

Quickly she climbed from bed and rushed across the room to flick on a light. She turned and glanced around and then noticed that she hadn't tripped getting to the light switch. Ana looked at the door and gasped when she saw that the small gilt chair she had wedged under the doorknob was no longer there. Now, even more disturbed, she searched the room for any other signs of intrusion.

When Ana entered the closet, she saw that the chair she had wedged under the doorknob, positioned before the vanity once again. 'I must have dreamt putting the chair beneath the knob,' she thought, but as she turned to leave the closet noticed there was now a wooden valet standing in the middle of the dressing area. Hanging there on the padded hanger was a simply styled gown made of lightweight amethyst silk. Pinned to the hanger, centered over the dress's plunging neckline, was a folded sheet of parchment. Seeing the dress and remembering the candle, Ana decided a servant must have come in while she slept to deliver the dress, and not wanting her to awaken in complete darkness, they had left a candle burning. That determined, she removed the paper and opened it to read a message written with crimson ink in flowing calligraphy.

Anastasia,

Please do me the honor of wearing this gown when you join me for dinner.

Gabriel

There, on a shelf next to the valet, were three different-sized velvet boxes. Ana opened the first and largest of them and found nestled in silver tissue paper a pair of high-heeled slipper-like shoes with satin ribbons, all dyed to match the dress. Removing one of the shoes from the box, she flipped it over, enjoying the way the smooth ribbon caressed her skin like cool water and discovered they were her size.

She put the shoe back into the box, then lifted the lid off the next box and gasped at the creations of satin and lace she found within. Stroking her fingertips over the silky fabric, she moaned with pleasure at the sensual shiver that ran up her spine. Pulling the lingerie from the box one item at a time, Ana "Oohed" and "Ahhed" each piece as it was taken out. First, she removed a black satin corset with an amethyst lace covering; the ribbon stays matching the ribbons on the elegant shoes. She held the corset up to herself to judge the size and noticed a deep 'V' down the middle that would match up with the plunging neckline in the gown. From the hem on both the front and back dangled four garters. Laying it aside, Ana lifted out a tiny pair of hip-hugging, lacey panties, and a pair of lace-edged thigh-high stockings. Gently returning the lingerie to the velvet box, Ana thought to herself, 'Someone definitely thought of everything.'

She looked at the third and final box and wondered what could possibly be contained in such a thin box, then picked it up and was surprised by its hefty weight. Depressing the small silver button, she unsnapped the hinged lid and allowed the box to open. Contained within, laying on a bed of black velvet and secured in place with small tabs, was a pair of earrings and a necklace. The earrings consisted of six pieces of thin silver chain, varying in length from an inch and a half to three inches. Each strand ended in a small, half-inch teardrop-shaped amethyst. Lifting an earring out of the box, Ana was delightfully surprised to find that it didn't seem to be as heavy as it appeared. Replacing the earring, she turned her attention to the necklace. Overall, it was a very simple piece of jewelry, a single strand of silver chain that would circle her neck, resting just atop the collarbones. This would create a "V," which started at what would be either side of her neck and, having the longest portion centered in the valley between her breasts, were many lengths of silver chains. The lengths of the chain started at an inch and became progressively longer until the point, which measured five inches long. Every third chain was studded with small amethysts down the entire length and ended in a half-inch teardrop-shaped stone. Also included in the box were two amethyst studded bangles, which looked like the bracelet portion of a pair of handcuffs, all the way to the patented latching mechanism.

Ana gently closed the jewelry box, returned it to the shelf, and then left the closet. She thought that Gabriel either had great taste in women's clothes and jewelry or perhaps he hired a very good personal shopper to work for him. Walking back over to the bed, she picked up the small alarm clock from a bedside table and saw that it was 8:15, meaning she only had forty-five minutes to get ready for dinner. She went back into the closet and softly caressed the dress fabric. "Well, the least I can do for Gabriel after all his hospitality is to wear this dress for him."

Part Four

Thirty minutes later, Ana walked out into the hallway and pulled the door closed behind her. Lifting the front of the dress off the floor with one hand, she started down the hall. Ana made it halfway to the stairs before she heard soft laughter coming from the courtyard below her. She stepped over to the railing, rested her hands on the balustrade, and leaned over, ever so slightly.

Ana looked down into the dark courtyard with its simple landscaping of grass surrounding a single fountain and quickly located the source of the laughter. Below her, laughing together and dancing around the fountain, were Giovanna and Angelica, beams of light from the full moon basking their nude bodies in an ethereal glow as they twirled around and around the lightly splashing fountain. Shocked and strangely intrigued by their complete lack of inhibition, Ana watched them for a few moments until the women suddenly stopped dancing and looked up at her.

Curving their fingers at her, the two women beckoned Ana to join them. "Anastasia, come down and play with us. We promise not to bite...hard."

Disgusted by the invitation and the knowledge that for a split second, she had actually felt the desire to join Giovanna and Angelica in their sensual frolicking, Ana moved quickly away from the railing and rushed off toward the stairs.

When she reached the top of the stairs, Ana slowed her progress and lifted the skirt of her gown higher, then continued downward, watching her feet as she went. Half a

492

dozen steps from the bottom, she saw someone standing at the base of the stairs, where he had apparently paused to look up at her. As she got closer, Ana saw that it was Jennings, awaiting her arrival with an arm raised to assist her. She took the old man's offered hand to move down the last steps and smiled. "Thank you, Mr. Jennings."

"This way, please," the older man whispered as he released her hand and bowed his head. He then led Ana through a doorway out of the courtyard and into the maze of corridors winding through the first story. After a few moments of moving through the confusing warren of rooms in utter silence, she asked, "Where are we going?" But Jennings continued on without a single word.

When they had walked a few steps more, she asked him, "Where is my brother?"

Jennings whispered, "You will see him soon," and then fell silent once more.

They traveled the remainder of the way in silence, and eventually, they came to a large oak door with iron studs protruding from the wood. The door opened silently when Jennings turned the handle, and he entered before her.

He turned to the room at large and announced, "Our Master's honored guest, Miss Anastasia Connor."

As she stepped into the room, Ana was met by a roar of applause and the pounding of fists on a tabletop. Looking around the room quickly, she saw that running its entire length was a huge dinner table, and of some twenty chairs placed alongside the table, only two were vacant—a large throne-like chair at the head of the table and a chair positioned directly to the right side of the throne. The wall behind the master's seat consisted of an open fireplace, large enough to roast an entire cow in one piece. Surprised by the brightness of the room when the only source of light was the fire, Ana looked up and saw that the ceiling was tiled in mirror panels.

"Follow me, please, Miss," Jennings said and then began showing her down the length of the room.

Moving slowly past the other diners, Ana couldn't describe the uneasy feeling that settled over her. Everyone seated at the table, while unusually pale, was exceptionally gorgeous. She didn't understand her feelings of discomfort; she had been around beautiful people before, and it had never affected her like this. Nervous and on edge, she plastered a smile on her face and tried not to stare. As she passed by, men and women alike looked at her as if she was a delicious dessert. A few of them began drooling as she passed, while half a dozen licked their lips hungrily and one particularly stunning woman with feline features gave her a sinister smile and then snapped her teeth at Ana.

Startled, Ana flinched away in surprise and caused her audience to begin laughing. When she finally reached the chair that Jennings held for her, she smiled weakly at the elderly man and once more asked, "Where is Nich?"

"Soon," he said, smiling down on her like a patient father placating an inquisitive child. "Could I offer you a drink?"

Wishing to steady her quickly unraveling nerves, Ana nodded, "A glass of wine, please."

Jennings chuckled and said, "We have not had that spirit here since 1969." At her shocked expression, he continued, "The Master does not like how it changes people."

"Water is fine," she said.

Jennings poured her a glass of water, then quickly left

the room. Left by herself in a room full of strangers, Ana looked down the table, turning to locate a friendly face. Not seeing any, she looked down at her plate for a few moments. She was just about to push her chair away from the table and leave when a small door next to the fireplace opened.

As if drawn by a magnetic force, Ana turned and saw Gabriel coming through the doorway. Instantly the room became deathly silent, and the diners assumed subservient bowed head positions. He crossed the room to her side, moving with the grace of a jungle cat, then smiled down at her. "Anastasia, my dear, you look ravishing tonight." Taking her hand from where it rested on the table, he lifted it towards his mouth and turning it over. He rested his lips in the bowl of her palm. When she drew in a shaky breath, he moved his lips up to her wrist and slid his tongue along her inner wrist, directly over her thundering pulse.

When he finally released her hand, Gabriel took his seat, and the first course of dinner was immediately served. Throughout the meal, he kept up a steady stream of conversation, constantly working to put her mind at ease. Every time Ana would ask about her brother, Gabriel would simply say, "I am sure Nicholas will be along soon."

A short time later, groups of servants silently entered the room, cleared away the dirty dishes from the latest course, and laid dishes for the main course, placing a large plate, knife, and fork in front of each diner. Four of the servants quickly moved among the diners and filled their wine glasses with effervescent pink champagne.

Lifting her glass to her lips, Ana slowly slipped the bubbling liquid and watched as two servants wheeled in a large, covered platter on a cart. Reaching the foot of the table, they attached large chains to handles on the platter and a smaller chain to a ring on the lid. Pulling on a hanging loop of chain, they lifted the platter off the cart, and as it was elevated off the cart, the platter became centered lengthwise over the table.

Hearing the frantic shuffling of restless people in their chairs and an excited murmuring, Ana looked down the table at her fellow diners. By the glazed eye expressions of intense anticipation on their faces, she figured they must know what culinary delight waited beneath the silver lid. As she watched, previously elegant and refined appearing guests began drooling and grabbing up their forks and knives in preparation. With the platter in mid-air, Ana could tell it was easily seven feet in length and at least three-wide.

Once it was centered, the servants tugged on the other side of the chain loop, and the platter dropped smoothly to the table, touching down with a solid thud. Jennings, who had silently entered the room as the platter was lowered to the table, stood to his master's left and said, "The main course is served. Bon Appetite." He then pulled a tasseled cord which caused the lid to rise off the dish.

Ana looked at the platter and watched as the lid was removed. She gasped when she saw what appeared to be human arms in the small gap between the lid and platter. When the cover was removed completely, she screamed in shock and jumped out of her chair, staring down at her brother lying before her. Ana's eyes widened as she took in the horrifying sight before her—Nicholas' body was stretched out in the platter trussed up like a pig at a luau, with a bright red apple shoved in his mouth to stifle his screams. His eyes were frozen open in terror, and as he turned his head from side to side, his eyes locked with Ana's with a shocked look of pain and fear.

She looked down the table, wondering what the other diners' reactions to her brother's horrible condition would be, but backed away from the table in fear at the hunger and joy she saw reflected on their faces. Ana watched in speechless horror as they rose from their chairs and their canine teeth lengthened into large glistening fangs. Their eyes turned red with blood lust; the ravenous group began jabbing at her brother's flesh with sharp steel knives, laughter punctuating the air as with each nonfatal laceration, another muffled moan was forced out around the apple. Holding wine goblets under each wound, they collected the blood like a fine vintage, as it flowed freely, blood spilling onto the table as Nicholas squirmed helplessly on the silver platter.

Terrified of the others and not wanting to turn her back on them, Ana slowly backed away from the table and began heading for the door, tears streaming down her pale face. When those hideous monsters started climbing onto the table to get closer to their meal, many drinking the blood directly from Nicholas' swiftly paling skin, she turned and ran for the door and escape. She had almost reached what she hoped would be safety when she heard laughter coming from behind her. She turned to see Gabriel rising out of his chair, his canines and incisors elongating into vicious fangs.

Slowly he moved toward her, stalking the young woman like a cat would a terrified mouse. Smiling cruelly, he said,

"Really, Anastasia, you don't know your history very well. What else did you expect from the only remaining son of Vlad Tepes?" Seeing confusion mingle with the horror he had already witnessed in her eyes, he continued, "Perhaps you would know him as Vlad the Impaler?" When he saw no dawning of recognition cross her face, he asked, "No? Then, possibly Dracula?"

Her eyes finally widened in recognition, and she tried to take another step back, only to feel the wall press hard against her. Gabriel moved forward and trapped her against the wall with his tall, muscular body. He reached up he traced the neckline of her gown, trailing his fingers over the edge of the bodice and down over the swell of her breast. Using the seductive power of his voice and the gentle caress of his hand, Gabriel hypnotized Anastasia and made her helpless to deny him. He cupped the back of her neck, tilted her head dramatically to the left, and leaned over, then whispered against her skin, "It's not so bad, my dear. It will only hurt for… an eternity." As his fangs punctured her flesh and his lips closed over her throbbing pulse, her weak scream of pain and ecstasy was drowned out by the sounds from the table of animals feasting.

The End

THE WORLD OF MYTH

MAGAZINE

POETRY

SELECTION

Christopher Bice

Growing up in Brantford Ontario, I moved West with my family to a small village in Northern BC.
After many years I returned to the East and met my wife. We later came to Coalhurst Alberta (just outside of Lethbridge) to retire. I enjoy fishing and camping and I find my inspiration while out in nature.

New Beginnings
By: Christopher Bice

I lost the forward stabilizers and I knew I was about to
die,
The Mother ship exploded like a fiery Fourth of July.
Like a surgeon's knife, the meteor cut through the
forward bridge,
Snuffing out those precious lives like a fiery burning
midge.

If only I can get to a pod I might escape this fiery fate,
I'll take my chances out there but first I must escape.
There's a small planet just off the port side,
I hope that I can make it, the pods on auto glide.

I landed on the deserted planet, glad to be alive,
Cautiously I opened the hatch to have a look outside.
A hazy looking atmosphere, a red sun is in the sky,

Christopher Bice

Steadying myself, I wondered what caused the locals all
to die.

Might have been a nuke, more likely quite a few,
It left the air quite hazy with this morning's heavy foggy
dew.
It's taken a thousand years, for life to grow up from the
ground,
Plenty of mutated animals are roaming all around.

Could have been worse places for me to crash and die,
Suddenly I see another streak across that crimson sky.
The pod makes a rough landing and she comes crawling
free,
I realize that she's the botanist; I think her name is Eve.

We come to realize that we alone survived that fiery fate,
Crashing on this little blue planet a thousand years too
late.
Hello my name is Adam, I believe that yours is Eve,
Could be a long time till we're rescued; let's wait under
this apple tree.

Kevin Adams

A board game enthusiast and loving father, Kevin has been surviving quite well since *The World of Myth* last saw him in 2012. Forced into early retirement then, he recently was 'tempted' back with the promise of writing and conducting *TWoM* interviews. His current line of work has him fabricating parts for turbine engines, he still tries to keep a simple relaxed life when not working.

Depression
By: Kevin Adams

Depression

Spiraling down
into a dark abyss
my emotions unchecked

I want to die
feeling the need to end my pain
a gun would be quick

My hurting would end
no more fake smiles
or false laughter

I could rest
no more looking for respite

Kevin Adams

among these thorns

Finally free of stress
nothing further expected
except my death

What stops me I wonder
my heart has had enough
and agony never fades

Blackened souls can't redeem
regardless of struggle
shrouded in shame

Walk in my shoes and survive
then we can talk
and have evil in common

Anguish is a slow killer
it hides itself inside
much like me from you

My cold walls are silent
much like my lips
conveying this wounded life

Sore bones hang on flesh
it is tired of this damage
so much brutal negativity

I can't pull the trigger
508

knowing one person might care
who is it though?

Rebecca Ilich

If something appears a bit familiar with Rebecca Ilich, it's because it's Rebecca C. Lofgren all grown up. Although she's in her 30s, she has an impressive publishing history behind her name, including being a part of this magazine since issue one and her book of poetry and art B*ook of Dreams* being consumed all around the world. Despite the success in the literary market, Rebecca left it to venture into podcasting with her husband & brother. She enjoyed robust achievement for the past five years, now living back in Southern California with her husband and furry children, Rebecca has returned for to *The World of Myth!*

Leave Your Box Of Empathy At The Curb
By: Rebecca Ilich

Sometimes I feel like life is too much.

I reach for the edge as my hopes and dreams are crushed.

Will I plummet today, will I hit the ground running.

I could reach for a hand but there are none coming.

I just need a chance a simple word or two.

But in this great big world we are all alone and that's nothing new.

We are born alone and we die alone.

I use to spend my days soul searching but the only thing I'm searching now is on my phone.

I live in a world where my greatest accomplishment is hiding all of my fears.

I smile and laugh while I hold back all of my tears.

With each drop I shed a little bit of pain.

But all these emotions are just too damn much I think

Rebecca Ilich

I'm finally going insane.

I'm sorry that I'm too sensitive, a cry baby, or a drama queen.

Things could be different, I could be different if I had just one person on my team.

That's just not meant to be and I will never be understood.

So I face the edge alone like a good little girl should.

Peggy Gerber

Peggy Gerber is a poet and short story writer from northern New Jersey. She has been a big fan of science fiction ever since she saw her first Star Trek episode at seven years old, and it still inspires much of her work. Her stories and poems have appeared in many publications including Daily Science Fiction, The World of Myth, Potato Soup Journal, Terror House Magazine and many others.

Cancer is a Four Letter Word
By: Peggy Gerber

I don't want to write about cancer,
I'd rather write about anything else,
like the miraculous new life growing
and blossoming inside my daughter's belly,
her tiny little hands and feet kicking and
pummeling my sleep deprived daughter as I
impatiently wait for my beloved to be born.

I don't want to write about cancer,
but all I can think about is the walnut
sized growth, crusty and decrepit
poisoning the body of the man
that I have loved for over forty years.
Or the surgery he will have to endure
as doctors cut through tendons and muscles
plucking out pieces of his insides

Peggy Gerber

as I sit by helplessly and wait.

I don't want to write about cancer,
I'd rather write about our family and friends
coming together to pray that his broken, battered
body will soon heal and his strength will return,
and we can declare to all the world:
We won this battle!

I don't want to write about cancer,
but rather about all the plans my husband
and I will make when he is recovered.

Christopher Bice

Growing up in Brantford Ontario, I moved West with my family to a small village in Northern BC.

After many years I returned to the East and met my wife. We later came to Coalhurst Alberta (just outside of Lethbridge) to retire. I enjoy fishing and camping and I find my inspiration while out in nature.

Genocide
By: Christopher Bice

Atop a boulder at the edge of the world
Flags of every country at my feet lie furled
The barrens before me dead and cleft
The end has come and what is left
As I'm gazing past all eternity
I dream a dream that I did not see

Civilizations ravaged turned to dust
All for would be gods and their power lust
I cry tears for the forgotten and lost
Wondering what has this genocide cost

It won't be long until I see
A last hazy sunrise for me
Sores on skin that do not bleed
A gift from false prophet's greed

Christopher Bice

Soon to succumb I will return to dust
Praying to God to forgive all of us.

Linda Imbler

Linda Imbler has eight published poetry collections and one hybrid ebook of short fiction and poetry. She is a Wichita, Kansas based author. Learn more at lindaspoetryblog.blogspot.com.

Old Time Religion after the age of Covid
By: Linda Imbler

Tiger cages masquerade as houses
to enslave our bodies,
but allow our souls to escape.
Divine rights of kings,
tear down the totem.
Righteous indignation, uprising of the masses,
love me or I'll destroy you,
worship me or I'll tear down your lands.

Social conventions, so well taught,
put aside in the name of survival.
Thou shall not kill or steal,
not in vain, covet, false idol,
no other before me.

What does my spirit say to you?

Linda Imbler

For truth is embraced there.
Too many conditions and we can't choose.
Back off, let me choose.
I'll find my own way to the center of all that is,
that light, that perfect synchronization
of what lives, breathes, thinks and grows.
Keep me in the tiger cage , if you will,
but the most important part of me will still escape.

Linda M. Sauve

An avid reader from a young age, Linda developed an addiction to books in her childhood that has intensified into an obsession that is getting more expensive by the day. Although she had been writing for some time, prior to publishing as "L. M. Mercer" her work had not been viewed by the public at large. Linda had mainly used (and still does use) writing as a release for life's stressful times (never intending for others to read her poems) , but she eventually allowed herself to be badgered into submitting some pieces by friend and coworker, Kevin Magnus, who told her to "Stop wasting your talent." She did finally admit to him that she is very grateful for his badgering.

Linda is returning to *The World of Myth* after years of consistent encouragement (pestering) from good friend, David K. Montoya. While making no guarantees on the frequency with which she will be able to submit pieces, Linda has decided to end her hiatus and return to *The World of Myth*.

Returned to Heaven
By: Linda M. Sauve

   I carefully laid you upon the bed, laying down behind
you.
   I leaned forward and placed my head next to yours.
   I looked out the window and saw the sky quickly
darken.
   But I didn't mind, it matched my mood.
   As tears filled my vision snowflakes began to fall.
   I startled when one of the nurses entered the silent room.
   She softly rubbed my shoulder and asked if we were
ready.
   Slowly I got down off the bed and placed a kiss upon
your brow.
   Daddy and I bathed and dressed you one final time.
   Outside the snow continued to fall, harder and harder
with each passing second.
   I brushed your bangs out of your face, knowing how

much it annoyed you.

I laid my cheek next to yours, drawing up some inner strength.

I whispered, "We will always love you baby girl."

With a final kiss we walked away from the bed.

The nurses watched silently as we left the unit.

Minutes later we walked out of the hospital and I stared into the snow'filled sky.

It hit me then, my Angel on Earth had Returned to Heaven.

Christopher Bice

Growing up in Brantford Ontario, I moved West with my family to a small village in Northern BC.

After many years I returned to the East and met my wife. We later came to Coalhurst Alberta (just outside of Lethbridge) to retire. I enjoy fishing and camping and I find my inspiration while out in nature.

Siren's Song
By: Christopher Bice

Off the calm waters
The sunrise twinkles
As do your eyes

Little sparks of love
Like dancing pixies
Fluttering across the water

Our lips brush
Tasting ocean waters
Gently lapping soft sand

Two bodies entwined
As the surf caresses us
Envelops us

Christopher Bice

Pledging our love
Each vowing to return
To this beach

But a sailor's heart
Beats for just one
His mistress is the sea

Returning each night
You sit and sing
Your sad song of betrayal

Beckoning all who hear
To save you from anguish
From a broken vow

Come lie at my feet
On my bed of rocks
Come die for me.

Jeff R. Young

When not dealing with his chaotic household consisting of four dogs, three cats, two late teen daughters plus the eldest's boyfriend, Jeff R. Young strives diligently to turn his love of writing poetry and fiction into a career. His hobbies include gaming, shooting darts, and drinking vast amounts of coffee.

Facebook:https://www.facebook.com/JeffRobertYoung
Twitter:@JeffRYoung1

Divine Spark
By: Jeff R. Young

It's your name I would whisper
If I need to speak of love
A name so delicate on my lips
Yet I wear it like a glove
I speak of you so gently
Like I handle fragile glass
I handle you so lightly
Or like dust in wind you'll pass
Your voice is soft and tender
Like a ripple on a lake
The tone of your expression
My ears can barely take
Your touch is so angelic
Sends shivers down my spine
It's all that I can say or do
When our bodies intertwine

Jeff R. Young

So please don't leave me wanting
Keep your body near to mine
Because when we're close together
Your love is just divine.

Christopher Bice

Growing up in Brantford Ontario, I moved West with my family to a small village in Northern BC.
After many years I returned to the East and met my wife. We later came to Coalhurst Alberta (just outside of Lethbridge) to retire. I enjoy fishing and camping and I find my inspiration while out in nature.

The Coin
By: Christopher Bice

I followed the path
Through the glen
It's an old trail
Used by many men

But today something
Caught my eye
I nearly missed it
As I was walked by

Just off the path
Was wee piece of gold
A smallish gold coin
Who knew how old

I bent to retrieve it

Christopher Bice

And what did I see
A little person hiding
Behind the tree

Excuse me good sir
I see my gold coin you found
It must've fell from me pocket
Onto the ground

If you pass it over
And give it back to me
I'll put me nose to my finger
Give one wish for free

What is it mister
Tell your wish to me
Give me the coin
Come sit by the tree

I told the wee man
My wife is about to give birth
Here's your coin
Can you promise heaven and earth

The wee man scrunched up his nose
Then pulled out his pipe
He packed it with tobacco
Calmly asked for a light

I'll tell you what mister
You'd better run straight home

542

Ya don't want to leave
Mother and child all alone

I ran home through the glen
I needed to see
If the wee man
Kept his promise to me

Oh daddy the wee girl said
Sitting on my knee
Don't you ever get tired
Telling the same story

The wee man gave me
A story that never gets old
He gave me a beautiful daughter
With hair of gold.

www.ingramcontent.com/pod-product-compliance
Lightning Source LLC
Chambersburg PA
CBHW071334020726
47502CB00001B/88